BLUE MOUNTAIN WEDDINGS

THREE-IN-ONE COLLECTION

CANDICE SPEARE
NANCY TOBACK

BARBOUR
PUBLISHING

Cover Design: Kirk DouPonce, DogEared Design

Published by Barbour Publishing, Inc., P.O. Box 719, Uhrichsville, Ohio 44683, www.barbourbooks.com

Our mission is to publish and distribute inspirational products offering exceptional value and biblical encouragement to the masses.

 Member of the
Evangelical Christian
Publishers Association

Printed in the United States of America.

Dear Readers,

The last thing we write for a book is a note to our readers. As always we're torn about what to say because many things come to mind. Things like: We hope you enjoy the sweet romance and the characters. We hope you're satisfied with the happy endings. But more than anything else, we hope through our fiction you catch a glimpse of a merciful Father God who loves all of us more than we can ever imagine. He is the preeminent author of true love. He's the ultimate mender of broken hearts, the fixer of the unfixable, the forgiver of sin, and the One who restores lives. And unlike fallible humans, He will never, ever forsake us.

If you wish to contact Candice personally, you may do so through her website: www.candicemillerspeare.com

Candice

A HERO FOR HER HEART

Dedication

We'd like to acknowledge the following people who helped us: Bryon and
Dawn Miller, who willingly answered any and all questions about Walla
Walla, and John and Diana Blessing, who helped us with Washington facts.
If any of our readers wish to learn more about Walla Walla or things we've
mentioned, here are some Web sites:
http://www.brightscandies.com/index.html
http://www.marcuswhitmanhotel.com/
http://wwvchamber.com/calendar.html
http://www.arbinifarms.com/
And last but never least, thank you, Wanda Dyson for the story.

Chapter 1

Sweat beaded on Allie's forehead as she adjusted her truck's air conditioner, but it didn't make a dent in the July heat. She headed onto a side street to avoid the Saturday morning crowds gathered for the parade to begin a series of events leading up to the Walla Walla Sweet Onion Festival scheduled for the following weekend.

"Excited?" She shot a glance at her eight-year-old nephew in the passenger seat. His black cotton T-shirt enhanced his bronze skin, and a familiar question crossed her mind. *What did his biological parents look like?*

"Yep." Smiling, Danny strained against the seat belt, dark eyes wide.

She winked at him, then backed her truck into a spot off the main drag. After she parked, she patted sweat off her brow and blew a damp piece of hair from her face. "Ready, Spiderman?"

Nodding, he unbuckled his seat belt. "We're going to Bright's before the parade, right?"

Allie leaned across the seat to kiss his forehead, but he backed away in mock horror. "Aunt Allie. I'm too old to be kissed in public."

"Oh, that's right." She sat back and sighed. "You're practically grown up. I'm sorry."

"That's okay," he said seriously. "But you need to try to remember."

"I'll try." Allie smiled. "Yes, we're going to Bright's. That's why I got us here before the parade starts."

The parade was the brainchild of Philip Maynard, mayor of Walla Walla and a member of the Walla Walla Valley Chamber of Commerce, whose close family owned nearby onion farms. Although Philip wasn't a farmer himself—he owned a law firm—he wanted to ensure that people didn't forget the onion farmers. Whatever Philip's agenda, her nephew would enjoy the event.

Danny scrambled from the truck, slammed the door, and stood on the sidewalk waiting for her. She watched a car pass, then hopped to the ground and locked the doors. A fine layer of dust covered her red Chevy truck. With a sigh she ran her fingers over the white magnetic sign on the driver's door, wiping the dust off the black letters that spelled out VAHN'S FARRIER SERVICES—the business she'd learned from her father and shared with her brother, Luke, before he died.

"Come on, Aunt Allie. I'm hungry." Danny bounced from foot to foot.

"Bottomless pit," she joked as she walked around the truck to join her nephew. His appetite was enormous lately, digging into their already slim grocery budget, but she wouldn't complain. It was preferable to the months he'd refused to eat after his parents died.

She suddenly caught sight of Michael Maynard, the mayor's son, in his BMW, and she jumped back behind her truck, dragging Danny with her. What a coincidence that Michael was passing by just when she'd arrived. Or was it?

Danny tugged on her arm. "What's wrong?"

She put a finger to her lips. "Shh. I know I'm acting like a kid. But I'm hiding from someone."

"Who?" He stretched his neck around the truck. "Mr. Michael?"

"Yes." She yanked him back by the shirtsleeve. "And the whole point is to stay hidden."

"Why?" Danny sucked in his cheeks, narrowed his eyes, and studied her. That was Danny—sharp beyond his years. He crossed his arms. "I thought Michael was your friend."

Friend? Michael had been her fiancé until he'd cheated with another woman nine months ago. Now he wanted to date Allie again, which was out of the question. She would never be able to trust him, and fending off his advances got tiring.

She peered around the truck. Michael's car was gone. "Um, he is my friend, but I don't feel like talking to him today."

"Aunt Allie, that isn't right, is it? Can't I talk to him even if you don't?"

Allie bit her lip. She had good cause to avoid Michael, but no reason to drag the eight-year-old into the fray.

"You're right, Danny." Leave it to a kid to point out adult idiosyncrasies. "I might be twenty-eight, but no one said I was mature. Next time we see him, feel free to do whatever you'd like." She tucked a stray piece of Danny's black hair behind his ear. "Let's go. I want some of those mint truffles. And I know what you want."

"Gummi animals." They spoke simultaneously and laughed. Allie leaned down to kiss his dirt-smeared face, caught herself, and gave his hand a squeeze instead.

Above them wisps of marshmallow clouds scuttled across the blue sky, driven by hot wind. The sun bore down on her back as they headed for Bright's Candies.

"Hey, Allie!" Out of the side of her eye, she caught a glimpse of her friend Shannon a half block away waving her arms. Allie smiled. Who could miss her in a long denim skirt, tie-dyed, bell-sleeved blouse, and waist-length, blond braid?

"I've got our seats!" Shannon shouted. "Main and Second."

Nodding her understanding, Allie pointed in the direction of Bright's. Shannon gave a thumbs-up and disappeared into the crowd.

Allie smiled to herself. She loved Walla Walla with its rich history, old buildings, and forever friends.

Danny and Allie walked past the wrought-iron fence, which corralled tiny tables and chairs in front of Bright's windows. The gleaming glass door swung open without notice.

Allie slammed into a hard chest and gasped. A plastic bag landed on her feet, and jelly beans scattered around her sneakers.

She reeled back and looked up. If there were still such things as pirates, the tall man in jeans and black polo shirt fit the bill, minus the eye patch. His black collar-length hair glinted blue in the summer sun. A razor-thin scar ran down his tanned face—from the top of his cheekbone to the corner of his mouth. His dark gaze latched onto hers.

Handsome, Allie admitted to herself.

The man looked down at Danny. He blinked, and his lips curved in a smile. Her perception of a pirate vanished. In its place was a man whose eyes emanated warmth. He suddenly turned his attention back to her.

"I'm sorry." Allie ripped her gaze from his and pointed at the sidewalk. "I made you drop your—"

"No problem." He stepped back and held the door open for them.

As she and Danny walked through the opening, she felt the man's eyes on them, but refused to turn around. She hadn't the time or desire for flirtation.

Allie placed her order at the counter while Danny moved toward Bright's chocolate city display, a massive concoction under glass made from chocolate and jelly beans. As she watched the perky teen behind the counter fill her requests, a voice from behind called her name. She recognized the distinctive baritone before she turned to see Philip Maynard's familiar and mostly bald head bobbing like a buoy amid the sea of waiting customers.

"I finally found you," he bellowed as he skirted others to reach her. The buttons on his short-sleeved dress shirt strained dangerously against his portly stomach. "I've got a blacksmith-type emergency."

An emergency. Of course. She just happened to be handy, which was why he didn't call his regular farrier.

"Hello, little man." Philip ruffled Danny's hair.

Danny wrinkled his nose and jabbed his finger in Allie's hip, an obvious attempt to remind her that this was *their* day.

Allie drew a deep breath, about to say, *Thanks, but no thanks.*

"I'll pay double your fee." Philip, always a sharp politician, had apparently read the hesitation on her face before she denied his request.

Double the fee? Yes, he probably knew she was strapped for cash. She had confided in his son, Michael-the-Cheat, and he must've relayed the info to his dad. Danny's adoptive parents, Luke and Cindy, had died with a will and a boatload of hidden debt against the business, which left her with guardianship and no money. Bottom line, she shouldn't turn down any job.

But. . . Allie pulled Danny closer. Today was different. She had no intention of working. "Sorry, Philip, but Danny and I are here to have fun."

"I know, I know, but the shoe on my Paige's horse is loose. She's part of this woman's club, and their group is riding in the parade in honor of the brave pioneer women who traveled the Oregon Trail—that was *my* idea." He paused, waiting for her appreciation.

Allie studied his red face. The Oregon Trail? Yes, that was a large part of local history, but this parade was supposed to be part of the onion festival. The connection between the two events eluded her, but she nodded anyway.

The mayor cleared his throat. "We can't have a spot missing from the formation." He dabbed his creased brow with a handkerchief. "Paige is on the verge of a meltdown."

Allie wasn't surprised. She'd known Paige, Michael's only sister, most of their lives. She was prone to emotional depths and heights that often left those around her dizzy. Even in a steady relationship with Allie's brother years ago, Paige had been a drama queen. And her hissy fits had only grown worse as she aged. How she'd ever gotten a law degree was beyond Allie's comprehension.

"Listen, Allie, all you have to do is hammer the shoe back on." Philip patted her arm. "I know you won't let us down."

Danny continued jabbing his finger into her hip. Allie gave him a warning glare and handed him his bag of gummi candy. That would keep his finger busy on something other than bruising.

Philip Maynard cleared his throat again. "Could mean more business for you, Allie."

Right. She recognized his words for what they were. An empty promise to use her services in the future.

Just hammer the shoe back on? Allie eyed Philip's hopeful face. Who knew why the shoe was loose? It could be bent. Or maybe the hoof had grown out. "You know, if I were your regular farrier, this wouldn't have happened." She always made it a point to know what her clients had planned for their horses, then ensured the animals were ready.

Philip's eyebrows twitched. "Could've sworn I told my secretary to give you a call." He wagged his head as if to blame the woman. "Why, just last week—"

"I'll do it." Allie saved him the embarrassment of expounding on his lie. Bills were stacking up. Danny's birthday was next week. The extra cash would be a blessing. Bottom line, she was in no position to refuse Philip's request.

Allie glanced down and offered Danny an apologetic smile, then looked at Philip's crimson face. "You want me to *hammer* the shoe back on the horse's hoof? What if I can't?"

"Why, I'm sure you can. You have your tools with you, right?" He dabbed again at the sweat running down his temples.

"Yes. In the truck. But if there's more wrong than just a missing nail, I won't be able to help you today."

Philip smiled. "Go get your tools, girl. I need you. Paige will have the horse at the market area at Main and Fourth." He whirled around, his portly body vibrating with tension as he pressed his way to the door.

"Aunt Allie, you promised." Danny's tone was whiny, and Allie felt a brief spurt of irritation, which she quickly squelched.

"I'm sorry, sweetie." She leaned close to his ear. "There's a reason I'm taking this job. A special event that's coming up. . ."

Danny's brow furrowed in concentration, then a big grin lit his face. "My birthday!"

"Yep." She high-fived him. "How about I get you settled with Shannon? That way you won't miss anything, and I'll be back as soon as possible."

Twenty minutes later, clad in her work chaps, Allie took the reins of a nervous chestnut gelding from Paige Maynard, who stood in a cloud of Chanel wearing a shorts outfit no doubt from the most expensive department store in the area.

"Daddy says this horse has good breeding. I don't care." She gave a one-shoulder shrug. "As long as he looks handsome riding in the parade."

"He's a beautiful animal." And a Thoroughbred, a breed used for horse racing and known for skittish nerves. Come to think of it, if Paige were a horse, this is exactly what she'd be like. White ringed his eyes, and his nostrils flared with his breaths. "What's his name?" Allie patted his muscled withers.

"Chester. He's. . ." Paige groaned and fanned her face, showing off a French manicure and a sparkling diamond bracelet. "My stomach hurts." Ever the drama queen, she rubbed her abdomen with jerky motions, and the horse tossed his head.

Allie positioned herself between Paige and Chester and began stroking his neck. How lucky she was that Paige had never gotten her way and married Luke.

Paige continued to fidget behind her. "Where's Danny?"

"He's with Shannon." Allie willed herself to be patient. Was God okay with her praying for Paige to disappear?

"How is the little guy?" Either Paige had been miraculously healed of her ailment or didn't have stomach pains to begin with.

"You mean Danny?" Allie kept her focus on the horse. For some odd reason, she was reluctant to discuss her nephew with Paige even though she'd handled his adoption for Luke and Cindy.

"Yes. Is he recovering? I mean, it's got to be hard, losing both his parents and all. Especially Luke."

Allie flashed a glance over her shoulder at Paige. Her tears at Luke's funeral had been more than show. She'd never gotten over her high school crush on him. "Danny's not so little anymore. And he's doing well, thanks. I had him in grief counseling. . . ." She felt like a mare, protecting her foal. "I'm thinking of adopting Danny."

Paige pressed her hand to her chest. "Adopting him?"

"Sure, why not?" Allie smiled. "It'll make Danny feel more secure."

"But you're already his legal guardian, right? Why go through the courts to—"

"Yep, I'm Danny's legal guardian." She fought hard to keep pride out of her tone. "But I think adopting him might make him feel more secure."

"I'm. . ." Paige took a deep breath and rubbed her stomach again. "I'm feeling queasy. I'm scared I might have heatstroke or something."

"You should go get a drink of cold water." Allie willed Paige to leave. She'd then be able to calm Chester without interference.

"Yes, I suppose you're right. Besides, I need to change into my costume. I'll be back."

Was that a promise or a threat? Allie listened to Paige's footsteps recede, then turned her full attention to the horse.

"You know, big guy," she whispered, "with an owner like that, it's no wonder you're jittery. She makes me jittery, too."

The white rings around his eyes slowly disappeared. She stroked his neck, and he whickered softly.

"Okay, fellow. I think you're ready. Let's do this." She pulled her tools near, lifted his hoof, and placed it between her legs. She'd appreciate her hoof stand, but hadn't felt like carrying it or bringing her truck with all her equipment to check a single shoe. Sure enough, there were nails missing. Fortunately, the hoof was fine, and the shoe wasn't bent. She'd be able to make the repair.

She picked up several nails, placing them between her lips, then grabbed the hammer. After driving in the nail, she bent it back, and set the next one in place.

A shadow fell over her, and she glanced up into the coal black eyes of the tall pirate she'd run into earlier.

Chapter 2

Allie's face heated. She dropped Chester's hoof and rose, hammer in hand.

He flashed a beautiful smile. "So we meet again."

The man made her feel discombobulated, something she rarely experienced. Allie found herself searching for a clever response. "Sorry I bashed into you earlier. I hope you didn't lose too many of your jelly beans."

He held up a bag of candy. "No, I still have some." His gaze swept her and Chester. "You're a blacksmith."

"Farrier. And I'm glad it's obvious. I'd hate to think I'm doing this with no experience." She smiled and realized she was flirting, so she toned it down. "I guess I could also be considered a blacksmith, but I don't do a lot of the heavier forging of iron or steel objects. I just shoe horses."

His smile broadened, and his black eyes snapped with the kind of interest that flattered her. "I'm Derrick Owens. I'm in town for business."

"Allie Vahn." She gave him a quick full-body glance. His jeans and polo shirt looked expensive. In fact, his persona screamed toned and well-to-do, which brought her back to reality. She'd had enough of spoiled men with a sense of entitlement like Michael.

The horse jerked his head, and she chided herself for allowing her attention to wander.

"I need to get back to work here." Allie gestured at Chester.

"Definitely a pleasure to meet you again." He nodded, gave her another hundred-watt smile, then sauntered away.

"I know where the term *butterflies in my stomach* comes from," she murmured as she turned her concentration back to the shoe and drove in the last nail. Finally finished, she stood, stretched, and began to remove her chaps.

Philip Maynard appeared as if on cue. "You done there?" He thrust out his chest like a banty rooster. "We don't have long now before—"

"I'm done." Allie set her tools on the ground and unsnapped the leg straps of her leather chaps. "I'll mail you a bill." She skimmed the crowd with a detached air. The dark-haired stranger was nowhere in sight—and she had no good reason to feel disappointed. She did not need another man to deal with right now.

"I'll get Paige." With labored breaths, Philip ambled away.

"Whatever." The horse shuffled nervously. Philip's presence had disturbed him. Allie rubbed Chester in a soothing gesture. How had a simple day at the parade become so complicated? She had to get back to Danny.

She rested her head against Chester's warm neck, breathing in the distinct pleasant odor of horse. "C'mon, Mayor, I've got to get going."

"Allie." Philip must have heard her thoughts. He was barreling toward her, waving frantically.

The horse twitched. Allie straightened and watched, openmouthed. How could Philip move so fast? What a red-faced, sweaty mess to behold.

"We've got a huge problem," he gasped when he reached her.

Paige wasn't the only one on the verge of heatstroke. Allie stepped back and attempted to hand the horse's reins to him, but he shook his head, shooing her away. "I don't know what to do."

Allie's stomach clenched. The look in his eyes told her his problem was about to become hers. "Do about what?" Her tone was snarly, but she wasn't about to apologize.

"Paige has worked herself into a fit. She's sick to her stomach."

"And?" The desperation in his eyes didn't move her. "Someone can just fill in for her, can't they?"

His eyebrows shot up, and he smiled. "Why, that's brilliant. You can do it."

"Oh no." She shoved the reins at him. "No way. I'm here to watch the parade with Danny. Besides, I don't have a costume."

Philip Maynard's slit-eyed perusal told her he was calculating the best way to get her to acquiesce. "How about I pay you *three* times your rate for hammering on that shoe? And you can wear Paige's costume. You're about the same size."

Allie opened her mouth to say no, but the cost of Danny's party and the mounting bills with late fees made her hold her tongue. Danny might enjoy seeing her ride in the parade, she reasoned. Or maybe not.

"I'll do it under one condition." She couldn't believe her own words.

Philip breathed hard, watching her as if he was afraid of what she was going to ask.

"You write me a check for that amount and give it to me today."

He nodded heartily. "You got it."

She handed him Chester's reins. "I'll meet you back here shortly. I need to explain to Danny what's going on."

The mayor smiled. "I'll have someone bring you Paige's costume. Tell me where you'll be."

She did while mentally chiding herself for not bartering for more money. Finally, she turned to the horse, who tossed his head and shuffled uneasily. "Get over yourself, Chester. We're about to become even better acquainted."

❧

The sun warmed his skin as Derrick strode down Main Street toward his next goal. Walla Walla was a charming town. He'd been here on business before, but had never walked the streets. The parade, which he hadn't intended to watch, would start soon. He was drawn by the simplicity of it all. When was the last time he'd seen a parade? He couldn't remember. Today he'd intended to go for a drive and scour the outskirts of town for land that had potential for developers, then he'd contact the owners and see if they were interested in selling—a partial ruse. He groaned. He had a client interested in developing property, but land acquisition wasn't Derrick's actual purpose for coming to Walla Walla, and he was having trouble staying on task.

Derrick reached into his bag of jelly beans and popped one into his mouth. He'd lost some of the candy running into the petite auburn in front of Bright's, but the loss was well worth it if his hunch was right.

Allie. A farrier? He smiled at the memory of her holding the hoof of the large horse. Tiny as she was, she likely had a magic touch with the animals in order to do her job effectively.

Derrick rested his back against the rough bark of a tree and dug into his bag of candy. Allie had special eyes—green and expressive. She was different from any woman he'd ever met—in what way, he couldn't exactly say. She had shown a flash of interest in him, too. He'd grown accustomed to that kind of attention from women and had used it to his advantage in the past. But Allie's interest had died as quickly as it had come. The old Derrick would have turned on the charm to engage her again, but the new Derrick lost the desire to lead women on. Besides, he wasn't here to find a girlfriend. He was here to get information and return to his own life and home.

Could his search be over already? If God was on his side, Allie and the boy held the answers he needed.

Derrick stuffed the last of the candies into his mouth and tossed the bag into a nearby trash receptacle. His cell phone rang, and he quickly snatched it from the holder on his belt, glanced at the number on the screen, and flipped it open.

"Hello, Dad." Derrick spoke around the chewy candy that threatened to glue his jaw shut. He could practically see his father holding a pen over the leather-bound planner on his desk opened to his to-do list. Now his father could put a line through "Call Derrick."

"Just checking in, son. Have you found any potential properties?"

"Not yet. I'll keep hunting over the next day or so. Today the town is caught up in this onion festival parade. It's rather charming the way—"

"Please keep me posted." Dad harumphed. "I'm glad you're taking the initiative to find more business for Owens Realty."

Guilt rattled Derrick. His interest in land in Walla Walla gave him a legitimate excuse to be in town, but truth be told, finding property wasn't his priority. He tapped his fingers against his thigh. Did the omission of certain information constitute a lie? Possibly. And untruths, whether white lies, out-right lies, or stretching the truth, had a way of coming home to roost.

"Your mom said to tell you"—Dad cleared his throat— "that Sandy. . .er. . . Sandy is eating well."

A euphemism that meant Derrick's sister was having a good day and her will to live had given her temporary victory over the lymphoma that was killing her. Their father would not show his emotion, nor would he concede that his daughter was going to die.

"Good," Derrick said, blinking back sudden tears. Sandy had little time left. He needed to find what he was looking for here. For her sake. He'd do anything for his sister.

After he signed off with his father, Derrick dialed Sandy's cell.

"Derrick." Her voice was stronger than he'd heard it in a while. "Have you got news?"

He stopped pacing and made way for a group of rowdy teens. "I think I do."

"Really? Already? I prepared myself to accept this was a wild-goose chase."

What if he was wrong? Last thing he wanted was to get her hopes up, only to squash them. "Today, just by chance, I ran into a boy who could be the one we're looking for, but I can't promise yet."

"Wow. How do you know he's my son if you just ran into him?"

"The family name is Vahn," Derrick said. "Granted, they might not be the Vahns who adopted your son, but he's got our eye and hair color."

"Oh, Derrick, that would be an answer to prayer." Sandy's strained breath-ing made him short of breath. "Remember, I don't want them to know who you are or who I am. I just want to be sure my son's happy with the people who adopted him, okay? Promise me."

Derrick was silent.

"I said you have to promise me."

"Yes, fine." Derrick kicked his booted foot against the hydrant. "I won't let on."

"Thank you." Sandy sighed. "How can you forgive me, D-man? Giving away my baby and not telling anyone?"

"I didn't let on how shocked I was at first. I was afraid my reaction would send you into a decline."

She laughed. "I'm already declining."

A hard knot formed in his throat. "That's not funny, Sandy."

"I think my prognosis gives me the right to laugh at whatever I please."

Derrick had to smile. His sister's humor in the face of death amazed him. "You were desperate, Sandy. Not in your right mind at the time you signed away your baby."

"That's putting it mildly." She laughed softly. "More like a drug-induced alternate reality."

"I know. I feel guilty because I didn't come and rescue you back then."

"I wouldn't have let you. Believe me." She paused. "It's funny how coming to the Lord changes your perspective, isn't it? You look at life so differently. The things that used to be important aren't."

"True." Derrick nodded, but sometimes he worried the process of sanctification was taking too long in his own life. "You gave me all the info you had, right? That's just the names of the parties involved and this one picture."

"Yes. It was a closed, private adoption. I signed a bunch of papers. I was given the picture of my son and his birth parents, but nothing more. I promised the lawyer, Paige, that I'd never attempt to contact the parents. It all happened right after he was born, and I was in a fog—worse than normal." Her voice grew raspy. "Knowing what I do now, I think they gave me more money than they should have. Of course, I promptly squandered it on drugs. It's been almost nine years, and the first three of those are like a nightmare sequence. . . . I can't even remember everywhere I lived up until I returned home." Her voice had weakened during their conversation. "D-man. . .I don't think I have much time left."

"I won't let you down, sis." Derrick released a jagged breath. "You take care, okay?"

"I will. And I'm praying God will guide you in the direction you need to go. I'm just so glad this all worked out the way it did with you having business in Walla Walla."

Derrick swallowed hard and severed their connection. He couldn't even be totally truthful with his sister. Would his newly found Savior bless his overall efforts, despite what he had to do to get there?

God, please forgive me.

❧

Allie sat in formation with the women's club members. A hot, brisk breeze blew against her face and moved the skirts of her pioneer costume. She felt baked in the sun. A good thing she'd remembered to slather on sunscreen this morning. The leader of the group told her they'd be riding in a perfect diamond formation, with Allie at the back point of the diamond and the rest of the group in front of her.

The parade began, led by the local VFW. Behind that was a float ordered by Philip to be built by the historical society, complete with a papier-mâché replica of an onion and a huge banner bearing the town's name. Several members of the historical society were on board, dressed in overalls and jeans, holding garden tools. The mayor trailed in a blue convertible, followed by two cars filled with town dignitaries.

Although Chester walked quietly, she sensed the Thoroughbred's tension. Allie relaxed her position, heels down, back straight, hands resting lightly on the saddle horn.

From the side of her eye, she thought she caught a glimpse of Derrick, the pirate. Then the folks on the float in front of her brought out a banner. As it unfurled, Chester danced a few nervous steps. She leaned and spoke to him gently while stroking his neck.

The banner snapped in the wind, the white material undulating like a wave of water. Chester reared, eyes wide with fright. The women gave her wide berth. The leader of the group was hollering, which only added to Chester's discomfort.

Heart beating wildly, Allie fought to control the horse. She finally got all four hooves back on the pavement and took a breath.

The banner snapped again, and the panicked animal squealed.

"Chester!" Allie screamed. His hooves slid on the pavement. He was about to fall. She loosened the reins. Chester reared, ears back, eyes rimmed white.

Allie weighed her options while Chester snorted and danced. She could ride the crazy Thoroughbred through the streets of Walla Walla until he threw her or slipped on the pavement and fell, possibly crushing her. Or she could try to jump from his back now, risking broken bones or—

Chester's muscles tensed.

Allie released her feet from the stirrups and prepared to leap.

Chapter 3

With no time to think, Derrick snatched the tiny farrier from the horse by her waist. She was heavier than she appeared, and her long dress wrapped around his legs, making it difficult to walk. As he carried her away from the horse, Allie squeezed his neck in a viselike grip. He held her closer and longer than necessary, guilty for liking the feel of her next to him.

Allie's grasp tightened, and the subsequent lack of air to his lungs quickly diminished his pleasure. He set her feet on the sidewalk, then peeled her arms from around his neck.

"You're okay now," he said, massaging his windpipe. "You can relax."

Her eyes jerked open, and she stared at him. "You!"

He pointed to himself. "Me?"

With her breathing still rapid and her face white, she continued to stare at him. He checked to see if he had a piece of a jelly bean stuck in his front teeth. After a long pause, she appeared to collect her composure, though her face remained ashen and her hands shook. "Sorry. I owe you a huge thanks."

Derrick nodded, then assured the bystanders she was okay.

Allie scanned the streets, wide-eyed. "Where is Chester. . .the horse?" she asked. "That Philip Maynard—what was he thinking, putting that animal in this parade? Poor thing."

Derrick made a quick mental note about the name *Maynard*, then put his hand on the small of her back and moved her away from the road. "The 'poor thing' took off around the float, but some people up ahead caught him. And it appears the parade is moving on without you."

"Good." Her gaze raked the crowd. "I've got to find my nephew. I hope he isn't worried." She brushed past him and headed for Second Avenue.

Derrick followed her. They didn't go far before he caught sight of the boy who spotted Allie and grinned widely.

"Aunt Allie!" He ran to her, slamming into her legs. Only Derrick's quick grasp of her shoulders kept her from falling backward. When she regained her balance, he released her.

"Aunt Allie, you were like a rodeo rider! Wow!"

She smiled and pulled him close. "I'll probably feel like a rodeo rider tomorrow. All bruised and battered."

Derrick glanced from Allie to Danny, whose black eyes looked so much like his own. Aunt and nephew. Where were his parents?

"You guys. . ." A blond walked up to them, denim skirt swirling around her ankles. She carried a large black bag, which she set next to Allie. "Your tools, Ms. Farrier." Then she looked over Allie's shoulder. "I'd say you're a hero, mister."

Derrick shook his head, about to protest, but Allie turned and faced him. "Without you my landing would have been awfully hard. I might have even broken a few bones."

"All in a hero's day's work."

Allie laughed and motioned toward the blond. "This is my friend, Shannon O'Brien. Shannon, this is Derrick. . ." She frowned. "Owen?"

"Derrick *Owens*," he said, acknowledging Shannon. He dropped his gaze to Danny, who had been staring at him with a wrinkled forehead.

The boy traced an invisible line down his own face, perfectly matching the placement of Derrick's scar. "Did you get hurt bad?"

Allie offered an apologetic smile. "Danny honey, it's not polite to make comments like that."

"It's okay." Derrick pointed to his cheek. "I got hurt a long time ago. It's a scar. Do you have any scars?"

The boy nodded. "On my leg. I fell out of a tree. I was pretending to be Spiderman."

"So I'm not the only hero around here then."

Danny shrugged. "I'm a hero when I wear my Spiderman costume, I guess."

Derrick laughed. Could this be his sister's boy?

Shannon reached over and hugged Allie. "I certainly hope old man Maynard paid you well for your services. He owes you after that ride."

Old man Maynard? Derrick's heart thumped. There was that name again.

"Yes, he's going to pay me *very* well." Allie tilted her chin. "We're going to have a real shindig for Danny's birthday."

"Good. You probably deserve twice what he's giving you." Shannon's gaze snapped to Derrick again. "You're a real, live hero, Derrick Owens, and they're in short supply around here. You new in town?"

A hero? If they knew why he was here, they might not think so. Derrick masked his discomfort with a smile. "I'm checking out a few opportunities in the area for the contracting company I work for."

Shannon's eyes lit up. "Are you looking to buy land? Allie might be selling her land."

"Really?" He glanced at Allie.

"Not a for-sure thing." Her smile had faded, and she was frowning at her friend.

Shannon patted Allie's arm. "Just remember that God opens doors when you least expect it." She stepped back. "Well, I'll let Allie explain if she wants to. I need to scoot. I have to get back to my shop to relieve my temporary help."

"Thanks for watching Danny," Allie called after her.

"Anytime. I'll see you after dinner tonight." Shannon waved over her shoulder and swirled away in her flowing denim skirt.

Allie took a breath as if she was going to say something, but before she could speak, an overweight man, red in the face, trundled down the sidewalk at a clip that surprised Derrick given his size.

"Allie!" His chest heaved with his breaths. "Are you okay? I thought you were going to get killed."

Allie scowled. "And I'd have *you* to thank for it, Mayor."

He sputtered for a moment. "The horse was a little temperamental, but we thought he'd be fine. We just got him, you know."

"Gee, now you tell me." Irritation sparked in Allie's green eyes.

Derrick observed the shade of the mayor's face and hoped he wasn't going to have to perform CPR.

"You okay? Danny okay? This isn't going to affect him, is it? I mean, I wouldn't want things to get worse for him, poor little man."

Allie's body went rigid, and the sparks in her eyes turned to fire. "Some things are best left unsaid, aren't they?"

The mayor flushed, glancing from her to the boy and back again. "Yes, well. . .do you need a doctor?" He drew a noisy breath. "Do you have, er, insurance?"

Derrick watched the exchange with interest. What things were best left unsaid?

"No worries, Mayor. I'll be fine. But we need to get going." She held out her hand.

He fumbled in his shirt pocket and pulled out a check. "Ink isn't even dry on this. Here you go." He nodded at Derrick, then turned and dashed off.

Allie's narrowed gaze followed him for a minute, then she opened the check and smiled. "Ha, five times my going rate is almost worth taking that wild pony ride."

"Is that a lot of money?" Danny asked. "Does that mean you and Granny can buy me that Game Boy?"

"Possibly, but only if you don't nag me." Allie stared fondly at her nephew.

"Birthday boy?" Derrick asked, taking mental notes.

Danny grinned. "My birthday is next Saturday. Aunt Allie and Granny are giving me a party. Now I might get better presents."

Allie thumped his head with her finger. "That's enough about presents, Spiderman."

Danny nodded, but his eyes still shone.

Derrick's breaths came more quickly. Could it be this easy?

"Shannon is right." Allie interrupted his thoughts. She refolded the check and held it tightly in her hands, then looked Derrick squarely in the eyes. "You are a hero."

Hero? "Could be because you've known me less than fifteen minutes."

Danny hopped from one foot to the other. "That was cool, the way you caught Aunt Allie. Where did you learn to do that?"

The force of the boy's enthusiasm was irresistible. Pretending solemnity, Derrick glanced around as if to make sure the coast was clear, then leaned down and whispered, "I learned it in hero school."

Danny's eyes widened. "Is that where your face got hurt?"

"No, but it does make me look more heroic. I graduated at the top of my class." He straightened and glanced at Allie. "And because I'm a hero, I insist I walk you to wherever you're going while I carry your tools."

"You don't need to do that," she said quickly.

"Oh, but I do." He lifted his eyes to the summer sky and scratched his chin as though he were thinking hard. "See, it's rule number. . .um. . .twenty-one, I think. 'After saving a damsel in distress, always see her safely home or to her vehicle, whichever applies.'" He crossed his arms. "I scored a perfect hundred on that test. Of course, I stayed up all night cramming. And it's been awhile."

Allie's lips twitched. "How does one study for a *hero test*?"

Derrick placed his hand on his chest as though making a pledge. "Sorry, I can't reveal the secrets of a hero. It's in the rules. Number one, and I quote, 'No method, secret, rule, or procedure shall be revealed to anyone at any time.'" He paused and winked again at Danny. "And number two says, 'No hero will ever be caught bragging on exploits, whether his own or those of a fellow hero.'"

The boy's wide smile brought cheer to his heart, but it was Allie's grin that made his insides warm. He'd have to be careful. Old flirting habits died hard, and he couldn't afford the complication of an attraction. He had information to gather, then he'd be gone. Most of all, she could never know why he was here.

"All right, Derrick Owens, hero extraordinaire," Allie said, unaware of his turmoil, "you may walk us to my truck."

Derrick fought another surge of guilt. He leaned over to pick up Allie's tools so she wouldn't see his eyes. As he did someone called her name, and he glanced up. A tall, slender man in creased jeans and a brand-name polo shirt was jogging toward them.

"It's Mr. Michael," Danny said in a stage whisper, glancing up at Allie.

"So it is." Her face was an interesting study in consternation. "Go ahead, Danny."

"Hi!" he said to the blond man.

"Danny, good to see you." He gave the boy a quick brush on his head, then stopped close to Allie and touched her arm possessively. "My father just told me what happened. Are you all right?"

The mayor's son. Derrick recognized the resemblance now. Both had the same classic Roman nose. He also recognized disappointment in Danny's eyes. Perhaps he hadn't gotten the response he'd expected from *Mr. Michael.*

"I'm okay." Allie shrugged. "Just stiff and tired."

Pointing at Derrick, Danny said, "He rescued Aunt Allie."

Michael frowned and shook his head. "I can't believe my father would allow anyone to ride that horse. If it had been Paige, she might have been killed. She's not nearly as good a rider as you."

Paige? Derrick's shoulders went rigid. *Lord, You are answering Sandy's prayers.*

"Why your father would allow your sister to even be near that horse is beyond me," Allie said. "Two nervous Nellies."

"Well, we owe you. How about I take you home?"

Allie straightened her narrow shoulders. "I'm just fine, Michael." She side-stepped him and snatched Danny's hand. "Derrick is walking us to my truck."

Michael turned to him, a flash of surprise in his eyes. . .and irritation. He extended his hand. "I don't believe I've had the pleasure."

The man didn't look like he was feeling pleasure. Derrick clasped his hand. "Derrick Owens."

"Michael Maynard." The guy stared at him with intense curiosity. "You aren't from around here."

"No, I'm from the Tri-Cities. I'm here on business."

"I've got to get going. We're hungry," Allie said, cutting off their conversation.

"I'll call you later then." Michael glanced from Allie to Derrick and nodded.

Allie didn't respond. She squeezed Danny's shoulder with her right hand and began to walk away, pulling him along. Derrick had no choice but to follow.

As he followed, her tools in tow, Derrick felt Michael's eyes on his back and fought the temptation to turn and look at him. He hurried to catch up with Allie, whose strides were long and fast for such a petite woman.

Could he have imagined Michael Maynard's possessive attitude toward Allie? Not likely. Maybe they were dating. Derrick loosened his tight grip on her tool case. None of his business if the two were involved. With Sandy dying, he had to find answers quickly. He breathed a prayer of thanks to the Lord for blessing his efforts so far. He'd been in Walla Walla less than two days, and he was confident he'd found his nephew. He needed a bit more information—then he'd hightail it out of this town.

Chapter 4

As they prepared for dinner after the parade, Allie laughed when Danny described the wild horse incident to his grandmother while she sliced ham at the kitchen counter.

"I could have been killed!" Allie feigned a scowl.

"Not you, Aunt Allie. You ride too good."

"Too well," Allie corrected. She popped two painkillers into her mouth, took a drink of water, sat, and stifled a groan. Stiffness had already set in.

Her mother chuckled. "I'm not surprised you're okay. You always were good with horses. And you were such a tomboy. So independent. That's your father's fault."

"You know you did just as much to encourage me."

Ma hid a smile and shook her head. She carried a platter of cold ham along with a bowl of onion, cucumber, and tomato salad to the dinner table. "Ah, the perfect summer meal." Allie's mouth watered.

After they prayed and passed the food, Danny went on to describe the tall hero who had even attended hero school.

Ma's eyes widened. "Who is this man? We don't get many heroes coming through town." She looked at Danny. "Especially ones who went to hero school!"

The sudden memory of Derrick holding her in his arms warmed Allie's face. He was a stranger—and maybe it was the severity of her predicament—but she'd felt safe against his solid chest. *Stop it, Allie.*

She needed time to heal before allowing any man to bowl her over with his charm. Michael had practically abandoned her at the altar, and Luke. . .

There had to be a reasonable explanation for why her brother left them deep in debt. *Please, Lord.* Allie stabbed at a slice of onion, then met Ma's glance. "His name is Derrick Owens. He's a stranger in town on business."

"Well I'll be!" Ma's shrewd gaze hadn't missed Allie's emotions.

"I'm sure he's only here for a few days. We won't see him again."

"Hmm, you never know." Ma's smile lit her face, only to be outdone by Danny's.

Allie grimaced. "No matchmaking, you two. Don't think I haven't overheard you talking about finding me a man after Michael and I split up. And this one? A total stranger? He could be an ax murderer for all we know."

"What a mind you have." Ma clucked her tongue.

"He's not an ax murderer," Danny said as he chewed his food. "He's a hero."

Allie wagged her finger at him. "Don't talk with your mouth full."

The two conspirators said nothing else, but their exchanged glance spoke volumes. Allie determined to forget the whole topic—and the *hero*—and enjoy her meal. She brought a forkful of salad to her lips when her cell phone started to vibrate, dancing on the table next to her plate. She glanced at the screen, held back a snort, and continued to eat.

"You going to answer that?" Ma asked.

"It's Michael." Allie forced a smile for Danny's sake. "And we're busy eating dinner."

Ma dismissed the phone with a wave. "Right, let's eat." She understood how badly Michael had hurt her. "I have some good news."

"Oh?" Allie salted her food. "Do tell."

"I'm going to work for Shannon."

Allie's fork hit her plate. "What?"

"She's thinking about expanding by adding a shop in the Tri-Cities. She'll need someone to manage her store here. I'm going to start part-time."

"Shannon's really going through with that?" Allie's appetite fled. Her best friend. . .leaving. "I knew she was mulling it over, but—"

"Seems she believes the Lord is leading her there, and she'll be closer to where her parents live."

"Miss Shannon's leaving?" Danny's eyes grew watery.

Allie could've given herself a swift kick for elaborating in front of her nephew. Danny had suffered enough loss. "Don't worry. The Tri-Cities are only an hour from Walla Walla."

"Right," Ma assured.

"Ma, you've already got a job cleaning the church." Allie shook her head. "No. I don't approve." As soon as the words left her mouth, she regretted them. A combination of the stressful day, a stiff body, annoyance at Michael, and worry about the future made her snippy.

Ma sat back in her chair and crossed her arms. "Young lady, I don't think you should be telling your mother what to do. And two part-time jobs equal full-time pay."

"I'm sorry." Chastised, Allie took a deep breath. "But I don't want you working so hard. At your age you should be looking forward to some time off."

Ma's blond brows nearly hit her hairline. "Are you insinuating I'm old?"

Danny's head swiveled back and forth between the two like he was watching a tennis match.

"Not at all. You're not old. In fact, if we looked anything alike, we could be sisters. But. . .we should talk later," Allie said with a slight dip of her head in Danny's direction.

"Yes, we should." Ma's eyebrows were drawn into a frown. "And we will."

Allie barely tasted the remainder of her meal. The minute dinner was over she stood and gathered plates.

"Stop." Ma stayed her hand. "Danny and I will clean up. You sit and rest and give those painkillers time to work. I watched you limp into the kitchen earlier."

Allie sighed. She couldn't deny that every muscle in her body ached. Regular exercise and her job kept her fit, but she hadn't the time lately to do much riding. Clinging to Chester with all her strength during his rampage at the parade left her sore in places she didn't realize she had muscles. "All right, thanks."

Danny popped out of his seat and took the plates she'd gathered. Allie shifted in her chair, trying to find a position that didn't hurt. She longed to lie down, but she had a date with Shannon tonight at which time she'd lecture her friend about offering Ma a job without first consulting her. Not to mention reminding Shannon that Allie didn't want Shannon to move away. What would she do without her best friend close by?

Allie looked at her mom and mentally rehearsed ways to get her to understand she didn't need a second job. When Danny had finished cleaning the table, Allie crooked her finger at him, and he came over and stood in front of her.

"Spiderman, why don't you go feed the horses."

He grinned. "You want to talk to Granny without me, don't you?"

She squeezed his hands and smiled. "You're too smart by far."

He tapped his head with his index finger, then skipped out the back door.

Allie rested her weary head against her fisted hand. "Ma, I can support all of us."

"No, you can't." Ma shut the dishwasher and began rinsing the sink. "We aren't making it, Allie. You know that as well as I do. You work so hard, honey, but you've lost business because you can't keep up the workload you and Luke maintained together. This property is too big. The place wasn't meant for two women alone."

The words cut deep. First Daddy died, a year later Luke, then the dissolution of her engagement to Michael. No adult men in their household. No heroes to save their property. "Maybe we won't have to sell. We can lease out more land."

"Not fast enough to catch up with the bills."

"Okay then, we sell off land like we talked about. Then we could pay off debt."

"Do you know how long that would take?" Ma shook her head. "We have bills due now. We don't have months to wait."

"It's not fair. Not to you, not to Danny. None of it is fair."

Ma crossed the kitchen, sat across from her, and took her hands. "You know what I'm going to say."

"Yes, I do." Allie snatched her hands from under her mom's. "What you always say. God never promised life would be fair. Just that He'd walk through the trials with us. You've said it a million times, but—"

"It's true. Nowhere in the Bible does God promise us a bed of roses."

"More like a bunch of thorns." Allie clenched her fists.

"Honey, I know you're still angry about a lot of things. Your daddy dying. Luke and Cindy's accident, and Luke leaving so much debt. You being unable to pull in the kind of money you want to—"

"Of course I'm angry. Especially at what Luke did." Allie bit her lip. Why hurl bitterness at her mother?

"Yes, I know. He misrepresented some things."

Allie slapped her palm on the table. "*Misrepresented things?* He got credit cards for our business without my knowledge. He kept a second set of books to cover the debts. And he had the bills sent to a PO box. That's worse than misrepresentation. He was living a lie."

"You're right. But you don't know why he did it."

"No. Neither do you." Allie glared at her mother. "That's even worse. I've been lied to by two men I loved more than anyone else in the world. The latest being Michael the Cheater."

"What Michael did to you was awful. I won't defend him."

"At least we agree on that." Allie groaned. "There is no good reason to lie. No excuse for it."

"I agree with you in principle, but we can't stand in judgment of someone else." Ma sighed. "Luke was my son as well as your brother. Don't you think I have questions, too? But I have to forgive him."

"I loved him so much," Allie said. "Looked up to him." Beyond what she could express in words. She'd had this discussion with her mom too many times. Exhaustion washed over her, and Allie got to her feet, ready to escape to the quiet of her bedroom.

"It's like you're trying to make up for Michael's transgressions and Luke's by being perfect." Ma tapped her finger on the table to emphasize her words. "You want to rescue Danny and me by yourself, and that's admirable, Allie, but you can't. Your stubbornness is not going to pay the bills. You have to learn to be humble. To ask for help. From me and from others. I'm ready to go to the pastor to get his advice."

Allie swiped angrily at the tears in her eyes. "I don't want people to know."

"I understand, I really do. But if we lose everything, they'll find out, and then we'll look foolish. I've been trying to tolerate your obstinacy, but I'm not going to let us go under."

The firm set of Ma's chin told her she was losing the battle, and she fought tears.

"How about a change of topic?" Ma, ever the peacemaker, smiled. "Remember that tomorrow Danny's boys' group gets their safety badges at church. And the picnic here afterward."

"I remember." A smile came to Allie's face. "I'm so proud of him. He's come so far in a year."

"Yes." Ma raised an eyebrow. "We should all be doing so well."

Allie ignored the jab.

Ma stood. "I'm going to finish making salads for tomorrow."

Allie stood, too, and couldn't stop the groan that came to her lips. "I'll stay and help you instead of going to Shannon's for our Scrabble game."

Ma shook her head. "No, ma'am, you won't. That's your weekly ritual. You go take a hot shower. That'll help the stiffness. Then go on and play Scrabble." Ma reached out and squeezed her arm. "Honey, you never allowed yourself to grieve. You became stoic and just kept working. So did I. Too many losses in such a short time. For both of us. Now we need to move on with our lives."

Move on? To what? Still, Allie nodded her agreement. "Yes, I do know." She wanted nothing more than to protect her mother and Danny, but instead she was acting like a petulant child, mad at everyone around her and mad at God.

꙳

Derrick grabbed the phone directory from a drawer in the hotel bed stand and leaned back against a stack of pillows he'd jammed behind his head. The luxurious room in the Marcus Whitman Hotel provided everything, including a wireless connection, but he preferred the yellow pages. He thumbed through the book until he reached the listing for churches. Since coming to the Lord, he rarely missed services, and then only due to circumstances beyond his control. Now he felt a special need to worship. More so because his good intentions were keeping him from being totally up front with anyone.

Oh Lord, I'm doing this for Sandy. She wants to know her son is safe.

The town's churches were limited, and he couldn't decide which to attend. He shut the phone book, got to his knees on the plush maroon and beige carpet, and bowed his head.

"Lord, I need Your guidance. Lead me in Your ways. Show me a church to attend. And I know You despise a lying tongue. I ask Your forgiveness for omission of truth. I want to keep Sandy's secret and remain a godly man. Only by Your grace and mercy. Amen."

Derrick stood. One niggling concern taunted him. What if someone recognized his last name and put him together with Sandy? Although that probably wasn't likely since eight years had passed between the adoption and now. His stomach growled a protest, and he glanced at the clock. Five thirty.

Time for dinner. He headed downstairs to the Marc Restaurant, which the hotel attendant had promised was one of the best in town. Once he'd been seated and served, and after one bite of the succulent steak, Derrick reminded himself to thank the attendant for his recommendation. He adjusted the cloth napkin on his lap and tried to put his thoughts in order.

Okay, what had he learned so far? Derrick sliced his steak, then took a sip of tea. At this point it seemed likely that Danny Vahn was his nephew. Sandy had been living on the streets as a runaway, but when she realized she was pregnant, she'd gone to a clinic run by a religious organization. Different churches provided volunteers, and that was where Sandy had met her son's adoptive mother, a nurse named Cindy Vahn. She'd convinced Sandy that her best option was to give up the baby. A local law firm handled the private adoption, and the lawyer's name was Paige Maynard. Derrick sighed. A case could be made for coercion, based on what Sandy had told him, but. . .that was then. This was now.

So where did that leave him on his mission? How would he meet Danny's adoptive parents and be able to observe their interaction with the boy? All he wanted was to reassure Sandy—and himself—that Danny was in safe hands. If the boy's parents were anything like Allie, he and Sandy had nothing to fear.

Derrick finished up his meal, paid his check, and headed out of the hotel. He strode aimlessly around the center of town, his stomach in knots. He'd eaten too much too quickly. Perhaps a walk would settle his stomach.

Though Walla Walla was not very far from the dry arid desert of the Tri-Cities where his family lived, it was like a green oasis. He appreciated the sight of the Blue Mountains in the distance, where he often skied in the winter. Had Danny ever skied? It would be great to have an opportunity to teach the boy everything. To make him a part of the Owens firm when he grew up. . .

No. What was he thinking? He had to keep his promise to Sandy. Check on Danny, leave town, and report back to her. His nephew would never be a part of his life.

After passing one tourist-type shop after another, Derrick found himself several blocks from the hotel, wandering up Second Avenue. He was about to turn around when a junk store snagged his attention. Piles of items littered the sidewalk outside. Just the type of shop he used to visit with Lynn, the woman he thought he'd marry. The gaudy sign read THE QUAINT SHOP, and Derrick peered through the window at a washboard like his great-granny used to own. He peered inside the store and caught sight of Shannon, Allie's friend.

Chapter 5

S hannon had mentioned she owned a store. This must be it. For some
reason it suited her. And having access to her alone suited Derrick.
Maybe he could pry some information from her.

He wasn't two steps into the shop when Shannon came bounding up to
him, a bright smile on her face.

"What do you know?" she quipped. "The hero's here!"

Derrick glanced over his shoulder. "Where?"

Shannon laughed. "It's time to close. Let me lock the door and you can
join me in the back kitchen. I'm brewing tea. Want some?"

She twisted the key in the lock, then guided him to the back of the store
before he could answer. Shannon pulled aside a beaded curtain, revealing a
small kitchen with a tiny white table and two chairs. She pointed at one. "Sit.
And don't worry, this is herbal."

Derrick eyed the delicate-looking antique chair and proceeded with caution.

"That is stronger than it looks, believe me." She held the kettle over a plain
brown teapot and glanced at him. "None of that caffeine in this. Kills the
liver, you know."

"That'll be fine." He'd be willing to put his liver on the line for a strong
cup of coffee right about now, but it was more important to be sociable.

While she hummed and brewed tea, he studied the kitchen. Shannon had
been born in the wrong decade. She would've been right at home in the
golden era of hippies. He sniffed and scanned the room to locate the source
of the strong scent.

"Jasmine and chamomile," she said as she poured tea from the pot to mugs.

He blinked. "What?"

"What you smell. Aromatherapy. Jasmine and chamomile. Good for end-
of-the-day relaxation."

"Oh," he murmured. How had she known what he was thinking?

Shannon shoved a stack of papers aside and set a smiley face mug in front
of him. "I'm thinking of expanding—opening a new shop in the Tri-Cities.
Could be lucrative, I'm not sure."

"I might be able to help you." The words slipped out. He couldn't imagine
a shop like hers in the upscale areas he serviced.

"Really?" Smiling, Shannon took a seat across from him.

"Yep. My father and I own a real estate company." He took a sip of tea. Weird.

"That would be totally awesome." She scooted to the edge of her seat. "Wow, what you did today. . ." Shannon sighed. "You saved my best friend from breaking something serious, that's for sure." She sipped from her cup.

"I'm sure Allie would've gotten that horse under control. She looks like a strong, capable woman." A memory of the wild-haired Allie atop the crazy horse made him smile. Allie was spunky, but something in her green eyes told him she was vulnerable, too.

Nodding, Shannon set down her cup. "Allie is capable, all right. And strong. I don't think I could've survived what she went through."

"Why? Are you afraid of horses?"

Shannon shook her head. "Oh, I didn't mean the horse incident. I mean she's emotionally strong. First her daddy died. He had a heart attack. No one saw it coming, although he was a lot older than Allie's mom." Shannon shook her head. "He was such a great guy. Anyway, then her brother and sister-in-law in that awful car accident."

Derrick held his breath—and his tongue—while he watched her slowly sip the tea. He couldn't hold back. "Danny's parents are dead?"

Tears pooled in Shannon's eyes. "Poor little guy. Allie made sure he got counseling." She jumped up, opened a cupboard door, and grabbed a box of tissues. As she peeled away the plastic from the box, Derrick scrubbed his jaw with his fingers. Danny seemed to be in good hands.

"Sorry." Shannon sat back down and blew her nose into the tissue, then fanned her flushed face with her hand, a silver ring on nearly every finger. "Anyway, Allie takes better care of everyone around her than she does herself. She might have done with some counseling as well." Shannon blinked, then looked at him as though she were surprised to see him sitting across from her. "Do you go to church, Derrick?"

What? The way her mind jumped from topic to topic could give someone mental whiplash. Patience. He had to get her to back up to where she'd left off in the conversation, but again, his gut warned him not to push. "Yes."

"Oh, I had a feeling you were a Christian. I can usually tell. It's something on people's faces. . .well, really, it's in their eyes. The eyes are the windows to the soul, you know." Shannon's bright smile was back. "Derrick, you must come to Walla Walla Tabernacle tomorrow morning! Allie will be there, too. And guess what else. Tomorrow Danny's boys' group will get badges during the service."

Derrick quickly sorted through Shannon's words, keying in on the most important fact. He sent up a silent prayer of thanks. If it turned out Danny was his nephew, he'd be able to tell his sister that Danny was active in church. Sandy would be ecstatic. "In that case, I'm there. Where is it, and what time is the service?"

"Oh, cool! I've got last week's bulletin with the address." She got up and rifled through a three-inch stack of papers. "Here it is! Service starts at ten." Shannon gave him the bulletin, then rubbed her hands together. "It's like you're part of the family already, saving Allie's life and all."

Guilt speared his heart. He had to keep playing his part, keep up the facade, despite the fact that it meant leading on such nice people. "Got any more tea?" He had forced down the strange brew, but he needed a reason to linger and keep Shannon talking.

Shannon was out of her chair, kettle in hand. She grabbed a tin can of. . . Derrick squinted at the label. What was he drinking anyway? "Pu-erh?" He didn't mean to say it aloud.

"That's right," Shannon said with pride as she made him another cup. "Comes all the way from Yunnan." When she was done, she dropped into the chair, mugs in hand. "Oh, don't worry, that's a province of China, not a different planet." She laughed. "You're funny."

"Me? Why's that?"

Shannon scooted closer to the table. "I study body language. And, well, the way you held your hand against your stomach when you said 'pu-erh,' I could tell you worried about what you were drinking."

Actually he was surprised his stomach felt settled since he'd drunk the tea, but best not to contradict her.

"And there's more to you than what's on the surface." She studied him with clear hazel eyes. "Sometimes the Lord shows me things about people, I think. Sort of a discernment thing."

Derrick held his breath. He certainly hoped not.

"I think you're a good guy, Derrick Owens."

He didn't feel as relieved as he should. He was a man with a secret, which didn't quite add up to being a good guy.

". . .but there's something." A frown creased Shannon's forehead.

Derrick forced himself to relax and meet her gaze. "Everybody has something, don't they?"

Shannon's gaze scoured his face, and the wary look in her eyes disappeared. Derrick released a pent-up breath. As he started to relax, a hard rap on the back door gave him a start.

Shannon jumped from her chair and went to the door. "That's Allie." She tossed him a sly grin. "She's come to play Scrabble."

And Shannon hadn't warned him? That meant Allie probably didn't know he was here either.

Allie stepped through the door, and her gaze slammed into his.

"Look who's here," Shannon said with a gleeful smile.

"I have eyes." Allie's smile wobbled. "I'm surprised to see you, Derrick."

"No more surprised than I am to see you," Derrick said dryly.

"One more for Scrabble. It'll be fun." Shannon looked like a kid in a toy store.

Allie drew a deep breath. "Sorry to be rude. It's good to see you again."

"I was wandering the streets after dinner, getting a feel for the town, and I saw Shannon in the store. Decided to come in and see what's up."

Shannon set a third cup of tea on the table. "Derrick is going to help me find a place to rent in the Tri-Cities for my expansion shop."

"Oh?" Allie raised an eyebrow in his direction.

"I'm a Realtor. Property is my business. I handle rentals as well as sales."

Shannon pointed. "Allie, sit. He doesn't bite." Shannon grabbed a worn Scrabble game from the top of the refrigerator.

Allie blushed and dragged another chair to the table. Derrick hid his smile with his teacup.

"Did your mother tell you the good news?" Shannon glanced at Allie as she dropped the box on the table, pulled out the game board, and unfolded it.

"She sure did," Allie snapped.

Shannon pressed her bejeweled hand to her throat. "Does it upset you that she'll be working here?"

"Upset me? My best friend is definitely moving and didn't let me know. And she hired my mother and didn't tell me? What do you think?"

"I'm sorry. I thought I told you." Shannon patted Allie's arm. "I was just so involved with all the decisions, I wasn't remembering everything."

Derrick could believe that.

"Well, you didn't." Allie tapped the table with more vigor. "Ma is already working, cleaning the church. I worry about her. I don't want her working so hard."

"Come on, Allie. It's not like she's senile or something. She's not *that* old. I think she can make her own decisions." Shannon handed out letter holders.

Irritation lit Allie's eyes. "I know that, but I'm allowed to be concerned about my own mother, aren't I? She's been through too much. I want to protect her *and* Danny. She's always worked so hard. I just want to take care—"

Her jaw snapped shut, and she glared in Derrick's direction. Obviously his presence had slipped her mind.

Shannon grabbed Allie's hand. "Please understand. I'm hoping she'll be able to work here full-time soon. Manage the place. That means she can stop the cleaning job. In the long run, that will be easier on her."

Allie inhaled, and her shoulders sagged. "Okay. I give up. You're right." She lifted one corner of her mouth—a poor effort at a smile.

Shannon took game pieces out of the box. "And it will be lucrative, too. I'm going to work it out that Betsy gets a percentage of sales. That'll help you guys pay—"

"Let's talk about it later." Allie slid another quick glance Derrick's way.

A distress signal shot through him that went beyond just caring for his nephew. It was concern for the petite farrier and her mother. He tried to stifle the feeling. He couldn't afford to get deeply involved. Yet their well-being did directly affect his nephew. And the things Allie had left unsaid raised some doubts in his mind. How could he pursue this without giving away his real purpose?

Derrick sighed inwardly as Shannon began to pass out Scrabble letters. He got the letter *X*. No matter. Perhaps he'd earn extra points by using the word *pretext*.

Chapter 6

A high-pitched blare startled Allie from sleep. She jolted forward in bed, her heart pounding. "Wh–what?" Was someone playing a poor rendition of reveille? Early morning sun glowed around the edge of her blinds. She scanned the bedroom through slit eyes, focused, and caught sight of Danny's dress shoes poking out from beneath floor-length curtains.

"What in the world?" Allie glanced at the digital clock. It was eight thirty. She'd forgotten to set her alarm. "Daniel James Vahn!"

Allie pulled back the covers, got out of bed, and groaned from stiffness. She tiptoed toward the window where the muslin curtain billowed, then settled back, outlining her nephew's wiry form. "Danny? You little monster." She poked at where she thought his shoulder would be.

Danny giggled. His face appeared between the two curtain panels. "It's Sunday morning. You were oversleeping. I had to wake you up."

She smiled but might've cried. He was growing so quickly. At almost nine, his facial features were more defined, emphasizing his coal black eyes. Before long he would be a man. A striking man.

He stepped forward, shedding the curtains like a cloak. Dressed in his uniform, he held his dented bugle in his left arm like a soldier and saluted her.

Allie planted her hands on her hips. "Soldier, that horn is for camping with the boys' group, not for use at home."

"Yes, ma'am." He snickered.

She bit back a smile. "Now skedaddle so I can get ready."

"Ma'am, yes, ma'am." Danny saluted again and hurried from the room, closing the bedroom door.

Allie sank to the edge of the bed and put her face in her hands. She hadn't rested well, tossing and turning, between worry about finances and the memory of Derrick. Playing Scrabble with him had been fun, with his bright smile and quick wit. Definitely a charmer and clearly a confident man. Michael had been that way to a degree.

While engaged to him she'd thought how nice it would be to marry and give Danny a family again—a mom and dad. Her heart ached for the losses Danny had suffered. He deserved better than he'd had in his life. She often wondered about his biological mother, but knew nothing except the little her sister-in-law, Cindy, had told her. His mother had been young and living on the street. She couldn't give him what he needed.

That was ironic. Allie was beginning to think she wouldn't be able to provide for him either. She stood and stretched. With so much debt left by Luke, she was on the verge of declaring bankruptcy. She wanted to give Danny a secure life. In her heart of hearts, she knew her mother was right.

"I've been proud and stubborn, Lord." But she had her reasons. She'd do anything to hide the extent of their family problems from outsiders. She wanted to protect Luke and hide what he'd done. Lying, keeping a second set of books...her own brother. But why had he done it? What could have driven a man who was otherwise so honest in his dealings to lead a double life? Worse, she had to admit she felt betrayed by the Lord. Why had He allowed so many bad things to happen?

She clasped her hands and closed her eyes. "Lord, we need answers. If You're really there, if You really do watch over us, please give me answers."

Forty minutes later Allie forced down bites of toast in the kitchen while she tried not to think about Derrick. *Stop it!* she told herself. Why was she dwelling on a virtual stranger? The phone rang and put a stop to her ridiculous train of thought. She snatched it off its cradle and barked, "Hello!"

"Allie, it's me. I forgot to tell you last night that I invited...so I...and he...then I..."

"Shannon?" Allie pressed the phone closer to her ear. "I can barely hear you."

"Oh...won't hold the cell to my ear..." Shannon said something else that Allie didn't catch. "Just read...same as sticking your head...microwave. Brain cancer."

Allie huffed out a sigh. "Well, why can't you wait until we get to church?"

"No! This is important!" Shannon's voice came through loud and clear. "Did you hear the part about Derrick coming to church?"

"What?" Heat burned her cheeks. Just when she'd been dreaming about him.

"I invited him last night, but I forgot to tell you."

Allie ignored the footsteps coming into the kitchen and focused on the phone conversation.

Shannon giggled. "I think he likes you, Allie. All that time we played Scrabble, he kept trying not to look at you. You know how I'm good at reading body language—"

"Shannon! Why did you invite him to church? I'm not interested in a man right now, no matter what his body language says. You remember what I went through nine months ago with—" She turned to see her mother standing in the doorway.

"Michael? Forget about him!" Shannon said. "You need to leave that in the past and move on." The timbre of her voice had changed to the one she used for animals and small children, making Allie feel stupid. "Besides, Derrick coming to church is really not that big a deal. If anything, we're being kind to someone who's temporarily in town. What harm can come from it?"

Ma cleared her throat, and Allie faced her, pointing at the phone.

"Shannon, I'm not—"

Ma pointed at Danny then at her watch.

"I have to go," Allie said.

"Okay. I'll talk to you at church." Shannon's voice was too cheerful.

As she hung up, Allie could have sworn she heard her friend laugh, and a bolt of irritation raced up her spine. She switched her attention to her mom. "Let me brush my teeth real fast."

"Okay. I take it the hero will be at church today?"

"I guess." Allie shrugged. "Thanks to Shannon."

"He will?" Danny smiled widely. "Yay!"

"Hurry, then. We'll be waiting for you in the car." Ma and Danny walked out of the kitchen into the utility room and then outside.

As Allie hurried to the bathroom, she mentally scolded her friend. Shannon had arranged this on purpose. Now there were three people set on match-making. Her mother, Danny, *and* Shannon, and she wanted no part of it.

✖

As Allie walked down the church aisle, her eyes burned and she glanced up at the wooden ceiling beams to hide her tears. Hard as she tried to please the Lord, to love Him, she was at odds with Him lately. Her anger caused her lack of faith in His goodness, and she couldn't find a cure for it.

I'm sorry, Lord.

Trailing Ma and Danny, Allie shuffled into the pew four rows from the front and sat at the end next to Danny. Her gaze automatically roamed to the second row. Shannon. They locked gazes, and Shannon winked, then she smiled at Ma and Danny.

Allie turned at the tap on her shoulder. She found herself staring up into Derrick's dark eyes, unable to utter a solitary word.

Derrick smiled. "Good morning."

His crisp shirt dazzled white in contrast to his tanned skin and black hair. She grew as breathless as yesterday when he yanked her from Chester's back and into his arms.

"Mr. Derrick!" Danny grabbed Derrick's attention, saving her the mortification of revealing her inability to form a coherent sentence, a rare occurrence.

Derrick greeted Danny with a warm smile. "How are you, Spiderman?"

"Great. This is my granny." Danny pulled on Ma's hand.

Allie's face heated. She should've made the introduction, but Derrick had her so tongue-tied, she'd forgotten her manners.

"Derrick," Ma said, "it's a pleasure to meet you. I'm Betsy Vahn. Please call me Betsy. Thank you so much for rescuing my daughter yesterday."

"I told Granny you're a hero," Danny added.

"And he told me all about hero school." Ma's grin was wide. "If we'd known you were coming, we would have saved you a seat." She leaned forward, indicating with her eyes that the pew was filled, and shrugged.

"Quite all right." Derrick pointed to the front. "Shannon saved me a seat."

A spot near Shannon? Allie felt a spurt of jealousy, then told herself to get over it. She wasn't interested in any man. Not now. Not for a long time. But despite her mental self-chastisement, she watched as he walked over to sit beside her best friend.

Allie's cell phone vibrated in her purse. She fished it out, peered at the text message on the screen, and saw Michael's name. ALLIE, WE NEED TO TALK. The man wasn't listening to her. She didn't want to talk. She wanted nothing to do with him.

The music commenced, and Allie stuffed the phone back into her purse and rose with the congregation, but her gaze kept returning to Derrick's broad shoulders. He seemed to know the songs by heart—not once looking at the lyrics on the overhead projector. She caught a glimpse of the side of his face. Eyes closed and hands lifted, he appeared to be sincerely worshipping God. Allie leaned forward, caught her mother looking at her, and swung her gaze to the screen. Great. Ma was grinning.

What was there to grin about? Who knew anything about Derrick Owens? Charming, friendly, and more than likely a professing Christian, but experience had proven even people she'd known a long time couldn't be trusted.

⁊

As the pastor wound up his sermon and asked the boys' group to come forward for the special ceremony, deep sadness washed over Derrick. Sandy should be here. She should see this boy who was her blood. He had to find an opportunity to snap a picture of Danny to show his sister. Though Allie and her mother obviously loved the boy, he had to get close enough to check if he was being raised in a good environment. Just to ease Sandy's mind and, if he was truthful, his own.

He couldn't resist turning his head to observe Allie and her mother. Betsy was tall and blond with brown eyes, so different in looks than petite Allie with her auburn hair and green eyes.

Allie met his gaze, and Derrick turned toward the front and looked at Danny. So many details pointed toward Danny being his nephew, like his age, birth date, last name, and the mention of a Paige Maynard that Derrick had heard yesterday. But Danny's eyes cinched it for Derrick. Black like his own and Sandy's, a trait they'd inherited from their father.

Derrick tugged at his tie. A part of him wanted to talk to Paige—the woman who had taken advantage of Sandy when she was only nineteen. But as much as he resented the lawyer and wanted to give her a piece of his mind, he reminded himself he had to keep his promise. Talking to Paige might lead to Allie discovering who he was and his relationship to Danny.

The pastor asked for the parents of the boys to come up.

Derrick's heart felt like it was cracking. Danny's parents were gone. His biological mother was slipping away, too. He fisted his hands and forced himself not to stand and take part in the ceremony.

But Allie ran up to stand beside Danny. Her face shone with love. Derrick couldn't pull his gaze from her. Something he'd never felt before put his senses on high alert. This feeling. . .it wasn't familiar to him. He'd dated many women, beautiful women. But Allie. Perhaps he was looking at her heart, far past the physical, warm and inviting.

She caught him staring, but he made no attempt to hide that he was watching her. Their gazes entwined, just for a moment, and his heart thundered in his chest. He had to get out of town. Fast. Before anyone discovered the truth. And before he lost his heart to a woman he could never have.

Danny left his friends to hug Shannon, then high-fived Derrick before running from the church.

"That kid's like lightning," Derrick said, glancing over at Shannon. "Thanks for inviting me to the service."

"I'm so glad you were able to make it. Danny is something else." Shannon's eyes searched his face and lingered. "Isn't he?"

Had she seen a resemblance between himself and Danny? "Yes, he's a great kid."

"I've often wondered about his real family. They have to be awesome." Shannon half-smiled and patted his arm. "I've got to run. Will we see you again?"

"I don't know," Derrick said. At least that was the total truth.

"Okay." Shannon turned abruptly and ran smack into Allie. "Hey, Al. You know what the Bible says, right? 'In all things God works for the good of those who love him, who have been called according to his purpose.'"

Allie fidgeted with her purse strap. "What are you talking about?"

Shannon glanced from Allie to Derrick. "Just keep it in mind."

Danny bounded back into the church whooping and made a beeline for them.

"Shh," Allie motioned with her index finger on her lips. "This is a church."

Smiling, Danny bounced on the balls of his feet. "When are we leaving?"

"Shortly." Allie combed her fingers through Danny's dark hair. "I was so proud of you today."

"Thanks, Aunt Allie, but I'm really hungry. Can we go—"

"Allie, I'll see you in a little while." Shannon pointed her thumb over her shoulder. "You should invite Derrick to the picnic today."

Allie opened her mouth to speak, but her mother spoke first.

"What a great idea, Shannon." Betsy's eyes were warm. "The boys' club is coming over for a barbecue and potluck. You come, too. It'll be my thank-you for rescuing Allie."

Allie's head snapped toward her mother, and her brows lifted.

"Cool! Please come." Danny nodded enthusiastically and tugged on Derrick's arm.

How could he refuse the boy? "All right, then. I'll see you there," he said, which earned him an unreadable glance from Allie.

Chapter 7

Derrick pulled his gray Silverado into the Vahns' driveway and sat behind the steering wheel, strumming his fingers on the dashboard. He shouldn't be here. He was getting too emotionally involved—and not just with Danny.

Even if an argument could be made for coercion when it came to Danny's adoption, that point was moot now. Sandy only wanted to know her son was safe and happy. She didn't want his life interrupted. Yet here Derrick sat in front of the Vahns' house, wanting to spend time not only with his nephew, but also with Danny's aunt, both of whom he'd be better off never seeing again. No way could he have a relationship with Allie. Wishing that things could be different only made the situation more difficult. He hardened his resolve to get a picture of Danny. That done, he'd walk out of his life—and Allie's—forever.

As Derrick strode up the gravel path to the house, he couldn't help but view the property with a real estate agent's eye. It was habit after years in the business. Despite the obvious efforts of the two women to keep things up, the property had a run-down air. The gardens were neat and tidy, but all the buildings needed a coat of paint, including the house. The land around the house was pretty. Flat fields with clumps of trees here and there. Some of the outbuildings in the back were falling down, but the barn remained in good shape.

He scanned the old, single-pane glass windows. From his periphery, he thought he saw Allie staring out one of the upstairs windows, but when he looked again, she'd gone.

No more stalling. Derrick rang the bell, and Danny was at the screen in two seconds flat. "Mr. Derrick!" He swung open the door with a warm, welcoming smile.

"Danny." Derrick gave the boy a quick hug and was rewarded with the feel of his nephew's arms around his neck, a bittersweet experience that he tucked away to cherish as a memory.

They stood in a tile foyer, and a long hallway spread out in front of them with a wide staircase on the right. To his left through an arched opening was a formal living room. Derrick surreptitiously studied the old farmhouse, which he judged to have been built in the early 1900s. Everything was neat and tidy and so clean. He would find no dust balls in the corners. But the furniture was dated and the sofa threadbare. Old water stains marred the ceilings. Signs of decay would be evident, even to someone without a practiced eye.

Derrick walked farther into the room, and his breath caught in his chest. There, on top of a spinet piano amidst an array of framed photos, was the same picture Sandy had given him of her son with his new parents. Only this one was larger and framed with gold.

"Come on," Danny said, tugging at Derrick's arm. "Let's go outside through the kitchen."

Derrick ripped his gaze from the picture to follow Danny. As they started up the hall, Betsy entered through a doorway at the other end where he could see a kitchen. She strode toward them, carrying a piece of paper.

"Derrick! I'm so glad you made it. Allie is upstairs. She'll be down in a minute." She held up the paper. "I've made a sign for the front telling everyone to go around back and join us. That way we don't have to keep answering the door."

"Yes, good. . .good idea." He had to get his bearings. He felt overwhelmed and couldn't think straight. If only Sandy were strong enough to be with him now.

Betsy taped the sign to the door, then turned to her grandson. "Danny, Pastor John is heating the grill. You go out and make sure he has everything he needs. I'll be out in a minute."

"You come, too, Mr. Derrick," Danny said as he bolted down the wood-floored hall and disappeared into the kitchen.

"Be right there." Derrick kept in step with Betsy's slower pace.

"This house is old," Betsy said, her tone apologetic. "It needs more work than we've been able to do."

She must've noticed him checking things out. "Oh, was I gaping? If so, I'm sorry. I love old houses and tend to imagine renovations here and there."

"That's fine. I understand." She sighed as they walked. "My husband never had time to do much. He was too busy with the family blacksmith business. Nor did we have the money to do a lot of renovation. We still don't."

"A lot of people find themselves in situations like that." Derrick wanted to kick himself for whatever she'd read on his face that had her making excuses for the condition of the house. Perhaps his facial expressions were too like his father's. A man who tended to look down on those who weren't in his social stratum.

The front door banged open. Betsy whirled around, and Derrick glanced over his shoulder.

Michael, the man he'd met at the parade, walked into the foyer.

"Oh," Betsy whispered. "I'd forgotten Michael was coming. Let me introduce you."

"We've already met. At the parade." Derrick couldn't help the irritable tone of his voice. He hadn't liked Michael at first glance and didn't like him any better now. But he was worried the reason was jealousy, and Derrick hated that emotion.

Betsy must have noticed. She sent him a fast glance. "Oh. Well then, please excuse me. I need to say hello."

Derrick let her go and made a quick exit into the kitchen. Since Paige was Michael's sister, there was always the possibility he would mention Derrick to her. And despite the passing of almost nine years, she might recognize his name and tell Allie or her mother. He could only imagine the hurt in Allie's eyes if she discovered he had misrepresented himself to her, Betsy, and Danny.

In the kitchen he skirted a large oak table covered with bowls and platters of food to reach the mudroom. There he exited the house onto a cement slab that served as a back porch. Under a large maple tree, Danny and the pastor were working on the grill, and Danny waved but was immediately distracted by one of his friends. People stood or sat in groups talking. No one paid much attention to him. This was a perfect time to snap a few pictures and just observe. He walked over to another maple, partially hiding himself, and held his phone up until he could see Danny on the display screen, then snapped. He took two more, glanced up, and noticed the spectacular view of the Blue Mountains in the distance so took a few shots of them, too.

"Taking pictures?"

Derrick jumped, almost dropping his phone. Shannon stood at his elbow.

"I love the scenery here," he said quickly.

"So it would seem." Shannon tilted her head.

"I don't have a view like this at home." Derrick opened the viewer on his phone and showed her the pictures he'd taken of the mountains. All the while his mind screamed, *Liar!*

&a.

Allie stayed upstairs as long as she could. Lack of sleep caught up with her, and she wasn't in the mood to see anyone, yet she had to go face a houseful. She'd watched Derrick arrive and then Michael. Their joint presence alone was enough to make her feign sickness. But she couldn't do that to Danny or Ma. And she had to start the burgers.

She ran down the stairs to the kitchen and took a platter of raw burgers from the refrigerator. A shadow fell over her, and she turned and saw Michael.

"You're avoiding me." Michael crossed his arms like he expected an explanation. "I saw you hide behind your truck before the parade."

Allie felt sheepish, but nodded, tired of pretense. "That's an accurate statement. I am."

Michael's blond brows drew together. "Why's that?"

"We broke up." Allie placed the platter on the counter with a sigh. "You were dating another woman when we were engaged. That's called betrayal."

"That's called a *mistake* on my part." The muscle in his jaw worked. "And I'm sorry it happened."

"Admitting it was a mistake and being sorry don't mend betrayal. Not for me. You were living a lie."

"Something I'll regret the rest of my life."

The pain he felt was obvious, but his duplicity had almost destroyed her. Allie shook her head. "I found you kissing another woman. Then you told me you weren't sure what you wanted—"

"I wasn't sure, but that made me realize it's you I want. Only you, Allie."

"If you weren't sure, you shouldn't have gotten engaged to me to begin with. I'm sorry, Michael." Allie picked up the platter. "It's over."

He drew closer. Too close. "Who's this Derrick?"

"Exactly who he said he was. A businessman passing through town."

"Then what's he doing here at the picnic?"

"Not by my invitation, and none of anyone's business."

Anger flashed in Michael's eyes. "Are you going to tell me you don't love me anymore? That you can forget what we had between us?"

Had he always been petulant and pushy, and she just hadn't seen the real Michael?

"There is no 'us.' It's over." She walked toward the screen door, but he jumped in front of her and held it open.

Outside she headed for the grill manned by the pastor. Ma stood next to him chatting. Michael hovered near the back door and began to chat with a local family, much to her relief. Allie studiously avoided meeting his gaze.

Pastor began to put burgers on the grill. "I'm not an expert, but your mother asked me to do this."

Allie shrugged. "You'll be fine. Thank you for doing it." She was relieved. She wouldn't have to man the grill. The way she felt today, she'd probably burn the burgers to a crisp.

She glanced around, not wanting to admit to herself she was looking for Derrick. She finally spied him with Shannon, nose to nose in conversation, partially hidden by a tree. Her legs felt frozen, and she couldn't tear her gaze from the picture in front of her.

Shannon's long hair hung free, blowing in the breeze. Her light skin and hair looked striking next to Derrick's dark hair and tanned complexion. How humiliating to feel jealousy over a man who meant nothing to her! Her cheeks heated. A good thing God allowed people's thoughts to stay private—but what was in her heart? Pining over Derrick Owens, a total stranger?

Ma joined her. "Honey, you look like you've been sucking lemons. What's wrong?"

"What *isn't* wrong?" Allie snapped.

"Allie," Pastor John said. "How about we sit and talk?"

Allie dropped onto the bench and held back a sigh. Everybody knew that a "talk" with the pastor meant a serious sermon. Why couldn't she keep her feelings to herself?

"Your mother was telling me about your financial situation."

Allie shot her mom a withering look. Great. On top of everything else, now everyone would know the Vahns were headed for bankruptcy.

The pastor smiled and touched her arm. "I know it's hard to share things like this, but we need each other. We can agree with you in prayer that God intervene and do a miracle."

"Seems we've been a little short of those lately," Allie blurted before she could stop herself.

Ma opened her mouth to speak, but Pastor continued. "I understand why you would say that. I don't have any pat answers for you. I wish I did. However, God is still in the miracle business. He still answers prayers."

And there in a nutshell was Allie's biggest issue. If God still answered prayers, why were things so difficult for her? For Ma and Danny?

But for her mother's sake, Allie agreed. They bowed their heads, and she tried to listen, but her thoughts were too loud. She wanted to believe. She wanted to return to the strength of faith she'd had several years ago, but her relationship with the Lord had been eroded by her experiences. Michael's faithlessness. Luke's deception. Luke's and Cindy's deaths. Logically she understood the Lord wasn't a puppet master. People made their own choices. Things happened based on those choices. But she still felt let down, and she'd grown cold in her faith. So why would God respond to her prayers now?

Chapter 8

After the picnic Allie was cleaning the kitchen with Shannon. Through the window over the sink, she saw Derrick and Danny helping Ma roll the grill to the old shed in the backyard. Odd. . .he looked so familiar, like he belonged.

"Michael didn't stay long," Shannon said.

"That's because I told him under no uncertain terms that our relationship was over. Completely over."

Shannon snorted. "You've done that already."

"And already and already and already," Allie said. "He seems to think dating another woman behind my back was just fine as long as it led him back to me."

"He's justifying himself." Shannon loaded the last glass in the dishwasher. "Like if his bad actions led to a good result, it's okay."

"Yeah." Leave it to Shannon to analyze the situation. "And it's not just that he did it or tried to justify it. The thing that bothers me most is he's never admitted it was wrong. He said it was a mistake and he was sorry, but sorry for what? That he got caught? It's almost as if I should be glad it happened because he ultimately decided I'm the right girl for him."

"I'm not surprised." Shannon wagged her head. "I never liked him, as you know. He was too good for a lot of the simple things in life. He would never have stooped low enough to drink my tea or play Scrabble with us."

Shannon's words were true, and she was sure her friend meant to point out a fundamental difference between Michael and Derrick. Michael was a snob. Derrick wasn't. Funny that would be so obvious even though they hardly knew Derrick at all. Or maybe Shannon was getting to know him better than Allie thought.

"I'm a fine one to talk about being snobbish, though." Allie shoved a plastic pitcher of juice into the refrigerator.

"What do you mean?" Shannon scowled. "You're nothing like Michael."

"Maybe not, but I have my own issues." She glanced at her friend, then at the floor. "I'm pretty mad at God right now, along with people—men—I can't trust."

"Oh, that. Don't worry." Shannon waved her hand in the air. "The key is to keep the communication open with God. Don't stop talking to Him. Ask for forgiveness. He'll deal with your heart, and the feelings will follow."

"I suppose." Shannon's encouragement didn't assuage her guilt; it only made her irritable that her best friend had an easy friendship with God. And maybe the picture in her head of Shannon and Derrick didn't help. "What were you and Derrick talking about earlier?" Allie inspected the countertop like the question meant nothing to her.

"Business," Shannon said, not looking up.

Allie attacked the sink with cleanser and a sponge. "What kind of business?"

"Yours and mine." Shannon dried a pot and put it in the cupboard. "I told you he's going to help me find a property to rent in the Tri-Cities, right?"

"Yes." That meant Shannon and Derrick would be working together. Allie felt the stab of jealousy again and shook her head. Ridiculous.

Shannon gave her a sidelong glance. "We also discussed your situation. He might be able to help you sell some land."

"That again?" Allie slapped the sponge into its plastic holder behind the sink. "Why is everyone talking to everyone else about my personal business?"

"Gee, that's an overstatement. I only meant to—"

Ma, Danny, and Derrick walked into the kitchen, all three laughing. Then Ma held up a rectangle of paper. "The pastor gave us a check, Allie. It's from a fund at church for parishioners in situations like ours. It will help get us through this month."

Allie wanted to shush her mother in front of Derrick. Not everyone needed to know their financial woes.

"Derrick!" Shannon flapped a dish towel in his direction. "Tell Allie what you said about the land."

Derrick dropped onto a kitchen chair, looking as if he'd been a part of the family forever. "I might be able to help you sell part of your land. I have a buyer looking for investment property—possibly to subdivide and build houses. That's why I'm in town."

"And that's not all." Shannon motioned for him to continue.

He nodded. "I thought you could give me a quick tour of the place. I'll go back to the office and poke around a little bit, look at other listings, run some figures on comparable properties. Talk to some people. Then if things look good, I'll have to come back for a longer look."

Allie swallowed. When all was said and done, she didn't want to sell. Especially to someone who was going to build a subdivision. She loved her home and the privacy it afforded them. But what choice did she have?

"Go show him around before it gets too late." Ma stuck a card on the refrigerator with a magnet. "Derrick's business card."

"I'm coming outside with you!" Danny crowed. "I want to show Mr. Derrick the barn."

Ma and Shannon exchanged quick smiles, then stared at Allie expectantly.

No need to wonder why Ma hadn't shown him around the property herself. She was matchmaking again, which was more than useless. Derrick was here on business, which was becoming more apparent by the second. There was the possibility that he'd already looked into properties and saw theirs as a good prospect. The thought occurred to Allie that maybe he was using them for his own ends.

Danny waited near the door, and her heart ached for him. He'd been attached to Michael. Looking back she realized Michael had given Danny attention until Michael had won her heart, then he'd backed off. Danny had noticed and kept trying to win Michael's approval to no avail. She could never allow that to happen again. Danny was vulnerable, and according to his counselor, going through a stage where he was searching for a father figure. Even now he waited impatiently, eager to show Derrick around. How could she protect her nephew? In just a day and a half, Danny had developed a bond. She couldn't bear to see him hurt again.

Derrick glanced at his watch. "I'll probably need to leave soon. I have to. . . um, I have another appointment."

Another appointment? Is that what he considered his visit with them? An appointment?

Allie tried to smile. If she were honest, she'd developed a bit of an attachment to Derrick, too. She chided herself for weakness and pointed toward the door. "Let's get to it, then."

As they walked out of the house and toward the barn, the wind mussed his thick black hair, sending wisps across his forehead. Their fingers brushed, and she had the sudden thought that it would be nice to hold his hand. Fortunately, Danny jumped between them and interrupted her insane desire.

"Hey, Spiderman," she said. "Lead the way."

Danny bounded ahead of them. Their footsteps were silent as they crossed the yard, and the crickets sang their familiar song. Would she lose all this?

Derrick looked over at her. "So how did you get into the blacksmith business?"

"My dad started it. Learned it from his father. He taught me and Luke." Her breath caught. "He was my brother—"

"Luke was my dad," Danny said over his shoulder. "He's dead. So is my mom. And they're in heaven. There's no time there, you know. So while I grow up, they're happy and waiting to see me again."

Oh the simplicity of a child's faith. And of course Danny was listening to every word she and Derrick exchanged. They reached the end of the backyard and began walking the fence line toward the barn.

Derrick motioned at a cottage beyond the barn. "What do you do with that?"

"Nothing at the moment. We rented it out for a while, but it needs a lot of work, and we haven't had time or money to do it."

Why was she opening up to this virtual stranger? Perhaps Pastor's prayer had helped after all, but was Derrick a safe person to open up to? She waved to the right. "We lease out these fields to a local farmer. That brings in some money, but it's not enough. Not with the amount of debt we have to pay."

Derrick stopped and looked at her intently. "There's got to be a way to fix this."

If not for his serious demeanor, she would've been amused. "I assure you, my mom and I have tried everything."

He seemed to be waiting for further explanation, and Allie hastened to change the topic. She pointed at a small building next to the barn. "That's our. . .my office. That's where I take care of the business." She motioned for him to follow her to the weathered barn. When she opened the door, Danny ran ahead of them and disappeared through a doorway in the back—his hiding place. "Danny's favorite place is the barn. I hope we can keep it when we sell property."

"Oh man, this is tough." Derrick almost spoke the words to himself.

"Yes, well. . ." She inhaled the familiar scent of hay and straw, and tears stung her eyes. Two horses in stalls next to each other stretched their necks over the bottom half of the stall doors, and she rubbed the mottled gray face of the first.

"The horses love you, huh?" Derrick smiled.

"I love them, too." Allie moved to the second stall where a stocky bay horse snuffled gently against her arm.

"Do you have just these two?" Derrick reached out, stroked the horse, and his fingers trailed over her hand. She didn't move. The rough feel of his fingers warmed her skin.

"Yes. We had to sell the others." A lump rose in her throat. The time was coming when she might have to sell these as well and her heart would break.

"They're both quarter horses. The gray is Storm. This guy is Pip. I named him after Dickens's character in *Great Expectations*. My dad used to read that story to me. He bought me Pip when I was fifteen." She hugged the horse's neck and buried her face in his mane. "Pip has been like a friend to me," she said almost to herself. "I used to hang on his neck and cry during the worst of my teenage angst."

Derrick went to Storm's stall and patted his neck. "Beautiful animals."

Beautiful, she thought. Derrick Owens definitely cut a striking figure. "Do you ride?"

"Yes. Not as well as you, of course." His laughter sent a shiver of delight up her spine. "I can't forget your wild ride at the parade."

And she couldn't forget the feel of being in his strong arms. She found herself smiling despite the prospect of losing the land she so loved.

Derrick sobered and looked her in the eye. "Shannon said your father died of a heart attack."

"Yes." Allie stared out the barn door in the direction of the mountains. "Seems he had a ticking time bomb in his chest. We didn't know until it was too late. He was quite a bit older than my mother, but they adored each other."

"And your brother and his wife died in a car accident?"

"Yes. A terrible tragedy. Sometimes I relive it over and over again in my dreams. It had already been a bad day. They'd been fighting and. . .shouldn't have been on the road." Allie took a deep breath. "Well, anyway, thank God Danny wasn't with them. Last minute, they asked me to watch him."

"Yes, indeed," Derrick murmured and cleared his throat. "We should talk business. I know the thought of selling part of your property is hard. You appear to love it, and it's part of your family history. I understand that."

"Yes." Allie met his dark gaze to see if he was sincere. Those eyes—expressive and sensitive.

Allie switched her gaze to Pip, gave him one last scratch, then walked back to the door. She wrapped her arms around herself and stared at the Blue Mountains. Lately she'd felt older than twenty-eight. She worked long hours, and when she did take a break, she felt guilty. The responsibilities were always there like clanging alarms waiting to be turned off.

"What are you thinking?"

She hadn't heard him walk up behind her. He was so close she could turn and fall into his arms. Being held, having someone to lean on, would feel so good. She shivered. Would Derrick stick around long enough for her trust in him to grow?

"I'm thinking that Shannon has a point when she says we all need balance in our lives." Allie shrugged. "For instance, I love the mountains in the winter. I ski. Cross-country. I pack food and just go all day. Sometimes Shannon goes with me, but she chatters too much." Allie snickered. "Though I couldn't ask for a better friend, sometimes I need the solitude. But when I do it, I feel selfish taking time for myself."

"I don't get the chance to feel guilty. My dad's the travel agent for guilt trips."

Allie laughed. "Is he?"

"Oh yeah." Derrick's eyes crinkled with a good-natured smile. "But I understand your need to be alone." His voice was low, like he was confiding secrets. "When I want to be alone, I hike into the bare hills around the Tri-Cities. I sit and stare out over the Columbia River. I also ski."

"Shannon and I are going on a spiritual retreat next week. At a monastery. We have to spend part of our time in silence."

Derrick chuckled. "That will be hard for Shannon."

"Yes, it will," Allie agreed, then she shuffled her feet on the floor. "I write poetry."

"Poetry?" Derrick's raised brows told her he was surprised. "Really?"

The heat of a blush inched up her face. "It's silly really, but writing poetry helps get my feelings out."

"Not silly at all." Derrick clamped his hands behind his back and looked her in the eye.

"Mr. Derrick!" Danny yelled from the back of the barn. "Come and see my hiding place."

Allie's heart pounded hard, and she was relieved by Danny's interruption. "You go on. I'll feed the horses. He'll enjoy showing you his treasures. Danny is so much like Luke, even though he was adopted. From a little boy, Luke would stash things in hiding places. Anyway, when you're done, tell Danny to bring you to my office."

Derrick headed toward the back of the barn, and despite her efforts to resist, she drank in his retreating form. He looked capable and strong, like he would protect the people he loved. For a dangerous moment, she found herself longing that Derrick Owens would fall in love with her.

Chapter 9

Sunday evening Derrick hovered in the doorway to Sandy's bedroom, trying to muster the courage to face his sister. This was his "appointment" that he'd mentioned to Allie and her family. He needed to tell Sandy everything he'd discovered.

The decor was so like her. Creamy yellow walls, bright white curtains open wide to let in the light. The room glowed, even in the dark of night.

He clutched the bouquet of flowers in his hand and stepped through the door. His mother rose from a blue cushioned chair next to Sandy's bed and came toward him. It seemed Mom had aged overnight, and he hoped his face didn't give away his concern. Dark roots were visible through her usually perfect blond hair. Lines carved around her eyes and mouth had appeared during the last month.

"Mom." He gave her a peck on the cheek.

"So glad you're here," she said. "Sandy ordered me to wake her when you arrived."

His sister looked pale and thin under her covers. "Please don't. I can come back later."

"I think we should do what she asked."

Because we don't have much longer to do it, Derrick completed his mother's thought while he fought tears. His mother wouldn't cry. His parents never did, at least not publicly. They regarded stoicism as admirable, to be worked at and sought after like some people worked at getting fit. His father alleged that displays of emotion made one vulnerable. Something others could use as tools to manipulate.

Derrick sighed. He agreed in part, but there was a time and place for emotional expression. To allow loved ones to know how much they were cared for. He'd seen and felt it this past weekend in Allie, Betsy, Danny, and even goofy Shannon. Allie was the one who withheld the most, but even she showed depth of emotion with her poetry, her horses, and her love for her family.

"Mom is right," Sandy's weak voice came from the bed. "You'd better do what I ask."

"You're not asleep; you're just pretending." Derrick crossed the room, smiling. "And what are you going to do if I don't do what you ask?"

"Don't mess with me, D-man. You know I have ways of getting even."

The light banter helped relieve the knot of dread in his stomach. No matter how ill, Sandy's sense of humor remained.

She pointed to the flowers. "Wow. A girl has to be dying for her brother to pay attention to her."

"Sandy!" Mom hissed. "What a horrible thing to say."

Sandy laughed softly. "Why should I deny it, Mom? I *am* dying. Laughing makes it easier to cope."

"I find nothing funny about it." Their mother edged toward the door. "I'll leave the two of you alone. Your father will be here soon; I'm going to wait for him."

Derrick watched his mother slip from the room, her high heels tapping hard on the wood floor of the hallway as if clicking their disapproval.

He placed the flowers on the nightstand and sat on the edge of the double bed. "Did you do that on purpose? To get rid of her?"

Sandy shrugged. "Not really, but I'm relieved. I feel bad for Mom. She's really struggling with this, but she acts like I'm already dead, walking around on tippy toes, turning off my happy worship music when she thinks I'm asleep, and putting on this heavy, funeral dirge classical music. As if she's afraid anything lively is going to kill me more quickly."

He laughed and cried at the same time.

Sandy's smile lit her eyes, making it easier to look at her thin, pale face. "The hospice nurse has been coming in. . .Leanne. She's wonderful, and we conspire together and think up practical jokes."

That was so like her, the joker. He feared if he took a breath, the tears he fought would come in a flood.

Sandy took his hand. "It's okay. You can cry. In fact, do anything you need to do. God's biggest gift to me is the realization that He isn't just a stern God, but He's also a loving Father who wants His children to enjoy life. We're allowed to laugh and even get mad. Sometimes I'm so mad at God, I could just spit." She sighed. "Yeah, I know. Some church people would tell me that's horrible. I should never be mad at God, but He knows my thoughts, so I might as well admit them. Mostly I'm peaceful. I'm beyond grateful I had the opportunity to be born again. And even better, that you and I were born again at the same time."

The memory of the altar call they'd answered together was clear, like a series of snapshots in his mind. Sandy's street-hardened expression had melted into peace, taking years off her face.

Derrick swallowed past the hard lump in his throat and kissed her forehead. "It's so good to see you." He pulled the worn picture of Danny as a baby with Cindy and Luke from his shirt pocket. "I wanted to return this."

"Thank you." Sandy pointed to her Bible on the bed stand. "Put it in there and tell me everything. All about this young man who is my son."

"I have good news, and I have bad news."

"Of course. That's always the way, isn't it?" She poked his arm. "So get on with it. I really don't have forever."

"Okay, here's the good news. His name is Danny. I'm positive he's your son. I saw a larger version of that picture you gave me on top of a piano in the living room of their house." Derrick tucked Sandy's copy in her Bible.

"Danny." She smiled. "Short for Daniel."

"The bad news. His parents are dead."

Her eyes widened. "What? How?"

"Car accident. A little over a year ago. Now he lives with his aunt and grandmother." Derrick pulled his phone from his pocket. "I have some pictures. I took these at a picnic at their house today." He went on to explain about Danny's award at church while she flipped through the photos. "And I have a surprise for you."

"You do?"

He pulled a photo from his pocket. "This is Danny and his grandmother. I e-mailed it to myself and printed it out for you."

"Wow, look at my handsome son. Aw, his grandma looks sweet." Sandy glanced up. "Whoa, D-man, I just realized what you said. You got invited to a picnic at their house? How?"

He grinned and saw himself pulling Allie from the horse. "I guess you could say it sort of fell into place." He explained in detail about the parade, meeting Shannon, playing Scrabble, and being invited to church. Then he explained about Michael and expressed his worry that Paige might recognize the Owens name.

"Maybe. But how many people have the last name Owens? She'd need good reason to tie you to Danny. Do you have a picture of Allie?"

Just the mention of her name sent a rush of adrenaline through his veins. "No, I don't." Derrick squinted at the photo for all the diversion was worth.

"I see. And she's not married?"

"No." Derrick massaged his forehead, hiding his eyes from his sister. Their relationship had always been close because they were together so much as children, tended by a nanny while their parents worked long hours. That bond gave them rare and precious insight into each other's thoughts.

"Danny," Sandy said softly. "Like Daniel, the Old Testament prophet. A man with great faith and conviction."

Derrick nodded. "His eyes are dark like ours."

"Danny's family are good people then."

"Real good people. Danny's Aunt Allie and his granny love him. . .adore him. But they're struggling financially." Derrick looked directly into her eyes. "A big part of me wants to do something. Intervene. He's family. He's our blood. I want him to know, and I want to help take care of him."

Sandy shook her head violently. "Derrick, no. The family has been through so much. A boy losing his parents and then just when he finds out he's got a biological mother, she dies, too? That would be cruel. And then there's Dad. If he found out, there would be no peace for Danny's family."

Derrick said nothing. Knowing Danny as short a time as he had, he wasn't sure the boy would struggle, at least not for long. But Sandy was right about their father. "I feel dishonest. And now I have to go back."

Her mouth fell open. "You're going back?"

"Yes." Derrick clarified about the Vahns' land. "Danny phoned me on my way here. He invited me to his birthday party next Saturday night. I've woven a tangled web." Derrick couldn't help but think of Sir Walter Scott's words, "*Oh what a tangled web we weave when first we practice to deceive.*"

Sandy was quiet for a moment, then drew a ragged breath. "It's risky, you know, but the land is a good way to help them. And I know you want to see Danny again. I want to see more pictures if you can get them. Close-ups."

"The Vahns could discover I'm a fraud, I suppose." A big part of him wished it would happen and save him the pain of an explanation. The more time went by, the harder it was to keep up the subterfuge.

Derrick squeezed Sandy's frail hand. "Are you sure you don't want them to know? I mean, the way you gave up Danny. . .I'm not sure it was on the up-and-up. At the very least, it was coercion. They took advantage of a young, drug-addicted woman."

"We've talked about this. No." Sandy's voice was surprisingly strong. " 'In all things God works for the good,' you know."

Strange, Shannon had said the exact same thing.

"The thing is, D-man, I couldn't have cared for Danny at the time. I was living on the streets. And I was on the outs with Mom and Dad and was afraid to face them with my story. Now, looking back. . .well, he wouldn't have been raised in a Christian home. Mom and Dad weren't. . .aren't. . ."

"I know." He and Sandy prayed for their parents. They thought their childrens' conversion to Christianity was an annoying but passing phase. "Remember when Dad said we were in a cult?"

Sandy laughed and shook her head. "Oh, it's not funny really." She pointed at him. "Have Pastor Clark officiate at my funeral. If anybody can bring down the conviction of the Holy Spirit. . ." Sandy's face lost all animation. "Seriously, if Mom and Dad hear him preach, they've got a real chance of coming to the knowledge of the saving grace of Jesus."

"If Jesus takes you home, I'll do that."

" 'If,' huh?" Sandy blew out a long sigh. "There's no 'if' about it."

Derrick wanted to argue, but he couldn't. Instead he vented his anger at the disease that was killing her. "Why cancer? You could have fought the hepatitis."

"I talked to the doctor about that. Hepatitis makes a person more vulnerable to lymphoma. Talk about reaping what you sow. I was in such a drug haze back then. I didn't care about anything but my next fix."

She grabbed his hand. "I was a fool. I didn't even know who Danny's father was. Could've been anyone, probably a dealer. I was a charity case in drug rehab. Scared to death. But God watched out for Danny. Cindy came along. She was a volunteer nurse at the clinic. She wanted a baby badly. Said she and her husband had been trying for a long time. She said if I agreed, she would adopt my little boy, and she seemed like an angel at the time. I never saw Cindy again, and before Paige disappeared, she gave me that picture I lent you."

"I'd still like to tell them the truth, sis."

Sandy raised his hand to her cheek. "Remember Danny's namesake? God protected Daniel even in the lions' den. His grace is sufficient. I'm dying, Derrick. Please let Danny be. God will take care of him." A little twinkle lit her eyes.

"Now what?" Derrick frowned. "You're up to something."

"Tell me about this Allie. I think you find her attractive."

Derrick leaned back on the bed and huffed out a sigh. Just as he'd dreaded, Sandy had seen through his facade. "It doesn't matter. She can't know who I am, remember?"

Sandy's smile died. "Yes, that's true."

"I'm invited back next weekend for Danny's birthday party, and I'm going to inspect their property and see what I can do for them. Then I'm going to disappear from their lives."

"I'm sorry." Tears came to Sandy's eyes. "I can tell you like this woman. Maybe more than like her?"

Derrick shrugged. "There are lots of women." His statement was ironic. He'd always said that after ending relationships in the past because no one had ever captured his heart. But this time the words felt hollow. Allie wasn't like the others. For the first time in his life, he realized he was truly capable of falling in love—deeply, madly, and forever.

Chapter 10

On Tuesday afternoon after she'd shoed the Armstrongs' two palominos in preparation for a show, Allie sat in her truck and consulted her planner. As she scanned her to-do list, she nodded. "Looking good." She and Ma had worked out their schedules with Mary, the mother of one of Danny's friends, so he could be cared for while Ma trained at Shannon's shop.

Shannon. What would she do without her best friend? Tears pricked the backs of her eyes, and her nose burned. Another loss. It seemed the Lord saw fit to strip her of everybody and everything she'd given her heart to.

Allie drew a breath and shook her head. She was just feeling sorry for herself. She still had Ma and Danny. They were more than enough to be thankful for. They were her life. Her reason to get out of bed in the morning and keep going.

She swiped a tear from the corner of her eye, returned her attention to the planner, and groaned. She had to check on Eddieboy, Frank Johnson's cranky pony, who was recovering from a bad case of thrush caused by a poorly cleaned stall. Frank, who was almost as cranky as his pony, could have treated the thrush himself, but Eddieboy was not cooperative, to say the least—one of the reasons he was often left to his own devices in his polluted stall. He had an enormous set of teeth and wasn't hesitant to use them.

Allie tossed the planner on the passenger seat and started down Highway 12. If she survived her encounter with Eddieboy, she'd call on Raymond Connor. He ran a stable of trail horses and had given the Vahns business for years. But after Luke died, Raymond had moved on to another farrier. He didn't believe women should be farriers, let alone work *outside* the home. Losing the man's business had been a hard financial blow. If only she could convince him that a woman was just as capable as a man.

"Good luck with that." Allie flicked the turn signal and hung a right.

So much to do today. She would stop at the bakery between her other appointments to ask if they were on top of Danny's cake.

And last. . .she didn't have to look at the planner to see what she wanted to avoid at all costs. She'd prefer to deal with Eddieboy and his teeth than to hear that deep voice and try to act casual.

Return Derrick's call.

What luck that she'd been in the middle of an appointment when he'd phoned. Last thing she needed was to be caught off guard with nothing clever to say.

Allie grabbed her cell phone from her purse. She'd already heard Derrick's message, but she wanted to hear it again. "Hi, Allie, this is Derrick. I've got a quick question for you. Call me back."

She sucked in a breath. His deep voice. . .the way he spoke her name. . . An involuntary chill raced up her spine.

"Call me back," Allie repeated. As though any single woman in her right mind wouldn't return Derrick Owens's calls. The man was not only self-confident and good looking, but also nice. Which was precisely what drew her to him and scared her all at once. She shouldn't waste her time. He was most likely only after her land. And she couldn't really fault him for that. He was a businessman. But he had the courage to save her at the parade. That said a lot for the kind of person he was.

Allie glanced at the clock on the dashboard. She wasn't due at the Johnsons' for an hour. Plenty of time to call the tall, dark hero.

She pulled her truck over to the side of the road, threw the gearshift into PARK, and rubbed her thumb over the clouded glass on her cell. Derrick was probably calling her with an offer. She'd either accept or reject. Nothing more to it. Then he'd walk out of her life.

"Oh, for Pete's sake." She had to grow up. Allie snapped on her headset, drew a breath, then dialed Derrick's number.

After three rings, her shoulders relaxed. He wasn't going to answer. She could leave a message and—

"Hello." Derrick's voice sounded close and intimate and sent a shiver of pleasure down her spine.

"Umm, Derrick. This is Allie. Allie Vahn."

"Allie." Was she imagining the smile in his voice? "I'm glad you called me back. I have a question for you."

"Sure. Fine." She readied herself for the worst. "Is this about selling my property?"

"No." Derrick laughed. "I want to get Danny a birthday present, and I wondered what he'd like."

A birthday present? Of all the things Derrick could've asked, this hadn't been on her radar.

"You don't have to do that." What was he really getting at? "Between myself and Mom and Danny's friends, he'll have plenty of—"

"I know I don't have to, but I want to. I'm not going to show up without a gift for him."

"Show up?" Allie pressed her hand to her heart. "Show up where?"

After a long silence, she shook the phone. Had their connection been severed? "Derrick, you there?"

"Yeah, um, this is awkward." Another pause. "On my way home on Sunday, I got a call from Danny. He invited me to his party. I assumed you knew."

"He called you?" Where had Danny gotten Derrick's phone number? Aha! The business card on the fridge. Smart boy. Wait till she got her hands on the kid.

"I'm sorry," Derrick said, "this should've been cleared with you first. I won't come."

"What? No, it's fine." Her heart hammered as hard as the day she'd nearly been thrown from Chester. "Danny invited you. But I want you there, too." Allie clamped her hand over her big mouth. What had possessed her? Heat traveled from her neck into her cheeks, stinging the tips of her ears.

"Are you sure?" The softness of his voice seemed to suggest a deeper question. But she could be hearing what she wanted to hear.

She summoned her most casual tone. "Of course Danny wants you there or he wouldn't have called."

"As long as you're okay with it, I—"

"Of course. It feels like you're a friend of the family already."

"Thanks for that. So. . .any gift ideas? I'm not up on the latest for nine-year-olds."

"Hmm, I'm getting him a Game Boy. How about you get him a game to go with that?"

"Easy enough," Derrick said, and the background noises suggested she should make a graceful exit.

Allie cleared her throat. "I guess—"

"I've got to—"

They spoke at the same time.

"Sorry." Derrick laughed. "You first."

"I was just going to say I have an appointment, and I guess I'd better go."

"Sure thing. I'm about to head out to a meeting with a client who might be interested in your property."

"Oh, that's great," Allie lied.

They exchanged good-byes, and Allie snapped her phone closed. "What's wrong with me?" She rested her head against the steering wheel. Derrick ended the call with business, taking all the wind out of her sails. *Not that you're in the market for a man,* she reminded herself.

Allie shifted the truck into DRIVE and headed toward her next appointment, her stomach aching and a dull throb in her head. Even if she couldn't save herself from her foolish emotions, she had Danny's feelings to consider. The poor kid had attached himself to any father figure she'd brought home. Derrick Owens had been in town to find land for a developer. She had Danny and Ma to consider. Time would tell if Derrick became anything else.

"Lord, if Derrick's got a fatal flaw, please reveal it to me. If he's nothing more than a real estate agent selling our land, please intervene and don't let us all get attached to him." Her prayer was heartfelt. Ever since Pastor prayed for her at the picnic, she'd found herself more expectant about God's answers. Slow but sure, she was beginning to give her life back to the Lord. To trust Him.

Trust. She didn't trust men, either, and she was surprised Derrick had wormed his way into her life so easily. Were she and Derrick two ships passing in the night? Allie sighed. She'd have to get it out on paper. She would have to write a poem.

❧

Good phone conversation or bad? Derrick frowned. Today Allie had shifted emotional gears fast enough to make his head spin.

Laura ran up to him and grabbed his arm. "Mr. Owens, your dad wants you in his office. . .ASAP." His secretary's whispered command startled him from his deep thoughts.

Derrick nodded, then rounded the corner and strode down the long foyer to the end of the hall. Now what? Surely he'd be called to task for not giving a full account of his whereabouts. His mind raced, and he dismissed one lie after the other.

Well, Dad, I was at a picnic with the woman of my dreams. Spending time with my nephew.

Yeah, Derrick. That would definitely work.

He tapped lightly on the cherrywood door before entering. He turned the brass knob and approached his father's ornately carved desk on cat's feet. "You wanted to see me?"

His father continued to study the computer screen. "I've been waiting to hear about your trip to Walla Walla." He turned finally and looked up. "Land? Ring a bell?"

"I found a likely prospect." Allie's property. Danny's home. Derrick took a seat in front of his father's desk. "It's farmland—"

"Good, good." Dad steepled his fingers, and his eyes narrowed. "Are we looking at a steal or a deal?"

He had once admired the real estate tycoon. Now the idiom made his skin crawl. Derrick shrugged.

"Don't disappoint me, son." He pushed back from the desk and stood. "I want to see *something* in writing." His face turned as crimson as Walla Walla's illustrious mayor's.

Derrick caught himself lifting his hands in a gesture of surrender, a motion he'd used so often through the years to placate his father. He purposefully lowered his arms. No more. "Nothing is settled. I've got to go back, do a bit more research before I—"

"For crying out loud!" His father paced like a caged lion. "First your sister, now you." He rapped his hand on the desktop. "Are you both going to turn out to be losers?"

Dad's words were harsher than normal and cut deeply. "I'm doing my job. I don't want to lose business by being careless." Derrick sprang from his chair. "I don't care what you think of me, but Sandy is no loser. She's a great kid. A little mixed up, but—"

"She's no kid." Dad sliced the air with his meaty hand. "And sure enough, neither are you." Breathing heavily, he clamped his hands behind his back. "What were you doing in Walla Walla all that time? Womanizing again?"

Derrick stood head-to-head with him, his face heating. Dad's attack today was worse than normal. He sent a silent prayer to the Lord for help. "I don't do that stuff anymore, Dad. And you know it."

"Sure, sure, you got religion." He wagged his head. "A zebra doesn't change his stripes."

Derrick's phone buzzed, indicating a text message. He glanced at the screen and put the phone back on his belt. "I have to go. That's my secretary. I'm needed." He turned and walked toward the door. Understanding hit. His father was stifling his grief about Sandy dying and taking it out on Derrick. He turned. "I'll keep you appraised of the Walla Walla details."

"I expect results that benefit us. None of this Christian namby-pamby stuff." Dad sat again at his desk. "And we'll speak again shortly."

The "results" would mean taking advantage of the Vahns. He'd taken advantage of desperate sellers before, raising his percentage by a few points with the promise of getting it done quickly. Could he do it again?

Chapter 11

What a day. Allie headed up the highway toward home, the worst part of her day divided equally between playing keep-away with Eddieboy's teeth and her visit with Raymond, who'd told her in no uncertain terms that he was done with the Vahns' farrier service.

"A woman, 'specially one your size, couldn't possibly be a farrier. Your brother, now we're talkin' a horse of a different color."

But when Allie pulled into her driveway and saw Michael's BMW parked in front of the house, Eddieboy's teeth and Raymond's scolding looked inviting. She didn't want a showdown with Michael, especially at her house. But if she disappeared, Ma and Danny would be worried and hunt her down.

On a deep sigh, she parked her truck next to her office and went to the barn to clean her tools, taking her slow, sweet time about it. Would Michael ever give up? Her pulse quickened with anger as she loaded her tools back into her truck.

By the time she was walking toward the house, she was ready to take someone down. She stomped through the yard to the back entrance, stopped at the sound of Michael's voice, and inhaled deeply to gather her emotions, reminding herself that anger profited little. She stepped into the kitchen, and there Michael sat at the table, working on a 3-D puzzle with Danny and Ma, eating ice cream. Michael made a snide remark, and Danny laughed.

Allie dropped her keys on the counter, and once again fury rose from deep inside her. Michael was using Danny again to get to her. She approached the table short of breath.

Michael looked up and smiled. "Hey, Al. I came by to bring Danny a birthday present." He motioned at the puzzle.

"I invited Mr. Michael to my birthday party." Danny smiled.

Anger constricted Allie's chest, and she could hardly breathe. Before she said something she'd regret, she needed to escape and gather her thoughts. "I'll be back," she managed. "I have to change my clothes and shower."

She crossed the linoleum, heels of her boots thudding hard, feeling everyone's eyes on her back, and ran up the stairs to her room. She sent up a silent prayer for peace and took care not to slam her door.

❧

That evening Derrick paced the parlor, reliving his conversation with Allie.

"Will you be joining your parents for dinner?" Hank, the chef and all-around housekeeper, as well as one of Derrick's confidants, stood at a discreet distance.

Who could eat? "Hey, Hank. No thanks. Maybe later."

"If you need to talk, you let me know."

Derrick nodded. "Will do." He needed to be alone with his thoughts. Hank disappeared before he could offer an apology for his rudeness, and he added another regret to his growing list, but he couldn't bear to speak with anyone right now.

"Oh Lord, give me wisdom." Derrick went past the back staircase, bypassing the dining room unseen, and quietly walked down the hall. *Lord, help me sort this out.*

He dropped into a comfortable leather chair in the library and closed his eyes. He hated having to make choices, but this was where he'd found himself—in the belly of the whale. He could disappoint his father, although that was nothing new, or he could shortchange Allie and her family. Or. . .

He could confess all to his parents in the hopes that they'd understand. But that would mean betraying his sister. Going back on his word. Then there was Allie.

Derrick massaged his aching forehead. He lived in a different reality than Allie. He had no money worries, didn't believe money in and of itself was evil, and was grateful for the blessing now that he'd come to know God.

"Derrick?" His father strode into the library. "I thought I heard you. I'd like to talk to you before dinner."

He acknowledged his dad with a nod.

His father sat across from him on the sofa. "Have you seen Sandy?"

"Earlier today, just briefly." He held tight to his reserve. No emotions allowed.

Dad shifted in his chair. "Have you seen Lynn lately?"

Strange question and out of left field. "Lynn?" Derrick shook his head. "I haven't seen her in months."

A frown formed a V in the middle of Dad's forehead. "You stopped dating her?"

Sad. But if he'd taken the time to talk regularly, his dad would've known. "Yes, we broke it off. A mutual decision."

"Ah. I see. She couldn't take the other women in your life, no doubt."

Derrick focused harder on his father. He barely knew the man. He'd grown up watching him come and go and bark into the phone incessantly, happy when his dad tossed him a few crumbs of attention, wishing for so much more. But Sandy—Dad's negligence was hardest on her. He often wondered if Sandy's daredevil antics were to get attention from the man she called "Daddy dear."

"I want to discuss keeping the business in the family."

"It *is* in the family." Derrick tugged at his tie. Where was this leading? "It's you and me."

"Yes, and therein lies the problem." Dad stood and paced the room. "Your mother mentioned that the Victors recently had a grandson."

Understanding hit like a sledgehammer. "Are you suggesting I get married and have children just to carry on the Owens name?"

"You're thirty-two going on twelve." Dad scowled. "Aimless. Don't you feel it's your duty to—"

"Duty?" Derrick slapped his hand on the arm of the chair and stood. "I'm not going to be the king of England. Do you think I'd marry a woman I don't love so I can give you heirs to the business?" Even as he said the words, his thoughts went straight to Danny. This confirmed Derrick's feelings. He'd never be able to tell his father he already had a grandson. Worse, that meant he couldn't be honest with Allie. Sandy was right. Dad would never leave the Vahns in peace, especially now that Danny's adoptive parents were dead. Where did that leave the Vahns legally?

Dad crossed the room and stood directly in front of him. Odd that they could be so physically similar and yet completely opposite in character. Strangers, in a way. "Sometimes we need to do things that aren't comfortable because it's best for the family."

Where had Dad been when he and Sandy were young and needed him desperately? "I'm not listening to this. It's archaic at the very least, and it's demeaning." In the past his parents had hinted at their hopes that he'd marry and have children, but he couldn't remember a conversation that had been this blunt.

Dad blinked, and his eyes reddened. He ran his hand over the back of his head. "Family is everything, you know."

It might be too late, Dad. Derrick took a deep breath. "I understand that family is important." He'd seen that connection between Allie and her mom and Danny, and at least he'd experienced it with Sandy in the last few years after she'd returned home.

"Try to understand." Dad strolled to the arched window and stared out into the night. "Sandy. . ." He squared his shoulders and cleared his throat. "Whatever. We forgive and forget. But she can't give your mother and me. . ."

Derrick saw his father through new eyes. The hotshot real estate mogul had turned into a fragile, vulnerable man in a blinding flash.

"Dad." Derrick strode toward him and rested his hand on his shoulder. Why hadn't he noticed his father disappearing before his eyes? Dad's independence and big personality had clouded his vision.

"Well then." Dad backed up. Derrick dropped his arm. "I'm glad we had this talk, son."

No. There was so much more to say—but Derrick stood speechless and watched his father leave the room.

ஃ

Allie awoke to the sound of knocking on her bedroom door. The room was dark, her hair damp and partially wrapped in a towel, and she was on top of her covers wearing a bathrobe.

"What?" She blinked and focused on her clock. Eleven-twenty. And this was. . .Tuesday night.

"Allie, it's Mom. I'd like to talk to you."

Allie switched on the lamp on the nightstand, tossed the towel on the floor, and sat on the edge of the bed. "Okay. Come in."

Ma entered and lingered in the doorway. "Were you asleep?"

"Yes. I guess I lay down for just a second and dropped off. I'm sorry." Sour memories came rushing back. "Is Michael still here?"

Ma shook her head and settled on the edge of the bed. "No, he left."

"Good." The word slipped out of her mouth before she could think straight.

"We need to talk." Ma smiled. "Are you up to it?"

"What about?" Allie combed her hair with her fingers. She would have to wash it again just to work out the tangles.

"Tell me what you're thinking."

Allie blinked. "Thinking? About what?"

"Your actions tonight were. . .rude."

Allie sat back, and the anger she felt when she'd seen Michael's car returned with a vengeance. "*I'm* rude? How can you say that? I walk into my own house after a hard day's work and find Michael sitting at the kitchen table as if everything is peachy. And you and Danny laughing and doing a puzzle with him. Gee, what's wrong with that picture?"

Ma's eyes flashed. "This is not just *your* house. Two other people live here who have feelings, too."

Allie's fury grew. "Michael was *my* fiancé. He cheated on *me*."

"Michael didn't come just to see you. He came by to give Danny a birthday present."

Allie shook her head like she'd been sucker punched. "Ma, that's pathetic." Her mother was sometimes naive when it came to people's motives. "I know you choose to see the best in people, but even you have to realize Michael's using Danny as a portal back to me."

"Then blame me." Ma shrugged. "I'm the one who invited him to stay awhile. I felt sorry for—"

"I thought you understood what Michael put me through." It was one thing for Ma to feel sorry for every repentant soul and quite another to invite Michael back into their lives.

"I do, but I felt bad for him."

"Are you implying that I should go back with him?"

"That's not what I said. Not at all."

Allie pulled in two long breaths. This was going to turn into a talk on forgiveness, and she had forgiven Michael, but she didn't want him to be a part of their lives. Next subject. "Why did you let Danny invite Michael to his party?"

"I didn't. Danny blurted that out. I couldn't very well say no, even though I didn't think it was appropriate given the circumstances."

"Did you know that Danny also invited Derrick to his party?"

"Did he?" Ma smiled. "I had no idea. How did you find out?"

"Derrick told me."

She chose to ignore her mom's blatant show of pleasure at the prospect of having the hero attend Danny's party. "I know we've spoiled Danny a bit. He's the center of our lives, but we can't let him run things around here, either."

"Danny meant well." Ma sighed and stood. "He's a sweet, sensitive kid. I sometimes look into his dark eyes and think. . ." She crossed her arms over her midsection. "Ever wonder what his biological parents were like?" She moved toward the door. "We could ask, I suppose, but Cindy said the records were closed."

I wonder all the time, Allie mused, but she'd save that conversation for another day. "All right, we'll make the best of it, but don't blame me if things go haywire with Michael at the party."

"You're bigger than that, sweetheart." Ma opened the bedroom door then turned. "So Danny really invited Derrick to his party?"

Allie grabbed a pillow and held it high over her head. "Another word about Derrick and—"

Before Allie could hurl the pillow, Ma ducked out of the room, laughing.

What did Danny have in mind, inviting both Michael and Derrick? Allie tossed aside the pillow and headed to the bathroom, her mother's query hanging at the back of her mind. *"Ever wonder what his biological parents were like?"*

Lately, and for no known reason, the question wouldn't leave her alone.

Chapter 12

Sunshine streamed into the kitchen window. Allie poured batter into the pan to make another batch of pancakes. Saturday. Danny's birthday.

"Allie!" Her ma's voice gave her a start.

Spatula in hand, Allie swung around. "I'm making pancakes."

"You didn't have to tell me. I followed the scent from my bedroom." Ma laughed and sidled up beside her at the stove. "Drown mine in syrup."

"Drowned in syrup, coming right up."

Her mother peered at her with a suspicious smile. "You seem very happy today."

"I am." Allie carried the two plates to the table. "Where's Danny?"

She needn't have asked. He thundered down the stairs and through the hall, skidded into the kitchen, and posed dramatically with his fists planted on his sides, hero-style.

"Do I look any different?" Danny puffed out his chest.

Allie exchanged a wink with her mom, then frowned and looked him up and down. "I don't think so."

Ma shook her head. "Except maybe your entrances are getting noisier."

"My muscles are bigger." Danny flexed his skinny arms, and she and Ma laughed.

"You're the light of our lives, kid." Allie set two plates stacked with pancakes on the table. "Now sit. Time to eat breakfast."

Danny bounced his fists and planted them harder on his hips. "Don't you remember what today is?"

"Today? Ma? Isn't today Saturday?"

"I believe it is. And I'm very hungry."

"Come on!" Danny yelped.

Allie laughed and pointed at his place at the table. "Silly boy. How could we forget? You've been reminding us for weeks now. That's why I made your favorite breakfast."

His ear-to-ear grin warmed her heart.

"Cool. I'm starving." He yanked back a chair and hopped into it.

Allie brought her plate to the table, and after they prayed, Danny began a litany of all the people coming to his party. She almost choked when her nephew mentioned Derrick's name, and she felt Ma's eyes on her.

"He's coming, right, Aunt Allie?"

"Yes. He said he'd be here." She sipped her juice, lids lowered. Her mom would surely be able to read her internal reaction. Allie focused on slicing her pancake. She was looking forward to hosting Danny's party. Her pulse kicked up a notch. And too eager to see Derrick Owens. In her head she wondered if his only motive for showing interest in her was part of his sales pitch. In her heart she wondered if there was more.

She'd better get her eyes off Derrick and a grip on reality.

"I almost forgot," Ma said. "Derrick called me this week needing information about the property." Her voice was light and cheery, as though losing the land Dad labored so hard to keep up was a simple necessity. There had to be other options. "He's going to be here this morning to pick up paperwork from me. Then he said he'll return for the party at five."

Allie's appetite fled. "Why didn't you tell me?"

"I didn't think it mattered much." Ma shrugged. "He won't be here long. So what are your plans this morning? Do you have appointments?"

"No, I'll be getting ready for the party. I've got to get caught up on paperwork, too. And I've decided to begin my long-term project of going through the old files in the file cabinet to clean them out." *In preparation for selling the property*, but she didn't say that. The pancakes tasted like sawdust.

A knock at the back door gave her a start. Allie's heart pattered erratically as Danny ran to get it.

"Mr. Derrick!"

"Hey, Spiderman. Happy birthday."

They came to the table smiling, and Allie was suddenly struck by the similarity of their eyes. Both coal black. The one difference was that dark circles hung like half moons under Derrick's. In fact, tension lined his face, making him look a bit weathered, which didn't take away from his good looks. It made him appear less polished and more human.

"Aunt Allie made pancakes." Danny pulled out a chair. "You wanna eat with us? Please?"

Ma greeted Derrick with a bright smile.

Derrick glanced at Allie as if gauging her reaction. She stood and pointed to the table. "We have plenty. I'll get some for you."

"Thank you." He slipped into the chair. "I already grabbed a bite, but pancakes are my favorite."

"They're my favorite, too." Derrick exchanged a high five with Danny then, head tilted, appraised Allie. Had he caught her staring? His gaze gave away nothing.

"If it's not too much trouble, Allie, could I have a cup of coffee?" His yawn said how badly he needed caffeine.

"Oh, sure." She piled a plate with buttermilk pancakes, her senses reeling, and set it in front of him and got the coffee. Her stomach felt like it was wrapped in a rubber band.

Danny, Ma, and Derrick held a lively conversation, but his presence turned her mind to mush, and she had trouble following their words.

"Delicious. Thank you." Derrick laid his fork on his plate, took a gulp of coffee, then cleared his throat. "Now, let's talk business. I need to look at the property more closely, take some notes. Nobody has to accompany me, but I need about an hour."

Ma stood. "Danny and I are off to pick up his cake and party supplies. Allie has paperwork to catch up on. But please, have another look around. If you need anything, Allie will be in her office."

"That works."

Allie felt heat in the sidelong glance he sent her way. She quickly averted her gaze, met her mother's eyes, and saw the faint smile on her lips. Match-making again.

❧

Derrick explored the cottage with land developer Les Links in mind. Les probably wouldn't be interested in the old cottage on the Vahn property unless it could serve as a decorative landmark. Too bad. It would be a shame to knock it down.

When he'd completed his inspection, Derrick dusted off his hands and pulled a notebook from his pocket. Now he'd have a report to show his dad. He sat on a tree stump beside the door and scribbled out notes, listing the pluses and minuses of the acreage. He worded his report in favor of restoring the cottage possibly as a community meetinghouse.

He eyed the building. The Vahns hadn't been able to keep it up. Weeds and plants grew in abundance. In the backyard was a massive blackberry bush that held berries just getting ready to ripen. Fixed up, the place would also make a nice home, smallish but charming, especially for a couple just starting out. But a developer wouldn't do that.

A couple. His conversation with his father slammed into his mind. Most of his adult life he had fought a serious romantic relationship. The closest he'd come was with Lynn. His parents welcomed Lynn with open arms. His mom wanted a grandchild and his dad an heir to Owens Realty. But when he'd made a decision to live for Christ, Lynn rebuffed his beliefs.

No matter. Derrick sighed. What he had with Lynn wouldn't have carried them through "till death do us part," especially with the fundamental difference in their faith. And worse—or better—he realized he hadn't loved her with a depth that would last a lifetime.

Now Allie. . .

Derrick got to his feet and stuffed the notebook into his pocket. Allie was unlike any woman he'd ever met, and they shared the same faith. He couldn't deny the growing attraction between them. But what about Michael? He still couldn't figure out Allie's relationship with the guy.

He glanced back at the building next to the barn that served as her office. He wanted to see her again, spend time alone with her. He had to find an excuse.

Derrick rubbed his hand over his jaw, searching his mind. Hmm. He could ask her permission to drive his truck into the field to look at the far end of the property.

A plausible request, he told himself as he strode up to her office door and knocked. He heard no sound coming from inside and rapped his fist against the door, a bit harder this time. He was about to call her name when he saw movement from the side of his eye.

Allie appeared around the corner of the building holding a bridle in her hands. "Are you looking for me?" Her voice was shaky and her face pale.

"Yes, but I didn't mean to disturb you. Um. . ." He suddenly felt awkward, like he'd intruded on a very private moment. "I'd like your permission to take my truck into the field to check out the pond."

She studied him for a moment, frowned, then seemed to reach some kind of conclusion. "I was about to go for a quick ride. Want to come along with me? You can ride Storm. I'll show you the boundaries myself."

What brought this on? Derrick agreed, too quickly perhaps, but he was more than pleased by her offer. Perhaps he'd misread the panic on her face a minute ago. Still, the cheer in her voice sounded forced.

As they saddled and bridled the horses in relative silence, Derrick stole glances at the petite, auburn-haired beauty. At least the color had returned to her face, but something in her eyes clued him in that she was troubled. He could easily imagine her mixed feelings. She loved the land she lived on. Sellers weren't always happy to see real estate people at their door—not when the sale was necessary to their financial survival.

"You ready?" Allie mounted. She looked regal atop the bay quarter horse.

Smiling, Derrick climbed atop Storm, and they took off at a leisurely pace into the field. A flock of birds flew up from a group of trees in the distance, and Pip danced a few steps.

"Derrick," Allie called over her shoulder.

"What?" He lagged a distance behind her. She was by far a better rider than he.

"I'm going to run."

Without waiting for his response, she lightly kicked Pip's sides. As if the horse had been hoping for his cue, he shot forward like he was leaving a starting gate. Storm didn't need much urging to follow, and Derrick felt the exhilaration of the wind in his face. Allie's hair blew behind her, and he loved the sound of her laughter floating on the wind.

For the first time since he could remember, he felt at peace, thinking of nothing but the moment. Allie radiated an inner beauty that had unlocked something deep and hidden in his heart. A tenderness he hadn't known existed.

As they neared the pond, Allie slowed Pip to a trot, then a walk. Following her lead, Derrick brought his horse alongside her.

"Beat you." Allie smiled.

Derrick pretended to scowl. "Are you kidding? I let you win."

Laughing, she stopped under a knot of trees and swung from Pip's back in one fluid motion. Derrick dismounted, too, and she took Storm's reins from his hands and tethered the horses loosely to a tree.

"They won't go anywhere. Danny and I come down here for picnics and to fish." She grinned. "Even if we never really catch anything. Come on. I have something to show you."

She held out her hand, and he hesitated half a beat before he took it. The close physical contact sent a rush of warmth through him.

"I don't know how much longer we'll own this place, so I want to enjoy it while I can, and I love to share the beauty with friends."

Her voice trailed away. She glanced at him, then back at the pond. A warning cloud engulfed him. A true "friend" would tell the truth and nothing but. He'd come to investigate whether or not Danny was taken care of properly. He had to be dreaming if he hoped for romance with Allie. She'd toss him out on his ear when she discovered the truth.

Derrick squeezed her hand and resisted the urge to pull her into his arms, hold her close, tell her why he'd come to Walla Walla to begin with. But he couldn't—not without betraying his dying sister's last wish. The only way he could help her was to get top dollar for her property. He glanced at her profile. Her pert nose and full lips. High cheekbones. What he wouldn't give to hold her, kiss her. . .

"Here we are." Allie led him along a path overgrown with plant life where the air grew cooler under the trees. They reached the pond's edge, and Allie turned to face him.

"So many memories." Her voice was resigned. "Daddy used to bring Luke and me here. Taught us both to fish. Then Luke and I did the same with Danny."

The catch in her voice tore at his heart. Derrick looked into her eyes. A stray tear zigzagged down her cheek.

"I feel like I've failed them," Allie whispered and backhanded the tear off her face.

He had to hold her, just this once. Derrick took her by the shoulders gently and looked into her eyes. "Please don't cry. We'll pray together that things work out and God will make a way for you and your family."

If only he could confess everything. Right now. *I'm Danny's uncle and—*

"Would you please hug me, Derrick?" Her jaw worked and then she swallowed. "I haven't had a big-guy hug in a long time."

She was asking for a hug? "Of course." Derrick pulled her against him, wrapped his arms around her slim shoulders, and inhaled the lilac scent of her hair. Was this what falling in love felt like?

She leaned back and looked up. She was so close he could see the kaleidoscope of shades that made up her green eyes.

"Thank you." She cast her gaze downward. "I don't really know you, but for some reason, I keep thinking I can trust you."

Derrick's heart pounded at Allie's words. She'd let down her walls, but he didn't deserve her trust. He slid his hand behind her neck. She glanced up at him, and her sweet breath feathered the corner of his mouth. He blocked the voice in his head urging him to tell her the truth. Leaning closer, he shut his eyes, touched his lips to hers.

Allie slipped her arms around his neck, and he held tighter to this woman who'd turned his world upside down.

He owed her the truth. But what about Danny? Sandy? Derrick pulled back, brushed his hands over her hair. "Allie," he whispered. "I. . ."

She nodded and closed her eyes, obviously thinking he was asking permission to kiss her again.

He proceeded to do so, and his runaway fervor shook him to his core.

Allie stepped back, and the expression on her face mirrored his infatuation. Surprise and wonder and. . .alarm.

She looked away first. "We should go back. I have work to do."

"Right." Derrick's hands slid from her shoulders, down her arms. He released her and instantly regretted severing their physical contact. "Good idea."

The ride home was quiet except for an occasional birdsong and the twigs snapping beneath the horses' hooves. He had almost told her the truth. Only the kiss had prevented a confession from spilling from his lips.

They reached the barn, and Allie stared straight ahead. Her walls were back up. As were his own. He couldn't allow the intimacy to ever happen again. He had to honor what his sister asked, and his respect for Allie had to override what stirred in his heart.

Allie dismounted without a glance his way. He helped her remove the tack, then they quietly brushed the horses, avoiding being near each other.

"I'm sorry," he finally said, unable to bear the silence.

She shook her head. "It's not your fault. It's no one's fault." She glanced at him. "I'm not upset, I'm confused. I don't know what to think." She stepped backward. "I'll see you tonight at the party."

As she walked away, Derrick's heart felt like it had collapsed on itself and become a black hole. What had he been thinking kissing her? The relationship could go nowhere.

Lord, what am I doing here? Why can't I just walk away?

Chapter 13

Allie clutched a bundle of check stubs in her fisted hand and paced her bedroom. Why had she chosen the day of Danny's party to clean out the file drawer in her office? How she wished she'd never come across Luke's check stubs, hidden at the back of the bottom drawer behind their old financial records. Luke had handled the finances; she'd never had reason to go there. . . .

How was she going to tell her mother?

Allie went to her bed, lifted the mattress, and stuffed the evidence deep in the crevice. Her own brother. . . And to finally know why they were flat broke now. He'd been paying money to Paige Maynard. The amounts weren't huge, but over a period of years they added up to a hefty sum. Why had he been paying her?

The most likely scenario. . .

Allie closed her eyes and pressed her hand to her thudding heart. Could it have anything to do with Danny? His adoption? No. Danny's adoption was paid for years ago. What about an affair? Nothing else made sense. Back in high school, Luke had a thing for Paige, and Cindy, even in jest, had shown jealousy. Luke would scoff at the idea of it. Was that an act?

The thought of Luke cheating on Cindy—and with Paige Maynard of all women—made her stomach churn.

Allie went to the vanity, looked into the old glass mirror, and ran her index finger over her lips. Her intense state of shock must've driven her into Derrick's arms today. The old glass mirror darkened her reflection, and she closed her eyes and relived Derrick's kiss. Romantic. Tender. Like a whisper, yet tingly. The setting had been perfect. When she was a teenager with the whole world ahead of her, naive about the future, she'd often ridden to the pond with a book of poetry to read and a notebook of poems she'd written. She'd imagine the man she would marry, living on the farm, maybe in the cottage.

That young girl still lived inside her, and she struggled against the cynical woman she had become. *But I have to protect myself. . .don't I?*

She heard gentle tapping at the door. "Allie?"

She spun away from the mirror. "Shannon. Come in."

Her wacky friend opened the door, and Allie smiled at Shannon's outfit—a gaudy peasant dress in reds and earth tones accessorized by her ever-present silver rings, bracelets, and chunky necklace.

"Vintage?" Allie asked, pointing at her outfit.

"Yeah." Shannon turned, and the gauzy material swirled around her ankles. "I found a bunch of stuff at an estate sale a couple of days ago."

"Very nice." The simplest pleasures made Shannon happy. Allie had often wished she was more like her friend. Content with the smallest things instead of so intense—so "on" all the time.

"I thought so, too." Shannon flicked back her hair and dropped onto Allie's bed. "Are you looking forward to our retreat this coming week?"

Allie nodded, although going away for several days seemed so unwise right now.

"What else is going on?"

Too much to tell. "Why does something have to be going on?"

" 'How do I love thee? Let me count the ways. I love thee to the depth and breadth and height my soul can reach, when feeling out of sight for the ends of Being and ideal Grace.' Elizabeth Barrett Browning." Shannon laughed. "A book of love poems *and* your Bible open on your bed stand. One of your poetry journals next to them. You're wearing your most favorite dress in the whole world, and your makeup looks like it did when we drove to Portland and had that lady at the cosmetics counter do us up."

Allie blinked. "Wow. You're right."

"Has he kissed you yet?"

No, she'd kissed him first. "You are way too nosy." Allie paced the room.

"I'll take that as a yes." Shannon lounged on her elbow. "As much as I like Derrick, I think you need to slow down."

"What?" Allie barked out a laugh. "You telling the tortoise she needs to move slower?"

"Yes," Shannon conceded. "I guess you're right. You are slow." She sat straight on the edge of the bed and studied her face. "You both have walls up. I know where your walls come from and why they're there, but his. . ."

"What are you telling me?" Allie's face heated. "You're not going to start up with the body language stuff, are you?"

"All I'm saying is that it wouldn't hurt to find out a bit more about Derrick." Shannon got to her feet. "Come on, gorgeous. People will be arriving soon."

❧

Allie answered the front door, and her breath caught. She stared up at Derrick, speechless.

He stood there in a light denim shirt and dark blue jeans holding Danny's wrapped present and looking wary. "Am I too early?"

She touched her lips. Could she forget his kiss ever happened and at least make a pretense of nonchalance?

"I'm sorry. Come in, of course." She had trouble meeting his eyes, turned her back to him, and proceeded down the hall.

Derrick caught her by the arm. "I'm early because I want to talk to you alone."

Alone? Could she trust herself? She turned and finally met his dark gaze.

"Can you come outside? For a minute?"

She hesitated, then nodded. Derrick stepped back and allowed her to go ahead of him. The scent of his cologne made her long for his nearness. One more hug...another kiss...

"Listen, Allie."

They stood on the front porch, and she couldn't look him in the eye again. Instead she stared at the Blue Mountains.

Derrick touched her arm. "I'm sorry about what happened today. I want you to know it won't happen again. I promise."

Ouch! As much as she appreciated his honesty, it stung.

Derrick cleared his throat. "I'm no more ready for a relationship than you are."

"Direct and to the point. I admire that." Her hard shell thawed a bit, and with that came a smile. "It wasn't just you, Derrick. I was a willing participant, if not the one who initiated—"

"Hmm." His lips lifted in a half smile. "Let's just say we were both willing participants and leave it at that." He drew a deep breath. "Can we be friends? Pretend this afternoon didn't happen?"

She laughed, part of her wishing he'd declare his everlasting love, the other part knowing what he said was for the best—especially with Shannon's warning ringing in her head. "Yes. I agree. And this is Danny's birthday party. I want to enjoy myself."

"Good. I do, too." Derrick directed his hundred-watt smile her way, which threatened to be her undoing. Her insides turned to melting butter, and her knees weakened.

"I have another idea," Allie said. "Why don't I take you to Bright's tomorrow? I owe you some candy."

After the words left her mouth, she wanted to kick herself. Spending more time with Derrick was dangerous on her emotions. Her heart leaped while she waited for his response.

"Tomorrow?"

Allie caught sight of Michael pulling up in his BMW, and new worries knotted her insides.

Derrick turned to follow her gaze, then looked back at her.

"Are you two—"

"No. No way." Her emotions must be so obvious. Now that Derrick had handed her the friend card, she might as well come out with the humiliating admission. "Michael and I were engaged. He cheated on me, then decided he wanted me back."

"He was a fool," Derrick blurted, and the words seemed to come from his heart. "Do you want to go back with him?"

Michael got out of the car, slammed the door, and walked toward them, a scowl on his face.

"No." Allie shook her head. "I can't abide lying."

A flicker of tension crossed Derrick's face. "Um, I'll leave you here. It appears Michael's not in the best frame of mind, and having another man with you isn't going to help matters."

Derrick disappeared into the house, shutting the door firmly before she could ask him to stay. Michael walked up the porch steps.

"Are you dating him?" He blew out a breath and strummed his fingers on his thighs.

"You can't say hello before you give me the third degree?" She was suddenly shaking. "I've had a long day. I don't need—"

"How can we talk? Whenever I see you lately, Owens is by your side."

The door opened again.

"Allie?" Shannon's voice came from behind her. "We need instructions to finish getting ready."

"Oh sure." Allie gestured for Michael to go inside. "I'm done talking. I don't owe you any explanations," she whispered to him. "This is Danny's birthday party, and he's the focus. If you must have a discussion with me, we'll do it later."

Michael opened his mouth as if to argue, then clamped it shut. He stepped into the house, and she followed. Waves of bitterness emanated from him, and she sent up a silent prayer that Danny wouldn't sense the hostility.

"Okay, more guests will be arriving soon," Allie said with false cheer. "Let's get ready to party."

Shannon gave her a thumbs-up. Allie smiled, looked across the room, and met Derrick's gaze head-on. All tension drained from her, replaced by the foolish thought that everything would be all right as long as Derrick was around.

Derrick returned her smile, and she was totally entranced by everything about him. He studied her frankly, and his gaze dropped from her eyes to her lips.

At that moment she knew. She and Derrick could never be "just friends."

❧

After Danny opened his presents, Michael announced he had to leave.

Good. Derrick slid a glance to the front door where Allie stood with Maynard. He'd like to speak with Maynard alone someday, grab him by his scrawny neck for hurting Allie.

No. That was the old Derrick. God had been working on his heart, and He was faithful to finish the good work He'd started in him. Plus, who was he to judge Maynard? Derrick hadn't been exactly up-front.

An hour later, everyone else had left. Danny tugged on his shirtsleeve. "Mr. Derrick! Can you stay and watch me play the game you gave me?"

"Did you ask Aunt Allie and Granny if it would be okay?"

Danny waved his hand. "Of course it's okay. They don't care about stuff like that."

"You sure?" Derrick laughed. Danny had the run of the house for sure. He followed the boy into the den.

Danny settled beside him on the sofa, his thumbs already working the game's controls. "My friends have this game. It's awesome. Thank you."

Derrick wished more than anything he could sit with Danny like this every night. After only a few minutes, Danny yawned. "I'm tired, Mr. Derrick." He swiped his eyes.

"Me, too." Derrick tapped him on the shoulder. "Did you have a good birthday?"

"Yeah. Really good, but. . ." Danny coughed, got up, and went to the bookcase. "I miss my. . ."

"What's wrong, Spiderman?" Derrick moved to the end of the sofa cushion. "You crying?"

Danny shrugged, swiped his hand across his eyes, then pulled an album from the shelf. "This is my first birthday without my mom and dad."

Yes, of course. The thought hadn't crossed Derrick's mind. "I'm sorry, Danny. Do you need to talk about them?"

Danny shrugged again. "Not much to say, really. They're dead. I know I'll see them again in heaven, but sometimes I miss them a lot. I want a mom and dad."

He studied his precious nephew, at a loss for words. What could he say to such raw emotion?

Danny opened the album and pointed to a photo. "This is them and me. Last year."

"Look at you on that roller coaster!" Derrick fake punched Danny in the shoulder. "Even I'm scared to go on those big rides."

Laughing through his tears, Danny punched Derrick back, and Derrick wrapped his arm around the boy's thin shoulders. "You're a chicken," Danny hiccuped. "I thought heroes were never chickens."

"Every hero has at least one flaw. Remember that." His heart broke for Danny's pain. "And your parents looked like a happy couple. You must've had lots of fun with them."

Danny wiped the tears off his cheeks, leaving wet smudges on his face. "At least I have my granny and Aunt Allie." He smiled despite his tears. "She's the best aunt in the whole world. She loves me, and she's not afraid of big rides."

"She'd make a great superhero, too," Derrick said.

"Yeah."

"I know she loves you. You're easy to love, Danny." Derrick released a pent-up breath. "But if she's not afraid of big rides, maybe you shouldn't tell her I'm a chicken. Heroes don't like to talk about their flaws."

"Scout's honor." Danny closed the album. "I think I'll go upstairs now. Thank you for the present." He crossed the room, turned back, and hugged Derrick, who felt his own eyes burn.

"Mr. Derrick," Danny said, "will I see you tomorrow?"

"I don't know if I'll be back." Derrick's heart pounded. What was the point of getting closer to this family? He was falling hard for Allie. Betsy Vahn felt like a second mother to him. And Danny. . . His nephew had stolen a chunk of his heart.

Danny backed away, and his smile faded. "Okay then, see you sometime." He walked from the room, head down.

The boy was getting too attached. *Lord, I've been completely self-centered.* He hadn't considered Danny's emotions before barging into the Vahns' lives. The poor kid didn't need anyone else to depart from his life. And even if Derrick spent more time here, sooner or later he'd have to return home. His facade couldn't continue indefinitely.

The time had come to leave Walla Walla. Tomorrow he would take Allie to Bright's like she suggested, then he'd return home and handle everything else by telephone and fax. No need to continue here.

He stood, stretched his legs, then headed to the kitchen to say good-bye to everyone. But before he could enter the room, he heard Betsy's voice.

"Allie, you mustn't overreact. I'm sure there's a reasonable explanation."

"This explains the debt he left, Ma. At least we know that much."

He heard the sound of a chair scraping on the floor. "I need to see what Derrick and Danny are up to. We'll talk more tomorrow."

Derrick was about to be caught eavesdropping. He hurried back into the family room and turned toward the bay window.

"Where's Danny?" Allie asked behind him.

"He's gone to bed." Derrick turned toward her. He needed to tell her about the photo album and Danny's tears, but not with the deep pain already etched on her face.

"Are we still on for tomorrow?" *Please say yes.*

Allie nodded. "Yes, of course."

Derrick smiled, reached out to give her a hug, but dropped his arms at his sides. Unless he could tell her the whole truth and nothing but, he didn't deserve Allie's affection.

Chapter 14

As he took Allie's hand to guide her into the truck, Derrick caught another whiff of her flowery perfume, reminding him of their kiss—a distraction he didn't need. He'd have to work hard to keep his wits about him today. Squelch the urge to kiss her at all costs.

He closed the door, came around to the driver's side, and started the engine. He wracked his brain to think of something to talk about so he wouldn't slip and say, *Hey, I know what I said about being friends, but I really liked that kiss yesterday. Could we try again?* Or, *Did you know you're Danny's aunt, but I'm his uncle? And may I kiss you again?* And then there was the conversation he'd overheard last night. *Hey, Allie. Not only am I not telling you that I'm Danny's uncle, I also eavesdropped on you. What's up with the debt?*

"So, I take it from the frogs I hear at night that the road is named Frog Hollow for a reason?"

"Oh yeah." Allie smiled. "I used to love trying to catch them at the pond."

Talk of the pond brought back a rush of fresh memories of their kiss. Derrick searched his mind for a change of topic. "I bet Danny enjoys frog hunting, too."

"That and picnics near the pond." Allie sighed. "I guess all that will have to end soon."

Poor Allie. She was suffering having to give up the land. That they would still have their house and a few acres wouldn't make things easier. She'd probably die a little bit with each house a developer built on the land she used to ride on. This was one time he hated his job. Maybe he could send her money anonymously. With everything in him, he wanted to do something to help the Vahns. Still, that wouldn't help them keep all their land.

"You can make a left here. I'm taking you to town a different way." Allie smiled at him with genuine warmth. If she had a clue as to why he'd come to Walla Walla, she wouldn't be friendly. Guilt washed over him. How had a simple search for his nephew become ugly and complicated?

Derrick hit the turn signal. "I've never taken this road." But he was willing to go wherever Allie wanted to take him.

"This is mostly farmland, but if you get bored—"

"No, I won't get bored." *Not with you sitting beside me.*

"Good." She settled back against the seat then turned toward him, her gaze glued to his face. Did she see the strong resemblance between himself and Danny? Derrick cleared his throat. It was dangerous for him to be alone with her. A part of him wanted to spill every secret—confide his purpose for coming to Walla Walla. But he did owe her one truth right now.

"About Danny, I think you should know that he showed me a photo album last night. Pictures of him and his folks. He said this was his first birthday without them." Derrick choked up, took a breath, and started again. "The kid was crying. I tried to cheer him—"

"Oh no." Allie's face lost color. "My poor little boy."

"I'm sorry." Derrick reached over and squeezed her hand. "I didn't mean to upset you."

"I'm glad you told me." Allie squeezed his hand in return. "My sister-in-law, Cindy, started the album as soon as she and Luke adopted Danny." She sniffed. "I can't believe it most days. None of this is real."

"I've got tissues in the glove compartment."

Allie released his hand and snapped it open. "Thanks."

"Does Danny know he's adopted?"

Allie nodded. "Yes, Cindy and Luke felt they owed Danny the truth. They let him know as soon as he could understand. They told him he was special, handpicked by God for them."

He felt Allie shutting down, but he needed more answers. "Sounds like Cindy and Luke were thrilled to get Danny."

"Oh, Cindy would only allow me to hold Danny long enough for her to take a shower." Allie laughed, and he loved the musical sound of it. "Luke and Cindy, they were a dynamic couple. So in love and happy." She glanced out the side window as though a new thought had stolen her attention. "At least most of the time, but at the end. . ."

Derrick held his breath, waiting. But as the seconds ticked by, he accepted that Allie had clammed up on the topic and he'd get no more from her. Pain was like that. You just had to shut it out sometimes.

Allie sat forward and pointed. "Did you know the Nez Perce Trail was located right here on Main Street?"

"No. Maybe I should brush up on Walla Walla's history since I live nearby in the Tri-Cities."

"My dad was a history buff, and I spent many Saturdays with him exploring this area. His research files fill a whole drawer in the cabinet in my office. I haven't had the heart to look at them until yesterday." She balled the frayed tissue in her hand. "He once talked about writing a book."

"No kidding?" The sadness in her voice cut him to the core. Time for a change of topic. "I do know that Walla Walla means 'place of many waters.'"

"Yep." She smiled. "Good job. See? You do know something."

"A bit. But I'd like to learn more from you."

"My pleasure."

Allie showed him all her favorite places in town, giving him a litany of history. A tour guide couldn't have done better. They finally parked near Bright's Candies.

"Weird, being here with you."

Worry wormed its way into his heart. "Why's that?"

"This is where we met for the first time."

Relief relaxed his stiff shoulders. As if he could ever forget. "You mean when you knocked my whole bag of jelly beans to the ground?"

She laughed. "At the time you said it was fine. Now you're changing your story?"

"Never." He squeezed her shoulder. "You're fast becoming one of my favorite people on the planet."

Smiling, Allie tilted her head. "That's sweet. Do you really mean it?"

He thought about what he'd blurted out, and yes, it had come from the heart. "I mean it." Derrick hopped out of the truck and walked around to her side before he did something stupid.

He opened the door for her, took her hand, and helped her out of the car. Not that she needed his help. She'd demonstrated physical and emotional strength he wasn't sure he possessed. She'd held up after her dad, sister-in-law, and brother died. Would he have that strength when Sandy passed away?

They entered Bright's, and he abandoned his morbid thoughts and instead inhaled deeply of the sweet scent that hung in the air. The mixture of chocolate and sugar. . .and Allie by his side. What more could a man ask for?

"Yum, what should we get?" Allie stood in front of the counter smiling.

Derrick eyed the goodies behind the glass, licked his lips, and pointed. "Fudge."

"I take it you like fudge?"

"Love it." He patted his well-toned stomach as if that was proof enough. "How about you?"

"I like their mint truffles." She looked relaxed now. Maybe he'd scaled the walls around her heart. Then again, maybe it was Bright's atmosphere. Everybody turned into a kid when entering a candy store.

After they ordered, they sat outside at a table in the sunshine and shared their sweets. "This was a good day, Allie. Thanks for taking the time."

"Uh-uh. No need to thank me. I should be thanking you. I haven't done anything for fun in far too long."

"That explains it then." Derrick pointed at her face.

"What?" Allie laughed. "What are you grinning about?"

"Can't take you anywhere." Squinting, he leaned forward. "You've got chocolate on your cheek."

"Do I?" She wiped her face with her fingers. "Did I get it?"

He shook his head, then picked up his napkin, reached across the table, and wiped the corner of her mouth.

Allie remained stone still. The look in her eyes made his heart beat faster. If they weren't in public, he would've kissed her again. "I guess we should—"

"Yes, let's go." Allie gathered their candy wrappers and tossed them in the trash.

He had to stop sending her mixed signals. Unless, and until, Sandy gave him permission to identify himself as Danny's uncle, their relationship didn't have a chance. And if he was able to admit the truth, Allie might totally reject him for leading her on. He would probably lose no matter what.

They walked to his truck, and his cell phone vibrated. Derrick pulled it from the holder on his belt and glanced at the screen. "My mother. . ." Fear weighted his limbs.

Allie walked a discreet distance from him.

Derrick hit the Talk button. "Mom?"

"Derrick, Sandy has taken a turn for the worse. They say it won't be long."

Chapter 15

E arly Monday morning a blaring alarm clock startled Allie awake. Grumpy from fitful sleep, she slapped the Off button, then stomped to the bathroom to get ready for the day. She had an early appointment to shoe an Arabian gelding nicknamed Goober. The name suited him. His markings and classic Arabian looks made him appear regal and distant, but only because he was too dumb to act any other way.

Scrubbing her face, she told herself it could be worse. She could be returning to work on Eddieboy, who was smart enough to pretend he was dumb before lashing out with his teeth.

In the kitchen her mood didn't improve when her favorite coffee cup shattered onto the floor, victim of her half-closed eyes and errant elbow.

What was yesterday about? Why had she been so silly to ask Derrick to go to Bright's? Why had he accepted? Derrick's quick end to their day in Walla Walla only compounded her confusion. She knew his mother called and there had been a family emergency, but she didn't know what it was. She had locked lips with a total stranger. But still, the ugly reminder emerged—knowing a person a long time meant nothing, either. She'd grown up with Luke. She'd looked up to him as her older brother, yet she'd discovered he'd been deceiving her for years and maybe his wife, Cindy, as well. Why all the checks to Paige?

Allie stared at the shards of ceramic on the floor. That's what her life felt like. As if a big hand had picked her up, dropped her, and pieces of her emotions were scattered all over.

She went to the utility closet and grabbed the broom. Once again since Pastor's prayer for her, she longed for a return to the kind of faith that would make her want to open her Bible first thing in the morning, meditate on the scripture, and get on her knees for a conversation with God. To return to the faith she'd drifted away from, captured by the cares of this world and her own resentments. It seemed a long way back.

ю.

Two hours later, after her session with Goober, Allie stopped by the coffee shop in town. She sat at a small round table next to the window, ordered a skinny latte with two extra shots of espresso, and stared outside. If only she could turn off her brain for a while—forgive and forget and get rid of the anger. Her mental churning made her head ache and her heart pound.

The young waitress, looking as carefree as a summer breeze, brought her the latte. Allie nodded and smiled a thank-you. Not so long ago she was as cheery as the server. That's when Dad was strong and full of life. And Luke and Cindy may have had their battles, but when they'd sneak peeks at one another across the table, they appeared madly in love.

Or was it all an illusion? Could anybody truly know another person? Allie sipped her drink and gazed out the window again. An older couple shuffled along the sidewalk, hand in hand. How sweet. Romantic. She closed her eyes and saw only one man with whom she'd love to grow old. A man she might never see again.

She opened her eyes, and the dream disappeared. Was that Paige Maynard crossing the street? Allie gritted her teeth. Just look at her! Perfectly groomed. Dressed to the nines. Were her clothes bought with Luke's money while she and Ma had to sell off their land to pay off Luke's company credit cards?

Allie stood and tossed her empty cup in the garbage, her throat suddenly dry. Despite a little voice in the back of her head telling her to take a deep breath and calm down, she threw open the door, charged across the street, and met a startled Paige on the sidewalk.

"Allie." Paige took a step back. "Wh—what's wrong?"

"We need to talk."

"Uh, what about?" Paige glanced around, and her gaze slid back to Allie. "Is this about Danny's adoption?"

Allie blinked. "Danny's adoption?" Ah, the parade. Understanding dawned. "I wouldn't use you as my attorney if I decide to adopt Danny, if that's what you're asking."

"Oh. . .that's fine, of course." Paige's shoulders sagged. "Still, I could do the paperwork. I handled the first adoption." She motioned toward the coffee shop. "Do you want to go inside and grab a cup of coffee with me?"

"No, I don't want anybody to overhear." Allie pointed to the park bench across the street. "We're going to need privacy and time."

Paige drew a deep breath. Did she know what was coming?

"Of course. I've always got time for you, Allie."

Allie stepped off the curb, and Paige followed. Something was very, very wrong here. Paige was too compliant and overfriendly. Must be the guilt.

They sat, and Allie looked her dead in the eyes. What had Luke seen in this woman? All the makeup. The opposite of Cindy with her natural beauty.

"I think you know what this is about," Allie blurted and took pleasure in the sight of Paige's guilty face going white.

"You look angry, and I don't even know what I've done." Paige's voice broke off. "At least give me a hint of what we're talking about here."

Allie snorted a humorless laugh. "All right, if you want to play stupid I'll spell it out for you. Hint number one: I found my brother's check stubs. That ring a bell?"

Paige shook her head. "I don't understand."

"Of course you don't." Allie scanned the expensive designer clothes, and fury rose up in her to a level she'd never known. "I'm going to warn you that I won't abide lying, Paige. I'll have more respect for you if you fess up and be a woman about this."

Nodding, Paige licked her lips. "Yes, Luke gave me money—"

"Because you and my brother were having an affair, right?"

Paige pressed two manicured fingernails to her frosted pink lips. Her gaze darted left and right before she blew out a long breath. "Can you ever forgive me, Allie?"

"No!" Allie's nails bit into her palms. "You knew he was married with a son." She choked up. It was true after all. The money worries slipped from her mind along with the anger, replaced by memories of Luke and overwhelming sadness. "Why you?"

Paige flinched like she'd been slapped. "It was wrong, I admit, but you don't have to be vicious." She shot to her feet. "We were in love. We had been for years, you know. Since high school."

"When people are in love"—Allie stood and came within an inch of her face—"it doesn't require an exchange of money."

"There was the rent on my apartment." Paige had the decency to look down at the sidewalk. "We needed a place to meet."

"A place to meet?" Bile rose at the back of Allie's throat. No wonder Paige had moved out of her father's mansion. "And you're trying to tell me *you* don't have money of your own with that wealthy family of yours?"

Paige shrugged. "Daddy is stingy, you know. I get my paycheck from the law firm, of course, but I needed more." She sniffled. "I loved Luke. It wasn't easy for me, either, carrying this secret."

"A secret?" Allie snapped. "That's not what I'd call it. Adultery is more like it."

"Please." Paige reached her hands out in supplication. "What are you going to do?"

Allie ignored the gesture and backed away. "I have no idea what I'm going to do." She whirled around and took long strides toward her truck. She looked over her shoulder and couldn't resist one last jab. "What do you think your father would do if he found out?"

"You wouldn't tell him, would you?" Paige's face was ash white.

Allie took no pity on her and didn't wait for a response. She pulled open the truck door, jumped inside, and turned the key. As she drove away, she burst into tears.

Derrick forked pieces of stuffed french toast around his plate, trying to force himself to eat. Last thing he wanted was to hurt Hank's feelings since the chef had prepared one of Derrick's breakfast favorites, as he'd done for the rest of the family this morning. Hank had faithfully served the Owenses for nearly two decades and took part in raising him and Sandy. Cooking was Hank's remedy for the bad things in life. When Sandy broke up with boyfriends, he cajoled smiles from her with her favorite oatmeal chocolate chip cookies. Derrick's broken arm in grade school was treated with a large dose of snicker-doodles. Hank handled pain by cooking, whether it was his own or someone else's. And today he was trying to fix everybody's grief with his delicious creations.

He was scrubbing the already spotless dark granite counter. Pots hung from hooks, their copper bottoms gleaming like new pennies. Hank kept a tidy kitchen, but today every inch of the room sparkled. Derrick wished he had the energy to work out his grief with something productive. Instead it was as if he were paralyzed. He could think of nothing else but Sandy lying in her bed upstairs, the hospice nurse by her side. Her lucid moments had diminished, and he understood why his parents were maintaining their vigil anywhere but in his sister's room. No words could express the pain of watching a loved one pass away from this world.

"It's okay. You don't have to eat." Hank dropped on a stool opposite him at the kitchen island.

Derrick looked up. Buried in thought, he hadn't noticed Hank walk across the kitchen. "Sorry. Any other day I would've devoured—"

"I understand, believe me." Hank blinked back tears. "Hard to let go of our little girl."

Feeling like a kid, Derrick wiped his nose with a napkin and stood. "I need to go be with her."

"Of course." Hank reached across the island and rested his hand on his shoulder. "I'm here if you get hungry."

As Derrick walked down the hall toward the main staircase, Dad popped his head out of the study. "Derrick, I'd like to speak with you, please."

Derrick sucked in a breath. He needed to see Sandy, but his father's tone demanded compliance.

Dad was ensconced behind his desk. Strain stretched the skin across his face, making it look almost like a mask.

"What's going on with the land in Walla Walla?"

Derrick summoned an all-business tone. "I've got preliminary papers drawn up. I need to get them signed."

"Good. Please stay at it. I may have another developer who's interested in a large piece of property for a new housing development." Dad grinned wolfishly. "We could begin a bidding war."

"That would be good." Now that Derrick had an idea of the extent of the Vahns' debt, he wanted to do everything he could to help them. Perhaps this would bring more money.

Derrick watched his father pull something from his desk. It was the photo Derrick had given to Sandy of Danny and his grandma. A tense silence hung in the room while he heard his pulse pounding in his ears.

"Do you know anything about this?" Dad asked, tapping the photo with his forefinger.

Derrick swallowed hard. Did his father know? "Where did you get that?"

"It fell out of Sandy's Bible." Dad squinted at it. At least the photo wasn't a close-up. He wouldn't be able to see Danny's eyes.

The less said, the better. Derrick waited, holding his breath.

Dad finally looked up. "Must be one of her friends' kids. She was always praying for someone." His harsh tone made it clear what he thought of prayer as a way of seeking answers.

Derrick nodded. He wouldn't have to lie. . .again. "I'm going to sit with Sandy for a while."

His father studied the photo again, and Derrick made a quick escape.

As he stood in the doorway to Sandy's room, Derrick whispered, "God, help me." A memory of Allie infused him with strength. She had lost three family members, but she kept on.

Leanne, the hospice nurse, stood and waved him in.

He tiptoed to Sandy's bed and whispered, "I'll sit with her for a while."

"I'll wait outside in the hall."

When she was gone, Derrick sat, and Sandy opened her eyes. "D-man."

"You're awake?" He reached for her hand.

"I won't be here much longer." She spoke with effort, and tears filled her dark eyes.

"I know." He swallowed, unable to see through the blur of his tears.

"Hey." She squeezed his fingers. "I know for a certainty I'll see you again. Meantime, you're going to be happy."

"Don't talk to me about happiness today." Derrick choked on a sob.

Sandy managed a weak smile. "My only regret is you and Allie."

Derrick wiped at the tears on his cheeks with his fingers. "What?"

"I think you're falling in love with her."

An automatic denial came to his lips. He opened his mouth, closed it, then leaned his weary head against Sandy's bony hand.

"It's true, and I'm standing between you two. I made you hide your identity."

Allie had been in his thoughts constantly, and he'd tried to push her out. He had too much grief to deal with right here in front of his eyes. Knowing he'd left behind a woman he could love with all his heart and a nephew he wanted to help raise made the pain of loss unbearable.

Derrick sat up. "Don't fade away on me, Sandy, please."

"Listen. I was wrong. Tell Allie the truth."

The truth. "I don't think she'll listen."

"Tell her, and send Mom and Dad in here now."

A deep sob ripped through his chest. Derrick leaned down and kissed her cheek. "I love you. I always will."

"I love you, too, Derrick."

He walked out of her room, knowing in his heart he'd never hear her speak those words again, never hear the sound of her laughter.

Tears flooded his eyes as he headed toward the office, but his dad already stood in the hall. "Sandy wants you to come—"

"I'm going to her room now." Dad swiped his hand over his face. "Your mother will join me." He walked past quickly, but not before Derrick saw the tears, the gray pallor of his face.

Leanne put a hand to his arm. "Will you be okay?" She handed him a wad of tissues.

Derrick wiped his eyes and nodded. "I'll be okay, but I'll never be the same."

"Loss does that, but God wants you to go on. Sandy's work here is almost done, but I suspect the good Lord has plenty for you to do yet."

A short laugh escaped his tight throat. "You've been talking to Sandy, haven't you?"

Leanne wrapped her hand around his wrist. "Sandy said to tell you that you *must* invite me to the wedding."

Chapter 16

Lord, I'd rather not have known."
Allie headed home and caught herself going over the speed limit. She had to get there before Jake's mom dropped Danny off.

She hated herself for grilling Paige. Instead of fond memories of Luke, she'd forever live with the ugly truth. An adulterer? How could it be so? Nearly every word Luke spoke, every romantic gesture toward Cindy, all of it a lie! Was that the reason Luke gave Paige money—to keep her quiet? "Let it be true, Lord." At least it would mean Luke wasn't in love with Paige. That he only paid her off to keep the truth from Cindy.

As she pulled into the driveway, Allie's hands shook. She saw Jake's mother, Mary, waiting in the car and drew a jagged breath. She wanted to expose Paige for who she was—even to Mary—shout it from the rooftops, but the Vahn family would fall into disgrace as well. Luke was the married man with a son.

"Hey, Allie." Mary pointed at the tire as Allie got out of the truck. "Your tire is low on air."

Allie sighed. One more thing to worry about. "Thanks, and thank you for bringing Danny home. We appreciate it."

"Anytime," Mary said. Danny exited the car and waved good-bye.

After they went inside, Danny headed straight to the fridge. "Aunt Allie, is Mr. Derrick coming over again?"

"Wash your hands before you eat." Poor kid. "I'm really not sure, sweetheart." *But I'd love to know.* "So tell me, how was VBS?"

"Good." Danny shrugged, dried his hands, and returned to the refrigerator. His forlorn look made her face heat with anger all over again. Yet another man in and out of Danny's life. She felt at a loss. Should she speak to him about Derrick? Or about missing his parents on his birthday? Or should she let it go? Maybe he needed more grief counseling. Come to think of it, maybe Allie did, too.

"What are you hunting for in the fridge?" She came up behind him and ruffled his dark hair.

"I don't know." He took out a carton of milk and looked up. "Can you call him? Mr. Derrick, I mean."

"How about I make you a peanut butter and jelly sandwich?"

"Okay, but. . ." Danny wouldn't be sidetracked. He poured himself a tall glass of milk. "Can *I* call him then?"

Now what, Lord? Allie assembled his sandwich. "I don't think you should be calling Mr. Derrick, hon." She cut the crusts off the bread, quartered it, and set the snack in front of him at the table.

"But he likes me." Danny took a hearty bite. "I could tell because—"

"You're talking with food in your mouth again." She grabbed a napkin and brushed at his face the way Derrick had done to her at Bright's. How long before she'd get Derrick out of her mind? "What were you going to say about Mr. Derrick?" Pathetic! Pumping her nephew for a few crumbs of information.

"He's fun. He calls me Spiderman, just like you and Granny." Danny's brows scrunched together. Yikes! Did he copy that facial expression from Derrick? She couldn't recall if Danny had ever pulled such a face. "I think he likes you, too." He covered his mouth and giggled. "He looks at you a lot."

"Danny!" Allie's pulse did double-time. "People look at people when they speak." Here she was again, mining for hope. "It's only polite."

He swallowed another bite and shook his head. "He was *staring* at you."

Allie heard the sound of a car in the driveway, jumped up, and went to the window. "Oh, Granny is home." All the excitement seeped out of her. She had the heartbreaking task of having to tell her mother what she'd learned from Paige this afternoon.

Chapter 17

On Tuesday, with his cell phone clutched tight in the palm of his hand, Derrick paced the upstairs hall. His parents had come out of Sandy's room and walked straight past him without a word. A moment later Leanne emerged. One look at her told him no words were necessary.

Sandy was gone—at her going-home party, dancing on streets of gold with Jesus. No more sickness and pain and sorrow.

But what about him?

He ducked into his room, closed the door, and dropped onto a leather sofa. Memories of their youth came rushing back. Sandy the tomboy. How many times had he bandaged her up before his parents got home, hiding that Sandy had done something dangerous—like taking flight with her pogo stick from the high porch? Climbing a tree to the top, hanging upside down, then falling?

"Lucky you've still got a brain," he'd told her. And Sandy quipped, "I'm smarter than you any day, D-man." And she was.

Derrick buried his face in his hands and wept. If only Sandy and Danny could've met, just once.

"Why, Lord?" Derrick stood, slammed his fist against the wall, then drew a breath. He went to the window and pushed aside the curtain. The hearse. They had come for her. He would not see her again until he, too, went to heaven.

❧

Allie zipped her suitcase closed, grabbed the handle, and shut her bedroom door. "Ma?"

"I'm right here, hon." Ma stood at the bottom of the staircase holding two brown bags.

Allie descended the stairs, smiling. Her mom was one of a kind. "You're sending us off with lunch?"

"Sure, you've got a long ride. In this bag I've got a sandwich for you." She waved her right hand. "This one's for Shannon. Tell her it's that weird, healthy stuff she likes."

"That's sweet." Allie laughed and gave her a hug. "Thanks." She stepped back. "But I still don't know how you and Shannon talked me into this. I'm going to lose a lot of money by not working."

"Tending to the spiritual is far more important for you right now," Ma said as they walked to the front door and Allie pulled it open. "It's only four days. You'll come back refreshed and renewed."

"What if you need me for something? What if there's an emergency? I won't be able to call you. There isn't any wireless or cell phone access on top of that mountain."

"Stop it! There is a phone at the monastery if there's an emergency." Ma gave her a light shove and followed her onto the porch. Then she stopped and pointed. "Oh my, are you going in Shannon's truck? Will that green thing make it?"

"My truck's got a flat, remember?" Allie smiled down at Shannon and waved. "Don't worry, Ma, it's only a three-hour drive."

"I won't worry, I'll pray." She gave her one last hug. "I'll get your flat fixed while you're gone."

With her bright smile, Shannon waved to Ma and blew a kiss.

Allie hurried toward the truck before she had a chance to change her mind. Three days. No communication.

She opened the rusted back door, and the tired hinges moaned a protest. Would the truck make it there and back? Allie sighed and tossed her suitcase atop a mess of random items.

"Isn't this exciting?" Shannon asked.

"Um. . ." Allie hopped into the passenger seat, set down the lunch bags and her purse, and shrugged. "I'm kind of worried that we'll be incommunicado for four days."

"Of course you're worried." Shannon pulled away from the curb, smiling. "You're Allie."

"Hmm." She couldn't argue the point. Shannon knew her too well. "Question. How will you *not* talk for hours every day?"

"You know, I asked myself that very same question." A serious expression crossed her face. "But Ray—I'm talking to him about taking guitar lessons when I move to the Tri-Cities—he told me the atmosphere in a monastery is so sacred I won't want to disturb the peace."

"So, this Ray—sounds like he knows you well." Allie laughed. "Any romantic interest?"

"No-o-o." Shannon wagged her head. "He's another—"

"Friend." Allie finished the sentence for her and sighed. "I envy you that. Michael started out as my friend, ended up a boyfriend, and now I avoid him like the plague. I guess I can't handle the friend thing with a guy, especially one I've dated."

"No way you could be friends with Michael now." Shannon turned onto Highway 11 toward Pendleton, Oregon. "He's jealous of Derrick. I saw that right away at Danny's party."

"I don't know why he'd be jealous of Derrick. It was over between Michael and me long before Derrick was in the picture."

"Aha! So he *is* in the picture."

A sinking feeling hit the pit of her stomach. "No. It's more like Derrick walked off into the sunset and disappeared. He hasn't phoned, even about the property." Allie snapped her fingers. "Gone. Just like that."

"Doesn't sound like Derrick." Shannon slid her gaze her way. "You're falling in love with him, aren't you?"

"No!" Allie's breath caught in her lungs. "I heeded your advice about slowing down. Now everything is at a standstill, and I think it's best I stay away from him."

"That's not what I told you to do! I told you to take it slow, that I felt there was more to Derrick than meets the eye."

"Apparently you were right." Allie gave a nonchalant shrug. "I haven't heard from him since Sunday." She stared out the side window and sighed. "Not that I care, but he came into Danny's life, and Danny misses him."

"You don't care?" Shannon waved her index finger. "And before you bear false witness, remember that we're going on a monastic retreat."

Allie couldn't suppress a burst of laughter. "What if I do care? Derrick *doesn't*."

"Yeah, sure he doesn't." Shannon smirked. "Something must've happened for him not to call. When we get back home, why don't you call the real estate office?"

"No way." Allie shook her head. "When Michael pulled his disappearing act, I did the calling, innocent that I was. I ended up finding him with that other woman. I've decided if a man is interested, he can pursue me."

"Michael was engaged to you. Derrick isn't obligated."

"Exactly." In her mind's eye, Allie saw Paige and her brother together and shuddered. "For all I know, Derrick Owens could be married."

"Uh-uh." Shannon wagged her head. "No way is Derrick married. I would've picked up on that." She sighed and looked thoughtful for a moment. "But there is something; I just can't pinpoint what he's hiding." She placed her hand over her heart. "I feel it in here."

Allie couldn't take another second of this conversation. Why waste time analyzing a relationship that didn't exist? "Ma packed you a lunch." She tapped the brown bag. "That crazy food you like to eat. Probably bean sprouts and hummus with fried tofu or something."

Shannon laughed. "Not quite, but she's a darling. She knows what I like." Her expression suddenly grew serious. "And don't think I'm not aware that you intentionally changed the subject."

Allie nodded. "I think we can both use this retreat."

Perhaps she'd be able to forgive Paige and Luke and. . .

Please, Lord, help me put Derrick out of my mind, too.

Chapter 18

By midday Thursday the last of the funeral guests were gone, and the temporary staff had finished cleaning up the dining room where Mom and Dad had graciously received condolences from their friends as well as Sandy's. Derrick now stood alone in the kitchen with Hank, who stared out the window over the sink.

"The service was nice," Hank murmured.

"Yes," Derrick said. "Pastor Clark gave a wonderful message."

Hank turned and leaned back against the counter. "It was exactly what she wanted. So many people got up to speak about her. It was a celebration of her life."

"I'm having trouble celebrating," Derrick said softly.

"I know. Me, too."

"The only thing that helps is knowing her pain is over. But I still want to ask God why. She had such a hard life, and when she finally got it all together, this happens."

Hank nodded. "I gotta admit I have the same questions."

"Life will never be the same." Derrick pulled out a stool and sat at the island.

"You got that right." Hank joined him and rested his hands on the granite. "Kinda makes you think about the future, too, doesn't it? Like maybe we should grab it by the horns and just go for it. Be real. Take chances for love. Not hold back."

"Hank, you're not thinking of anyone in particular, are you?"

The big man who had always been in charge of himself, his emotions, his kitchen, blushed.

Derrick grinned. "That's what I thought. A certain nurse named Leanne would be my guess."

"I'm not saying."

"Yeah, you don't need to." Derrick sighed. "I always thought that's what I was doing. Taking life by the horns. Living day to day. But I wasn't loving. I used people. I didn't know what love really was until I met the Lord."

The two sat quietly for several minutes, then Hank broke the silence. "It's going to be quiet around here, I think. Too quiet. I don't imagine you'll be living in the guest cottage much longer. I need someone to care for." He went to the massive stainless steel refrigerator and peered at the leftovers. "I didn't have an appetite before, but now I'm getting it back." He glanced over his shoulder. "How about you?"

Derrick nodded. "Yeah, the knots in my stomach are starting to come undone."

"Your sister would have wanted us to enjoy the food. You know how she liked to eat. Especially things like this." He took a package from the fridge and brought it to the island.

Derrick leaned forward. "Spring rolls? Philadelphia rolls? I didn't see these earlier."

"I didn't put them out earlier. I hoped we'd have a chance to talk, and I know how much you like them and how much she liked them. It'll be our little celebration." He retrieved some paper towels and gave Derrick two. "One for your plate, the other for hands. Totally informal. For her."

"Sandy was a fireball, wasn't she?"

"Yes, and if she can hear us now, she's having a good laugh." Hank stopped cleaning and looked him in the eye. "I'm sure you already know, but Sandy loved you with her whole heart and soul."

Nodding, Derrick swallowed past the dryness in his throat. "I know, Sandy always wanted the best for me, and near the end she gave me guidance." He couldn't tell Hank all that lay on his heart. "I'm going to heed her advice."

"Is this about her son?"

Derrick felt the blood drain from his face. "How do you know? Does my father know?"

"I don't think your dad knows, but Sandy called me to her room the day before she passed away." Hank's watery gaze searched his face. "Your secrets are safe with me."

"I don't doubt that for a second." Derrick took a deep breath. "But if Sandy told you, do you think she mentioned anything to Mom and Dad?" Worry stirred in the pit of his stomach. Sandy had wanted Derrick to tell Allie the truth. *But what if Dad beats me to the punch?* Dad, short on patience and long on agenda, might contact the Vahns first. Knowing his father, he might even threaten to take Danny. Without an opportunity for Derrick to explain himself to Allie, she'd believe he was an outright liar.

❧

For the third time Thursday evening, Derrick dialed Allie's cell, only to hear an automatic message. Why would she have shut off her phone? Maybe she was out shoeing horses. He snapped off his phone without leaving a message, then dialed their landline.

"Hello?" Betsy picked up on the first ring.

"Hi, Betsy, this is—"

"Derrick! How are you, and where've you been?" There was a smile in her voice, and it hit hard how much trust she'd put in him.

"My sister passed away," he said. "The funeral was today." Sandy's death registered anew, bringing with it a tidal wave of raw emotion.

"Oh, Derrick. . ." A long silence ensued. He heard her sniff and thanked God again that Sandy's son belonged to a sensitive, caring family. "I don't know what else to say except I'm sorry."

"Thank you." Derrick's eyes burned. Would the tears ever stop? "I know you've been through your own losses."

"Yes, too many." Betsy's voice cracked. "I'd tell Allie to call you back, but she won't be home until Saturday."

"Away." A myriad of thoughts darted through his mind. Where'd she go and with whom?

"She's with Shannon at a retreat in a monastery."

"Um, a monastery, you said?" Derrick frowned. The way his luck was running, Allie would become a nun.

"Yes, it's lovely. I've been there once. Peace and quiet and meditating on God's Word. Thing is, no talking allowed, so she's keeping her phone turned off. Besides, they can't get a cell signal up in the mountains."

Now there was an interesting concept. Overprotective Allie with no cell phone, unable to check for messages from Danny. Exhaustion fell on him like a wet blanket. He needed to get it all out there, tell her the truth. "So I guess I won't be able to speak with her until Saturday."

"Yes, she'll be back in the afternoon." She paused. "Do you have questions about the land? Is this an emergency? Or did you want to tell her about your sister?"

The land was the furthest thing from his mind. "No emergency. And it's not about the land, either. I did want to tell her about my sister." There he went again, avoiding the truth. Yes, he wanted Allie to know about Sandy, but that was not his priority.

"Hang on for a moment, please, Derrick."

He heard Danny's voice in the background.

Betsy inhaled. "Derrick, I must go. And again, I'm sorry. I'll have Allie call you the second she gets in."

"I would appreciate that—" She'd already hung up. Danny must have gotten into some kind of mischief she had to straighten out.

Derrick clipped his cell back to the holder on his waist and turned to see his father in the doorway. How much had he overheard?

Chapter 19

A s Shannon rounded the corner onto Frog Hollow Road, Allie smiled. "There's no place like home."

"True," Shannon said. "But the time away was worth it. I can't believe it's just Saturday. I feel like I've had a month's worth of weekends. I feel renewed and invigorated."

"Absolutely. I feel like I'm ready for anything now. Like I can face the giants." Allie dug into her purse and pulled out her cell. "I have no voice mails. I assume everything is okay at home. And then there is that one voice mail from Derrick just saying hello. He said I didn't have to call back, so I'm not going to."

"You could, you know."

"I don't have to, you know."

Shannon laughed. "Playing hard to get will just attract him more."

"Great," Allie said. "I spent the last few days keeping my mind on the spiritual. I don't need to start thinking about him again."

"I don't think he's going away," Shannon said.

Allie ignored that. "I can't wait to see Danny and Ma. I felt a bit guilty about leaving her alone to care for Danny."

"She said she was going to take Danny to work with her on some days. I bet your mom sold more at my shop than I ever did. She's so good with the customers."

"Yes. She's just great with people." Allie noticed a fast-food restaurant.

"Hey, I'm starving," Shannon said. "You want to stop?"

"How about I make us something at home?" Allie smiled.

"I know." Shannon flashed her a grin. "You just want to get home to see Danny."

"You got it." Allie eyed her house in the distance.

Shannon slowed the truck and turned onto the long drive. "I prayed a lot for you while we were there. And I prayed that something would happen so you wouldn't have to sell any land."

Allie had told Shannon everything on the way to the retreat. Paige, Luke, the checks.

"I prayed about that, too." She glanced at Shannon and shrugged. "It just seems impossible. Though some people might not think the debt Luke left is that bad, he wrote checks against our business credit card accounts. Add interest on top of the amount owed, and I'm not making the minimum payments."

"I know," Shannon said. "But God does miracles."

"Yes, and there's been a minor miracle in me. I prayed that your new business would succeed, and I wouldn't be so selfish about missing you. I prayed and meant it from the heart."

"An hour trip back and forth isn't bad. We can still have our Scrabble nights."

"Yes, we can." But with so many things changing, Allie wondered what the future was going to hold.

As they pulled up to the house, Danny ran out the front door to greet them, a broad smile on his face and his arm in a sling.

"Guess what, Aunt Allie? I broke my arm."

&

Derrick's mom darted about the reception office of Owens Realty, her pasty face swollen. Derrick had no doubt she was crying in the night. The stately woman who'd worked beside Dad for the past thirty-five years had become a shadow of the vibrant woman she'd once been. He wondered if Sandy's death had marked him, too.

"Sorry to interrupt," he said, "but where's Dad? He left me a list of things to do, including going by the mortgage company to drop off some papers. I have a question, and he's not answering his cell."

"Your father?" She set down a stack of files on the sleek reception desk. "He mentioned something about the Kents. . .buying land in. . .oh, I don't know. I'm trying to straighten up, keep my mind occupied before I lose it."

How could Derrick be such a clod? "Mom." He went to her side, leaned down, and gave her a hug. "I'm sorry. I understand."

"No more Sandy." She sagged against his shoulder and sobbed. A first. He'd never seen her cry, and it tore at his heart. "Your kids are never supposed to go before you."

Derrick wrapped his arms around her and held her for a moment. When she finally pulled away, he tried to figure out a way to ask if Sandy had confessed to them about Danny. "Mom?"

"Yes?" she murmured.

"Did Sandy give you or Dad any last-minute requests?"

"Like what?" Mom stepped back and blinked. "Sandy could barely speak. Did you say you're going to the accountant?"

"No, the mortgage company." Her series of questions caught him off guard. The past few days it seemed her thoughts followed no pattern, which added to his worry. All Mom needed was the shock of hearing she had a grandson—or did she already know?

Derrick searched his mother's eyes carefully for any clue that Sandy might've made a deathbed confession, but there were no signs.

"So you don't know where Dad is?"

She perked up just slightly. "Since when has your father ever given me a detailed account of his whereabouts?"

Had Mom taken issue with his dad's long absences throughout the years like Sandy and himself? If she had, she'd kept it well hidden and stood by Dad's side through every crisis and every business deal with never a complaint. She fanned her face and sighed. "Just the Kents, that's all I remember."

"Okay." Uneasiness still plagued him. If Sandy told Hank, would she have told someone else? Especially if she was under the influence of pain medication? He didn't want to imagine his father driving to Walla Walla and intimidating the Vahns.

Derrick kissed his mom on the cheek. He had to see Allie. "Will you be all right?"

"Yes, of course. I'm going through these files. The work distracts me." She smiled through her tears. "I've been around Hank too long."

Derrick shot out of the office and hurried to his car. He'd get to Allie and calmly explain all. He could only pray she'd give him a chance after that. She made it obvious on more than one occasion that she couldn't abide lying, but maybe she'd find it in her heart to forgive him for avoiding the truth. Because of Sandy.

He stuck the key in the ignition of his Silverado, and it roared to life. As he pulled onto the street toward the mortgage company, he yanked his cell phone from his belt, dialed Allie's number, and waited.

"Derrick!" Allie said after he greeted her. His heart sank at her panicked tone. Did she know? "Ma told me about your sister. I'm so sorry."

Relief. "Thank you," he said. "I know you understand."

"I do."

Derrick wanted to blurt out everything right then and there, but he couldn't. They needed to be face-to-face.

"Oh, if you're coming, you need to know. Danny broke his arm," she said. "I feel like it's my fault. I was away and left all the responsibility to Ma."

"How did he break his arm? Is he okay?" Worry twisted his stomach. He hadn't been there for Danny, either.

"Well, he's fine." Allie paused. "He fell out of a tree. That's my fault, too."

"Why?" Derrick drove toward the mortgage company as fast as the speed limit allowed.

"I taught him to climb that tree, and he was playing Spiderman."

Derrick couldn't help himself. He chuckled.

"I'm not sure it's funny," Allie said, but he could tell she was smiling.

"You know how I got my scar?"

"How?"

"I fell out of a tree playing a superhero."

After a moment's pause, Allie laughed. "You understand then."

"Absolutely. All young boys can fly."

"So. . .you called for a reason, right?" The laughter in her voice died.

"Would it be all right if I came by tonight?" Derrick massaged his aching neck. She just had to agree. This couldn't wait another day.

"Um, sure. Is it about our property?"

"No. But we need to talk." No more half truths.

"Okay then, sure." The tone in Allie's voice made him realize she did care for him, and she'd probably missed the signs that should've told her he'd fallen for her. Too bad he was about to tear up her world.

Derrick pulled into the parking lot. "I have one errand to run, then I'm on my way. I should be there in a little less than two hours, okay?"

"Definitely okay." Allie's voice became muted. "Derrick, I've got to go now, somebody's at the door. See you later."

"Later," he said and fought the fear he couldn't put a name to.

Chapter 20

With her heart pattering pleasantly, Allie stuffed her phone in her pocket and headed for the stairs. Derrick was coming to see her. Not about the property. She couldn't help but feel a shiver of excitement.

Murmurs of voices came from downstairs. Ma had gotten the door; Allie didn't need to bother. She stood in front of her full-length mirror smiling and fluffed her hair. Then Danny came bounding into the room.

"Aunt Allie, there's a man at the door."

She turned toward him. "Who is it?"

"I dunno." Danny stared at her. "Why are you fixing up?"

She smiled. "Just getting ready for—"

"Allie?" Ma's voice came up the stairs. "I think you should come down here."

Why so serious? Allie left the room and descended the stairs, followed by Danny.

Ma stood in the living room, staring up at a tall man with dark hair. The man had his back to her, and Ma motioned her into the room.

"You need me?" Allie picked up her pace.

The man turned. Allie stepped back and stifled a gasp. An older version of Derrick studied her, then clasped his hands behind his back.

"Allie. . ." Ma said. "This is Richard Owens. Derrick's father." His eyes, black like Derrick's, skimmed over her.

"Mr. Derrick has a father?" Danny stood next to Allie.

Richard's gaze flickered to Danny. His eyes warmed, and a tiny smile played in the corner of his mouth. "Yes, Derrick has a father."

"I'm sorry about your daughter," Allie said.

He finally looked at her again, and the semblance of warmth on his face died. "I appreciate the condolences."

"What happened to your arm, son?" Richard asked.

Danny laughed. "I was Spiderman and fell out of the tree. I always climb that tree."

Richard frowned. "I see."

"Are you here about the property?"

"Call me Richard," he said. "And no. I'm not here about the property.

That's Derrick's job."

"Then—"

"I should get right to the point." He took a deep breath. "I'm here about Danny."

"Me?" Danny asked, bouncing on the balls of his feet.

Allie rested her hand on her nephew's shoulder. "Danny? Why?" A bad feeling slammed into the pit of her stomach, and she turned to her nephew. "Honey, why don't you go upstairs and wait for me to call you?"

"But Mr. Derrick's father said—"

"Sweetie, listen to Aunt Allie," Ma said. "Please go to your room now."

Danny must have picked up on her urgency. He left the room with no further argument.

Richard's eyes followed Danny with emotion Allie didn't understand. She felt so totally discombobulated. Richard looked like an older version of Derrick, but the resemblance ended there. Except when he looked at Danny, Richard was coldly businesslike. No easy smile, no warmth in his coal black eyes.

"Please sit." Ma pointed to a chair, then she sat on the sofa.

Allie eyed his fine clothing. He reeked of money. She hated feeling like she wanted to apologize for the worn furniture, which had seen its better days, but Richard Owens sank into a chair, seemingly unfazed.

"So what's this about Danny?" Allie sat beside Ma, and fear lodged in her chest, growing with each passing second.

Richard crossed his legs. Even seated informally, his presence commanded attention. "In her last days when she was under the influence of painkillers, my daughter talked about having a son. After she died, I found photos and paperwork in her belongings, along with phone messages and texts from Derrick confirming the truth of her words. I immediately contacted my attorney."

A chill raised hairs on the back of Allie's neck, and she opened her mouth to speak, but Ma grabbed her hand and squeezed, signaling her to allow Derrick's father to finish.

"The truth of the matter is that Danny is my grandson. Derrick was here to find him."

Allie clapped her hand over her mouth. The room spun. Danny's eyes. . . and Derrick's. The facts came together in a sickening flash of clarity.

"So Derrick didn't come to Walla Walla for land." Her voice shook. She turned to her mom. "He lied to me. . .to us." The words came out in a hoarse whisper.

Richard scowled. "If it brings you any comfort, you're not the only one my son lied to. He told his mother and me he was in town on business, then went about searching for Sandy's son, investigating your family. I don't know what

Derrick hoped to accomplish, but—"

Allie jumped to her feet, fists clenched. "Why are you here?"

Richard held out a placating hand, like he was humoring her. "Please sit down. I'll explain."

For a satisfying moment Allie imagined the little pony Eddieboy going after Richard Owens and clamping his eager mouth on the man's arm. She felt the pressure of Ma's hand, and the moment passed. "Sit, sweetheart. This will all work out."

Allie slumped onto the sofa. "Not if they intend to tell Danny his biological mom just died." She glared at Richard. "Danny's been through enough."

Richard sniffed. "Sandy, as well as the rest of my family, has also been through a lot. My daughter died never seeing her son. A son she was coerced into giving up for adoption."

"Coerced?" Allie shut her eyes and sank back onto the sofa. *Don't yell. Don't cry.* She continued to glare at Richard. She would not allow him to intimidate her. "How can you say that? My brother wouldn't have participated in anything questionable." Even as she spoke, she saw the illogic of her words. Luke had been having an affair with Paige, which was questionable to say the least. But...hadn't Paige handled the adoption? A formless thought wriggled in the back of her brain, struggling for clarification.

"Richard," Ma said, "even if that were true and your daughter had somehow been coerced, where is this going?"

"And what is it you want?" Allie asked.

"My grandson." He ran his hand down his tie, nodded, and tilted his head. "I'm open to shared custody. Danny is my daughter's son. Possibly the only grandchild I'll ever have."

Allie stared in disbelief. "Shared custody? Why would we agree to that? Danny doesn't even know you."

"He does now. And he knows Derrick."

"I don't think you have a legal leg to stand on, Mr. Owens." Ma's voice was sure and confident, and Allie drew strength from her.

"Danny's adoptive parents were killed in a car accident. He no longer has parents, just a legal guardian." Richard stood and drew back his broad shoulders. "My wife and I and Derrick are family by blood. If you're not agreeable to informal shared custody, we will do this through the courts. If we do that, you risk losing him altogether."

Allie leaped to her feet. Lose Danny? No! Of course they'd fight. But they had barely enough money for necessities lately, let alone legal fees. Frozen to the spot, strength drained out of her and she could only stare up at him.

"We don't want to confuse Danny or hurt him." Ma stood and draped her arm around Allie. "We've nothing to be ashamed of, Mr. Owens. We love him with all our hearts."

"But it seems you're in financial difficulty. My lawyer's investigator discovered that. You're selling off land. Perhaps you can't provide for Danny like we can." Richard's gaze roamed the room. "Nor does it appear he's well supervised based on his broken arm. I could make a case of that. Would you like to reconsider?" Richard crossed his arms over his chest.

"Money doesn't grow happy children." Allie crossed her arms in imitation of his. "We may not have a fat bankbook, but Danny's the happiest kid you'd ever want to meet."

"We probably should consult our own lawyer," Ma said. "In the meantime, I think our discussion is over, Mr. Owens. I'll see you to the door."

Richard's face seemed to sag. "I'm sorry you feel that way. I can find my own way."

They watched as he walked from the room to the front door.

The door closed with a *snap*, and Allie wheeled around to face her mother. "What a nightmare."

"Yes, so it seems." Ma rubbed her temples.

"Should we have agreed to joint custody?"

Ma shook her head. "No. At least not right now. We don't know the truth for a certainty. And we don't know the Owenses. Except Derrick, and now that's in question. I just can't believe he would deliberately deceive us." Ma focused her eyes on her. "Last thing I want is your faith to be hurt more than it already has been."

"It's not your fault." Allie dropped into a chair, dead exhausted. "He played me, too."

"I'm not sure about that," Ma said. "Time will tell. But one thing for sure, they can't take our little boy."

"What if the adoption was illegal? They've got the money. They can hire hotshot attorneys who'll make the case."

"He said coerced, not illegal," Ma said with a slight smile. "If it had been illegal, a man like Richard Owens would have been here guns blazing. Besides, the Lord is in control." She took a deep breath. "I'm going to make cookies and pray."

They both turned when they heard footsteps on the stairs. "Aunt Allie? Did Mr. Derrick's father leave?"

"Yes, he left." Allie glanced at her mother for guidance.

"I'm going to make a batch of chocolate chip cookies." Ma held her hand out to Danny. "Come and help me."

"Goody!"

"I'm going out to the barn," Allie said.

"Remember who is in control," Ma said over her shoulder as she guided Danny to the kitchen. "We serve a good God."

Allie hated the thoughts that coursed through her head as she walked to the barn. Resentment and anger that flew in so many directions and at so many targets. The Lord, who hadn't promised a rose garden as Ma always said. And there was Luke, the brother she'd looked up to all her life. What had he done? Participated in a questionable adoption? Betrayed his wife? Then there was her own romantic life, if it could even be called that. Michael the cheater and now Derrick the deceiver. Had he really gotten to know her—kissed her—just to get to Danny?

Allie felt the tears start halfway to the barn. Once she was inside, she draped her arms around Pip's neck and let the waterworks flow. The horse stood patiently as he had for so many years. When the tears finally dried, she felt drained of all emotion and went to the storeroom for her shovel and wheelbarrow. Then she retrieved two bales of straw and placed them in the aisle.

Lord, I feel so lost. I'm not in control. I can't do this anymore.

As she scooped a pile of manure from Pip's stall, she heard the barn door squeak. She turned. Derrick's outline was silhouetted in the setting sun.

Chapter 21

The second he met Allie's scorching gaze, Derrick's greeting died on his lips.

"What do you want?" She heaved a load of manure into a wheelbarrow, and he could just imagine where she really wanted it flung.

"I talked to your mother. I know my father was here." Derrick slipped his hands into his trouser pockets, heart constricting, remembering the cool greeting he'd gotten from Betsy and the disappointment in her eyes. He'd never felt so shut out in his entire life.

"Yes, he was."

"I'm sorry." He uttered the words, but knew they couldn't begin to express his regret.

"So am I," Allie said.

Derrick took a couple of steps farther into the barn. "Please hear me out."

"No." Allie shook her head. "I don't want to hear you out. I've had enough listening. I want to ask questions."

"Can we sit, then?" Derrick dropped his gaze. He couldn't bear to see the wounded look in her eyes.

With a wave Allie indicated the bales of straw. Once they were seated, she faced him.

She flicked back her long auburn hair, then clasped her hands in her lap. "The only reason we're talking now is so I can get closure. Don't take it as another opportunity to lie."

Sorrow like a dagger stabbed Derrick's heart. He'd honored Sandy's desires, despite his reservations. Now he'd lost everything. But looking back, could he have done anything differently? He spread his hands. "Ask me anything."

"You came to Walla Walla looking for your nephew, right?"

"Yes," Derrick said.

"Was everything a lie? All of it?"

He wagged his head slowly. "I didn't lie to you, Allie. I just never told you my original reason for coming to Walla Walla."

"Did you come to town in search of your nephew and pretend to befriend me and Ma—worst of all, Danny—just to get your foot in the door and investigate us?"

"At my sister's request, I came to town in search of my nephew, to make sure he was okay. But I didn't set out to befriend you or deceive you. You fell into my life, so to speak. The befriending was real." He leaned toward her. "When I felt myself becoming attached to Danny and Betsy and attracted to you, I made the decision to stay out of your lives. I couldn't allow any of you to become more attached to me. That's why I didn't call you. But when I suspected my father found out, I came to talk to you. I knew how he would react. I can only imagine what that was like."

"You don't have to imagine. I'll tell you." Allie backed away from him, the conviction in her green eyes sure and strong. "He wants joint custody. He said he'd have no problem dragging us through a legal battle to get *his* grandson. He knew, thanks to you, that Danny's adoptive parents were dead."

"Stop," Derrick said. "I know how he came across. I've lived with the man all my life. But you have to believe me. I told him nothing."

Allie stared at him, tears in her eyes.

"I had a good reason for doing what I did," Derrick said.

"I really don't care." Her voice was so small and sad. "I have just one more question. If you hadn't met me the way you did, snatching me off Chester, would you have inserted yourself into our lives?"

"Probably not. I would have tried to find out what I needed to know without bothering you at all." He swallowed. "But if I had met you in other circumstances some other way, some other time, I would have ended up kissing you just like I did."

A long silence stretched between them, and he searched his mind for the right words, but the wall Allie built around her kept him silent. He knew unless God intervened and a miracle happened, the possibility of a relationship with Allie was gone.

"I'm sorry you lost your sister," Allie finally said. "I'm also sorry things turned out the way they did. I don't know what's going to happen now, but I do know that our friendship is broken. I don't think I can trust you."

Derrick's hopes died. He'd lost her.

She shrugged and got to her feet. "I think you'd better leave now."

He stood and stared down at her, remembering their kiss and how she felt in his arms.

"Mr. Derrick?" Danny's voice came from the barn door.

Allie gasped, and Derrick's muscles grew taut. How much had the boy heard?

He strode toward them and looked up into Allie's dazed face.

"Danny." Allie dropped to her knees in front of him. "I thought you were helping Granny make cookies."

"We finished. She thinks I'm in my room, but I wanted to see Mr. Derrick."

Derrick wanted to sink into the floor. Of all his regrets, the worst was hurting Danny.

Danny shuffled his feet. "I heard you talking." He looked up at Derrick, eyes watery. "I don't understand. Why is your father going to take me away?"

Allie glared at Derrick. He grasped Danny's shoulder. "Nobody is going to take you away from your aunt or grandma. This is where you belong."

"But why does he want to?" Danny asked.

"I'll explain in a little while." Allie met Derrick's eyes and nodded toward the door, silently demanding that he leave.

Derrick exited the barn, feeling like he was leaving his beating heart at Allie's feet on the dirt floor. As he got into his truck, he wondered how he could keep his promise. Could he stop his father? The man was accustomed to getting his way. He'd even made sure Derrick was detained at the office so he wouldn't interfere with his visit to the Vahns'.

His mind turned over all his options. He had to have someone on his side. As he turned onto Frog Hollow Road, he headed for his final destination before he left Walla Walla.

Chapter 22

Allie and Danny walked to the house from the barn.

"Is it true? Derrick's father is my grandfather?" Danny frowned and pursed his lips. "Does that mean Mr. Derrick is my father?"

"No, he isn't." Allie felt an urge to slug something. Now she was forced into telling Danny who his real mother was and that she was dead.

"Why did you make Mr. Derrick leave?" Danny looked at her. "He's my friend."

He's more than that, Allie thought bitterly. "Let's wait and talk with Granny, okay?" She walked into the mudroom with her arm wrapped around Danny. Let Derrick, his dad, or anybody else try to take Danny away from them. Over her dead body.

Ma looked up from cleaning the last remnants of baking in the kitchen. "Danny? I thought you were in your room."

"I wanted to see Mr. Derrick."

"He overheard us talking in the barn. Now he wants to know why Derrick's father is his grandfather and. . ." Allie swallowed. Where did she start?

"I see." Ma set down her dishrag and pointed at the kitchen chairs. "Let's sit." She looked across the table at Danny. "You're nine years old now. I know you'll be able to understand what we tell you. Are you ready?"

Danny nodded solemnly, minus his usual rambunctiousness.

As her mom began to talk, Allie's body went rigid. *Lord, please soften the blow. Give Danny peace.*

❧

Thirty minutes later Allie left the kitchen to make a phone call while Danny continued to hammer his grandmother with questions. Amazingly, he didn't seem terribly disturbed. Perhaps because he'd never met Sandy—or maybe because the Lord had actually softened the blow. Danny had become animated, focusing on the fact that Derrick was his "real uncle."

Derrick. She'd begun to trust him. She'd put her faith in love again, but he'd left her faith in ruins. The irony of that thought struck her, and she could hear the Lord whispering, *"Your faith should never be in a man, but in Me. No man is perfect. No man ever will be."*

That slowed her thoughts. It was true—no one was perfect, including her. She made plenty of mistakes. And wasn't her anger and resentment and lack

110

of trust in the Lord just as bad as Derrick's sin of omission? He was right. He had never outright lied to her, and he had finally come to her to tell the truth. At least what he knew.

But Allie had more questions. She needed to know if Danny's adoption had really been coerced. And there was one person who probably knew most of the answers. Paige Maynard. She pulled her cell phone from her pocket and walked to the living room, her long strides fueled by anger. Paige—what had she really done? Yet without Paige, would they have Danny? She began to punch numbers into her cell with trembling fingers.

Lord, I need answers.

Allie hit the last digit of Paige's number, held her breath, and listened to the first ring, then the second endless ring. "Lord, please," she whispered, "let her pick up."

"Paige here."

"This is Allie." She drew in a breath. "I had a visitor today. He told us that Danny's adoption had been coerced."

A long silence ensued. "Paige? Are you there? Hello?"

"I don't understand." She spoke in a clipped tone. "Who told you such a lie?"

Allie hesitated a beat. Paige had admitted to the affair with Luke, and what could be worse than that? Yet something in her gut told her to press on. "This person has evidence to the contrary."

"What type of evidence? And who is this person?"

"Richard Owens. The biological mother's father." Allie paced. She wasn't about to show her cards, not without knowledge of all the facts. Her thoughts returned to Luke, the money. She just couldn't accept that her brother had carried on an affair with the likes of Paige—the woman who'd chased him through high school and beyond.

"That money Luke gave you. . ." Her thoughts were a swirl of confusion. Too much had happened today. Allie sent up another silent prayer and started again. "You persuaded a drug-addicted young woman to give up her baby."

"Oh, wait just a second. That's right. Cindy was working in the rehab clinic when Sandra Owens came in pregnant, desperate, and begging for help. *Cindy* did all the talking and made the arrangements. Fine, I drew up the papers, but I'm not going to take the rap for this." Her breath hissed through the phone. "I'm talking to Michael. You'll see. I did nothing wrong. I was helping three people achieve what they wanted."

"Are you trying to tell me you put your reputation on the line for Cindy? I thought you hated her for marrying my brother."

"Well, the adoption was helping him, really. I would've done anything for Luke."

Allie's heart thudded with a sickening thought. "And the money? What was that for? Were you telling the truth when you said Luke had an affair with you?"

"Why would I lie? It's embarrassing enough."

Through the front window of the Quaint Shop, Derrick saw Shannon unpacking a cardboard box. The CLOSED sign hung in the window, but he banged on the front door.

Shannon looked up, dusted off her hands, and smiled warmly while she ran to unlock the door.

"Derrick, nice to see you," she said breathlessly. "I'm so sorry about your sister."

Allie must not have phoned her yet. "Thank you." He didn't know where to start. "Would you have a couple of minutes to talk?"

"Of course! It's been quiet today." With a wave, she summoned him to the back of the store. "How about I make us some tea?"

"That would be nice." Derrick followed her through the tie-dyed curtains and took the same chair that he'd sat in when he'd last drunk tea with Shannon. When he'd stayed and played Scrabble, sitting next to Allie.

Shannon busied herself filling the pot at the sink.

"I won't beat around the bush. I had an agenda the day of the parade when I walked in here for the first time."

"I knew that." Shannon didn't miss a beat. She set the pot on the burner, lit the pilot light with a strike of a match, then came to sit across from him. "Does Allie know?"

Derrick nodded. "I just left her. She has every right to loathe and distrust me, but I wasn't able to tell her everything. She shut down on me. Wouldn't let me tell her everything."

"She does that," Shannon said.

"I thought maybe if you'll give me a chance to explain, you could talk to Allie. At the very least, it might take some of the pain away."

Shannon took a deep breath and sat back in her chair, studying him with her clear gaze. "I told you I liked you when we first met. I have instincts about people, and how I feel about you hasn't changed. But I can't promise I'll talk to Allie until I hear what you've got to say. I won't manipulate her. She's gone through too much emotional pain already."

"Fair enough." He clamped his hands together on the tabletop and looked into her compassionate hazel eyes. "I'm grateful she has you to lean on because I've added to that pain. For that reason I wish I'd never come to Walla Walla."

"Then you never would've met Allie and Danny." She pointed in the direction over her shoulder. "Never tasted my tea." She smiled good-naturedly. "God brought you here for a reason, Derrick. His ways are far above our ways."

"Yes, but I'm not sure He can condone what I've done, yet I didn't feel I had a choice."

"Wow, that's quite an introduction." Shannon lounged with her back against the chair like she had all day to listen, and he sensed no judgment from her.

"I originally came here on my younger sister's behalf. Her name was Sandy. She had cancer. When she knew she was dying, she confessed to me about her past—the extent of her drug use and that she'd given birth to a son."

Shannon's eyes grew wide. "Danny," she whispered.

Derrick nodded. "All Sandy had left of the memory of her son was a worn photo and a couple of names in Walla Walla that I could follow up on."

"Wow." Shannon rose to tend to the whistling kettle. "I wondered if it was my wild imagination." She poured tea into two mugs. "But you and Danny. . .it's not just your physical resemblance." She set the cups on the table and sat. "It's something intangible, like your passion for life and magnetic personalities."

Derrick smiled. "You should have met my sister."

"She must've loved having a big, protective brother like you. I'm an only child." She shrugged, then refocused on him. "Why didn't you come right out and tell Allie when you discovered Danny was your nephew? It wasn't like you'd come to town to steal him from the Vahns."

"I couldn't tell her. Sandy made me promise. She wanted me to check on Danny, make sure he was with a good family, and leave town without revealing her identity or mine. She didn't want to disturb his life in any way. We were worried about what my father would do if he discovered he had a grandson. Turns out our fears were well-grounded." He took a swallow of tea. "Anyway, everything was going well enough until I—"

"Started to fall in love with Allie?" Shannon pressed her hand over her heart, and he would have laughed if not for the bitter ending.

"Yes, I started to fall in love with Allie. I also loved my nephew as though I'd known him all my life. And Betsy felt like a second mom to me. I didn't have that kind of warm upbringing." He sighed. "I was selfish for spending the time with them that I did. I should have gone home as soon as I saw Danny was fine."

"I understand why you did it." Shannon played with the handle of her mug. "So Sandy finally gave you permission to tell Allie?"

"Yes, right before she died."

Shannon sat back in the chair. "So you went to Allie after your sister's passing? Confessed everything? And she wouldn't forgive you?"

Derrick snorted a humorless laugh. "No, it gets much, much worse." He felt the pain anew and drew a breath. "My father found out about Danny."

Shannon's eyes widened. "Oh no. And he got to Allie first?"

"Exactly. He went to the Vahns' house and informed them the adoption was coerced. He demanded joint custody and threatened Allie and Betsy with a legal battle if they refused."

Shannon blew out a breath of air. "I know what Allie's reaction was. She came up angry, hurt, and fighting." She frowned. "Was it true? Was the adoption coerced?"

He nodded. "Yes, in a manner of speaking. By law the adoptive parents should have been investigated and approved. Sandy should have been given time to reconsider before signing papers. Instead she signed as soon as Danny was born, and he was whisked away."

"Man, oh man. And Paige handled the adoption, right?"

Derrick nodded. "Keep in mind that my sister had no regrets. She was living on the street at the time and couldn't have cared for him. But she wanted to make sure he was okay. That's where I came in. I wanted her to go home with a peaceful heart."

Shannon frowned in thought. "Do you remember the story of Rahab in the Bible?"

That came out of left field. Derrick just nodded.

"How she hid the Israelite spies from the local authorities and got protection for her family?"

"Yes."

"Well, in a way, you were doing the same thing. You were hiding Danny from being hurt while you got information for your sister. You were protecting everyone. And you never outright lied." Shannon slapped her hands on the table. "We've got to straighten this out." She stood, went to the counter, and picked up her cell phone. "The Bible says if we know the truth, the truth will set us free."

"I don't see Allie ever trusting me again. She's been deceived too many times." Derrick's shoulders sagged with defeat. "But if you're willing to try."

Shannon tossed her phone on the counter. "I won't call. I'll close the store and go pay Allie a visit instead." She picked up a big ring of keys. "I hate cell phones. You may as well stick your head in the microwave."

"Um. . .I never thought of it that way." Derrick followed her outside.

She patted him on the shoulder. "Pray, Derrick." She whirled away to her truck.

Derrick headed for his vehicle. Did God answer those kinds of prayers? He had deceived the very people who'd treated him with nothing but kindness.

Allie's words came back to haunt him, *I can't abide lying.*

Chapter 23

Allie and Danny returned from the blackberry patch with two buckets of berries. She handed them to him. "Take these inside to Granny."

"Wow, I can't believe Mr. Derrick is my uncle," Danny said for at least the eighth time, his eyes filled with wonder as he headed inside.

Just great. Her nephew was still impressed with "the hero" and glad he was related by blood.

Allie's cell phone vibrated in its holder on her belt. She snatched it up. *Michael.* "Hello?"

"Allie." His voice sounded strained. "I just talked to Paige. She's hysterical. I want to verify what you told her." He repeated her conversation with his sister.

"That's right," Allie said. "And did she tell you about the payments Luke made to her?"

After a long pause, Michael cleared his throat. "Payments?"

Allie explained the check stubs she'd found. "She claims she was having an affair with Luke and he helped support her."

Silence from the other end. "Michael, are you there?"

"Yes—yes, I am." He cleared his throat again. "Listen, no matter what you think of me, please know I don't want your family hurt. I'm looking into this. And, Allie, you'd do well not to talk to any of the Owenses until you have legal representation. I had my doubts about Derrick all along. I'm here if you need me."

Of course Michael would use this opportunity to make himself look good, to get Allie back. As she hung up, she heard a vehicle approaching and walked to the front of the house. It was Shannon in her old green truck, tearing up the driveway like a maniac, spewing dust in every direction.

After she slid to a stop, she hopped from the truck. "We need to talk!"

"Yes, we do," Allie said. They exchanged hugs. "I'm so glad to see you. You'll never believe—"

"I already know." Shannon sank onto a porch step and patted the place next to her, suddenly composed and relaxed. "Let's sit. It's a lovely day."

Allie complied. "What do you mean?"

"The sun is shining and—"

"I'm not asking about the weather, Shannon! I'm asking how you know what happened to me. Are we on the same page here?"

Shannon folded her hands in her lap and nodded.

"You spoke with Derrick, didn't you?"

Shannon inhaled. "How cool that you picked up on that. Maybe you're getting more in tune with body language."

"I doubt it," Allie snapped. "Otherwise I would have picked up on Derrick's lies."

Shannon waved her hand in the air. "I was thinking about what deception really is."

Allie blinked. "What?"

"And then I thought about Luke and Michael. Especially Michael. Anyway, I'm not sure 'lie' is the right word to use for what Derrick did." Shannon's eyes were filled with compassion. A sure sign that Derrick had gotten to her.

"Derrick *did* lie."

"Did he?" Shannon twisted her thumb ring. "He never told you anything that wasn't true, did he? Did he purposefully set out to deceive you with malice in his heart?"

"What does that mean?" Allie gave an inpatient shrug. "This wound can't be healed with soothing words. I know you mean well, but I—"

"Okay, stop." Shannon held up her hand. "This is one time you're not going to cut me off. You're not going to stop listening like you do sometimes. It's too important to your life and Danny's."

Allie's breaths came fast and hard with irritation. "Go ahead then. I don't have all afternoon. I have to make calls and fill my schedule with more work to earn enough money to hire an attorney to keep the boy who already belongs to us." She felt the threat of tears all over again. "Did Derrick tell you that, too?"

"Yes." Shannon patted her back. "That's not what Derrick wants, Allie. And I believe him with my whole heart."

"Of course you would. You have an almost unnatural ability to see only the good in people. Like my mother. And speaking of liars, guess who called me?"

Shannon raised her brows. "This is the only conversational digression I'll allow you, then I get to talk."

"Okay." Allie told Shannon what Paige had said and then about Michael's call.

"Hmm. Trying to get on your good side." Shannon nodded. "I think God is at work here. I'm imagining a big creaky mill slowly turning. It might seem to take forever, but the grain is getting ground up."

Allie wasn't sure she could see it. Shannon was particularly confusing today. "Okay. . .God is working."

"So now it's my turn. Remember the story of Rahab in the Bible?"

"What?" Allie asked.

"When you hear why Derrick did what he did, maybe you'll open your heart enough to forgive him."

Allie sat back and closed her eyes, hoping it might help her understand. "All right. Spill it."

※

Derrick walked into his father's office late that night without bothering to knock. He sat at his large cherry desk and looked up.

"Why'd you do it, Dad? Why did you threaten the Vahns?"

"You know why." Dad stood and tossed a folder toward Derrick and pointed at it. "This is all the information I need to go to court. I'm not going to change my mind."

Derrick approached the desk, but ignored the file. "So if you win this court battle—and you won't—you'll do what? Force a nine-year-old who adores his adoptive family to love you?"

Dad's eyes glittered. "If they don't agree to shared custody, I will do whatever I have to."

Derrick fought the anger that burned inside him. "You might want to reconsider."

"Are you threatening me, son?" He dropped to the edge of the desk and crossed his arms. "Your very generous paycheck comes from Owens Realty. You'd do well to remember which side your bread is buttered on."

Money. Again. "You can keep your money." Derrick put his hands, palms down, on his father's desk. "You think money can buy anything, don't you?" *Even love,* he was tempted to add.

"All of a sudden you're the poor little rich boy, are you? Never heard you complain over the years when you squired your many women around town in expensive sports cars, spending money without a second thought." Dad drew a noisy breath, went behind his desk, and sat. "I've got work to do, if you don't mind."

"I do mind," Derrick said. "Why do you always play the womanizing card with me? You know I've changed."

"Hmm, that's right, you found religion," Dad said, a trace of laughter in his voice. "But I think we're more alike than you'd care to admit. Could be I've met my match."

Derrick shook his head. "I used to wish that. I tried to emulate you. But now the last person in the world I'd be like is you."

Dad's head snapped back as if Derrick had hit him.

"You're trying to intimidate and bully an innocent family. Danny is theirs, and that's exactly how Sandy wanted it. Danny's a happy kid, he's well cared for, and—"

"And nothing!" Dad shot out of his chair. "His adoptive parents are dead.

He's being raised by a blacksmith and a cleaning woman when he could have all this." He waved his arms, then his brows drew together and he snorted. "What's that look on your face? If you and Sandy had come to me with this situation first, I could've handled things. You"—he pointed a shaking finger—"are the cause of all this confusion!"

"A *situation*? Is that how you refer to Sandy's son?"

"Ah, now you're talking sense. Danny is *Sandy's* son." Dad punched his right fist into his left hand. "*My* grandson. An Owens. Not an orphan meant to live on a dirt farm in the middle of nowhere. Left alone to break his arm." Looking satisfied with himself, Dad dropped into his leather armchair.

Derrick backed toward the door.

"Where are you going?"

"I'm leaving, Dad," Derrick said quietly. "I want out of the company, out of this family for good." At the slack-jawed look on his father's face, anger seeped from him replaced by great sadness.

"You're leaving us for them? You're going to walk out on us after we lost Sandy?" Dad came around to the other side of the desk and clamped his hands behind his back. "And your mother, what about her?"

"I'm leaving because I won't be a part of what you're doing. Mom will always be a part of my life—I'll be in touch with her regularly." He studied his father intently, but the man's face gave away nothing. "Mom doesn't know Danny exists, does she? She's got nothing to do with this idiotic threat."

"No, she doesn't. It would kill her to know Sandy's son is being raised by strangers."

"Hogwash!" Derrick's muscles went rigid, and he drew a breath and asked God to give him peace. "You don't know the Vahns. Allie and Betsy love Danny with all their hearts. Yeah, they have financial problems, but they work hard to give *your* grandson everything he needs." He had his father's full attention now, and Derrick took another breath lest he choke up. "You should've seen the birthday party Allie had for Danny. It must've cost her a week's pay."

Dad stared over Derrick's shoulder.

What was the use? His words were falling on deaf ears. "I'd rather Danny be raised without all the things I had. You gave me plenty of material things, but I needed your heart. That's what Danny needs, too, and he's got that with Allie and Betsy." Derrick swiped his suit jacket off the back of the chair and headed for the door.

"So just like that, you're walking out?" Dad asked before he could read the message.

"I'll have everything out of the guest house by Monday. And if you pursue action against the Vahns, I will use everything in my power to help fight you." Derrick opened the door and stopped. Standing there in the hall was

Mom, her face whiter than it had been, if that were possible. Tears wet her face.

"How long have you been here?" Derrick whispered.

Chapter 24

On Monday morning Allie loaded her truck with supplies, then zipped her bag closed. She had one appointment with a normal horse, then she'd have to deal with Eddieboy again. Seems he had spent two days hock-deep in manure in his stall, and the thrush grew worse. Not that she should complain. Frank paid her well, and she was able to slip in the appointment between two others. But today she was going to lay down the law. No animal, no matter how cranky, deserved to be treated like that. Besides, dealing with Eddieboy would keep her mind off everything Shannon had told her about Derrick. Allie didn't know how she felt or what to think.

As she pulled down the driveway, a big blue Lincoln headed toward her. She got closer and recognized Philip Maynard. The mayor hailed her, waving his chunky hand out the window.

Allie pulled onto the side of the drive and waited. He stopped his car alongside her. "Allie, I need to speak with you."

Her first question was, "Why?" Lately every encounter with a Maynard spelled trouble. In fact it was her encounter with Philip at the parade that had led to her meeting Derrick. "What can I do for you?"

"Um, got some place we can sit?" He cut the engine and tugged at his shirt collar.

"Yeah, sure." Allie indicated the picnic bench near the house, a myriad of scenarios passing through her mind. Did he come in peace or to threaten them in some way?

After they settled at the table, the mayor smiled. "How's everybody doing? Everybody okay?"

"Philip, I know you didn't come here for small talk. Please just get on with it."

"Right." He nodded, and his smile disappeared. "I'm ashamed of my daughter."

Allie gasped. "Paige told you about the. . ." *Affair? Adoption? Money?* The words stuck in her throat.

"Paige confided in Michael, and he's the one who told me everything. You know, my son's got plenty of faults, but he's letter of the law when it comes to business."

Her mind raced. "Business? Luke gave Paige—"

"Close to fifty thousand dollars. I know." Philip sighed. "And I intend to give you back every red cent."

"Why?" As much as her family desperately needed the money, her suspicions grew. This show of humility from Philip Maynard was out of character to the extreme. "What did Michael tell you exactly?"

Philip's eyes narrowed. "Paige misled you." He pulled a hankie from his pocket and dabbed sweat from his brow. "When Cindy was a nurse in the rehab clinic in the Tri-Cities, she met Sandy Owens, Danny's biological mother."

"Yes, I know all this and that Paige handled the paperwork."

He breathed heavily and wiped his balding head, and she felt a pang of compassion for the man. Mayor Maynard looked her in the eye. "Did you ever ask yourself, 'Why Paige?'"

Allie nodded. "Yes. She said it was because she loved Luke. She also told me she was having an affair with him."

"That's not true, Allie. Your brother was a good man, completely blind to what was going on. He wasn't aware the adoption was questionable."

"If she didn't do it for Luke, then why? Paige would've never handled the adoption out of the goodness of her heart. Cindy and Paige disliked each other intensely."

"Paige didn't do it out of the 'goodness of her heart.' She used it as an ace in the hole to endear herself to Luke. She never did get over him."

"Endear herself how?" Her heart pounded in her ears, and she struggled for breath.

"Then Paige could come to him with the cold facts later, in hopes that he'd leave Cindy for deceiving him. When that didn't work, Paige got angry and blackmailed your brother. If Luke didn't give her money, Paige threatened to expose Cindy, even at the expense of losing her law license." He wagged his head. "I don't know where I went wrong with my daughter. Gave her everything till she took advantage and I cut her off."

That explained all the fights Luke and Cindy had. Cindy's bitterness toward Paige. As Allie digested the information, she took pity on the mayor. Tears rushed to her eyes. "I'm so relieved to know my brother wasn't cheating on his wife. It was killing me to think Luke was a fraud."

"No, Luke was only protecting his wife and Danny. He hid things from you, but that's what a good man does—anything to protect family."

Just like Derrick had been protecting his sister. What Luke had done to protect Cindy—who wasn't dying—Derrick had done for his sister, only in a different way. He'd even tried to protect Danny, her, and Ma. In her mind's eye, she saw him sitting on the bale of straw, trying to get her to understand, but she'd refused.

"Why did you tell me all this?"

"Yes, well," Philip said with a wave of his hand. "Don't mistake me for being altruistic. I'm protecting my own family. If I didn't tell you, Michael would have. He wants to get back into your good graces. Besides, from what I understand, the Owenses might try to sue for custody. All this might play out in court, and I'm not going to risk my reputation for what my daughter did."

"That's why you're offering me the money?"

"Well, if you take recompense and don't press charges against Paige, the DA, who is a friend of mine, won't take this to court, and we'll avoid a public scandal. Unless Owens raises a huge stink, which I hope he doesn't. But Paige's future remains to be seen. She may lose her license to practice law."

"I don't want a scandal either, and I don't want to see Paige behind bars, but I might need that money for legal fees to fight the Owenses."

Philip swung his heavily jowled head from side to side. "Try to settle out of court. Take it from an old man. Maybe you could see it in your heart to let the kid see his grandparents. I know how I'd feel if I knew I had a grandson somewhere."

He struggled to his feet, and Allie followed him to his car. "Again, I'm sorry for what my daughter did, Allie. And the part Cindy played in all this."

Cindy. Paige. The Owenses. Philip's words rang in her mind as he drove off. She walked toward the house feeling lighter. They wouldn't have to sell their property. They would be able to battle the Owenses if they chose to fight. Despite all the bad that had happened, she could tell her mother Luke was innocent of wrongdoing. Ma would want to pray together to thank God, and for the first time in a very long time, Allie was eager to join her with a grateful heart.

❧

The full weight of what he'd done hit Derrick as he glanced around the empty guesthouse. Along with moving his belongings to a small apartment, he'd talked to his financial advisor. Though he had money of his own, walking away from his family meant he would no longer live a privileged life. Oddly enough, that idea challenged him and gave him the strength to follow through with his painful decision.

"So you finally stood up to the old man." Hank's voice came from behind him.

Derrick turned and saw him in the doorway. "Yes, I guess I did."

Hank dropped into a leather chair in the corner. "I'm not surprised. It was inevitable. I saw it, even when you were a kid. No need to wonder where you and Sandy got your willful streaks."

"Yeah, right. Maybe the showdown was inevitable, but not what I wanted." He zipped his suitcases closed. "Promise me you'll look after Mom?"

"You got it, but I think you'll discover your mother has a backbone of steel. She might have appeared vulnerable and acquiescent all these years, and especially the last few weeks, but believe me, the woman knows how to run the show."

"I hope so," Derrick said.

"Let me help you carry those to your truck."

The two men walked in silence out the door to the driveway.

"Will you fight for her?" Hank asked.

"What?" Derrick stacked the suitcases in the back of the Silverado.

"That young lady you like so much. . .Allie. Seems to me she might be worth fighting for."

Derrick shrugged. "She hasn't called me. Danny has, but nothing from Allie. I can't go back to Walla Walla on just my nephew's invitation. I need her permission."

"She won't call you. From what you've told me, Allie doesn't seem that sort." Hank slapped him on the back. "If I were you, I'd go see her. Tell her what you've done in the name of love."

❧

Derrick stopped at a light and pondered Hank's words. How about a happy medium? He'd call Shannon, get her opinion. By now she had spoken to Allie, and she'd know whether or not a visit from him would disturb the Vahns.

He dialed.

"The Quaint Shop, good afternoon."

"Shannon, it's Derrick." He infused his voice with cheer he didn't feel.

"Derrick! I was going to call you, but my pastor's wife pulled me aside after our prayer meeting."

She paused, and he heard murmuring in the background. "Shannon, you there?"

"Yes, sorry, a customer asked a question. Anyway, Portia, that's Pastor's wife, told me that I give out too much unsolicited advice. How embarrassing. Portia said she knows I mean well, but I have to allow God to do the work."

"Um, let's back up a sec. What does that have to do with me?" Derrick took an exit onto the highway toward Walla Walla. Was that where he wanted to go?

"If I keep talking right now, I'll end up giving you my advice."

"Shannon? I'm the one who asked you to speak with Allie. Therefore your advice wouldn't be unsolicited." He went on to tell her what had transpired with his father. "I want to tell Allie that I'm going to help them fight if they have to."

Another long silence. "Shannon?"

"Yes. I'm thinking."

Shannon was nice, but one of the most confusing people he'd ever talked to. "I'm on my way to Walla Walla, but I'm wondering if I should turn around and head home. I don't want to upset Allie or Betsy. If there's a chance that I'll make things even worse by going over there, I don't want to come."

"I've decided I'll tell you exactly what I think. You must come. Allie has some appointments. Call me when you get into town, and I'll confirm where she is and give you directions. I don't think you'll make things worse." There was a smile in Shannon's voice, and a tiny flicker of hope came alive inside him.

Chapter 25

Stop that!" Allie ducked to avoid Eddieboy's third attempt to chomp her arm as she walked past his head.

He snorted.

"Yeah, yeah, whatever. Carnivore." She checked his hoof one more time. "Frank needs a serious talking-to. If this keeps up, your foot is going to rot away." For some reason she felt sorry for the little pony, despite his rotten disposition. If he'd been better cared for, he'd have half a chance to bloom.

The barn door squeaked open. "Frank!" Allie yelled. "You and I need a word. I know Eddieboy is cranky. So are you, but you can't allow him to continue this way."

She heard footsteps, but no response. "Do you want me to call the ASPCA?"

Allie put the pony's foot down and stood to face Frank. "Oh no," she whispered and ducked quickly behind Eddieboy's neck. "It's Derrick. I don't know what to say to him after all this." She smoothed back her hair. After any encounter with Eddieboy, she looked like a tornado victim.

Derrick glanced around, noticed her peering at him over the pony's mane, and held up his hand. "Don't run away," he said softly.

She straightened and lifted her chin. "What are you doing here?"

"Looking for you." He took several steps toward her.

"How did you find me?"

"Shannon told me you'd be here."

Why had she bothered to ask? Shannon had just called her twenty minutes ago to ask her if she wanted to go out to dinner. The traitor. "What do you want?" Allie sounded rude, but she still wasn't sure how she felt about anything right now. She was too numb. "Did you come here to try to sweet-talk me?"

"No." He moved toward her again and stopped a couple of feet away. "I'm here to tell you I'm on your side. I'll hire a lawyer myself if my father insists on this ridiculous fight."

Of all the things he could have said, that wasn't what she expected. "What exactly do you mean?"

Derrick shoved his hands in his jean pockets. "I told my father I won't be working for him anymore. And I won't be living on his property." He shrugged. "I guess I disowned myself."

Eddieboy took another swipe at her, and she shoved his nose away. "You walked away from your family?"

"I did. I don't expect you to let me back into your life, but I want you to know that I'll do whatever it takes to see that Danny stays with you and your mother."

Allie stared, struggling to process his words. "You disowned yourself?"

"Yes." Derrick took a deep breath. "I'll call you if I hear anything. If you hear anything, get served with papers, or whatever, you call me, okay?"

She let his words sink in. "Yes, fine." Derrick hadn't tried to charm her like Michael always had.

He took his hands from his pockets and extended them toward her, but suddenly dropped them to his side. "Please hug Danny for me?" he asked as he backed away.

She nodded. Her mind was computing very slowly. "Right. Sure. Will do." *He came to tell me this in person when he could have called.* That took courage.

"I've got one more stop to make," he said. "I need to tell your mother the same thing. I owe it to her."

"She's at Shannon's shop," Allie volunteered. "Danny's at the sitter's." Now he risked Ma's cold shoulder.

"Right. She's working then."

She nodded like her head was on a spring.

He opened his mouth and snapped it shut. After a moment's hesitation, he turned and walked from the barn.

Allie watched the door shut. Derrick had walked away from his family because he cared enough to fight so that Danny could stay with her and Ma. Did someone who wasn't trustworthy do something like that? The Bible said there was no greater love than if a man laid down his life for his friend.

"Derrick?" Allie whispered, willing her feet to move.

The slam of his vehicle door met her ears.

"Derrick!" she yelled. Eddieboy jumped. "Oh, get over yourself," she told the pony. She left him tied in the barn aisle and ran outside.

"Derrick, wait!" As she watched the retreating taillights, she jumped up and down, waving her hands in the air to get his attention, but he didn't see her.

≈

Derrick felt his cell phone vibrating on his belt, but couldn't bring himself to answer. Right now it was best he didn't speak to anybody. He needed a few minutes. The hope he'd had for reconciliation with Allie had died. He hadn't been able to find the words to ask her forgiveness, perhaps because he didn't feel deserving.

He drove toward Shannon's shop as quickly as the speed limit would allow, prepared to tell Betsy everything. Get it all out, then leave the Vahns alone.

Lord, I want to do the right thing, no matter what the cost.

He parked, then walked toward the Quaint Shop, dreading the look of disappointment on Betsy's face when she saw him.

As he pulled open the door, he lingered at the front of the store for a moment, but the cowbell had alerted Shannon and Betsy to his presence. They turned, and both greeted him with bright smiles. Why?

Moving toward them slowly, Derrick tilted his head. "Good afternoon, ladies."

"I already told Betsy everything," Shannon blurted out. "Figured it would save you time."

Betsy came from behind the counter and hurried over to him. "Did you talk to Allie yet?"

"Well, I tried." Derrick shrugged.

"And?" Shannon clasped her hands like she anticipated good news.

"Allie was dealing with that scraggly pony." No. Truth was she used the creature as a diversion. "She didn't say much."

Shannon and Betsy exchanged glances.

"I'm going to call her." Shannon turned, then searched under the mess on her counter. "Where's that stupid phone?"

Much as she meant well, he couldn't expect Shannon to run interference for him. "No, don't call her."

Betsy and Shannon stared at him, eyes round with sympathy.

"It's okay, really." He backed away. "Allie has to make decisions for herself."

The front door banged open with a crash. Shannon and Betsy's eyes widened, and Derrick turned.

Allie stood in the doorway.

"I have something to say." She stared at him, her auburn hair as wild as the day he'd dragged her from Chester's back.

His breath caught in his lungs. The silence that followed was deafening.

She took a step toward him. "Derrick."

He couldn't decode the look on her beautiful face. "Yes?"

Allie ran at him and flung her arms around his neck. "Derrick," she whispered into his shoulder.

He held her close and swung her around in a circle. When he finally put her down, he gently kissed her cheek.

She backed up. "I know what you did was for your sister's sake." She clutched the lapels of his shirt. "You never meant to hurt anyone. You were trying to protect everyone, including my family."

"I would never hurt you on purpose. Never," he whispered into her hair. "I want to love you for the rest of my life." He kissed her soundly.

The sound of applause came from behind him, followed by a whistle.

Derrick lifted his head and laughed. "I forgot we had an audience."

Allie peered around Derrick and winked at her mother and Shannon, then looked back into his eyes, smiling.

Derrick's cell phone vibrated again, and he decided he'd better pick up this time.

"That better be important." Allie kissed him before joining the other two women at the counter.

He glanced at the screen and was hit with a pang of worry. "It's my mom." She rarely called, and when she did, it wasn't good news.

"Hey, Mom. What's up? Something wrong?"

"Not a thing." Her voice was cool, as if she'd returned to the woman she'd been before Sandy died. "I know about Danny. I know what your father has tried to do. I want you to go to Danny's family and tell them they will have no further trouble from us."

Stunned silent, he waited for more.

"I love your father, but I've learned over the years the only way to deal with him is to let him experience the consequences of his actions. After you left, I told him I would move into a hotel if he insisted on threatening the Vahn family. We want to see Danny, of course, but I will appeal to Allie and her mother myself. The Vahns need no longer fear legal recourse."

"Mom, thank you." Derrick smiled. "I'm right here with them."

Allie, Shannon, and Betsy stared at him.

"Pass on the message. I'll deal with your father." She paused. "And I think it's time you tell that young woman how you really feel."

"How did you know?"

"I know you confide in Hank. I cornered him in the kitchen and threatened to dent his pots and pans."

Derrick laughed. "So Hank caved."

"Of course he did. You know how he loves his cookware. Now, dear. You call me soon. Let me know how things are going with your young lady. And tell Betsy and Allie the next Owens they talk to besides you will be me. Ask them. . ." She paused. "Ask them to please consider allowing me to see my grandson."

Epilogue

Allie stood at her vanity mirror and adjusted her pearl necklace.
"Allie, you look beautiful beyond words." Shannon joined her at the window and fussed with her bridal veil. "A princess, that's what you look like."

Tears filled Allie's eyes, and she fanned her face. "Don't make me cry. I don't know how to redo my makeup like that professional artist."

"Okay, I won't." Shannon laughed and hugged her. "I've imagined my own wedding day, but never dreamt of anything this lovely." She stepped back and sighed. "Wait till Derrick sees you."

"Derrick." Allie smiled. "At the mention of his name, my heart pounds harder than the first time we met."

Hands clasped to her heart, Shannon exhaled heavily. "Oh how romantic."

"Tell me I'm not dreaming."

"You're not."

Allie reached out and smoothed the satin collar of Shannon's lavender dress. "You're so special. No girl could ask for a better friend or maid of honor."

"Now *I'm* going to cry. . .again." Shannon grabbed a tissue and dabbed at her eyes. "I hardly ever wear makeup. Talk about not knowing how to fix my face."

Allie grabbed her hand and walked her to the mirror. "This is how you should dress all the time. You're too gorgeous to hide under baggy clothes."

Shannon tilted her head and smoothed her hands down the sides of her gown. "Only under duress." She shot Allie a telling look, and they both laughed. "I can't see myself changing my style, but if it'll catch me a winner like Derrick, maybe I would."

"God's got someone extra special for you, too." Allie flounced to the window and looked out. "People are filling the chairs."

Shannon came to her side. "So they are. Look at your mom and Mrs. Owens. They're like best friends already."

"Mrs. Owens said Sandy was responsible for all this." Allie's eyes blurred. "She said, 'Death brings rebirth.'"

On the back porch of Allie's house, Derrick glanced at the flower-adorned gazebo where he and Allie would be married. Danny stood next to him in a black tux much like Derrick's.

"You nervous, Uncle Derrick?"

"You betcha. Have you got the rings?" Derrick stepped back and scanned his nephew. "You're one handsome kid."

"Grandma Owens says I look like you." Danny appraised himself in the mirror. "That's probably good because you got Aunt Allie to marry you. It means you're handsome."

Derrick laughed. "Hey, you're right. I'm the one who got the best of the deal. Now check your pocket again for the rings."

"I got 'em."

"Okay then, are we ready?" Derrick felt his heart pounding through his shirt. He swallowed past the lump in his throat and put his hand on Danny's shoulder. "Did I ever tell you you're my hero?"

Danny stared up at him, frowning. "What do you mean? What did I do?"

"You always believed in me, and that's one of the best things a hero can do for someone. It gave me the courage to face your Aunt Allie."

"I'm only a kid," Danny said, "but even I knew you liked her. You were always staring at her."

"I know," Derrick headed for the gazebo. "She might've stared at me a couple of times, too, you know."

"Yeah, maybe," Danny conceded and walked tall beside Derrick, passing family and friends that had come to celebrate with them.

Derrick sent up a silent prayer of gratitude to God for restoring his family, for Allie, and for giving Allie and him the greatest kid on earth. And he thanked God for his sister. She would be so proud today.

He stood with the pastor beside the gazebo, Danny at his side. The wedding march commenced, and he set his sights to the back door of the house. Allie emerged with Derrick's dad, their arms looped. His father's chest was puffed out with pride. He was growing to love Allie like a daughter.

She looked like a princess in a white satin ball gown. Tears rose in his eyes as she walked toward him, smiling.

His mom and Betsy held on to each other. They'd foregone the traditional bride and groom sides and stood side by side.

After Allie reached him, Derrick took her hands in his, and they faced one another, repeating their vows after the minister.

"To love, honor, and cherish. . .as long as we both shall live."

"You may now kiss your beautiful bride."

He lifted the veil, leaned down, and kissed her soundly on her welcoming lips. When he was done, the attendees cheered.

"Derrick?" Allie whispered in his ear.

"Yes?"

"You are the hero of my heart."

BOXED INTO LOVE

Dedication

Authors don't write in a vacuum, and this book is no exception.
We'd like to thank John and Diana for Tri-City details, and we want to
send a special thanks to Tracy for her help with Benton City information.
We also want to mention our wonderful editorial team—JoAnne Simmons,
Rachel Overton, and April Frazier. You guys are the best.

Chapter 1

Sleigh bells over the front door of the Quaint Shop jangled, distracting Shannon O'Brien from the task of sorting month-old invoices. As she nudged the door to her office shut with her foot, she decided she preferred the clang of cowbells over the door at her Walla Walla store than this shop in Kennewick. She forced her attention back to her desk. She'd promised herself she'd get this work finished today and didn't need any interruptions. Her clerk, Venus, could take care of customers.

Shannon returned to thumbing through the invoices, but couldn't get her mind to settle. After a quick glance at her guitar leaning against her antique safe, she abandoned her task to find something that required less concentration. Only an hour till closing time, lots to do, and then she had to practice for her guitar lesson with Ray Reed tomorrow night. If only she could better organize her time.

She opened the desk drawer and flipped through three days of mail. Why hadn't she received a new lease from her landlord? Her old lease would expire at the end of the month, and he hadn't returned her calls.

With a long sigh, her dog, Truman, stretched out next to her. "I fed you," she said. Her own stomach growled in complaint. She'd forgotten to eat lunch, and dinnertime was still a few hours away.

The murmur of voices from the shop drifted through the closed door as Shannon began to punch figures from her checkbook register into the calculator. Truman's ears twitched. She hit the button for the grand total, blinked, and took a sip from a cup of lukewarm herbal tea. The number came up much lower than she'd hoped. How could she manage to keep two stores in two cities when she was earning barely enough to cover her expenses? Somehow she had to make the store more profitable. Betsy Vahn, the woman she left to manage her store in Walla Walla, was doing wonders. Profits from that store were helping keep this one afloat.

The voices were clearer now, and Shannon strained to concentrate over the din. As Venus chattered on and on, the deep rumble of a man's voice followed. Truman sat up, ears cocked toward the door.

Shannon inhaled, breath hissing through her teeth. Not just *any* man— Glen Caldwell, owner of the upper-crust, art deco antique store next to hers. Possibly the most attractive man she'd ever met.

BLUE MOUNTAIN WEDDINGS

And the most irritating.

The tired floorboards creaked outside her office, followed by a rap at her door. "Shannon, may I come in?"

Oh, that British accent! Truman's tail wagged as fast as her heart thumped. Wasn't twenty-eight too old to have a crush on a foreigner? Shannon motioned for Truman to stay and spun her chair around. "Yes."

The door swung open. Glen hovered in the entry, his head only inches below the door frame, appraising her and her office with one brow raised.

Truman whined.

"I, um, told Mr. Caldwell you were back here," Venus chimed from behind him. Her usual piercing tone was breathy and girlish.

Glen Caldwell had that effect on women with his charming persona and captivating British accent. That's what made listening to his grievances too easy.

"I hope it's okay." Venus peered around Glen, her eyes brimming with curiosity. "I know you said you didn't want to be interrupted, but. . ." She patted down her short, white-blond hair streaked with red and blue, colored to please her new boyfriend, Louis.

"Sure, it's fine." Shannon averted her gaze to the papers on her desk while she tried to put a name to what she felt in Glen's presence.

Magnetism. Glen Caldwell oozed the self-confidence that Shannon felt she'd lost during the last few months.

Shannon pointed to a chair next to the door that hid the stairs to her apartment above the shop. "Come in. Hang up your coat and have a seat." She glanced back at Venus who hovered in the doorway, bouncing from one foot to the other. "Why don't you shut the office door and finish unpacking that Willow Ware."

A frown clouded Venus's eyes, but she sighed and acquiesced, leaving her and Glen alone in her office.

Glen remained standing, staring down at the leather chair beside her desk. "That's a new addition." He stated the obvious. "Well, a *used* new addition."

"Yes, I bought it at an estate sale." The chair didn't look like much, marred by scars and discolorations, but she loved it, and Glen's reaction annoyed her. She pointed. "Sit."

He hesitated.

"It doesn't have bugs." Shannon couldn't help chiding him. "Maybe traces of dog hair. Of course it's not the ritzy stuff you sell, but it's comfortable, dependable, and it happens to be my favorite place to relax now. Take off your coat and sit down. Please."

After he drew a deep breath, Glen hung his black wool coat on a hook on the back of her door and sank into the chair, which put him at eye level with her. The coffee-colored leather sighed as it molded itself around his body.

134

He quickly disguised a look of pleasant surprise before he met her gaze. Perhaps a miracle had happened, and he'd come by to shoot the breeze. She could sit and be mesmerized by the cadence of his speech and—

"This is not a social call," he said.

No, of course not. Shannon adjusted the daisy slipping out of her hair, leaned back, and noticed Truman had crawled over to lie at Glen's feet. She didn't bother to correct him. He adored Glen, and though she refused to dwell on it, she did, too.

"Can I get you something to drink? I've been practicing making proper English tea, not that I drink a lot of it. I don't want to kill myself with caffeine."

Glen sniffed, a nearly imperceptible gesture he often used to indicate his skepticism. "Thank you, no, though I appreciate the offer." He leaned over to scratch Truman's head.

"Herbal tea, then?"

"No." He cleared his throat and once again settled back into the chair, much to Truman's disappointment.

"So, why are you here?"

"The problem is that your shop has once again been mistaken for mine. This time by the mother of one of my most important clients. How that could happen is quite beyond my comprehension."

Indeed, as he would say. His long list of grievances included her show windows filled with cluttered displays. Her sidewalk sales when she and Venus piled bric-a-brac high on assorted pieces of furniture, which, he claimed, was hazardous to the safety of his clients. Truman's messes in the alley behind the stores, which she often forgot to clean up. The hand-lettered, "garish" sign hanging over the entrance of her store, and her friends and acquaintances— some of whom might be considered unsavory. The thought of her shop being mistaken for his was amusing. What harm could come of it? But for Glen, the mix-up wasn't a mere inconvenience but a personal affront.

"I've explained this to you before, Glen." She took a deep breath, folded her hands in her lap, and made ready to repeat her defense of her store, only with a twist. "When the middle classes of America go antiquing, they're drawn to shops stuffed with junk. Makes them hopeful they'll find something worth thousands that the poor store owner—meaning myself—is too ignorant to identify. That's why they come into my shop first and probably what happened with your client's mother." She spoke with exaggerated patience, very slowly. "Your shop is all retro—glass, steel, wood. That window display of yours is pruned to the point of boring. It discourages the average shopper from entering. In fact, it bleats expensive."

Glen's brows, the same dark brown as his hair, drew together in a frown over eyes that glittered like blue ice through his dark-framed glasses. "Bleats?

My window bleats? What precisely does that mean?"

Did she finally have his ear? A sense of satisfaction washed over her. Shannon smiled. "Ever heard a sheep that's stuck? When I was little, we owned one that was so stupid she'd wedge herself between the watering tub and the fence, and since she didn't know how to back up, she'd stand there bleating until someone came to her rescue. It's a sound you can't miss. Like no one can miss your stark, cold window displays filled with art deco stuff that the average customer can't afford to buy."

Glen recovered from her indirect insult with remarkable speed and studied her with a raised brow and slight grin. "I'm not interested in the *average* client. And as much as I find your unique descriptions, er. . .interesting, we need to discuss my client's misplaced spice box."

Shannon's smile slipped. She enjoyed egging him on, if only to keep him around longer, but today he obviously wouldn't be sidetracked. Besides, she still had work to do. "Spice box?" She tilted her head. "Okay. Shoot."

He adjusted his glasses. "The box belongs to Amanda Franklin."

Shannon's hands and stomach clenched at the name of the interior decorator who owned a shop five doors up. "That certainly explains your intense reaction." *And mine*, she thought.

Glen's eyes narrowed. "Some of the wealthiest people in the Tri-Cities and beyond utilize her interior design business, and she's one of my best clients."

"I know that." Shannon held up her hand to stop him. The less she heard about Amanda, the better. The woman disturbed Shannon's equilibrium. "So how am I involved in this? And what do I have to do with her spice box?"

"Well," Glen said, "her mother, Edna Franklin, has senile dementia." His eyes lost their focus like they did when he was about to go off on a tangent. "It's a problem the elderly develop when—"

"I know what it is, Glen." Shannon strummed her fingers on her leg like she was picking guitar strings. "What does that have to do with me?"

He blinked and focused on her again. "Yes, well, Mrs. Franklin made the decision to sell an antique Pennsylvania spice box—part of a valuable collection belonging to Amanda, and she wants it back. In fact, she's threatening legal action, something I see her doing without hesitation. She can be quite unpleasant when she doesn't get her way." He paused and sighed.

Shannon reached for a bag of raw almonds on her desk and held it out to Glen. "I'm well aware of Amanda's unpleasantness from personal experience, but again, what does this have to do with me? I don't understand."

He shook his head at her offer of almonds. "Apparently Mrs. Franklin found my business card on Amanda's desk, called a taxi, and slipped out of the house without her nurse noticing. A call to the taxi company revealed she was dropped off in front of our stores—spice box in hand. She returned several hours later, empty-handed."

"So how do you know she came in here?"

"I don't for certain, but she didn't come into my shop, and I've checked with the other shop owners. If that truly is the case, the poor woman must have confused your shop with mine, influenced, of course, by her dementia."

Shannon fought the brief stab of irritation and reached into the bag for ten almonds—her ration before dinner. "Of course. Anyone of her caliber coming into my shop would have to be demented."

Glen looked sheepish. "Well, you have to admit some of your clientele are—"

"Don't say it." She shoved almonds into her mouth to prevent banging heads with him. She was aware that some of her friends and acquaintances appeared odd, but firmly believed that the outside of a person never told the whole story. Her parents may have had their shortcomings, but they'd taught her to value people for who they were—not for how they looked. Glen wanted the Quaint Shop to be a mirror image of his sterile store, with upscale clientele. But short of a miracle, she would remain herself—a messy perfectionist, a contradiction in personality she'd never understood.

She swallowed. "I'll help you in any way I can."

"Thank you, Shannon."

The sound of her name on his lips usually sent tingles of delight up her spine, but his serious demeanor made her nervous. "Have you seen Amanda's collection of spice boxes?"

"Enough to know that she owns some valuable pieces, but I haven't seen them all. Amanda is eccentric, to say the least. Very touchy about her belongings. However, for this item, she says she'll take no amount of money. Seems this particular box has sentimental value."

"*Sentiment* and *Amanda* are not two words I would ordinarily use in the same sentence." Shannon forced herself to breathe. Amanda was not worth losing her peace.

Glen's lips twitched.

Shannon relaxed and smiled. "Except she might be a tad sentimental when it comes to you. If you could call it that." When Amanda looked at Glen, her gaze often held a predatory gleam. "In fact, her eyes shoot daggers at any woman who approaches you."

Glen's mouth turned down, as if he were considering the validity of her statement.

Shannon laughed and dropped the subject. "So, what does the box look like?"

"It's William and Mary style, made of walnut, pine, and white cedar," he said in a rush. "About eighteen inches tall and seventeen inches wide." Glen demonstrated the approximate size of the box. "I believe its origins are. . ."

Shannon stopped listening and focused on his hands. Strong and capable.

Enough to make a girl feel secure. But she had to be reasonable. Dreaming of anything more than a casual acquaintanceship with Glen Caldwell was a waste of time. In his tweed jacket with leather patches on the elbows, he looked exactly like an English lord who should be puttering about in a manor house on a drizzly English moor. Even if he were to take a sudden and miraculous romantic interest in her, their backgrounds were so dissimilar she'd want to challenge him to a duel at dusk within two months.

"...a woman who matches that description in your shop?" Glen leaned his wiry frame forward as best he could with his body ensconced in the puffy chair.

"Huh?" Shannon realized she'd missed part of what he'd said.

He exhaled. "I asked you if you've seen a woman like that in your shop."

"A woman?" She desperately tried to recall all of what he'd said, but her mind went blank. "I'm sorry. Please tell me again what she looked like."

"You have a habit of daydreaming." Glen sighed. "You do it often."

She could say, *only when I'm around you*, but didn't. In truth, she dreamed all the time, especially about Glen. Instead she shrugged. "Sorry."

"Well, according to Amanda, her mother is tiny, thin, with sparse white hair and, if you can believe this"—Glen cleared his throat—"she wears flesh-colored trifocals." His lips quirked in a half smile. "Ah, yes, and floral-print dresses."

"*Flesh*-colored trifocals." Shannon laughed. "That could be any number of older women who come in here. I don't recall anyone who matches that description exactly. Well, not the glasses." Shannon thought for a moment. "But I was out this morning. Venus opened the store. She didn't go to school today. Perhaps she remembers something."

"Oh, quite right," Glen said, and his direct gaze made her face warm.

"Venus!" Shannon called out.

"Be right there." Venus used the breathless voice again. The immediacy and clarity of her response told Shannon she'd been close by, probably eavesdropping. So much for the Willow Ware.

Venus burst into the office. "There was somebody with a box like that in here this morning, before Shannon came in. The woman got here really early, like, before I unlocked the door." She stopped and sucked in a deep breath.

Yes, Venus had been listening behind the door.

"Please, do go on." Fingers steepled, Glen leaned forward. "Tell us everything." He used his silky sales voice, the one that had helped him persuade customers to buy thousands of dollars of very expensive antiques.

"Okay, that old lady came in. She was almost creaky, she was so old. She had wrinkles on her wrinkles. Actually, she didn't come in on her own. I mean, the reason she came in is I invited her. I felt sorry for her. She was standing out on the sidewalk, looking cold and lost and. . ."

Venus looked at Glen from under brightly painted eyelids. He nodded and smiled with all of his charm, giving her the full Caldwell treatment. Venus's reaction was immediate. She stood up straighter, a grin lighting her face, making her eyes sparkle.

Like a fire sprinkled with bacon grease, Shannon mused, dismayed by a niggling jab of jealousy. Her teenage clerk was the recipient of the Caldwell charm while Shannon rarely enjoyed that pleasure.

"I told her to come in out of the cold," Venus continued. "I told her she would freeze to death. Her coat didn't look heavy enough—"

"Sweetie," Shannon said, "why don't you get to the point?"

"Oh yeah. Right. So she came in, and I gave her tea. She said she wanted to *dispose* of the box. She wouldn't have peace until she got rid of it. She said something about a secret." Venus frowned. "Strange. I mean, what secret? The box was empty. How weird is that? She reminded me of the ladies in the nursing home where we sang at Christmas last year. Remember, Shannon? Most were old and shaky, but they loved the Christmas carols. Singing at the top of their lungs in those squeaky—"

"I remember." Shannon glanced at Glen. The glint in his eyes reflected her hope that the box was in her shop. She disguised her impatience with Venus under a smile. "Now what about the box?"

"Gee, I felt really sorry for her. She walked bent over, and she looked worried. When I took the box, she was so relieved she almost cried."

Shannon heard Glen's sigh of relief over her own. Though she hadn't spied the spice box amongst the clutter, it had to be in her shop. Maybe this would be a good time to tidy things up—or not. She clasped her hands and turned to face Glen. "It doesn't sound like a case of mistaken identity. Sounds more like the early bird gets the worm." Shannon allowed herself a superior smile. Her shop opened an hour and a half before his.

"Well then, where is it?" Glen snapped, pulling himself to the edge of the slouchy chair, no small feat, and then staring hard at Venus. Her long-winded, convoluted explanations could make the most patient person explode.

Venus bit her lip. Silence filled the room. A mantle clock in the showroom ticked.

"I'll give you three times what you paid for it." Desperation leaked out in Glen's voice, making it low and husky. Decidedly attractive and almost enough to make Shannon daydream again. "Please," he said, "I need that spice box back."

Wow. She would love to hear him say "please kiss me" in that tone. But she had a better chance of performing a classical guitar piece for Ray Reed. Glen asking her for a kiss was the impossible dream, and she was nothing if not pragmatic when it came to love. Shannon returned to the topic at hand. "Venus?"

The girl shifted nervously, looking at the wall, the ceiling, her feet—everywhere but at her or Glen. Shannon's heart sank. Venus had done something with the box and knew they'd be upset.

Venus glanced covertly at Glen. "Yeah, I couldn't get her to take money. Not that I knew what it was worth, so I wouldn't have been able to pay her. And she wouldn't give me her name, so I couldn't do that consignment thing Shannon does." She looked at Shannon and picked at the tight-knit shirt that barely covered her stomach. Was that an earring dangling from her belly button?

Shannon made a mental note to have a discussion with Venus about proper working attire. It would save her one less complaint from Glen on how his classy clientele worried about the "riffraff" who hung around her store.

Glen shifted in the chair and tapped his loafer-clad foot on the floor.

"I didn't know what to do." Venus dragged her fingers through her hair, making her blue tips stand on end. "So I told her to come back for the money. She said she couldn't. She didn't care. She just wanted someone to take the box. She shoved it at me. It was freaky. I got goose pimples all over my body, even on my feet. Then she had me call her a cab. And I did." Venus ended her soliloquy with a dramatic arm flourish.

Glen's foot now kept a rapid rhythm that matched the movement of his fingers on his knees. For someone whose body language indicated agitation, he was acting remarkably patient.

"Venus, honey, where is the box?" Shannon asked the question in the slow, mild tone she used when she tried to obedience-train Truman.

"Right. That's what I'm getting to. Next, this mom and little girl came in. The little girl, around nine, spotted the box and wanted it, so I asked the mom what she'd pay for it. You know, I was, like, bargaining."

Glen stopped moving and groaned.

Tension stiffened Shannon's lips, and she had trouble speaking. "Tell me you didn't sell the box." Amanda already disliked Shannon. This would add fuel to the fire. Amanda's accusations might not stand up in court, but a threat of legal action would force Shannon to hire a lawyer, something for which she had no money. Visions of bankruptcy filled her mind. All her hard work to build her business flushed down the drain.

Venus looked at her feet again as though the leather boots she wore had suddenly caught fire. She mumbled something inaudible.

"What did you say?" Shannon asked. "You need to speak up."

Venus inhaled a gulp of air and glanced up at her with tear-filled eyes, then at Glen.

"I'm really sorry. I sold the spice box."

Chapter 2

Cold air slapped Glen's face as he emerged from Shannon's shop. He closed the door with a gentleness that belied his agitation. A gentleman and a Christian did not slam his way out of impossible situations. He inhaled, breath hissing through his tight lips with the exertion of maintaining his composure. As he exhaled, streams of white air ballooned toward the steel gray sky, giving veracity to the weather forecaster's prediction of an unusually early snow shower.

How would Amanda Franklin take the news of this bizarre series of events? She'd immediately pounce on Shannon, demanding the return of her property. Perhaps she'd make good on her threat of legal action. As bullheaded as Shannon could be, she was no match for Amanda, even though a lawsuit like this had no teeth.

Glen hunched his shoulders against the cold and picked his way around the battered benches and scarred chairs and tables placed in front of Shannon's shop for her sidewalk sale. The furniture held everything, from old kitchen utensils to Depression glass. "Clutter," he mumbled and examined his window display. Shannon's comments wouldn't leave him alone. Was his window too stark? Too cold? *Bleating* expensive?

Glen shook his head. What did Shannon O'Brien know about aesthetics? Nothing, if her front windows were any example. And the furniture she placed at least once a week on her sidewalk was a hazard, leaving little room for pedestrians—a complaint he'd given up lodging with her. Had she ever heeded his advice? No. Other store owners had complained as well, Amanda in particular.

Ah well, no matter how often Shannon ignored him, he was persistent if nothing else. He was determined to find a way to get the flower child next door to clean up her shop—for her own good.

The chill November wind penetrated his wool coat as he reached his shop. Would he ever get used to the winds that blew year-round across the desert of the Tri-Cities? Who would have thought there could be such a dichotomy of climate in one state? Rain in one corner and desert in the other. He shivered and pushed open the door, welcomed by delicate tinkles from silver chimes. Not sleigh bells like Shannon's.

Charlie Wyatt, his clerk, greeted him with a smile. "You're back, Mr. Caldwell."

"Yes." Glen glanced at the teen's khakis and black polo shirt, comparing him with Venus and her inappropriate attire. The conservative young man would never play owner at Caldwell Antiques the way Venus had in Shannon's shop.

"You were next door for a while." Charlie frowned as if to say, *What happened this time?*

Glen met his wary gaze. "Yes, why do you say that?"

Charlie shrugged. "Venus and I have some classes together at CBC."

"That's the community college?" Glen asked.

Charlie nodded. "Columbia Basin."

"I see." But Glen didn't really see why that fact bore mentioning. "Did I get any calls?"

Charlie jumped to attention. "Oh, yes. Sorry. Four calls. One from Mike Carroll about that possible expansion of your store. Says he'll see you after work Friday at that new French restaurant in Richland. They have a piano player, which he knows you'll enjoy. The other three calls were from Amanda Franklin. She wanted to know if you found the spice box. And she said something about that petition again." Charlie's narrow glance told him he hadn't yet figured out the relationship between Amanda and Glen.

Glen nodded. "Thank you." He hadn't figured out his relationship with her either. Her purchases brought in 30 percent of his income. He had no choice but to cater to her eccentricities while avoiding her obvious attempts to change their relationship from business to personal. Lately Amanda was obsessed with collecting signatures for a petition about renewing storefronts. She cajoled Glen into signing it early on, and he hadn't paid much attention to what it said. He just added his signature so she'd go away and leave him alone. She told him she planned to present the signatures to Mike, the landlord. Glen hoped that perhaps renewing the storefronts would encourage Shannon to clean up her act.

Glen took the written messages from Charlie. Mike Carroll's message was a follow-up to a conversation they'd had a week ago. "I wonder if the gift shop next door is going out of business. Have you heard anything, Charlie?"

"No, sir."

"Hmm, must be if Mike's offering me more space." Joe, the gift shop owner, had implied that business hadn't been good recently.

Charlie cleared his throat. "Venus texted me and told me about the spice box."

Glen looked over his glasses at the teenager. "Did she?" Odd that Venus would text Charlie. He couldn't imagine the two being friends, but what did he know about kids?

"Yes. She feels really bad about it."

"As well she should. What she did was irresponsible."

"She said it must be worth a lot if everyone is so worried about getting it back."

"I'm sure it is, but it may be more the sentimental value." Even as Glen said the words, he remembered Shannon's comment. Amanda was anything but sentimental.

Charlie's phone vibrated in his pocket, and he snatched it out and opened it to read a text message. When he was done, Glen eyed him. "I hope you don't spend all your time on your cell phone when I'm out."

"No, Venus is just upset, that's all." Charlie looked as if he wanted to defend Venus's honor, but didn't follow through. Wise of him. Glen wasn't in the mood to be delicate.

He strode through the store, soothing himself by admiring the clean lines of the furniture he had for sale, all made from smooth wood, metal, and glass. He reached his office in the back, dropped into his chair, and rested his elbows on the spotless top of the desk. How did Shannon find anything on her cluttered desktop? He leaned back, tucked his hands behind his head, and closed his eyes. He had to figure out a way to pacify Amanda and save Shannon from her wrath. Beneath Shannon's harebrained, carefree exterior, he had a hunch she worried a great deal about everything. And her friends—many of them outcasts and oddballs.

So why did thoughts of the outwardly unflappable Shannon keep him up nights? Glen sat forward and caught a flash of movement in the back alleyway behind their stores. "Shannon," he whispered. She sat on an old painted bench she'd placed there, chatting with Truman while stroking his massive head. She'd found the dog along the side of the road and immediately gone on a mission to locate his owner. When she couldn't, she adopted him. The dog was quite possibly the ugliest he'd ever seen.

Glen stood and positioned himself between two tall file cabinets where she couldn't see him. Spying! That's what he'd resorted to. For the past year he'd tried valiantly to ignore her charm and whimsical colloquialisms. To close his eyes to the beauty of her fresh-scrubbed, heart-shaped face and hazel eyes that brimmed with warmth and wonder.

Shannon rose, straightened her wool poncho, then adjusted her peasant skirt and tugged at her embroidered, bell-sleeved blouse. Glen grimaced. He had an eye for fashion, a necessity in dealing with his type of clientele, and Shannon's style made her look like a throwback from the sixties. Hair in a gold-streaked plait reached the middle of her back and enhanced the look. Her skirt swirled as she walked in the direction of her store. He could almost see her hair loose and windblown, sparkling in the—

Whoa, Glen! He had to stop right there. He was mad for even entertaining the thought. The woman was the most annoying creature he'd ever met—this side of the Atlantic or the other. And then there was that crazy dog of hers.

Glen sat at his desk, opened the Johnson folder, and scanned the invoices.

The order Amanda had placed for her client was near completion, but what if he didn't get that box back to her? And Shannon. . .would Amanda retaliate?

The phone rang. A welcome distraction. Glen promptly swiped it off its cradle without checking caller ID. "Good afternoon, Caldwell Antiques. How may I help you?"

"Glen? This is Shannon."

Odd that she would call just as he was thinking about her. Perhaps he thought of her too often. "Hello, Shannon. What can I do for you?"

"I'd say it's more what I can do for you." She laughed.

His shoulders stiffened. "And what might that be?"

"Weeelll," she began, taking her sweet time about it. "I reached the lady who bought the box. You know? The spice box you're looking for? The one Amanda is frothing at the mouth like a rabid dog to have back?"

Another colloquialism that exactly suited the situation. He couldn't help but grin. Shannon was baiting him, and he would avoid the hook. "Yes?"

"It seems the little girl took the box with her to a friend's house for a sleepover. At least that's what Lucy Jennings, the girl's mother, told me."

"And?" He refused to give in.

"And? You want to know the rest, do you?"

Glen heard laughter in her voice and sat back, waiting patiently for more. He enjoyed this game.

"Okay, I'll have mercy on you. The little girl will return tomorrow morning. I'll run over to their house then and buy back the box. They live in Benton City." She paused. "A place I'm all too familiar with." She said the words so softly, he almost missed them. "Anyway, Lucy Jennings has agreed to our very generous offer of five times what she paid for it."

"Wh—what?" Glen jolted forward in his chair. "I said *three* times the price, not five."

"Glen, the mom seemed hesitant to take the box from her daughter. I had to up the price and beg her to have mercy on me. Of course, I'll pay you back the fifty dollars Venus got for it."

"Fifty? That box is worth at least four hundred."

"How would Venus have known that? Anyway, this means I saved you over a hundred dollars, right?"

"A hundred dollars? What are you talking about? That doesn't make sense at all. I hope that isn't how you keep your books. You'll go bankrupt." Dismissing her skewed logic, he considered the offer. What choice did he have? "Fine," he said, "and I'll go with you to pick up the box." Glen shook his head. His offer had *big mistake* written all over it.

Shannon was silent, a rare occurrence. Glen paced his office, gratified that he'd found a way to render her mute.

"No you won't," she finally said.

He couldn't help but smile. "Yes I will."

"No you won't."

"I'm going. And that's final."

"No. I'm driving, and you can't come."

At last he'd gotten a reaction from her. The exasperation in her voice was music to his ears. Such a difference from the laid-back woman with the daisy in her hair and a sedate smile, floating around her disorganized shop like an angel in an embroidered blouse.

"Yes, I am."

He was silent, breathing into the receiver and wondering what possessed him to argue like a child with Shannon O'Brien—and enjoy it.

"Why?" she finally demanded. "Why must you go with me?"

"Perhaps I feel like a jaunt in the countryside. I am a foreigner, after all. A stranger in a strange land. Besides, I'm providing the money for a mistake made by *your* employee."

"Oh, please. You've lived in this country long enough now. And don't go blaming Venus. She meant well. If Amanda had taken better care of her belongings—and her mom—this would've never happened."

"Okay, all right." Glen blew out a breath. My, she was defensive of her friends. "So I'll see you tomorrow?"

Shannon sighed, long and loud. "I'm leaving at seven. That's seven in the morning. That's early, and you hate early. I'll see you then. . .Old Chap." She chuckled and hung up.

Grinning, Glen replaced the receiver, relishing his minor victory.

"That went well." Of course he was now obligated to be in Shannon's rattletrap truck for the drive to Benton City. His smile faded. What if she drove in the haphazard way she tended her shop? Worse, he would be in close quarters with a woman who drove him crazy in too many ways. Avoiding her was easier than trying to figure out his feelings. His victory didn't look good when viewed in that light. In fact, the whole thing was a bad idea. A horrible idea. What had he done?

But perhaps he could put the drive to good use and try to convince her to clean up her eyesore of a shop.

The door chimes sounded, and Glen peered through the glass walls of his office. Amanda Franklin stood at the counter. Charlie turned, looked beseechingly at Glen, and motioned for him to come to the rescue.

Glen strode from his office into the shop area. "Amanda, hello."

She turned her impeccably made-up face toward him. Her black hair bounced in loose curls over her shoulders. A silk blouse, expensive jeans, and a wool jacket were snug on her model-thin figure that Glen was sure she achieved with constant diet and exercise. She had looks, money, and a certain vibrancy and confidence that many men would find enticing. Not Glen. She was also abrasive and self-consumed. Besides, she had no curves like Shannon.

"Hello, Glen, have you located the box?" Long fingers tipped with perfectly manicured nails grasped a designer purse that had to cost at least a thousand dollars.

Why did the box deserve so much attention? It wasn't for its monetary value. "I discovered that your mother left the box with my colleague next door."

"Shannon?" Amanda hefted her purse strap on her shoulder and took a step toward the door. "I'm going to get it."

Glen put his hand on her arm. "Unfortunately, it was sold, and no wonder. I'm sure it was exquisite."

He felt the tension in her arm muscle as she drew herself up to full height. "Please tell me you didn't just say, 'It was sold'?"

"I'm afraid so, but we intend—"

"How could that woman be so ignorant?"

Glen took a deep breath. "Shannon didn't sell the box. Her employee did."

"You mean that blue-haired, skinny creature that looks like she belongs in a freak show?"

Charlie squared his shoulders and opened his mouth, but Glen caught his eye and shook his head. Fortunately, Amanda was too enraged to notice the exchange.

"I'm going over there right now."

"Wait, please. We can work this out."

"I won't be charmed, Glen. I want the box back."

"I know that. We've located the buyer in Benton City. We're going there tomorrow to get it."

Amanda clutched her purse so tightly, her knuckles turned white. "Who's the buyer?" Her lips thinned. "I'll attend to the matter myself."

"How long have you known me, Amanda? Long enough to know I keep my word." Glen looked her in the eye, smiled, and took her hand. "The buyer is Shannon's customer, and even if I did know the name, the information is confidential. But I promise I'll get that box back to you."

The emotion in Amanda's eyes was a curious mixture of fear, irritation, and attraction to him. Her lips moved as she struggled to speak—probably deciding between demanding her way or acceptance of his word. She scanned him head to toe. "Your colleague next door has been nothing but trouble, Glen. She and her ilk stand out like sore thumbs in this neighborhood. You really should make it your business to deal with her."

Glen swallowed his desire to rally in Shannon's defense. "She means well. I'm sure—"

"You're truly chivalrous, Glen." Some of the fire left her eyes. "That's certainly admirable, but she doesn't belong here. My Renew Our Storefronts idea will improve the neighborhood. Shannon's signature is not on my petition, by the way."

Glen didn't miss her implication that the remedy would have a negative impact on Shannon, and he didn't know how to counteract that. "She will come around. Straighten things up. I'm certain of that."

She drew a long, dramatic sigh, and her face hardened. "I plan a heart-to-heart with Mike Carroll when I present my petition to him." Amanda narrowed her eyes as if in challenge. "I will *make* him remedy the situation." She sighed, headed for the door, then turned. "I've done business with you for the past five years. I wouldn't want to have to stop now. . . ." She let her voice trail off, whirled on her heel, and exited his shop.

Glen blew out a breath and wondered why Amanda disliked Shannon so. The reason couldn't possibly be just the condition of Shannon's store. He glanced at his watch and turned to Charlie who had listened with interest to the conversation. "I'm sorry you had to be privy to that exchange."

"Are you kidding, Mr. Caldwell?" Charlie snorted. "I'm learning more from you than in any classroom. You're a real communicator. Smooth talking."

Was that what he was? A smooth talker? Not at all flattering. All he meant to do was restore peace and tranquility—and save Shannon's hide.

Sudden fatigue hit. "It's half past five. Why don't we close up shop? I don't think we'll get any more customers on this blustery evening."

Charlie's eyes widened, and he fairly ran to lock the front door.

With the Closed sign in the window, Glen poked around in the cash register. "Go on, Charlie. I'll see you tomorrow." He recalled he would be out. "Wait a minute, I forgot. I'm going with Shannon tomorrow morning to find that box. Take a spare key home so you can open the shop if for some reason I'm not back when you arrive after school." Glen removed a key from the cash register drawer and held it out to him.

"You're going with Shannon O'Brien?" Charlie stared, eyes round with disbelief. "Out? Together?"

Glen frowned. Why did people tend to imagine nonexistent liaisons in the simplest actions? "Charlie, listen to me. We are going to get the spice box. It's *not* a date. Okay?"

"Okay." Charlie grinned, took the key, and left in haste.

Glen sighed. That was a quick getaway.

❧

Shannon stared at the calendar above the counter. Venus walked up behind her. "Is something wrong?"

"No," Shannon said. "Well, just a little. I give my testimony at church on Sunday morning, and I'm already nervous."

"I'll come to support you for sure," Venus said.

147

Shannon smiled at her gratefully. "Thank you. That would really help me. Hey, it's slow today. I'm going to unpack a couple of boxes. You can leave if you'd like. And thank you for your help pulling the sidewalk sale stuff inside." She headed to the storeroom, then stopped. "Have you seen that pair of antique salt and pepper shakers? The dog and the cat? Did someone buy them?"

Venus blinked. "They aren't here?"

"No. That's odd." Shannon began walking again and gave her helper a backhanded wave. "No matter. They'll turn up. Just lock up when you go. And make sure you have your key in case for some reason I'm not here when you come in after classes tomorrow. I'm going to pick up that spice box."

"Do you have a guitar lesson tonight or tomorrow night?" Venus asked.

"Tomorrow night, and I haven't done much practicing. Fortunately Ray is patient."

"Has he kissed you?"

"What?" Shannon skidded to another stop and turned to face Venus. "Ray? Of course not! He's like a brother."

"Are you sure? He's nice-looking in a dark way, like Heathcliff in a leather jacket."

Shannon laughed at Venus's description of the hero from *Wuthering Heights*. "I'm positive." She headed once again to the storeroom, and Venus followed closely on her heels like Truman always did. Which reminded her. "Where's the dog?"

"In the alley on his leash."

"Oh good. Thanks for letting him out. He loves the cold. I sometimes wonder if he really is part wolf."

"Yeah, me, too," Venus said without humor. "Do you think the old lady was crazy?"

"I don't like to use that word *crazy* when it comes to anyone." Shannon heaved a cardboard box filled with antique books onto a table. "Everyone has their own reality." She pulled the top open. The distinctive, dusty smell of old paper wafted up to her nose. She ran her hands gently over the frayed bindings, then looked at Venus. "We need to get that box back before Amanda hires a lawyer and claims we took advantage of her elderly mother."

Venus shifted from foot to foot. "I'm really sorry I caused this problem."

Shannon shrugged. "It's okay. Now you know, and next time you won't take things into your own hands. You're not experienced enough yet. But I'm willing to teach you this business if you've got the passion." She dusted off her hands and glanced at the repentant young woman. "The problem is, I'm suffering for your mistake. I have to drive to Benton City with *Glen* to get that box."

Venus's eyes grew wide. "Wow. I'm sorry. I know how you feel about Benton City. Is that why you're suffering? Or is it—"

"Imagine being in an enclosed space like my truck with the man who is so critical of my store." Shannon clamped her mouth shut. She was about to say Glen was critical of her, too, but he'd never treated her with disdain—only as if she were a strange creature from another planet.

"I wouldn't mind being in a car with him." Venus wore a dreamy smile. "He's really good-looking."

Shannon blinked. So, Venus did think Glen was attractive. "What about his British stiff upper lip?"

"Stiff lip?" Venus frowned. "No. He's not stiff. Not at all." She looked wistful. "More like those well-bred, gentlemanly types I see in old movies. Don't you just love when he says things like 'perhaps' and 'quite'?" She giggled and turned to go. "Well, see you tomorrow afternoon."

Shannon folded her arms on the edge of the box and rested her chin on top. Glen was certainly good-looking in a royal sort of way, with tousled brown hair and crystal blue eyes.

Stop there, Shannon. The man was so her opposite. She could only imagine what his family was like. Probably upper-crust breeding all the way.

She shook her head as if it would help clear her mind of the antique dealer next door, then reached into the box. Better to think about books. Safer on the emotions.

৵

Glen exited the back of his store, locked up, and tossed a bag of trash into the rusted receptacle. He heard noises, turned, and saw Charlie walking toward him, head down.

"What are you still doing here, Charlie? You left a good twenty minutes ago."

"Don't look now, Mr. Caldwell, but Venus is at the end of the alley with that boyfriend of hers, Louis."

Glen couldn't help but look. Venus stood beside a red sports car, smiling up at the fellow. "My, he's stocky. Like a wrestler. Where did she meet him?"

"Through some friends at community college. He doesn't attend, just sometimes hangs around." Charlie's expression darkened. "He's got money and spends it on her."

The teen sounded envious. "Money isn't everything," Glen said.

"Yeah, well, it means a nice car and lots of money to spend on a girl. I don't have that kind of extra money. I'm just scraping by."

Glen nodded his understanding. Charlie lived alone with his mother, and they struggled. Charlie had to pay for college as well as contribute to household expenses.

"I wish she'd break up with him. I really don't like him."

Glen blinked, but kept his surprise to himself. Until this afternoon he hadn't been aware that Charlie and Venus knew each other. In fact, he didn't know much about the kids at all. He should've taken the time. Charlie continued to stare toward the end of the alley, his mouth quirked to one side, blinking rapidly. Were those tears in his eyes?

Truth dawned, and Glen looked away from him. Charlie was in love with Venus. How odd. Charlie was a good boy, worked hard in school and on the job. Venus was, well, Venus. An airhead. A bit like Shannon. Glen patted Charlie's shoulder. "Don't worry. God has a way of working these things out. You just concentrate on your education." Great. A cliché response with nothing of real meaning to console the teen. Still, only the young would be so naive as to think a relationship of such opposites could work.

Charlie offered a polite smile and walked away, and an eruption of noise sent a shudder through Glen. He spun around. Ray Reed turned his motorcycle into the alley, roared past Venus and Louis, at the last minute swerved past Glen, and stopped at the back of Shannon's store. Her infamous guitar teacher whipped off his helmet and nodded hello.

You nearly ran me down, was on the tip of Glen's tongue, but Shannon emerged from the back door of her shop and gave Reed a welcoming hug, a distraction that rendered Glen tongue-tied. She then looked over Reed's shoulder, and her eyes widened. "Oh, Glen. I didn't see you."

Neither had Ray when he'd almost run over him.

"Good day." Glen turned and headed toward his car. Here he was, trying to protect Shannon from Amanda, but Shannon continued to befriend questionable people. Ray was a recent addition to her stable of strays—except that a stray wouldn't be able to afford a Harley like Reed's.

Glen sat behind the wheel of his car, staring at the back of the Quaint Shop. Shannon lived above her store. Who was he besides her guitar teacher, and why'd she hug him like that? Would she invite him upstairs for dinner after her lesson?

Glen threw the gearshift into DRIVE. She was a magnet for oddballs and ne'er-do-wells. None of his business, except that he wanted to help the flower child who refused to help herself.

Chapter 3

Early on Wednesday morning, Glen stepped out of his car and groaned. Shannon was right. He was not a morning person. Especially not a wintry morning person. The cold, dry desert wind cut through his jacket like a sharp blade. As he tramped toward Shannon, he adjusted his foggy eyeglasses and tried to wipe the painful scowl off his face. Why give her the satisfaction?

"It's quite brisk this morning, isn't it?" Shannon stood beside her rusted truck, smirking.

She was baiting him again. "*Brisk* is not the word I'd use to describe it. *Glacial, arctic,* or *frigid* are more apropos. But. . ." Glen released his grip on the lapels of his coat and looked up. "Refreshing, isn't it?"

As he drew closer to her truck, it appeared that the seat was stuffed with something large. He blinked, pulled off his glasses, and took a step back. *Oh, fantastic!*

A pair of bright eyes stared at him through the window. Truman's massive, furry body wriggled in anticipation of his approach.

"Hope you don't mind Truman is coming." Shannon hopped into the truck and slammed the door.

And my presence on this trip was my idea. I am a complete idiot. Glen opened the truck door and dove in.

Truman seized the opportunity to stick his cold nose in his neck, wetting his ear with a doggy kiss. Glen shuddered and pulled a handkerchief from his pocket.

"Sorry." Shannon laughed as she started the engine. "He adores you, and he's happy you're going with us. I told him on the way here, and he got all excited."

Not only does she take her dog to therapy, she talks to him and thinks he's listening. "I thought wolves were supposed to be vicious and unfriendly." Glen pushed away the dog's persistent, hairy muzzle.

"Oh, come on, Truman's not really part wolf. I'm sure that vet was exaggerating." Shannon pulled away from the curb and started up the street at a sedate pace. "I'm sorry I ever shared that story with you." Her smile broadened.

Shannon began humming, and the dog tilted his head and stared at Glen, who in turn pressed himself against the passenger door. Even so, Truman's body was glued to his.

Glen stared out the window. It was too early and too cold to be out, let alone in a truck with a loony woman and her overly enthusiastic, part-wolf attack dog. There had been no time for a proper cup of tea or relaxed Bible reading—something he enjoyed every morning. On the positive side, at least the dog's body offered some warmth.

Shannon stopped humming and looked at him. "Glen?"

He grunted and turned his head toward her.

"I brought a thermos of tea for you." Shannon pulled out a steel canister from behind the seat, reached around Truman, and handed it to Glen with a pleased expression.

Shannon's ever-present herbal tea. Great. "Er, thank you."

He had no choice. She'd been kind enough to make it for him; now he'd do his utmost to pretend to enjoy it.

"I added sugar and cream." Shannon glanced at him with those hazel eyes that seemed to see right through him.

"In herbal tea?" What a horrific combination.

She laughed, a pleasing and contagious sound. "Not herbal tea, Glen. This is English tea. And I made it just the way you like it."

"How do you know what I take in my tea?" Glen glanced at her suspiciously, then unscrewed the lid and poured some into the plastic top. Proper English tea should be steeped in a porcelain teapot. Not stainless steel. Well, at least it would be hot.

"First off, I'm a woman, which makes me hyperobservant. Women see lots of things men miss." She pulled onto the interstate. "Also—and only my closest friends know this—I'm a student of body language."

Glen laughed. "I guess that means I'm one of your closest friends because I knew that already. You've mentioned it before." Body language, indeed. He inhaled deeply. Perhaps this trip would not be a wash after all. He needed a refresher course on why he should not be attracted to the messiest store owner in town. Shannon, with her Bohemian lifestyle, could not possibly be the woman for him.

Satisfied with his conclusion, Glen settled back in his seat. The steam drifting from the plastic cup smelled marvelous. He must be quite desperate for tea. Blowing gently on the liquid, he lifted it to his lips. The first sip made him blink. There had to be some mistake. The tea tasted almost as good as his own. He took another sip. No mistake.

"You're surprised."

He studied Shannon's profile. Light freckles dusted her nose and cheeks, and a small daisy was tucked behind her ear. Wisps of hair escaped the customary braid. The desire to reach over and stroke them back into place came over him so suddenly that he almost dropped the cup. He had to stop this nonsense. He'd do well to remember the last twelve months of owning a shop next to hers. Frustrating months filled with disputes he could never win against Shannon's illogical logic. The piles Wolf-dog left in the back alley that she "forgot" to clean up. Her sidewalk sales—a lawsuit waiting to happen. But then there were all the times she made him laugh and think. The times she surprised him. Like right now.

She blushed. "Quit staring. I am capable of doing *some* things right."

"Indeed." Glen took another sip. "Thank you. It's excellent."

Silver slivers of snow began to fall as the tea warmed his chest. She pushed a button on the dash. The sounds of Mozart from a surprisingly good stereo filled the vehicle. Thank heavens it wasn't the strange music that usually came from her store—or her noisy attempts at learning guitar from Mr. Leather Jacket—Ray Reed.

"Nice sound," he murmured.

"Ray brought the stereo to me and helped me install it. He said he got it from a friend in town."

Ray Reed again. "He certainly does a lot for you."

"He's like family," she said, smiling.

Family. Glen shoved Mr. Leather Jacket from his mind and chose to daydream about a warm, misty English countryside. He imagined walking around a small pond where frogs croaked in peaceful syncopation. The croaking grew louder. Glen's pleasant interlude came to an abrupt end when he realized what he heard wasn't frogs at all. It was gagging.

"Wh–what's that?"

"Truman." Shannon sighed and cut the dog a sympathetic look. "Oh, my poor baby."

"I know it's the dog," Glen snapped. "What is he doing?"

"He's about to lose his breakfast. I need to pull over."

"Lose his breakfast?" Glen moved forward in his seat, as far away from Wolf-dog as space would permit. "That's revolting. Does he do this often?"

"There's an exit right here," she mumbled.

"Please do it quickly," Glen murmured. The dog was gagging in a rhythmic way that left no doubt time was running short.

Shannon whipped the car right onto an exit ramp and pulled over on the shoulder.

Glen shook his head. "Do you mean to tell me the dog is going to retch here? On the side of the exit ramp?"

"*Hurl*, as Venus would say. Would you rather he do it in your lap?" Shannon flung open her door. As if rehearsed, Truman hopped out, ran to the grass, and deposited the contents of his stomach in the dramatic, unpleasant way dogs do.

Glen felt as if the tea in his stomach curdled. He looked away but couldn't eliminate the sound from reaching his ears. He concentrated on deep breathing until the dreadful interval finally ended, and he heard Shannon murmuring to the dog. Venturing a look, he saw her caress Truman's head as he stood on wobbly legs, sides heaving.

"That's better, isn't it, Truman?" The dog wagged its hairy tail. And just like that, the incident was over. Shannon fetched a bottle of water and a dish from a bag behind the backseat and offered the dog a drink.

"Should you do that?" Glen's stomach tightened. Suppose it all started again ten miles up the road?

"It's just a sip." Shannon had already taken the bowl from Truman. "The whole thing was my fault. He slurped too much water on top of his breakfast. He's got a sensitive stomach, especially in a car."

Great. The dog had a sensitive stomach. He was trapped in a vehicle with a dog liable to retch at any time, and it had been his idea to come along. It was like a British comedy of errors.

"Are you ready now?" Shannon cooed, as if he were a child.

"I'm more than ready to get on with this," he grumbled.

"I'm not talking to you. I'm talking to the dog."

Truman's answer came in the form of hopping back into the truck. Glen tried to move away, but Truman landed an enthusiastic lick on his cheek.

"Dreadful," Glen groaned, not even bothering with the handkerchief as he leaned forward to avoid another smooch from the wolf.

"Truman, sit," Shannon said. The dog obeyed, perching happily between them and once again leaning against the back of the seat to stare at Glen.

"I'm sorry, Glen. That was unpleasant for me, and I'm used to it. I'll see that he doesn't drink so much on top of breakfast next time."

There won't be a next time, Glen thought.

❧

Farther down the highway, Shannon chanced a glance at Glen. He hadn't moved. Eyes closed, he held the empty cup in very still hands.

"You look sort of greenish. Why don't you have more tea?"

"I'm fine. I don't want more." He sounded like a petulant child.

"You need more. It'll make you feel better. Don't make me stop this vehicle." She used her dog-training voice, then grinned at his stunned expression. "Do it, please."

He picked up the thermos without further argument, much to her surprise.

"Anybody ever tell you you're pushy?" Glen elbowed Truman's nose away, poured the tea, and placed the thermos back on the floor. "And stubborn?"

"That's the pot calling the kettle black." She paused and sighed. "Maybe it's a survival technique."

He stared at her. "What do you mean by that?"

She wasn't about to reveal her past to this pampered English gentleman.

She had never expected pity from anybody and wouldn't start mining for it now. She shrugged. "It's not important."

As they entered the outskirts of Benton City, Shannon felt around in her purse for the directions to the Jenningses' house, keeping one hand on the wheel. Unable to locate the paper, she looked down into her handbag.

Glen cleared his throat. "I'm not comfortable when the driver of a vehicle I'm riding in isn't looking through the windscreen."

"I can't find my directions. The piece of paper wasn't on my desk where I left it, so I assumed I'd shoved it into my purse." Shannon tossed the bag in his lap. "Would you mind looking for it?"

Truman sat up and jabbed his nose inside the bag. Glen pushed away his snout and stared inside. "In *here*?"

"Yes, in *there*." Shannon caught a glimpse of the Kleenex and pieces of paper that overflowed the zippered opening. She had meant to clean it out, but forgot.

Holding it open with the tips of his fingers, he peered inside. "This is a bit like maneuvering around your store."

"I'm not laughing," she said.

"Will I get hurt if I stick my hand inside? I'm not sure when I had my last tetanus shot."

"Ha-ha. Very funny, Glen. It's not that bad."

"You're quite mistaken." With a slight grin, he dangled a lint-covered Life Saver in front of her face. "Do you have plans for this?"

"I'm ignoring your snide comments. The directions are on a purple piece of paper with black writing." Glen's criticism disturbed her balance despite his smile. Recently, what he thought of her had become important. When had that changed? Perhaps when she'd talked herself into believing he looked at her in a certain way. Held her gaze longer than what was required for polite conversation. Pathetic! Shannon dismissed her fantasies and drew deep, calming breaths.

One by one, with dramatic flourishes, he pulled all the contents from her purse onto his lap. Truman's head bobbed with each of Glen's movements. Finally Glen stared around the dog at her.

"What?" Shannon frowned.

"I found two pieces of gum—unwrapped. A package of crushed Saltines, unopened. One Life Saver, mentioned previously. Innumerable tissues—used or new, I'm unable to determine. One torn leather wallet stuffed with everything *except* a piece of purple paper. A date book complete with addresses and phone numbers, but no purple paper. Two sets of keys, three dog biscuits, assorted hair ties, three tubes of lipstick—one missing its top, and—"

"All right!" Shannon clenched the steering wheel. "You've made your point. My purse is a mess, and yours—if you carried one—would be as pristine as that shop of yours. Anyone can see you're nearly perfect. I'm sure you have blue blood flowing through your English-bred veins."

"Actually, my family comes from—"

"I don't really care right now, Glen."

"Sorry. Still, that doesn't change the fact that the directions are nowhere to be found."

She glanced at him. "Stop smirking."

"What do you mean?"

"And stop acting superior."

Glen arched an eyebrow. "Me?"

Shannon bit back a grin. "Please put the stuff back in my purse. The last place I recall seeing that paper was on my desk. I guess I left it there. Now I'll have to remember how to find this house."

"Shall I tidy your bag up a bit while I'm putting all these things away?" Glen asked. "I'm sure I'll have ample time, given that you'll have to remember your way."

With a sidelong glance, Shannon cleared her throat. "Whatever floats your boat. Tidy away if you must. But no worries. My memory is quite impressive. We'll be there in a jiffy." She smiled. No need to exaggerate. Excellent recall was one of her strong points.

With only one wrong turn, she found the Jenningses' house. It stood solitary with lots of tall trees growing in the yard, thanks to irrigation. The tan-sided one-story rancher blended into the tans and browns of the surrounding treeless hills. In the driveway, a minivan was parked next to a Benton County Sheriff's Office patrol car. As she pulled up behind them, ugly memories surged to the surface of her mind.

"Are you sure you have the right house?" Glen pushed his glasses up the bridge of his aquiline nose.

Shannon looked away from his handsome face. *Lord, please don't let this be an embarrassment to me.* "Yes, I am. Told you I had good recall." She looked at the cars again. "Maybe the man of the house is part of the sheriff's department."

"We'll find out soon enough." Glen opened his door and got out.

Truman whined, and Shannon turned her head to tell him to behave while she was gone. She heard her door open and swiveled around. Glen stood there, hand extended, waiting for her to get out. She was baffled as to what to do next.

"I *am* a gentleman, no matter what else you think of me." He smiled—a brilliant, flash-of-teeth smile.

Mute, Shannon glanced from his face to his outstretched hand. As she reached out, a flood of bewildering emotions shut down her brain and made her breathing erratic. Finally, she knew what it felt like to touch his hands.

Wonderful and strong, just as she'd imagined. Her only rational thought was to ask herself why the notion of holding Glen's hand made her feel sorry for herself. The memory came back in a flash. She was the wallflower at the high school dance, and the prom king, a sweet, good-looking guy, took pity on her and asked her to dance. Nice of him, but a little humiliating because everyone knew what he was doing.

Glen's hand closed around hers, and warmth coursed through her. She met his gaze, held her breath. She didn't like what was happening to her heart, and just as bad, now she had to face one of Benton County's finest. She prayed he or she wasn't someone she knew.

ᴥ

Glen didn't know what to think. Shannon's expression was that of someone who had witnessed an accident. Had his innocent gesture of helping her out of the car made her uncomfortable? Or did she dislike him that much? Glen glanced over his shoulder. She lagged a good distance behind him, gaze glued to the patrol car. No, Shannon didn't dislike him. He knew that. Something else was going on.

A deputy with graying hair walked out of the house, saw them, and crossed the yard with long strides. Glen nodded a greeting.

"Can I help you?" The uniformed man tilted his head.

"I'm here to talk to Mrs. Jennings."

"Might not be the best time at the moment." Squinting, the deputy looked over Glen's shoulder. "Is that Shannon O'Brien? She looks so much like her mama, I'd know her anywhere."

Glen turned to see her nod in the deputy's direction, but she took her sweet time reaching them, first brushing back the stray hairs that had come loose from her braid. This was a small town, so it wouldn't be unusual for the deputy to know residents, but why the undercurrents?

"Hi, Sam. Uh, Deputy Kroeger." Her voice was a bare whisper. She was acting awkward, even a bit intimidated—rare for Shannon.

Kroeger eyed her, and his mouth twisted into a grin. "How're those folks of yours doing? I hear your daddy lost his job. Too bad after all those years of—"

"He's okay." Shannon swallowed. "Mom is great, too."

Frowning, Glen looked at Shannon. She rarely spoke of her parents.

"Nice to hear, darlin'." The deputy nodded. "Hope he's not self-medicating again. Reminds me, I've got to go check up on them sometime soon."

Self-medicating? Glen could only imagine what that meant. A spasm of some unpleasant emotion passed over Shannon's face. Fear? Dread?

Glen held his tongue. An intriguing exchange, to say the least.

A petite woman walked out the front door. "Oh, you must be Shannon. I'm Lucy. I should have called, but I forgot in all the trouble." She frowned at Glen.

Shannon appeared relieved to focus elsewhere. "This is Glen." She pointed at him. "He's the one I told you about. He owns the shop next to mine." She glanced quickly at the deputy, then straightened her shoulders and looked back at Lucy. "Are you okay?"

"No." Lucy rubbed her arms. "My house has been broken into."

"That's dreadful," Glen said, a feeling of apprehension flooding him. "Is everyone all right?"

"Yes." The woman waved her hand. "And I don't have your box right now. Amber took it with her to her cousin's house last night. They live near us, and the girls go to the same school. They were working on a project together, so I just let her spend the night. I was going to pick her up this afternoon." She clenched her small hands together. "I went grocery shopping this morning, but my house was broken into while I was out. Lucky it wasn't the weekend. Amber wasn't home when that gun-toting killer ransacked our home."

Glen winced. "A gun-toting killer?"

"Now, now," Kroeger said. "We don't have much violent crime in these parts. Mostly minor things. Drinking to excess. Drugs." His gaze fell on Shannon, then back to Glen. "Must've been a teen looking to make a fast buck, then got scared and ran away."

Lucy shuddered. "But nothing was stolen. Not even my new TV. I feel so violated."

Shannon patted Lucy's arm. "I'm sorry. You must be terrified."

Lucy nodded. "Yes. I'm waiting for my husband to come home. I'll have to get back to you about the box, okay? I know you need it. I have your number."

Glen could hear himself trying to explain the delay to Amanda Franklin. "I'd appreciate that." He looked at Kroeger, whose dark, bushy brows were drawn in a frown. "Thank you, Deputy."

Kroeger nodded his way, then smiled at Shannon who whirled around and walked back to the truck with hurried steps. The deputy's radio crackled, and he spoke into it as Glen turned and followed Shannon, questions running through his mind.

How would he explain this to Amanda? And what was the meaning of the odd exchange between Shannon and the deputy?

Chapter 4

As she mindlessly picked at the strings of her guitar, Shannon looked across her kitchen table at Ray. "I'm glad you came when I invited you for tea. I've had a lousy day. Sheer madness. I want to get it all thought through before I go to Bible study tonight."

Ray wrapped his hands around his mug. "Okay, shoot."

She hugged her guitar closer to her chest. "My past came back to haunt me." *In front of Glen Caldwell of all people.* She recalled seeing Deputy Kroeger, and her peace of mind was severely challenged. She gave Ray a brief rundown about the spice box, then jabbed her index finger on the tabletop. "Do you want to know what that officer of the law did?"

A tiny smile quirked the side of Ray's mouth. "I have a feeling you're going to tell me."

"He said he was going to visit my parents. Yeah, that's what Daddy needs after losing his job and all." She scowled. "My folks don't do the things they used to do. Why'd he imply that? I hate to say this, Ray, because I'm a Christian, but I don't like cops."

"C'mon, Shan. You know they're human like anybody else. You got the good and the bad. And sometimes it's easy to misinterpret their actions and tone." Ray rested his arms loosely on his thighs. "Hey, girl. You're not going to let a visit to Benton City take you to the bad place, are you?"

"It's strange, but living back in this area has diminished my self-confidence. I don't understand it." She set aside her guitar and shrugged. "Glen picked up on Deputy Kroeger's remarks, even though he didn't ask questions on the way home. Glen's as perceptive as they come."

"Well, to change the subject, I think you like this guy," Ray said matter-of-factly. "In fact, I think you more than like him."

"Guy? You mean Glen?" Shannon's heart thumped. "Wow. Is it that obvious to you? If it is, then it must be true, and I haven't really faced it."

"'Fraid so." Ray shrugged.

"Is it my body language?"

He stroked his chin thoughtfully. "It's in your expression plus in your voice when you talk about him."

"Wow. That's scary. I wonder if Glen sees it, too." She looked into Ray's eyes and recalled their conversation a couple of months back. He'd spoken of an ex-fiancée named Bailey. That he'd fallen for her the first time he laid eyes on her until the day he'd caught her dating a guy whom Ray had considered a friend.

"I'm not sure that Glen's on to you, though. Men are dense sometimes. Don't see what's going on right in front of our noses."

"Well, I'm not sure *like* is the right word," Shannon said. "Glen and I always quarrel."

"Whoa." Ray blew out a long whistle. "I hope you like him. It'd be a problem to fall in love with someone you don't like."

"Is that possible?" A spate of nerves weakened her stomach.

"Absolutely it is. It's more like infatuation, I think. You see what you want to see, and in your head they are what you think they are, not what they *really* are."

"Yikes, that sounds like something I'd say." Leaning back in her chair, she considered his weighty comment. "I know I'm idealistic. I'm a lot like my parents that way. I'm scared, Ray. I've never felt this way about any man. I'm not sure what I see in Glen. I'm tofu; he's meat and potatoes."

Ray laughed, crossed his arms, and studied her for a long moment. "Opposites, right? That was me and Bailey. You and I are emotional and driven by our feelings. People like them have a lot of self-discipline and. . ."

And we don't. He didn't have to finish the sentence.

"But what do I know, Shan? Look at me." Ray spread his arms. "I left my career behind. Now I'm going on thirty, doing a gig in a coffeehouse."

Ray never talked about his career, but he'd walked away from whatever work he'd done. Now he lived in a room in someone's basement, played in a band, and gave guitar lessons. How did he survive? He'd said something about taking leave, but never went into detail, and she never asked. Tears stung her eyes. God had put Ray into her life for a reason, and she wanted to encourage him.

"Don't put yourself down, Ray. You're a musical genius." She meant it from the heart. "What I wouldn't give to play like you. You're following your dream is all."

"When do dreams become escape from reality? When does running from reality and following a dream become irresponsibility? And as far as Bailey is concerned? No sense going over that again." Ray jutted his chin to the wall adjoining her apartment with Glen's shop. "Maybe it wouldn't be that way with you and Caldwell—maybe it'll be okay."

Shannon shrugged. "Well, he does make me laugh. He's always giving me advice like he wants me to succeed. He tells me how to keep my books, how to hire employees, and how to clean up my store. I can't figure out if that means he cares or if he's a control freak." She paused and then stared intently at Ray. "You never talk about your past except in snippets."

The words were out before she recognized the deep sadness in Ray's brown eyes. Shannon held up her hand. "I'm sorry. I didn't mean—"

"It's okay. Don't apologize. But the past has no place in the here and now."

"I don't know if I agree with that," Shannon said. "Don't you think the past defines us? At least in part?"

Ray shrugged and stared at the wall. "I'd like to think not. When the Lord comes in, He wipes the past away."

"Yes, but He doesn't erase it. Neither does He change our personalities. What we become is formed by what we've lived, as well as who we are." Shannon picked up her guitar, plucked at a string, and it snapped. "Oh man, I don't have any others."

"I'll bring you a new set tomorrow. I have an appointment in town, anyway."

"Thanks." She leaned her guitar against the table. "I can't tell you how many times I've asked God to give me a personality transplant. So I could be organized and not so weird. And then maybe I would make someone a suitable girlfriend. I have so many doubts about myself lately. Like I'm going through a second adolescence or something."

Ray laughed. "Moving to a new place and everything that's happening here will do that to you." The sadness left his eyes. "Shannon, when you find the right man, he will love you for exactly who and what you are. I've often thought it was too bad you and I don't feel that way about each other."

Shannon grinned. "Yeah, there is that. Venus thought we were dating. But I feel like you're my brother."

"Ouch." Ray mockingly winced and put his fist on his heart. "Handed the brother card."

She laughed. "I guess there has to be some of the opposite traits in a romance. Opposites are drawn to each other, that's for sure. Like my best friend, Allie, and her husband, Derrick. Opposite in many ways, but they're a perfect match."

Ray nodded. "True. It depends on the people involved and whether or not they're willing to accept certain things. Iron sharpens iron." He eyed her from under lowered lids. "So, what about Glen?"

"I don't know." Shannon's gaze scanned her kitchen and the odds and ends piled around that she promised herself she'd get rid of some day. "I'm thinking it would be Oscar Madison and Felix Unger."

Ray laughed. "Yeah, something like that, but I'm beginning to suspect this goes much deeper."

Shannon nodded her heartfelt agreement. "Much."

❧

Dreams of Shannon, her hair shining in shades of gold and her outrageous outfits, filled Glen's mind. Unfortunately they were mixed with thoughts of the difficulties she was causing in his life. All that added to his concern about the missing spice box. The growing list of problems rattled uncontrolled through Glen's brain, keeping him up half the night. He finally fell asleep early Thursday morning, only to wake to the alarm an hour later with a dull, throbbing headache—and the knowledge of what the day would bring. The prospect of facing Amanda Franklin this morning made him want to burrow deeper under the covers. She would be out for blood—Shannon's.

All this trouble, and for what? Because Shannon hadn't heeded his advice. Instead of hiring help based on an outstanding job application and solid references, Shannon used some sort of pity meter with which she favored the likes of Venus. He'd tried to talk to Shannon about the urgency of improving the appearance of her shop on the way home from Lucy Jennings's house, but she interrupted him with chatter about diet and health. He hadn't gotten a chance to ask about her father. She was so frustrating at times, yet he had to admire her ability to accept people and see beyond their outer appearance. She gave people the world saw as losers the benefit of the doubt, a second chance, and wasn't that what the Lord did, too? So what if she sometimes made a bad judgment call? What had Venus really done wrong besides try to imitate Shannon? Yes, it was irresponsible, but she was still a teenager.

Glen sighed. He had no choice but to face the day. He threw back the bedclothes, rolled to the edge of his king-sized bed, put his feet to the wood floor, and shivered.

Amanda would continue to make life miserable for Shannon, and as long as she refused to heed his advice, he couldn't defend her the way he wished. And there he was, back to that issue again. Getting Shannon O'Brien to listen to him.

He staggered to the kitchen and put a kettle of water on for tea. While he soft-boiled an egg, he smiled. Fred, the man he'd bought his antique store from, had gotten him hooked on soft-boiled eggs. They'd had many a talk about the antiques over breakfasts. The old family friend, who had moved to Kennewick to be near his mother, had noticed Glen's interest in antiques when he was a teenager. After he moved to the States, he'd kept in contact.

Glen put two slices of bread into the toaster and waited. Once everything was ready, he sat at the table and opened his Bible. "Lord, please speak to me. I need wisdom."

Glen turned to the book of Matthew. A passage in chapter 18, which he'd highlighted in yellow, caught his eye first.

"See that you do not despise one of these little ones. For I tell you that their angels in heaven always see the face of my Father in heaven. What do you think? If a man owns a hundred sheep, and one of them wanders away, will he not leave the ninety-nine on the hills and go to look for the one that wandered off? And if he finds it, truly I tell you, he is happier about that one sheep than about the ninety-nine that did not wander off. In the same way your Father in heaven is not willing that any of these little ones should perish." He reread the passage twice, then again.

A stab of conviction tore through him. In his way, he had been looking down at Shannon, at Venus. Even Ray. He'd held Amanda in a certain odd esteem for far too long, and why? Because she was a major source of his income. Who was the lost sheep in this situation? Himself, or Shannon and her friends?

His cell phone trilled, and Glen scanned the room and discovered it on the kitchen counter. Squinting, he examined the unfamiliar phone number before curiosity got the best of him.

"Glen Caldwell here." There was a long moment of static before he thought he heard his brother's voice. "Thomas, is that you?"

"Glen, I can hear you now. Yes, it's me. I'm calling from a hospital in Haiti."

"What? What's wrong?" The sound of Thomas's voice brought home just how much he missed his younger brother who hadn't had a furlough from the mission field for a long time.

"I can't stay on too long. I'm borrowing a cell phone. But I could use your help."

"Anything, Thomas."

"I know you send us a lot of money monthly, and I hate to ask for more . . .but Melissa. . .the doctor's found a lump. They say it's cancer." Thomas paused with a ragged breath. "We need to get back to London to get her treated properly, and our monthly support doesn't cover these kinds of costs."

Worry knotted Glen's stomach. This was a grim reminder of how badly he needed Amanda's business and why he pandered to her like he did. "How much will you need?"

"Airfare for the six of us. We're taking the kids in case. . .in case we have to stay home for a while. And we need enough to cover a place for us to stay—Mom and Dad don't have room for all of us. And I have to close things down here, pay people to help. I haven't told Dad yet. I'll call him next, but you know his church isn't big. Not a lot of money there."

"Yes, quite true." Glen tried to keep the worry from his voice. Thomas told him how much and where to send the money. "I'll be praying," Glen said when his brother was finished.

"I love you," Thomas said.

"I love you all as well." Glen's throat seized up. "Good-bye for now."

He stood for a long time. Where would he get the money? He'd invested much of his spare cash in large purchases of rare antiques for a job Amanda was doing. She'd given him half as a down payment, but hadn't paid it off yet.

He had no choice but to talk to his friend and banker, Blake. He could add to Glen's revolving line of credit. Reluctantly, Glen dialed the number.

After explaining his situation, he snapped his phone closed. Blake had been more than willing. He would do what Glen asked first thing that morning. Of course Blake was willing. The man might be his friend, but he was also a businessman. He would profit from the interest.

He paced. The sooner Amanda paid him, the faster he would be able to restore the money. He opened his phone again and called Amanda, but she didn't answer and he left her a message requesting a meeting that morning.

As he cleaned up his breakfast dishes, the urgency to locate the spice box pressed in on him. Finding the box might mean more time with Shannon, too.

In the bathroom, he grabbed his toothbrush and drew a straight line of paste on the bristles. "Glen, you've never let a woman affect you like this before. Why now? Why Shannon?" He brushed his teeth with a vigor sure to remove enamel. While he swished water in his mouth, he jammed his toothbrush into the holder. Staring into the mirror, he made up his mind. He would try again to reason with Shannon.

❧

Shannon jogged down the stairs from her apartment and stepped into her office. There were a lot of advantages to living where one worked. No commute, for one. But there were also disadvantages. She could never really escape. Truman followed her closely, and she opened the back door to let him outside to do his business.

As she waited, she yawned and rubbed her arms, chilled by the sudden exposure to cold. She hadn't slept well the night before, troubled by thoughts of Amanda, Deputy Kroeger, and, worst of all, Glen and what he must've surmised from the deputy's remarks.

"Come on," she hollered at the dog. She'd pick up his mess in a few minutes. Truman galloped past her and headed for his food bowl. Once inside, Shannon closed her eyes and inhaled deeply of the musty scent of old things mixed with the fragrance of her latest scent passion—cinnamon candles. She opened her eyes again, crossed the room, and glanced into the showroom. Mismatched pieces of furniture were interspersed with shelves of knickknacks, all for sale. The store might look a mess, but she enjoyed repeat business. It felt like home. Her friends loved and accepted her. So why should she care about living up to Glen Caldwell's unrealistic standards? The man was always ready to tell her how to do things better. More efficiently. Glen meant well with his attention to details, but did he really see the big picture? Stop to smell the roses? Was he capable of becoming so absorbed in a project that he engaged the right side of his brain and forgot about the big picture for a little while?

Shannon sighed. She wasn't being fair. Glen wasn't *that* bad. She blew out a breath and withdrew back into her office. Then something caught her eye. On the floor, right beside her desk, lay the purple paper with directions to the Jenningses' home. Why hadn't she seen it there yesterday? She thought back to the day before and couldn't remember. Yes, she was messy, but surely she would have noticed. Was stress making her lose her mind? A good possibility, given what she'd studied about the negative effects of stress on the body. She leaned down to pick up the paper when a pounding at her back door made her jump. Truman leaped to life, barked once, and danced around her ankles.

"Who is it?" she yelled, heart pounding.

"Shannon, it's me, Glen."

That figured. Just when she'd been thinking about him. Truman was beside himself, whining with happiness. She shoved him back with her leg and opened the door. Glen's tall form filled the opening. Truman whined louder, and she understood how he felt. Glen looked devastatingly handsome.

"Shannon, you look like you've seen a ghost or something. Can you stop staring and let me in? It's cold."

"Oh, oops. Sorry." She opened the door all the way and stepped aside so he could enter.

Truman greeted him with an enthusiastic bark, and Glen patted the dog's head with a leather-gloved hand.

"What are you doing here?" Shannon asked.

He stepped back and peeled off his gloves, frowning. "What's wrong?"

"You, pounding at the door, scared the wits out of me!" Shannon dangled the paper in front of his eyes. "Look at this. I found it on the floor."

"And?" Glen took another step back. He stared at her as though she'd lost her marbles.

"I know this paper was on the corner of my desk, under the stapler. Then it disappeared, remember? And nobody's been here since our trip to Benton City."

"Yesterday you said it was in your purse."

"That's what I thought, but it wasn't in my purse. You looked. That meant it had to be under the stapler, but it wasn't because I would have seen it. It was on the floor. But I didn't notice it there last night, either."

Glen glanced pointedly around her office. "How would you know?"

Shannon slapped the paper on the desk. "Because I would. It was important."

"All right." Glen held up his hands in a gesture of surrender. "Maybe Venus moved it. And wasn't Ray here?"

Judging by the scowl on his face, Glen had added Ray Reed to his riffraff list. "This paper wasn't here when Venus left last night. And yes, Ray was here." She frowned at him. "Are you spying on me?"

Glen cocked one brow and straightened his already perfect posture. "Spying? Not likely. But who can miss his comings and goings? The sound of his bike echoes off the buildings in the alley like thunder." He looked her in the eye, sending warmth through her that chased away the chill of the morning. "Perhaps this is a mystery that won't be solved at the moment. In fact, there are more pressing matters at hand. The purple paper aside, we need to have a talk, Shannon."

Why did he have to go and speak her name that way? So warm and inviting. She averted her gaze to the window and the alley behind the stores. "What would you like to talk about?"

"Have you heard from Lucy Jennings?"

"No, not yet." Through the window, Shannon saw a shiny, expensive-looking vehicle pull into the parking lot beyond the alley. It came to a stop, the door opened, and out came Amanda.

"Uh-oh." Shannon swallowed. Amanda marched a straight path to the back door of the Quaint Shop, a fur coat swirling around her leather boots. Shannon's heart banged against her ribs. All she wanted was to remain centered, and here she was filled with dread and a weird jealousy. Amanda was rich and beautiful, with legs to die for—and it was obvious she was attracted to Glen. Shannon read it time and again in Amanda's body language.

"What is it?" Glen asked, coming to stand beside her, so close the scent of his soap made her want to snuggle against him. "Oh great! Amanda. She wasn't due to meet me"—he pulled back his coat sleeve and glanced at his watch—"for another hour, at least."

Shannon had a sudden desperate thought. "I'm going to invite her in for tea and try to reason with her." She reached for the knob on the back door.

"Are you serious?" Glen placed his hand over hers on the knob. "Let me, um, let me take care of this." With his gaze on the fast-approaching Amanda, he said, "You can't handle her."

Shannon jerked her hand from under his, stepped back, and tilted her chin. "Thus far you've done a bang-up job of handling her yourself. Just look at her. Even someone who doesn't know how to read body language could read hers."

Glen nodded. "Yes, well, to use one of your colloquialisms, she looks like she's about to spit nails, but. . ."

Both of them inhaled when Amanda sidestepped the solid door, cupped her hands around her eyes, and glared at them through the windowpane. Why should she bother to knock when she could try to intimidate them through the window with a slit-eyed glare?

Shannon lifted her hand to wave, but Glen grabbed her arm before she could do it.

She tried to shake him off, but he didn't let go. "Stop it, Glen. I was going to do a beauty-queen wave. That hair of hers reminds me—"

"No need to make things worse. Go ahead and open the door," Glen instructed through a tight-lipped smile.

"Oh, now I'm making it worse?" She yanked her arm away from him and glared. "First you say don't open the door, then you say open the door. And they say *women* can't make up their minds." Shannon twisted the doorknob.

Chapter 5

Glen opened his mouth to remind Shannon that her lack of discretion in hiring quality personnel had caused this problem, but he didn't have time before Amanda pushed her way inside.

"Good morning, Amanda. Come on in," Shannon said in a cordial greeting that only Glen noticed was sarcastic.

"I almost stepped in a pile that dog of yours left." Amanda tried to shove past Shannon, but she stood firm even though her face reddened.

"I'm sorry. Truman was just out, and I haven't had time—"

"Never mind. I wouldn't expect anything else." Amanda stepped around Shannon and directed her gaze straight up into Glen's eyes. "Well, where is it?" She was trembling as she removed her gloves.

"I've already explained to you where it is. Didn't you get my phone message?" He said nothing else as he waited for his anger to subside. Amanda had a colossal nerve dismissing Shannon as if she wasn't there. Shannon's eyes glittered, but Glen had a feeling it was anger more than hurt.

Amanda patted her billowy mane of curls, then laid her fingertips on his arm. Glen resisted the temptation to pull away from her touch.

"You said you were going to get it yesterday; then you call me and tell me you didn't. You said the woman who bought *my* property let her daughter run off with it like it was some sort of insignificant plaything. This is ridiculous." Her hand was shaking despite her bold tone of voice.

"Well, Lucy didn't know any better." Shannon's voice was low but firm, and now Amanda did turn to look at her.

"Lucy? Who is Lucy? Your incompetent help?"

Shannon's lips thinned, and Glen knew she was biting her tongue. She'd be proud that he was reading her body language. The cloud of hostility in the office, coupled with the thick scent of Amanda's musky perfume, increased the intensity of his pounding headache, but he kept his face placid.

"Lucy is the woman who bought the box. We're waiting to hear back from her after her daughter returns." Glen cut a glance at Shannon. "Did you get a call from her yet?"

"A call?" Amanda's high-pitched voice pierced his ears. "I won't wait for a call. I'm going to pick up the box myself, which is what I should've done to begin with." She stood between him and Shannon and gave them both a look of disgust. "Now then." She lifted her hand, palm up. "I want that address."

"No. She was my customer. I'll deal with her." Shannon tilted her chin defiantly. Glen was simultaneously irate at Amanda and proud of Shannon. He saw her surreptitiously slip the purple paper into the pocket of her floral skirt. "As soon as Lucy phones, I'll go out to her house to get the spice box."

Amanda's eyes flashed, and her face colored. "Glen? I'd like to have a word with you. . .outside."

"Yes, yes, of course."

Shannon began humming. Something familiar. Glen concentrated and then almost choked. It was the song "Cruella de Vil" from *101 Dalmatians.*

Glen took Amanda's arm and hurried her out the back door. Then he glanced over his shoulder at Shannon. Arms crossed, she tossed him an impish grin and shut the door. Hard.

He fumbled with his keys, opened the back door to his store, and held it for Amanda. She brushed past him, then dropped to the edge of his desk. "I didn't want it to come to this," she said through tight lips, "but I've got a thirty-six-thousand-dollar order pending with you."

Glen heard the threat before she spoke it. "The furniture for the Johnson project is nearly complete. We searched high and low for the breakfront you requested." He pushed a smile to his face. "We'll add that piece, and the shipment will arrive tomorrow."

Shaking her head, Amanda slid away from his desk and stood face-to-face with him. "I want that address, Glen, or I'm cancelling the Johnson order."

Her eyes were flashing, and he wondered why the spice box was so important. Its monetary value didn't warrant her behavior. She was known for her fiery temper, but this conduct was over-the-top even for her.

He couldn't afford to lose this order. He couldn't afford to eat the cost. And now his brother needed help desperately. He had no choice but to try to make amends with the unreasonable woman. He was tempted to follow Shannon's example and hum the Disney movie tune.

"I cannot divulge the name of the person who bought the box, but please, will you give me until Monday to get it back to you?"

Seconds ticked by like long minutes while she paced his office, her heels clicking against the tile. Her eyes finally snapped up to his face. "For old time's sake, I'll do it."

His shoulders sagged with relief. "Thank you, Amanda, you won't be sorry."

"Of course I won't be. I hope you won't be." She hoisted her purse strap higher on her shoulder and smiled. "I hope you and I can continue to work together in harmony." Her smile dissolved. "But we have one big thing between us that I want to take care of. Shannon O'Brien. I'm going to see Mike Carroll with the petition."

"What does that mean? How will the petition take care of Shannon?"

What kind of hold did she have over Mike to give her such clout?

"You yourself have expressed a desire to have our stores tidy. You expressed interest in the Renew Our Storefronts project. . .and might I add, you signed the petition."

"Yes, but not at the expense of closing down businesses. I would like to see that petition again."

"I don't have it with me." Shaking her head, Amanda's eyes narrowed, and Glen felt nailed to the wall.

"What?" Glen shrugged. "What is it?"

"I've suspected this for quite some time. Now I know for a certainty." Amanda clucked her tongue. "Shame on you, Glen. Shannon is not your type. Of course you're probably using her. I will need to teach you to have better taste." Her gaze raked him head to toe. "She looks like a peasant from—"

"That's quite enough. You know nothing about Shannon." Amanda had just crossed a line. Client or not, she had no right to speak to him like that about his personal life.

Amanda paled, eyes flashing with anger—Shannon wouldn't have to interpret this body language for him. But he couldn't bring himself to apologize. Instead he walked to the door, grabbed the handle with a tight grip, and pulled it open for her. An icy blast of winter air whirled around him, a perfect accompaniment for Amanda's words and attitude. She'd make him regret what he said. A woman scorned was dangerous, and he'd chosen Shannon over her. Asking for her mercy on Shannon would only strengthen her resolve to get revenge.

He heard the roar of an approaching motorcycle and over Amanda's shoulder saw Ray Reed pull up. Perfect timing. Glen's jaw clenched.

"I am not a small-minded woman," Amanda said.

Glen choked back a rude laugh. The engine noise stopped.

Amanda's brittle smile did not reach her eyes. "I will still allow you until Monday to find the box. And I hope within that time frame you will give thought to the situation at hand." She turned and swept majestically through the opening.

The *situation at hand.* Glen snapped the door closed behind his client.

He could warn Shannon or. . . He paced his office and debated with himself. The sound of raised voices sent him running to the window to look outside. Amanda was in a shouting match with Reed, who looked worse than usual in old, worn jeans and beard stubble on his face. Shannon stood against her door, her big dog at attention beside her. Her eyes looked impossibly large as she watched Amanda and Ray argue. Someone had to do damage control, and she obviously wasn't up to the job. He snatched his coat from the tree stand.

❧

Hand clenched tight around Truman's leash, Shannon could do nothing but watch in silence at the ugly scene before her. She loathed angry confrontation of any kind and wanted only to make peace with Amanda, but the goal somehow eluded her grasp.

"You can't talk to Shannon like she's garbage." Ray slammed his helmet against the seat of his Harley.

Amanda clenched her fists. "No one speaks to me in that tone of voice."

The two glared at each other when the back door to Glen's shop swung open, and he stepped out and walked over to stand next to Shannon.

Amanda sent a scathing glance to Glen, then back to Ray, who was leaning against his bike, arms crossed, staring at Amanda. Truman growled low in his chest.

"Ray was just standing here," Shannon explained in a hurried whisper to Glen, whose face was a mask of controlled anger. "Amanda began yelling at me, and he defended me."

Amanda fisted her hands and jammed them on her hips. "Glen, what are you going to do about this—this riffraff?"

Shannon's heart sank.

"Pardon me," Glen said. "What—"

"He insulted me." Amanda leaned forward, eyes narrowed, savoring the exchange.

Truman stood and pulled at the leash. "That's not true." Shannon wrapped the leash tighter around her fisted hand. "I saw the whole thing. Please, calm down. You're upsetting my dog." She'd never before heard Truman's menacing growl or seen the fur on his back raised. A sense of dread washed over her.

"Are you calling me a liar?" Amanda stomped her high-heeled boot on the sidewalk. "Glen? Are you listening to me? I may call the police."

Ray snorted rudely. Glen faced him and seemed oblivious to Amanda's query. Neither man backed down.

"Please, Ray, drop it," Shannon said.

Her plea snapped him back to reality, and he raised both his hands as if in surrender. "I don't want any trouble, Caldwell."

"I don't intend to give you any." Glen's promise and his mild tone of voice didn't match his challenging stance. For once, Shannon was stumped by his body language. He glanced over at her, then back at Ray. "But perhaps you could, er, apologize to Amanda for your rudeness."

"Rudeness?" Something unspoken flew between the men; then Ray seemed to reach a conclusion. "Sure. Why not?" He turned toward Amanda, who wore an arrogant grin. "Sorry, ma'am, for any inconvenience." His cold smile was unlike anything Shannon had seen from him before. His gaze snapped to her, and he motioned with his head. "Come on. Let's go inside. I'm ready for some pleasant company."

As Shannon turned to enter her store, the last thing she heard was Amanda Franklin say to Glen, "Now do you see what I mean?"

Glen trailed Amanda to her car and braced himself for her wrath. Amanda would expect him to take sides, a lose-lose proposition in this situation. How could he protect Shannon—and his business—and not lose the money he so desperately needed to keep his commitment to his brother?

"Amanda," Glen said to her back when she stopped next to her car. He sent up a silent prayer for conciliatory words. "Remember what I said? If for whatever reason the spice box is gone, I will pay you for what it's worth. Then I will help you find another just like it. Please understand that."

"And remember that I said it's insured," she snapped. "The money is not the point. I want *that* box."

"I'm sorry. I'm doing everything I can. Shannon's clerk, Venus, didn't sell your spice box with ill intent. Your mom—"

"You're allowing your feelings for Shannon to take precedence over the safety concerns of your neighbors and faithful clients." Amanda didn't face him. *Whatever that had to do with the box.* "I don't know what 'feelings' we're discussing here, but I've always addressed every one of your concerns." *The whole stinking lot of complaints*, he was tempted to add.

She whirled around. "Your love life is of no consequence to me, not unless it interferes with business. Shannon O'Brien's been nothing but trouble since the day she parked that filthy truck full of broken furniture on our street."

Her anger-laced words said more than anything else that his "love life" was indeed of consequence to her. And suddenly the root of her anger at Shannon became clear. She was jealous.

Amanda crossed her arms over her midsection and blew out a breath. "And worse, people are afraid to shop here. Look at the type of element she brings around."

Glen couldn't agree that things were that bad. Still, if Shannon had cooperated with him, he could counter Amanda's claims, but he found himself at a loss.

"You've got until Monday to get me that box. Then I will present Mike with the petition and proceed with a lawsuit, and you will never work for me again." She spun around, opened her car door, and got inside. Without another glance at him, she started the engine and drove away. Gritting his teeth, he headed back to his shop.

Ray Reed had defended Shannon against Amanda, and Glen had tried to defend her in his own way but couldn't to the extent he wished without alienating his client.

On a sigh, Glen went back inside his office and sat at his desk. Amanda might be jealous, but that had little to do with her desire to get back the box. Something wasn't adding up here.

His thoughts were interrupted by the dim sound of voices and off-key plunks on guitar strings coming through the wall from next door. A sudden burst of jealousy pumped lava through his veins. Glen stood and jammed his hands in his pockets.

Despite late-night arguments with himself about Shannon, he was losing the battle with the logical part of his mind. His feelings for her had been growing for a long time, but he'd kept himself busy, avoided being with her, and compartmentalized his emotions. He kept reminding himself that he needed a mate who was orderly and rational, not a goofy flower child who wanted to befriend the world and didn't seem to have an organized bone in her body.

Glen returned to his seat and flipped open a folder on his desk. Time to get to work. He had to get Shannon off his mind and concentrate on business. His dad told him to trust God with every problem. Until Shannon O'Brien barged into his life and rattled his cage, he thought he had a handle on "let go and let God," but she forced him to take the reins again. "God, please help me put all of this in Your hands."

Tomorrow he'd meet with Mike Carroll. Find out how badly Amanda had already poisoned Mike's mind against Shannon and convince him that she wasn't a lost cause. Then he'd help Shannon fix up her store. . .if she'd allow him.

Chapter 6

There you go." Ray handed Shannon the guitar from where he sat in the leather chair. "The new string is on, but you'll have to keep tuning it for a few days. New strings don't hold their tune well."

"Okay, thanks." She took the guitar, strummed a few chords, then started to cry.

"Hey," he said softly and patted her arm. "Don't let that skinny hag disturb your balance."

Shannon giggled through her tears, almost choking herself. "That's not nice, Ray. Well, she's skinny, but she's not a hag. She's beautiful."

He rolled his eyes. "That's a matter of opinion. Or should I say, *taste*. But she's definitely not nice. Beauty is what beauty does, you know. And she's got it in for you."

Placing her guitar on her desk, Shannon sniffled, then swiped her arm over her face. "I do pray for her, and I ask God to forgive me for my awful thoughts. I just don't understand. I haven't done anything bad to her. Well, I guess I have. Amanda almost stepped in a pile of Truman's poop. I forgot to clean it up." She sighed. "What's wrong with me?"

"You have faults like everyone else," he said. "It's just that yours are manifested on the outside. Some people seem perfect because their faults are more internal."

"That sounds weirdly like something I would say." Shannon frowned. "Is that why Amanda doesn't like me? That's why she's upset? Because I'm a slob?"

He grinned. "You really don't know why she's upset?"

"I figured it was my shop. I'm a blight to the other store owners."

"That might be part of it, but it's not all." Ray grabbed her guitar and expertly picked at the strings.

"Okay, I'll bite. Why does she hate me?"

Ray's grin widened, and then he laughed. "That's one of the things I find so refreshing about you. Your total naivete."

Shannon frowned while she watched his fingers pluck the strings. "I don't think I'm naive at all. You know about my past. How my dad got busted for drugs. They did it around me. I—"

"You are still amazingly innocent despite your past." Ray stopped playing the guitar. "Your parents weren't the hardened criminal types. I'm not saying what they did was right—it wasn't. They were just free spirits who lived the way they wanted. Unfortunately, illegal activity is illegal activity, and you saw the results."

"That aside, why does Amanda hate me?"

"Because Glen more than likes you."

"What? You think so?"

"I made a special effort to watch him today." He put the guitar down and zipped his leather jacket. "I gotta get going, but trust me on this, Shannon."

❧

That afternoon Shannon ran from her office, waving a piece of paper and punching the air, yelling, "Thank You, Lord!" She'd been waiting all day for Lucy's call, and finally it had come.

Venus was staring at shards of ceramic on the floor. "I'm sorry. I broke a vase. It's kind of crowded in here." The teen glanced at Shannon with wide eyes rimmed on the bottom with dark half-moons.

"So I've heard. It's okay. Just sweep it up." Shannon tripped over an unopened box in her way and dropped the paper. It landed near the pieces of vase, and Venus picked it up. "What's this?"

"The address where the box is. Lucy called. Her daughter left it there. Mystery solved." Shannon paused. "You know, the whole thing is really weird. The person who broke into the Jenningses' house didn't take anything. It makes me wonder. . . . Anyway, the Allman family is expecting me tomorrow morning."

"Good, Shan. That's great."

"Are you okay? You look tired."

"I'm fine." Venus handed Shannon the directions, took a broom from behind the counter, and began to sweep with lethargic movements. Her cell phone began playing a popular tune, and she jumped.

"Yes, I think it's great, too." Shannon put the paper with the Allmans' address next to the cash register. "Go on and get your phone. I'm going next door. I'll be right back."

Shannon exited her store, circumvented the stacked furniture outside her shop, and turned into Glen's doorway.

"Shannon, um, Ms. O'Brien," Charlie said with a warm smile. "Can I help you?"

"Call me Shannon, please. Is Glen here?"

"Yes, I am." Glen appeared from the back of the store and strode toward her. Ray's words came back to her, and she felt suddenly shy and awkward. Her gaze scattered, first on Glen's broad shoulders, then his hair, and finally his face.

Big mistake. His crystal blue eyes held her gaze. Charlie said something, but she was focused on trying to interpret the meaning behind Glen's expression. Was Ray right?

"I, um. . ." Shannon pointed in the general direction of her store. "Got a call from Lucy."

Glen slipped his hands into his pockets and leaned against the counter.

Charlie cleared his throat. "Did they find where the box went?"

Glen continued to look at her in an odd, assessing way. She didn't know whether to be worried or elated, but she was leaning toward worried.

"Yes." Shannon glanced at Charlie, then swallowed and started again. "Lucy's daughter left the box at her friend's house in her upset state over the break-in." She dug in her coat pocket. "Oh, I must've left the address in my store." She brushed her hand over her long braid. Why was Glen staring? "Anyway, the place is only a couple miles from Lucy's house." She took two steps backward toward the door. Glen pushed off the dresser and walked toward her. "And—and I'll leave first thing tomorrow morning to get it. Everything will turn out fine after all."

"I'm going with you, of course."

Wagging her head, her pulse soared. Her emotions were making it impossible to read Glen's body language. He leaned toward her with a trace of a smile on his handsome face. Was Ray right?

"You won't want to join me, Glen. Remember last time?"

"Mr. Caldwell." Charlie cleared his throat. "May I go next door for a minute?"

"Yes," Glen said, but kept his gaze on her.

Shannon heard the chimes, felt the cold draft sweep in from the door as Charlie walked out.

"I suspect Charlie's taken with Venus."

"Do you?" *And are you taken with me?* she wanted to ask. *Do you want to hold me in your arms?* "What makes you say that?"

Glen took a step closer. "Body language."

Shannon giggled nervously. "What do you know about body language, Glen Caldwell?"

He looked directly into her eyes again, and her heart pounded madly. "I might know a bit more than you suspect, Shannon O'Brien."

Did he mean he could see through to her heart? Her face heated. "So then, I've got to get going. I'll have the box back to you by tomorrow afternoon."

"I am going with you."

"No way!" She couldn't be in a closed vehicle with him again. She was afraid her feelings for him had grown to the point that she wouldn't be able to conceal them. "I'm taking Truman with me. You know what happened last time."

"You know, Truman's starting to grow on me." Glen's little smile made her heart pound faster. He was so close she could reach up and. . .

"What time will you be leaving, Shannon?"

Why'd he have to go and speak her name again in that subtle tone of his? "What time?" Yikes, she sounded like a parrot. "You're not a morning person, Glen. I'm leaving very early."

He chuckled at her reminder. "Tomorrow will be nothing like our first trip." His eyes held a mischievous twinkle. "I think I'm prepared this time."

His gaze traveled over her face. He might be prepared, but she wasn't—not at all. She tried to regain her balance, but it had totally left her. *Lord. . .* "It's up to you. I'm leaving at seven thirty so I can be back to open my shop on time."

"I'll be there."

Shannon pivoted and ducked out of his shop before she had a chance to open her mouth again. "Okay," she whispered and began to pray. As she walked into her shop, she settled in her mind that she'd fallen in love with Glen. In His time, the Lord would iron out the wrinkles in their relationship—or not.

Chapter 7

On Friday morning as Shannon's truck jounced over the interstate and Truman lapped his ear, Glen settled back stoically. He had no choice but to accompany her on the early morning trip. He needed to hold the elusive spice box in his hands and then give it to Amanda on a silver platter if necessary.

Anger heated his face. What could be worse than to be beholden to Amanda—to be unable to defend Shannon publicly just to keep Amanda happy? Today his mission was twofold: Get the box and hope that would quell her antagonism toward Shannon so Amanda wouldn't pressure Mike Carroll to kick Shannon out—and at the same time hold on to Amanda's brisk business in order to pay off his debt.

"Want tea?" Shannon reached around Truman and handed him a thermos.

He gave her an appreciative nod and met her gaze for a moment. "Thank you." Who was he kidding? His mission was threefold. While listening to Shannon and Ray practice guitar through the thin wall that separated their shops, it hit him how deeply he'd grown to care for her during the past year, and much more during the past few days. He wanted the disorganized shopgirl to stay in her store. To stay in his life. Perhaps nothing would come of their association, but he was willing to try.

"You're awfully quiet." Shannon shot him a curious look. "I'm worried. You haven't even complained about Truman yet."

Glen concealed his smile under a frown. "I was just about to lodge a complaint, but after yesterday's display of Truman's temper, I figured it was best not to get on his bad side."

"I'm sorry about that. It was unexpected."

"Amanda was hostile, and it was directed toward you. I can't fault Truman for his actions."

Truman flopped his immense head against Glen's shoulder at the mention of his name, panting warm moisture on his face.

"Truman, back off," Shannon ordered in a soft tone. Wolf-dog obeyed immediately. "I wonder if I've got better animal skills than people skills. You think?"

"I think your people skills are fine. You care deeply, and people know that. . ."

"But," she said. "I can hear the 'but' at the end of that sentence."

"You don't always use wisdom." In fact, her life could be much easier if she'd allow him to help. How could he get through to her? "You've collected a few foes along the way. People who don't understand you. It happens to everyone."

"I know I'm different." She shifted in the seat and swiped a stray hair from her face. "It was always that way," she added softly.

"Truly?" Glen took another sip of the delicious tea, staring, waiting with interest for a deeper revelation. The rusted truck idled loudly at the STOP sign, and Shannon looked at him with her quizzical hazel eyes as if to see if he were serious or perhaps if he could be trusted.

"What I meant to say was. . ." What exactly did he mean to say? Searching the depths of her eyes, he'd be sure to slip out with something he'd later regret. "You're charming, is all. And some people just don't see it."

Shannon's face colored, and she quickly looked away from him.

"I meant that as a compliment, of course." Glen adjusted his glasses and studied her. There seemed to be a hiccup in their communication—an unbreachable chasm that prevented them from fully understanding one another.

"Thank you," Shannon said belatedly. "Um, Bible study this week at church was about sowing and reaping—"

"Ah yes. A good topic to study," Glen said. A discussion on scripture should be safer terrain.

"You know what I don't get? I'm trying to sow good things with Amanda, but it's not working." A small line formed between her brows, and he resisted the urge to lean over and press a kiss to her full lips.

"Out of control," he whispered.

Her head jerked toward him. "Huh?"

Wait. That's how he felt about her. "That is, er, some situations are out of our control. Amanda overreacted. Unfortunately, I depend on her business."

Shannon's frown deepened. "You *need* Amanda's business?" She slowed the truck to a crawl. "I guess I imagined from the looks of your store that you were wealthy."

He laughed. "Don't I wish. Despite appearances, I don't have oodles of cash, and Amanda's purchases bring in a good portion of my earnings."

❧

Shannon's heart sank. "You're scaring me, Glen. I feel like crying for the trouble I've caused you." She took the exit to Benton City with greater urgency. "Don't worry, we'll get the spice box and make Amanda happy—whatever 'happy' means to Amanda Franklin."

His lips turned up in a half smile, bringing her a measure of relief. She didn't have Glen figured out. She had put him in a box—confident, organized, and bossy, not to mention wealthy. Believing those things had made her feel he deserved her jabs. She, who prided herself in reading body language and understanding people. She'd failed with Glen. Perhaps her acceptance of people was reserved only for those who needed her. Those who didn't, she either avoided or believed they were too good for her. She rubbed her forehead with her left hand. It was all too complicated, and thinking about it made her head throb.

"I've said it before, but I'm sorry, Glen."

"No need to apologize. I can come off as overbearing, even when I'm just trying to help. I've got to work on that." Glen patted Truman's head. "But I do need Amanda's business. My brother is a missionary, and his wife is ill. She has to travel back to London from Haiti to get the treatment she needs, and they don't have the money."

"Can't their home church help? And don't they have monthly support like most missionaries? What about the organization they work under?"

Glen's sad smile didn't reach his eyes. "Their home church is my dad's church, as well as the organization they work under. My father is the pastor. But it's small, and right now things aren't great financially for the congregation. Yes, they have monthly support, but it won't cover these expenses. I borrowed money to wire to Thomas. I didn't really have it to give."

"Wow, your father and brother are in the ministry?" Shannon felt a sinking sensation in her stomach.

"Yes. I wasn't called to the ministry, but I work to support both of them as I can. If I lose Amanda's business—"

"You won't. I promise." Shannon scanned the directions to the Allman house. This time she had taped the paper to her dashboard. "We'll be there in five minutes. We'll get the spice box and give it to Amanda."

"All's well that ends well."

Would this end well? Maybe for Glen, his family, and Amanda, but a romance between her and Glen? The divide had just grown deeper. He might not be the blue blood she'd imagined, but now it was worse. Introducing a man from a good religious family to her parents. No, she could never do that.

"So where's your father's church?"

"Back in London."

Time for a change of topic lest their chat turn to questions about her family background. Lois and John O'Brien were still in their broken-down trailer. They had always meant to do better—just as she always meant to get her act together. Finish projects she'd started, just like her father and mother whose yard, trailer, and outbuildings were stuffed with things they'd never completed. A loom and spinning wheel from the time her mother raised sheep in order to spin wool. And the table her father built for a train set he'd never bought. She forced her mind back to Glen. "So what church do you attend?"

"Tri-Cities Tabernacle," Glen said. "How about you?"

"I'm at Sanctuary of Praise."

"Ah, Pastor Zach's church. I know him. That was the first church I attended when I moved from London to the Tri-Cities."

Shannon's throat grew tight. Pastor Zach and his wife, Laurie, would never reveal anything she had confided in them. Still, the idea that Glen knew her minister made her want to run away and reinvent herself all over again. "Why do you attend Tri-Cities Tabernacle if you've got a friendship with Pastor Zach?"

A long silence hung between them, and she told herself not to jump to an ugly conclusion. The people in Glen's church were wealthy. She'd hate to think he'd made his choice based on the opportunity to network.

"I guess I began attending there because many of my clients did." He took a deep breath. "That doesn't sound great, does it?"

She said nothing. Glen put a high priority on business, but in a different way than she did. She also cared just as much for people, and that was often her downfall. Maybe men in general prioritized differently than women.

"Come to think of it, I think I'll attend your church this Sunday. Say hello to Zach and Laurie."

Shannon wanted to scream no. She was scheduled to give her testimony in front of the congregation this Sunday. She'd shrivel in embarrassment if Glen was there listening. "Maybe you should try for Sunday after next. We're having a Thanksgiving service and fellowship afterward. I think you'll enjoy it more."

Glen leaned forward in the seat. "Look at that. Either we have a deputy escort waiting for us or there's trouble up ahead."

"What?" Shannon squinted, and her eyes lit on the flashing lights up ahead. "Oh no. Don't tell me that's the Allman house."

They got closer, and one of her least favorite people was there. Deputy Kroeger stood with his hands fisted on his hips. When she pulled in front of the house, he pointed to a spot behind his car. She parked and turned off the engine to the tune of her pulse roaring in her ears.

ॐ

Glen tightened his hands into fists. Was this to be a repeat of last time? If he couldn't get the spice box, Amanda would make good on her threat to take business away from him. And there would be no way to talk her out of trying to get Shannon evicted.

Glen exited the truck and Shannon jumped from her side with her purse over her shoulder, leaving Truman inside.

Deputy Kroeger approached them with long strides. Glen felt Shannon shrinking against him, and he enjoyed the sensation, even while he wondered at her reaction. He put an arm around her shoulder, and she allowed him to leave it there.

"What do you folks want?" the deputy asked. He turned his full attention on Shannon. "You know anything about this?"

"About what? What's happened?" Shannon jabbed her elbow into Glen's side. Did she mean for him to speak up on her behalf?

"We're here to buy back the same antique from the Allmans that we wanted from Lucy Jennings. Her daughter left it here." Glen eyed the rundown house. "Is there a problem?"

"So, they were expecting you?" Kroeger nodded slowly, like he was onto something big.

"Yes," Glen said. "What's going on?"

"Another break-in." Kroeger tilted his head. "What are the odds? I'm wondering. What's the deal with this box? Tell me what you know about it."

That was a good question. Glen was beginning to think the "deal" with the box was much more than what appeared on the surface. "It's a valuable antique that was sold accidentally. The original owner wants it back."

Shannon pulled away from him, and he let his arm drop. "Where is the family?" she asked. "Are they okay?"

"George took his wife and daughters to his parents' house. I'm waiting for him to come back. I guess they forgot about you in the trauma of having their house broken into."

Glen nodded, feeling selfish. He hadn't even considered the family's feelings.

"So this box is valuable, you say?" Kroeger's expression had changed. His eyes lost their focus, and a deep groove appeared between his eyebrows.

"Yes, a bit," Glen said. "Surely you can imagine why the owner is eager to have it returned."

Kroeger's attention snapped back to Glen. He removed a notebook from his pocket, along with a pen. "Who owns this box?"

Glen exchanged a glance with Shannon. Looking vulnerable, she shrugged and waited for him to talk. "The owner is a woman named Amanda Franklin."

The deputy met Glen's gaze. "Franklin, you say? You mean the James Franklin family in Kennewick?"

"Yes." Glen prayed Kroeger wouldn't hassle Amanda. That was all he needed.

"I see." Kroeger scribbled something in the notebook, then slapped it shut. "I need numbers where I can reach both of you."

Glen pulled a leather business card holder from his shirt pocket. Shannon began digging into her purse. "Do you know if the spice box was stolen?" She glanced up at the deputy.

"Don't know." Kroeger eyed both of them in turn.

Shannon finally found a business card. Glen eyed the crinkled card with dog-eared corners.

"If you folks don't mind now, I have a job to do. I might even call you and tell you if the box is here. And Shannon, tell your daddy I said hello." He turned and with his slow, sure gait walked back to his vehicle.

❧

Shannon realized her fingers were going numb and released her death grip on the steering wheel. *Stop it!* She was a new creation in Christ. She wasn't the six-year-old girl, shaking and wrapped in a blanket on her bed as deputies rummaged through her parents' trailer in search of their stash while they were handcuffed in the living room. She especially remembered the young Deputy Kroeger, standing in the doorway to her bedroom, staring at her with a blank expression before going back to scream at her parents and arrest her father.

Glen cleared his throat. "Shannon?"

Now what? She wished Glen hadn't come along. Not only had they run into the deputy again, she'd made a fool of herself, pressing up against Glen like a lovesick teenager. But she had to admit that his strong arm felt so good around her shoulders.

Leave the past in the past, she ordered herself. Too many things were pressing in the present to dwell there. "Two burglaries, Glen. Kroeger's right. What are the chances?"

"Right." Glen shoved Truman's head away as the dog made several attempts to lick his face.

"What's with that box? It's like a trouble magnet." Shannon drew deep breaths. "You don't think it's possible that Amanda. . ." She let her words drift away.

Glen's gaze snapped toward her. "You mean you wonder if Amanda is behind the break-ins?"

"That's horrible of me, isn't it? Especially since we don't even know if the box is missing yet." Shannon shook her head. "I can't believe I'd think something so ugly." She understood Glen's long silence to mean he was furious with her. "I'm sorry."

"Don't be. The thought crossed my mind as well. I just don't know how she'd know who had the box."

"What will we do if it's gone?"

Glen shrugged. Shannon fought rising fear that raised goose bumps on her arms. "I'm sure Amanda will go into cardiac arrest if we can't find it." Biting hard on her lower lip, she vowed to stay away from her old stomping grounds. The memories brought on by the close proximity dredged up old fears and brought out the worst in her. She totally lost her balance and any confidence she had worked hard to develop. She took a deep, cleansing breath and asked the Lord for peace. After a minute she slapped her hand on the steering wheel.

"If the box is gone, I'll find it if it's the last thing I do, pay whatever it costs

183

to get it back, and put an end to all this craziness. Although I don't know how."

"It's obvious that box is worth more than Amanda is letting on." Glen clutched the dashboard in a white-knuckle grip. "Please slow down."

Shannon lifted her foot off the gas pedal. "Sorry, I didn't realize I was speeding." The truck slowed, and Glen sat back again. "Will you tell Amanda about this? About the break-in?"

Glen snorted. "As you Americans say, 'No way, José.' I'll put it off as long as possible and hope the box is sitting in the Allmans' house. Amanda gave me until Monday to find the box or—"

"Or what?" Shannon's heart filled with dread.

"She'll take her business away from me."

Shannon's stomach turned over, and she thought she might have to stop the truck so she could be sick on the roadside. "Amanda said that?"

"Yes." Glen glanced at her around Truman. "I have to trust the Lord is in control. There's no point in getting uptight."

"Uptight? Uptight?" Fear and anger made her voice high-pitched and loud. Anger at Amanda for her controlling ways. Fear that she'd take business from Glen. Anger at Deputy Kroeger for reminding her of the past. Fear that Glen would find out just what her childhood was like. Anger at her parents for being weird. And even anger at Glen for talking to her in hippie-speak. She'd heard that expression enough times from her parents to make her stomach twist in knots. "I'm not *uptight*. I think everything is just *groovy*."

"Groovy?" Glen raked his fingers through his hair, then stared out the passenger-side window.

She'd done it again—managed to scare off another normal guy. And this time she had unleashed anger on top of it. Try as she might to reinvent the Shannon who reflected the image of her parents, Benton City brought it back home to her. Now things were worse. She was developing a temper. She shook her head. Of all people to see that, why the handsome, charming Glen Caldwell?

She glanced around Truman at Glen and saw his shoulders shaking. "Are you crying?" she asked in disbelief.

Glen shifted his gaze to her again, and she saw the grin on his face. "No. Have you cooled down a bit?"

"You're laughing?"

"Yes."

"There is nothing to laugh about here. Stop it."

"Oh, but there is," he said. "It's a comedy of errors. Us chasing a box all over the place." Truman stuck his nose in Glen's ear, and he shoved it away. "So why are you irritable? It's not like you."

"Oh, let me see," Shannon said. "We both might be sued. Amanda hates my guts. The box is missing, and Kroeger looked at me cross-eyed."

The dog rested his head on Glen's shoulder. "Cross-eyed? Is that another one of your American colloquialisms?" He pushed Truman's snout out of the way and continued to stare at her.

"Yes." Shannon snorted a laugh. "I saw the look in Deputy Kroeger's eyes. Another house was burglarized. I happen to show up at the scene of another crime. I grew up there. Can you see where I'm going with this?"

Glen scrubbed his hand over his jawline. "I'm genuinely perplexed. I don't see the connection between—"

"Doesn't matter." Holding her breath, Shannon took the exit out of Benton City. "Want to hear my favorite scripture verse?" She didn't wait for his response. "'Therefore, if anyone is in Christ, he is a new creation; the old has gone, the new has come!' From the book of Second Corinthians, I believe."

"I'm impressed." Shannon studied his profile. If he had any questions about her outburst, nothing showed on his face. A class act. "Chapter five and verse seventeen," he said. "Good life verse."

Pop! Boom! Her body started to vibrate with the shuddering steering wheel, and she gripped it hard to control the truck. "Oh no." She felt near tears. "A blowout."

"Pull over." Glen opened the window and waved at oncoming traffic, signaling them to go around.

Of course. She'd been driving on four bald tires since she'd left Walla Walla a year ago. Why today? Shannon pulled onto the shoulder, put the truck in PARK, and jumped out. Glen joined her at the rear of the truck, knelt, and examined the deflated tire.

"It's no wonder." He stood and gave her a look of disbelief, then strode to the front and leaned down. "The tires are threadbare, actually. Do you have any idea how dangerous this is? You need four new ones."

"I don't *want* four new tires." Shannon went to the cab of the truck, reached behind the seat, and began a search for her jack.

"What are you looking for?" Glen pulled his cell from the holder on his belt.

"This!" She held it up as proof that she had everything under control. "I know how to change a tire."

"I'm sure you do, but where is the spare?"

Her triumph died quickly when she was hit with the sickening realization that she'd made use of the spare on her drive from Walla Walla to the Tri-Cities. The tire it had replaced was unfixable.

Glen was chatting on his cell, requesting a tow truck. She paced and felt a strong urge to wring his neck for his take-charge attitude. As he gave instructions to the tow company in his commanding British accent, her agitation increased. Where would she get the money for a tow truck? A new tire?

Glen snapped his phone shut. "That's settled then. They'll be here soon." He replaced the phone into its holder and buried his hands in the pockets of his black wool coat. Then he smiled up at the clear sky. "Cold but lovely day, isn't it?"

Shannon huddled deeper into her corduroy jacket. "Right. It doesn't get much better than this. Are you trying to annoy me?"

He grinned. Then her phone trilled, and she fished it out of the depths of her handbag. "Like a switchboard around here," she mumbled. "Hello?" Shannon inched away from Glen and kept her voice low.

"Shannon, this is Deputy Kroeger."

Chapter 8

Poor Shannon. Glen sneaked another peek at her in the backseat of the tow truck, which reeked of cigarettes and stale coffee. Eyes closed, she rested her head against Truman's shoulder. Her vehicle, hooked to the back of the tow truck, looked as pathetic and battle weary as she did. He wished she was leaning against him again so he could hold her tight. He wanted to protect her from everyone, including Deputy Kroeger. The lawman had brought out the same reaction in Shannon today that he had witnessed the last time they'd encountered him. Some sort of fear.

Glen sighed, struggling to make sense of the interplay between her and the deputy. Something about her upbringing and her parents made her insecure. On her own turf at the store, Shannon didn't appear needy or downtrodden. She was the eccentric young woman with silver rings on each of her slim fingers thoughtfully staring out her shop window, a faraway smile on her pretty face and a flower in her golden hair.

The phone call she'd received before the tow truck arrived replayed in his mind. Shannon's face had grown pale as she listened to Kroeger telling her the box was gone. The news was unwelcome but not unexpected.

Glen had no clue what to do next or how they could locate the box. At the moment there seemed no way to stop the approaching train wreck of Amanda's vengeance.

"Got a cigarette?" The tow truck driver slapped his big paws against the pockets of his shirt.

"I'm afraid not." Glen glanced at Shannon again. The morning had been hard on her. He'd like to take her to dinner, as a friendly gesture, but he was meeting Mike Carroll this evening. "How much longer before we get to the gas station?"

"About five minutes. Why? Your girlfriend sick?"

Girlfriend? Did he and Shannon look like a couple? More like Felix and Oscar from *The Odd Couple*. Glen bit back a laugh, but at the same time, he felt good. "No, she's fine. Just a little tired."

"That dog back there bite?" The driver, with RICHIE embroidered on his torn shirt pocket, glanced in the rearview mirror. "I don't like the way it's lookin' at me."

Too bad Shannon had fallen asleep. She would've jumped to Truman's defense, explaining that the dog was not an "it" but a "he."

"Actually, we suspect he's part wolf." Glen felt privileged that Truman was his friend. "But he's harmless. Perfectly harmless."

Richie frowned and moved closer to the door, as if he was about to bail. "Dog bites me, I'll sue."

"Understandable." Glen hid his grin behind his hand. No wonder Shannon had such fun with her wolf tale. She was positively adorable, even if she was a study in contradictions.

"Here we are." Richie pointed in the direction of the gas station on the corner, and disappointment washed over Glen.

He should be pleased that this jaunt with Shannon and Wolf-dog would soon be over, but he longed for more time with her.

In the gas station office, Richie broke the news to Shannon and him that they needed to replace all four tires.

"No." Shannon shook her head. "Just fix the one that's flat." She wouldn't look Glen in the eye, just fiddled with her purse strap.

"He's right." Glen decided to try sound reasoning again. "You can't keep driving on those bald tires. It's only a matter of time before another one goes."

The mechanic jutted his chin toward Glen and wiped grease from his hands on an oily rag. "You keep those ones on your truck, you're gonna kill yourself. I ain't gonna replace just one. It'll be like committing murder or something."

"Um, let me see." Shannon turned her back toward the men, dropped her purse on a table cluttered with old magazines, unzipped her bag, and rifled around inside. Was she looking for her credit card? "What'll it cost? The four tires—"

"I've got it," Glen said and handed the mechanic his card.

Shannon's head snapped up. "No, no, no. You just told me about Thomas and—"

"Forget it."

The mechanic was already swiping the credit card through the machine while Shannon continued to shake her head. "Glen, please, I'll get new tires next month."

"No, we'll get them right now." He signed the receipt, and the mechanic walked into the garage, shaking his head.

She looked on the verge of tears. "Okay, the truth is, I won't be able to pay you back till next month. So please"—she pointed—"tell that man you've changed your mind."

Glen slipped his hands into his coat pockets and walked toward her. "But I haven't changed my mind."

"Didn't you hear what I said?" She released a jagged breath, then pointed to the clock on the wall. "Besides, we're going to be late opening our shops."

"Consider it a loan." Glen shrugged. "I can afford that for now. And we won't be that late." He'd caught on quickly that she was broke, and the thought of her driving on threadbare tires made him feel sick inside.

Shannon opened her mouth, no doubt to protest, but she instead placed her hand on his arm. "Thank you. I. . .just. . .thank you." Her eyes filled with tears.

What matter the cost? To be able to do something to make the flower child's life easier made him happy.

&.

Shannon pulled her truck into her parking space in the alley. Silently all three of them got out of her truck. Truman went off to sniff along the building. Shannon slipped a glance at Glen. His expression was pensive.

"I don't know what to do," she said quietly. "I need to fix this spice box problem."

He blinked. "It's not *your* problem; it's *our* problem."

"You mean it?" she whispered.

He frowned. "Of course. Despite how I came across when Venus first sold the box, I don't hold you responsible for its loss."

Relief washed through her, and a genuine smile came to her face. Glen wasn't accusing her of wrongdoing. Even better, she didn't have to feel alone.

"I still don't know how to find the box, but I know someone who does."

"Deputy Kroeger?" She stared at him hopefully.

Glen smiled. "Possibly, but I'm talking about the Lord." He reached his hand out toward her. "Why don't we pray and ask for the Lord's help?"

Shannon took his proffered hand, and his fingers closed around hers. While he prayed, she asked God's forgiveness—she couldn't concentrate on anything but the warmth of Glen's grasp.

After they were done, they said good-bye twice, then stood awkwardly beside the back door of Glen's shop. "So then," he said.

Hold me, please.

Without warning, Glen pulled her to himself and hugged her tight. "We'll get through this."

After he'd disappeared inside, Shannon walked to her door on numb legs. A real hug. Glen was so strong and handsome. He smelled so good. She opened her shop, snatched the phone from her desk, and dialed. She was suddenly desperate to hear Allie's voice and get her best friend's insight into the situation. She missed living in the same town as Allie and being able to see her regularly. Smiling, she punched in the phone number. By the fourth ring, she was about to hang up.

"Shannon? I'm here." Allie sounded breathless. "You're calling from the store phone and not your cell. I take it you're still worried it's like putting your head in the microwave?"

"Jury's out." Shannon paced with the cordless, smiling. "I didn't wake the baby, did I?"

"No, our Natalie sleeps like a log." Allie gave a contented sigh. "I'm glad you called. I miss you. What's the latest?"

"I think I'm . . ." . . .*in love.* No way to open a phone conversation with her logical friend. Shannon dropped onto the bench behind the counter and drew two long breaths. What if nothing came of this between Glen and her? Shannon shook her head, refusing to dwell on the negative, cleared her throat, and started again. "When you fell in love with Derrick, how did you know it was the real thing?"

"What? Are you in love?" The panicked pitch of Allie's voice made Shannon giggle. "It's impossible. We talked two weeks ago, and you didn't mention anybody. You didn't fall in love in that short span of time, did you?" She paused. "Well, knowing you, anything's possible. I'm surprised you haven't eloped or something."

"Ha-ha. Very funny. And no, not exactly. It's been a long time coming, and yet it happened in a short amount of time." Shannon closed her eyes. Where should she start? She'd been complaining to Allie for months about the British shopkeeper who nagged her all the time. "I mean, it's somebody I've known for a while. I was always attracted—"

"Don't say it. It's the guy who gives you guitar lessons. The one who helped us move you into the shop because he happened to drive by and notice your beat-up guitar. The one with the motorcycle and leather jacket." Allie laughed. "He sounds like he'd be your type even though you say he's got secrets."

"Oh no. It's not Ray. I mean, he's a great guy, but I don't know why you'd think he's my type."

Allie laughed harder. "He's unconventional and also seems to be a contradiction in personality. Plus he's a musician, that's why."

"Laugh all you want, but it's not him. Ray's like a brother to me." Shannon stood and began pacing again. "So, do you want to guess?"

"Yes. Don't tell me. I like this game." The clang of pots and pans followed Allie's request. "Is it someone you went to school with?"

"Yeah, one of the many who lined up to dance with me," she said sarcastically. "No."

Allie laughed. "Okay then, let me think."

In her mind's eye, she saw Allie multitasking. Thinking, doing chores. The kitchen spotless and her papers in order. Had Shannon not inherited one neat gene? "Are you working on dinner already?"

"Yeah, we're going to have fish tacos tonight. I found a great source of recipes online, and I bought a program for my computer that helps me plan my menus and my grocery lists for a month." More kitchen noises.

Planning meals for a month? Imagine being that organized.

"Is the guy local?"

Shannon stopped chewing the knuckle of her index finger and sighed. "Yes and no. You'll never believe me."

"Yikes, please don't tell me that it's Bozo. He was truly unconventional."

"Bozo?" Shannon frowned. "I don't know anybody by that name."

"The transient guy you allowed to sleep in your store."

"Oh." Shannon laughed. "That was *Bongo*. A sweet soul, just a bit confused. And he wasn't a transient, just temporarily homeless. I let him stay in exchange for painting my office walls. He left some drips, but overall I liked it. Sort of a muted tangerine—"

"Shannon," Allie injected, "you're getting away from the topic."

"Okay, it's not Bongo. And, by the way, he's got an apartment and a job now. He's doing really well."

"Good for him. Now, let me see. Process of elimination. I know it's not the Brit next door. The annoying one who's been haunting you for the past year to—"

"That would be Glen Caldwell." Shannon suddenly felt foolish. She shouldn't have phoned practical, rational Allie. "You know, sometimes people aren't what they seem to be on the outside. Like Venus with her blue-tipped hair. You of all people should know how that is. Remember how you met Derrick?"

"Huh?" Allie's sharp intake of breath told Shannon she'd figured it out. "It *is* Glen Caldwell!" Her tone made Shannon wince. "Oh my heavens, Shannon, if what you've said about him is true, how can you conform to his type? You're…well, you're unconventional. You've got your own way of doing things. You're different. In a good way, of course."

Shannon scanned the kitchen. Her mom would love to hear Allie characterize her as "different." The O'Briens were as different as they came. But was she so different from Glen that a relationship was impossible? And what would Glen think if she invited him into her apartment? People like her parents, Ray Reed, Bongo, and Venus didn't give a second thought to the chaos. But Glen…"Okay, Miss Know-it-all. Does Derrick love you for who you are, or did he ask you to change before he married you?"

"Good point. I guess we all make compromises to make things work." Allie laughed. Ouch! Shannon stopped pacing, pushed the curtain aside, and stared across at the parking lot. Glen's sleek silver BMW was parked in its usual spot, as was her truck. She didn't need a better picture of their differences. She let the curtain fall and began to tell Allie about the missing spice box, Amanda, and the two trips she and Glen had made to find the box.

"So it was stolen?" Allie interrupted her litany.

"Yes." She went on to explain how Glen had put his arm around her when Deputy Kroeger was there and how he'd paid for her tires. "And when we got back, he held my hand and we prayed about the situation. And Allie. . .he hugged me. . .tight."

"That's interesting," Allie said softly. "Very interesting."

Shannon sighed. "Maybe I made too much of today." She dropped into the fat leather chair. "But I've been seeing another side of Glen lately, not just the guy nagging me about cleaning up my shop. He's also kind and generous."

"Sounds like it." Allie cleared her throat. "And really, there's nothing wrong with cleaning up, right? Look what happened when my mom organized your Walla Walla shop. Business picked up."

Ouch again. A double whammy of irritation and hurt shot through Shannon. "It's not like my shop was a disaster area." She pressed her fist against her forehead and closed her eyes. "I think I'd better get going. Take Truman out for a walk before he has an accident on the floor."

"Are you crying?" Allie's voice was full of regret. "I'm sorry. What did I say? I didn't mean to discourage you. Maybe Glen *is* the one. Maybe—"

"I'm not crying. Just a bit choked up. I am so disorganized and can't seem to get my life together. I feel like such a failure."

"Why? Because you're not perfect? Because God is still working in your life? You know what? Everyone has stuff they have to improve. Sometimes God puts people in our lives to sharpen us—iron sharpens iron. And sometimes He gives us people who complement us and fill the places where we're weak."

Ray had mentioned "iron sharpens iron," too. Maybe it was a sign from God that there was hope for her and Glen. "True," Shannon conceded.

"I'm really sorry," Allie said. "I love you so much, and I didn't mean to hurt you."

"It's okay, Allie. And I love you, too. It's fine. Give Natalie a kiss for me, and send Derrick my best."

Shannon hung up and leaned back, staring at an old water stain on the ceiling. Her folks had always let her pursue her passionate interests with single-minded purpose. They applauded her unconventional attitude. If she didn't keep things tidy, they laughed and said it was her self-expression. They accepted her no matter what, but they were the only ones. How had that affected her? Perhaps she was too thoughtless about how she impacted other people. She drew a jagged breath. She was having a lot of trouble accepting herself right now. She didn't really fit in. She'd always have to strive for acceptance.

❧

The pianist at the Left Bank Café played a haunting rendition of a familiar love song. Glen found his mind wandering to Shannon. His thoughts ran the gamut from fondness to a desire to protect her. Was this what falling in love felt like? He'd had other relationships, but no other woman had made him react so strongly in so many ways.

He checked his coat, then located the table where Mike Carroll sat waiting for him. He would listen to what Mike had to say about leasing more space, but things were iffy right now, particularly because of Amanda. Then he would broach the topic of Shannon. He just wished he'd paid more attention when he signed the petition. He approached the table, his hand extended.

"Glen." Mike stood and shook his hand, looking pleased to see him. "Hope you don't mind, but I ordered us appetizers."

"Not at all." They both sat, and a server appeared. "Sir, may I get you a drink?"

"Sure, I'll have a Sprite," Glen said as the rail-thin waiter switched his attention to Mike. "Another drink, sir?"

"Sure, why not?" Mike drained his glass, then scooted his chair closer to the table. "Got a call from Amanda today. The woman's livid, I tell you."

Had Amanda broken her promise? Approached Mike with the petition before Monday? "Amanda's livid most of the time, isn't she?"

Mike let loose a congested laugh. "Spunky."

That's not how Glen would describe her.

The server set down their drinks. "Whenever you're ready to order, gentlemen."

"Later." Mike sent him away with a dismissive hand motion. "All kidding aside, the Franklins carry weight in this town. What Amanda wants, Amanda gets."

She must have some kind of hold over Mike. The certainty of his statement deflated Glen's hope, puncturing holes in his plan to appeal to Mike's lighter side. Glen shrugged. "What is it exactly that Amanda wants?" As if he needed it spelled out.

"Besides you?" Mike chuckled and leered at him, and Glen shifted in his chair uncomfortably. "The other thing she wants is what you want, too, Glen. You want Shannon out of the store next to you."

"I never said that."

"Amanda told me you did."

"That simply isn't true. Either you misunderstood her or she lied to you."

Mike shrugged. "That's what she said. Well, she usually does what it takes to get what she wants."

That was a true statement. He was so deep in thought he hardly noticed the server leave a tray of raw clams. Not his thing. "Mike, what do you know about Amanda?"

"Besides the fact that she's rich as Croesus and she wants to invest in my properties?"

There it was. The hold Amanda had over Mike. She had a way of wriggling her way into greedy pocketbooks. Glen huffed out a sigh. "I mean, what do you know about her family?"

Mike shrugged. "Daddy was rich. Other than that, no clue. They aren't from around here. Moved in about ten years ago." He leered again. "You could have her, you know."

"I'm not interested," Glen stated adamantly.

Mike laughed again. "Can't deny, Shannon is a looker. Shape in all the right places. At least from what you can see of her in those weird clothes she wears. Certainly doesn't show off her assets."

Glen clenched his fists to avoid reaching across the table and popping Mike in the jaw. The obnoxious man lifted his glass and waved it at the server, rattling the cubes, then nodded for another. "C'mon, Glen old boy. Dig in." He slurped a clam off its shell, and Glen's stomach did a backflip.

"This is not about Shannon's looks," he said through gritted teeth. "I believe Shannon is open to my assistance at this point. You've got my word that I'll help her fix up her shop, change her sign." He searched Mike's pale eyes. "Whatever you ask."

Mike summoned the waiter with a snapping finger. When he arrived, Glen gave him a subtle, sympathetic shrug.

"I'll have the Chicken Francese," Mike bellowed. He turned to Glen. "What'll you have?"

Glen shook his head. "Nothing. I ate a late lunch." In reality, he'd lost his appetite.

Mike eyed him. "You sure?"

"Yes."

The server slipped away. Glen put his elbow on the table and leaned toward Mike.

"Now, as I was saying, I can work with Shannon."

"I don't know, buddy," Mike said with his mouth full. "Amanda's been talking to all the store owners, and the majority seem to have complaints about O'Brien's shop. I gotta keep my store owners happy."

Glen wondered if they really wanted Shannon shut down or if Amanda had bullied them like she bullied everyone else.

Mike swallowed loudly. "I can make you happy, too. I'm offering you more space to expand. You've got a successful business."

"To expand means someone is moving out," Glen said, sudden dread making his muscles tense. "Do you mean Shannon?"

Mike shrugged and sat back in his chair, looking at him with glassy eyes. "I haven't made any decisions yet about anything. But if something becomes available, are you interested?"

"Probably not at this time." Especially since he suspected it would be Shannon's space. Besides, at the rate things were going, Glen might be out of business as well.

Mike shook his head. "Well, I've got some advice for you. Take it or leave it."

Glen leaned in closer. There had to be a way out.

"Don't let any woman, I mean *any* woman, mess with your head."

That was laughable coming from a man who allowed Amanda to push him around. "That's it?" Glen asked. "That's your advice?"

"Yeah. You're a clean-cut kid. Well, a kid compared to me. You want to get fat and bald and unhappy? Marry the wrong woman." He leaned in closer. "Money helps, you know. A rich woman with long legs and a nice car."

Like Amanda? Glen shook his head and pushed back his chair. "I've got to go."

Mike shrugged. "The deal still stands, at least for a little while."

As he began to leave, a dapper man in a blue pin-striped suit approached the table.

"Ah, William." Mike stood and shook the man's hand. "Glen, this is William Shepherd. He owns this hotel and several others. William, this is Glen Caldwell. He has an antique store in one of my buildings in downtown Kennewick."

William stretched his hand out to Glen. "I've heard the name. You're the British fellow who sells art deco."

"That would be me," Glen said, shaking his hand.

"Pleased to meet you. I have a friend who bought some pieces from you. Exquisite."

"I'm always happy to hear about satisfied customers." Glen offered an appreciative nod.

"Join me for dinner, William," Mike said, waving at the seat Glen had vacated.

Glen took that as his cue to leave, and it couldn't be soon enough. As he retreated across the room, he massaged the back of his neck and tried to block out the sad lyrics coming from the woman at the piano. A song about lovers saying good-bye.

Short of a miracle, Shannon would have to close down her shop. Would she blame him? What were his options? He could appeal to the other store owners, but Mike was ultimately the one to make the decision, and he had already made it, though he hadn't stated it outright. All thanks to Amanda.

Should he warn Shannon? What good would it do now? If she were forced to close her store, she'd move back to Walla Walla. The thought of not seeing her daily made him feel frantic, even when she made him so confused he couldn't think straight. *Lord, I need wisdom, please.*

The song lyrics broke into his thoughts again. Taunting him.

His heart was in trouble. Big trouble.

Chapter 9

Shannon pulled into the church parking lot on Sunday morning as the radio announcer warned of high-wind conditions the following evening. Low visibility on the roads was expected due to a probable dust storm. She sighed. One of the drawbacks of living in the middle of the desert.

After she'd exited her truck, Shannon caught sight of Venus getting out of her little Toyota.

"Hey, wait up," Shannon called out.

Venus stopped, and Shannon walked to her and opened her arms wide. The teenager's hug was less than enthusiastic, and Shannon stepped back. "Is something wrong?" She took note of the dark circles under her eyes.

"I didn't feel like getting up today." Venus shrugged. "I was up way too late last night." She shot her a covert glance. "I came like I said to support you, and I also invited some friends. Will that make you more nervous?"

"Not your friends. I'm glad they're coming. But Glen said something about coming, and I told him next week would be better. I don't want him hearing my testimony."

"Huh?" Venus finally gave Shannon her full attention. "I don't understand. You're the one who taught me not to judge people. You accept everybody, and you're worried about Glen accepting you for who you are? If he doesn't, he's not good enough for you. Isn't that what you told me? It's something I'm still working on."

Shannon stared, mute. There was nothing worse than people using her own words against her.

Venus rubbed her foot on the ground. "You've accepted me from the beginning. I hope you always will."

"What? Of course I will." And she meant it from her heart. "Take it from me, you shouldn't crave approval, except from God." Words she needed to apply to herself.

"Sometimes God feels very far away," Venus said softly.

"I know how that is. I usually feel like the odd man out. I think I flaunt my differences just to prove. . ." Shannon shrugged. "I don't know. Just to prove I can? And all my life I've had relationships with people I was positive wouldn't reject me." *Many of them people who were lost and broken.*

"I want Louis to accept me," Venus said, her voice filled with longing. "I'm meeting him this afternoon." She blinked away tears. "I feel like he's going to break up with me."

Louis? Shannon tried not to wince. She had met the boy once and didn't like him much. He was arrogant and treated Venus poorly. But Shannon could see there was a certain "bad boy" appeal to Louis.

"Is he from a wealthy family?"

"Not really." The faraway look returned to Venus's eyes. "He works hard to get nice things."

"Works hard doing what?"

Venus shrugged. "I'm not totally sure. He says he does something with his dad."

"Oh." What exactly would that be, and how well did her employee know her boyfriend?

Venus took a deep breath. "My friends are excited to hear you speak. It'll be good. They'll hear your testimony and realize if you could turn your life around, anybody can."

Shannon managed a smile. "That's good. I hope what I have to say will help them." She had prayed that prayer as soon as she'd agreed to get up in front of the congregation, but the reminder of public speaking brought a stab of nerves that hit her square in the pit of her stomach. What could be worse than speaking in front of a large group?

"You will help them." Venus finally smiled. "You helped me even though I don't deserve it."

"What?" Shannon's concerns fled. "What do you mean you don't deserve it? Of course you do. Everybody does." She pulled at Venus's arm. "Come on. Let's go inside."

As they walked up the front steps, Venus slid a glance at Shannon. "Charlie talks to me a lot. He thinks Glen's got a thing for you."

"Really? Ray says that, too. I'm not sure what to think. I know I frustrate Glen out of his mind. I've caused him so many problems, and we are so totally opposite." She opened the church door for Venus. "I think Charlie's got a thing for you, by the way."

"Charlie?" Venus stopped cold in her tracks and shook her head. "He knows I'm seeing Louis. I mean, Charlie's a really good friend. I can tell him anything. He'd never, ever give away my secrets, but Louis. . ."

Other people walked up behind them, and Venus shoved the door open. Shannon pulled off her Native American wrap. "It's precious that you can entrust Charlie with your deepest, darkest secrets. Don't take that for granted. That's how it is with me and my best friends like Ray and Allie. We tell each other the absolute truth."

"The absolute truth." Venus sighed. "I'll save a seat for you with us on the front row." She gave Shannon a genuine hug and walked away.

Shannon looked around at the congregation gathering. She didn't know most of the members well, but all of them had been kind to her. They would be a good audience. If only she could calm her nerves.

Someone tapped her on her shoulder. Shannon whirled around and found herself looking up into Glen's blue eyes.

"It's you." She sucked in a deep breath.

"Indeed." He looked down at himself, then back at her. "At least it was me when I woke this morning." He felt his face and head with his open palms. "As far as I can tell, it's still me."

"Funny," she said. "What are you doing here?"

"Going to church."

"Yes, I can see that, but I told you not to come today." She wanted to run away, but her legs were anchored to the floor.

"If I recall correctly, you didn't tell me *not* to come today. You *suggested* I come next week."

"Yes, okay. So why didn't you?"

"Why didn't I?" His brows lowered into a frown. "I might come next week as well. Why would it make a difference? You're a little snippy this morning."

As more church members entered, Shannon's nerves felt like twisted rubber bands. Not only was she going to speak in front of a bunch of people, that bunch would include Glen. And today he would hear about her past. She held tight to the paper in her hand with the testimony on which she'd worked for weeks. Breakfast churned unpleasantly in her stomach as she reminded herself that she should be proud of what the Lord had done in her life, not worried that it would turn off a man like Glen.

"Shannon?" Glen said.

She took a deep, cleansing breath and looked up at him. Wasn't Venus right? If Glen really liked her, even as a friend, wouldn't he accept her for who she was? Shannon relaxed a smidgen and smiled. "I'm sorry I snapped. I'm nervous about giving my testimony at the end of the service."

"You're giving your testimony? Really?" His frown deepened. "And you didn't want me to hear it? Is that why you didn't want me to come?"

She nodded.

"I thought we were friends. I even know your secret about reading body language."

Was that hurt in his eyes? "We are friends. I'm sorry. I really am nervous." Shame heated her cheeks.

Glen shifted the leather Bible in his hands. The gold on the edge of the pages was worn, attesting to the fact that the book was well used.

Shannon laid her hand on Glen's arm. "I have to go find the pastor. The service is going to start in about twenty minutes, and we have to pray." She opened the door that led to the sanctuary.

Glen hesitated. "Will you come back to sit with me?"

The plaintive tone in his voice sent a pang of regret to her heart. "I'm sorry. I can't. I have to sit up front, and as far as I can tell, the rest of the front row is taken up by Venus, her friends, and the youth group. But you can sit there." She pointed to an empty seat halfway down the third row.

"All right." He smiled. "Go get 'em, tiger. I know you'll do well." Then, with one more backward glance at her, he walked down the aisle. She watched his retreating back. Though he had smiled at her, a wall had formed between them. Her fault. She'd hurt him by trying to protect her own feelings.

I'm not fit for polite society, she thought as she walked through the foyer and down the hall to the pastor's office. Perhaps she could worm her way out of speaking today. She wanted nothing more than to go home, drink tea, and practice her guitar.

As she raised her hand to knock on the pastor's door, someone clutched her arm. "Shannon, I need to talk to you."

She turned and met the gaze of Yvonne, a young woman who had recently begun attending the church and the niece of Joe, the man who owned the gift shop on the other side of Glen's store. Yvonne helped Joe some weekends, and afterward she'd drop by the Quaint Shop to chat—at least that's what Yvonne called it. Shannon called it gossip, which she despised. She looked around now and wished for a way to avoid a conversation. She didn't need anything else to disrupt her balance.

"I'm sort of in a hurry," Shannon said. "I'm giving my testimony today, and I have to talk to Pastor Zach."

"I'll only be a minute." Yvonne left her hand on Shannon's arm and looked at her with a wide gaze that might have been sympathy. "I was surprised to see you talking to Glen Caldwell."

Shannon frowned. "Why?" Did everyone think he was out of her league?

"Listen, Shannon." Yvonne tugged at her arm to bring her closer. "Amanda Franklin is Glen's best customer."

"I know that," Shannon said.

"That means he'd probably do anything to please her."

Shannon shrugged. "I wouldn't think so."

"I don't think you understand," Yvonne said. "Amanda has it in for you."

"That's not news to me," Shannon said. Where was this going?

Someone called Yvonne's name, and she waved. "Be there in a sec!" Then she turned back to Shannon and leaned close. "Just watch your back. My uncle said she wants to get you shut down. She's doing whatever she can."

"Shut down?" The words stung like a slap to her face. No wonder Glen had been telling her to fix up the shop. Confused, she looked Yvonne in the eye. "Why are you blaming Glen? In his own bossy way, he tried to warn me."

Yvonne huffed out a breath and shook her head. "You're not listening.

Glen Caldwell and Amanda are thick as thieves, according to my uncle. That means he must have it in for you, too, don't you think?"

Shannon's breath stopped in her lungs. Was that possible? The look of pity in Yvonne's green eyes, coupled with the surge of irritation toward the gossiping young woman, made her want to run for the nearest exit. She reminded herself to take deep breaths and not allow the young woman's poison to infect her and influence her mind.

Yvonne dropped her hand from her arm. "Just remember, forewarned is forearmed."

Shannon watched as Yvonne sped away. *Like a hit-and-run driver.* Forewarned about what? Seemed to her that the only thing she had to arm was her heart. Still, the damage was done. Yvonne had planted a seed of doubt in her mind. As she knocked on the office door, tears stung her eyes. How would she give her testimony now? Perhaps Pastor Zach and Laurie would let her off the hook.

Chapter 10

Glen smiled as he watched Pastor Zach wind up his sermon, arms flying in all directions as he made his final points. The exuberant minister, in his late fifties like Glen's dad, had a similar personality. Enthusiastic, warm, and inviting. Just like Glen's brother, Thomas. Glen knew he could be charming, but he often felt the friendly, warm personality genes had skipped him.

Once more Glen caught a glimpse of Shannon's shining hair, and he felt flat, like a balloon without air. The hurt he'd felt before church when he realized she hadn't wanted him to hear her testimony surprised him. He had known he was attracted to his flower-child neighbor, but his depth of emotion this morning made him realize he was falling in love with her. If only he could be more like his father and Thomas. Warm and expressive. But wishing wouldn't make it happen, and somehow he had to find a way to reach her. Make her trust him. Prove his love. He'd start today by telling her about his meeting with Mike Carroll. Together they would find a solution.

The pastor closed his Bible and smiled at the congregation. "Now we have a special treat for you. We're honored to have Shannon O'Brien give her testimony."

Glen settled back into his seat. Perhaps what she said today would give him better insight into how she'd become the sweet oddity who'd stolen his heart.

"About a year ago, my wife and I saw Shannon sitting way back there." Pastor Zach pointed to the rear of the church to sounds of laughter. Glen smiled, too. "She was forty-five minutes too early for service." More laughter.

That's the early bird, Glen mused, still watching the back of her head.

"With time on our hands, Laurie and I started to chat with Shannon, and well, you know Laurie and Shannon. They kept chatting and chatting." The congregation laughed, and Pastor shook his head. "Then the two continued to discuss a myriad of topics, among them the value of observing body language."

Glen laughed out loud. Shannon was unique. A very special woman.

"Shannon has a heart for the lost." The pastor smiled down at the front row. "And one thing I'll bet most of you don't know is that while Shannon can talk the ears off a mule, she does not like speaking to groups. Go easy on her." He glanced over the congregation and met Glen's gaze. "So without further ado, I'd like to invite Shannon O'Brien to talk about her life."

Shannon stood and walked to the pulpit with hesitant steps. Glen blinked when he saw her dress. He hadn't noticed earlier because of her coat. The pink outfit had to be retro. A throwback to the sixties, but unlike the baggy stuff she usually wore. This dress showed off her figure like nothing he'd seen before, and he had to quickly remind himself he was in church. He forced his eyes back to her face, then noticed the paper in her hand was shaking. Glen had to stop himself from jumping up and joining her at the pulpit to bolster her courage.

Her eyes met his, and Glen smiled. *You can do it, Shannon*. She averted her gaze quickly, nodded at Pastor Zach, and then adjusted the mic to her height. "Thank you, Pastor."

⁊⁊

Shannon forced her stiff fingers to straighten her notes on the podium. If she survived this without throwing up, she would never offer to give her testimony again. She raised her eyes and looked out over the congregation of two hundred plus. Big mistake. A sea of eyes focused fully on her. Even the most familiar faces looked foreign in her shaken state. She glanced at Glen. He nodded and smiled. She wanted to smile in return, but Yvonne's poisonous words came back into her mind. She looked away and ordered herself to focus. Clearing her throat, she repositioned the mic.

"I can't say I'm thrilled to be standing in front of you. Like Pastor Zach said, this isn't in my comfort zone." She swallowed. "And that's putting it mildly."

"You can do it, Shannon!" Venus called out from the front row. The teens next to her hooted and whistled. The chain reaction of laughter that followed loosened Shannon's tight muscles, and she managed a smile.

"I am a walking miracle." She paused, and the reality of the statement hit her like an electric bolt. *It's true. I really am a miracle, and I should be proud of that.* "I grew up not knowing a thing about the real God. If He existed at all, He was whatever a person defined Him—or her—to be." She inhaled. "My parents taught me to respect every religion, every god; meaning, if somebody believed in receiving wisdom from crystals and amulets and that made them feel good, I should go along and join in so I could understand where they were coming from.

"In one way, that was good." She paused to think. "I mean, I learned to love people and accept them for whatever and whoever they are. But while I agree that we need to live at peace with our fellow man, we should not compromise our own beliefs. The thing was, like so many lost souls, I had no real belief system to use as an anchor, so I was plain confused." She caught Glen's gaze again. His smile encouraged her to continue, but she couldn't smile back.

"My parents were true hippies in that era and continued to maintain that lifestyle after I was born. They lived off the land and grew their own food . . .and drugs. Because of their friends and acquaintances, the police—the *establishment*—often paid visits to my house, but things didn't stop. I saw things that no child should see." She swallowed and shoved bad memories from her mind. "When I was six, my dad collapsed on the dirty linoleum floor. Mom wasn't able to talk, so I had to call 911 myself. After that, my father was arrested and jailed for several years. That was a tough time. I blamed myself, but my parents never held it against me. We didn't have much before then, but after my dad went to prison, my mother and I were officially poor.

"According to my mom, fashion and social acceptance was part of how the 'establishment controlled us.' As a result, I didn't buy the latest fashions. I wore hand-me-downs. All the wrong clothes." She stepped out from behind the pulpit and mock frowned. "But now I make a fashion statement wherever I go, don't you think?"

The congregation's spontaneous laughter paved the way for her to finish. "When Dad got out of jail, things didn't improve. He had trouble finding a job. But the good thing was they stopped the drugs. I saw firsthand what the substance abuse did, and it hurt when I couldn't reach my parents in their haze." Warmth washed over her.

"My junior year I gathered the courage to join the yearbook committee. Interestingly enough, the kids there were an eclectic group that accepted me for who I was." Venus's friends were watching her intently. "There was this one kid named Nick who headed up the yearbook committee." Shannon placed her hand over her heart. "A senior with thick dark hair and warm chocolate brown eyes that could melt snow. He was nice to me." She shrugged. "I thought, 'Here we go. He feels sorry for me.' One day he gave me a small Bible, asked me to read it, and said if I had any questions I should call him.

"I started reading the Bible in order to make a list of questions as an excuse to call Nick." The memory was so clear; Shannon smiled to herself. "But in the midst of my reading, my focus switched to Jesus. I believe that's what Nick intended in the first place. I talked a lot to my folks about all of this. They were fine with it. Called it 'cool.' But I'm still praying that they will come to believe like I do." She paused. "After Nick graduated, I continued to read my Bible. I discovered the most awesome truths. You don't have to clean up your act before coming to Jesus. Even if you're an outsider in the eyes of this world, standing around in silly clothes without direction, Jesus wants you to come to Him."

Shannon chanced a glance at Glen. This time his smile held a touch of sadness. She folded her papers, and Pastor Zach joined her at the pulpit.

In her relief to be done, she didn't hear much of what he said, but she exited to another round of applause and disappeared out a side door. The adrenaline that had given her energy while she talked was giving way to complete exhaustion. She didn't have energy left to stay and talk to anyone. Especially Glen. She grabbed her wrap and purse from the pastor's office where she'd left them and headed outside through the back exit.

Giving her testimony reminded her, like she'd said at the pulpit, that her life was a miracle. Things could have turned out so differently. So wrong. *Thank You, Lord.*

Hot tears began to stream down her face. She had no reason to cry, but she couldn't stop. Digging in her purse for tissues, she took long strides toward her truck. Dark clouds gathered over Horse Heaven Hills. Cold air snaked its way under her wrap, chilling her to the core and making the tears on her cheeks feel like icicles.

As she drove, Yvonne's words wormed their way back into her mind, attacking like poison darts. Had she imagined Glen's warmth at church? The hurt in his eyes when he discovered she hadn't invited him to hear her testimony?

By the time she reached the parking lot behind her shop, the idea of moving back to Walla Walla brought her a sense of serenity. She could give Glen an out. Maybe he'd pound through the wall that divided their shops and expand Caldwell Antiques. One long, clean line of art deco. Amanda would watch with a victorious smile. Heat exploded in Shannon's chest, and her hands shook when she thought of Amanda getting her way.

No! She silently berated herself. Anger released toxins in the body, and worse, anger and unforgiveness caused bitterness to take root in the soul.

Shannon leaned back against the headrest, closed her eyes, and breathed deeply. Emotional extremes weren't her norm. She'd lived through enough of those as a kid. She had to do something to get off this crazy roller coaster. Glen. The moment she'd acknowledged to herself that she was in love with Glen, her simple life had become unbearable. Full of fear and uncertainty. Her past had rendered her incapable of a real romantic relationship, and the sooner she departed, the better.

Her desire to go back to the tranquility of Walla Walla deepened. She'd be welcomed there with open arms by Allie, Derrick, and the rest of her friends.

Shannon opened her eyes and stared at her shop across the way. *Too much trouble*, she thought as she hopped from her truck.

She leaned against her back door while she fished her keys from her purse. The door opened of its own volition. Had she left it open? A cold draft sent a hard chill up her spine. She inched the door open while Truman barked wildly in her apartment above the shop. She gasped and froze. Papers littered the floor. One of her desk drawers stood open. Someone had been in her office. . .and they might still be in the shop.

Shannon backed away and spun around. She dug in her purse for her cell phone.

"911, what's your emergency?"

"My store's been broken into."

Chapter 11

After a pleasant chat with Pastor Zach and Laurie, Glen left church with a single-minded purpose—to find Shannon and try to make things right. It would hurt her, but he had to impart his suspicions regarding Mike Carroll's plan to evict her.

She'd be at her shop, hopefully. He forced himself not to drive like a madman through Kennewick. As he pulled into the alley behind their stores, he noticed a police car next to Shannon's rusty truck. Truman was tied outside her shop, whining.

Glen's heart began to hammer. All manner of horrible thoughts went through his mind. Shannon hurt. Shannon scared. Shannon needing him and his not being there.

He cut the engine, jumped from his car, and hurried to the slightly ajar back door. Before he could enter, he heard a man's voice.

"Ma'am, are you sure you didn't just leave the door unlocked? It doesn't look like it's been jimmied. No damage to the lock."

"I suppose it's possible, but that would only give someone easier access. . . ." Shannon's voice trailed off.

Glen knocked and entered. Shannon and a Kennewick police officer turned to face him. Glen's gaze flew to Shannon's pale face. "Are you all right?"

"Glen. Yes, I'm okay." Shannon pointed behind her. "This is Officer D'Amato. He's come to investigate a break-in."

D'Amato jutted his chin in Glen's direction. "And who is this?"

A myriad of emotions crossed Shannon's face. "My friend, um. . ." She shook her head. "I mean, Glen Caldwell, the guy who owns the store next door."

Didn't she consider him a friend? Glen looked from Shannon to the cop. "What happened here?"

"Someone broke into my store."

D'Amato glanced around with slightly raised brows, and Glen sidled over next to Shannon. "What do you intend to do about this?" he asked.

D'Amato shrugged. "I'll make a report, keep an eye out, maybe drive by on my shift, but without any evidence of anything missing, we can't even be sure someone was in here." He turned to Shannon. "You admitted you may have left the door unlocked."

The cop's tone told Glen the most they could hope for was a written report.

"Yes, but Truman was barking his head off. He never barks that way." Shannon sent a pleading glance in Glen's direction.

"That's true," Glen attested. "I've never heard the dog bark continually in the year Shannon's had her shop next to mine. Perhaps one woof when somebody enters."

Shannon turned her grateful smile on him, and his heart soared. Finally he could defend her, for whatever good it would do.

D'Amato closed his notebook. "I'll do what I can." He took a step into the shop, banged into a totem pole, turned, and caught it before it hit a row of brass candlesticks on the floor. "Sorry. That would've caused a domino effect."

Shannon blushed, and Glen quickly looked away from her. The cop was trying to say that the store was a wreck. "Officer"—he cleared his throat—"if Shannon believes someone broke in—"

"Listen, I *know* someone was in here." Desperation rang in Shannon's voice.

D'Amato looked more than a bit doubtful. "Uh, ma'am, I don't want to sound rude, but how could you tell?"

"Shannon has a great memory," Glen said. "She would know how she left things."

"Like whether or not she left the door unlocked?" D'Amato tucked his notebook into his shirt pocket. "Like I said, I'll do what I can." With a nod, he exited through the back door.

"He's not going to do anything," Shannon said bitterly. "And it's my fault. I'm such a slob."

Glen held his tongue. Trying to say anything right now would be navigating a conversational land mine.

Shannon looked up at him, and he struggled with how to comfort her. Perhaps a change of topic would be best. "Your testimony this morning was touching."

Shannon's shoulders dropped. "Yeah, I bet."

"I mean it, Shannon. You reminded me why I need to get closer to God and trust Him."

"That's a blessing, but I imagine you were shocked."

"Why would I be shocked? Everyone has skeletons in their family closets."

"Not like mine. And that was the cleaned-up version," she said quietly. "I didn't reveal all that happened."

"Who says you should have? You are who you are, and that's more than good enough."

"Good enough? What just happened with that cop"—she glanced around the shop—"just goes to prove it."

"Are you serious?" He'd never seen her so discouraged. He took hold of her arms and pulled her close. "Of course you're good enough." His gaze dropped from her eyes to her lips.

"You're kind, but—"

"Shannon." His patience reached the limit. He couldn't resist her anymore. He leaned down and touched his lips to hers softly. She inhaled, and for a moment he thought she would pull away, but she laid her hands on his shoulders and leaned closer. She felt warm and wonderful and alive.

He wasn't sure who ended the kiss, but when they parted, they stared at each other for a full minute.

"I'm sorry—"

"I'm sorry—"

They spoke at the same time, still looking deep into each other's eyes.

"That was unexpected."

"But nice." Shannon pressed two fingers to her lips and stared down at the floor.

His heart pounded. Their relationship had crossed over the friendship boundary, and they could only go forward from here. Going backward was impossible, at least for him.

Shannon began shoving papers around her desk.

Glen watched her with nothing of value to say. "I suppose you should determine if anything was stolen from your shop. If so, you'll have reason to contact the police again."

She nodded, turned, and walked out into the showroom. He followed as she wandered up and down the crowded aisles, looking lost. "I can't tell." Shannon swung around and met his gaze. "That police officer was right. How would I know if something was missing?" She leaned against the counter. "I know someone was in here. I just don't know how to prove it." She stepped behind the counter and opened the cash drawer. "I checked before. There's no money missing."

"You leave your money in the drawer?" he asked.

"Yes." Shannon blushed. "I think this has something to do with the spice box." She narrowed her eyes. "I have no clue why. It's just my gut feeling."

He nodded. "Maybe someone is still looking for it here. Not everyone knows it's been stolen."

"And Amanda is so concerned about recovering it. I know it's valuable, but her behavior is over-the-top, don't you think?"

The thought had occurred to him, but he had pushed it to the back of his mind. "Could be. Perhaps she doesn't believe us when we tell her it's gone. Meantime, why don't you look around and make sure nothing was taken. I'd help, but I wouldn't be able to tell."

"Are you saying my store is a mess like Officer D'Amato insinuated?"

Based on the set of her lips, there was no safe answer to her question. "I think you're having a reaction to the stress of the break-in."

"I'm having a reaction? What does that mean?"

This was not going well. Glen heard the roar of a motorcycle engine approaching. *Please, not Ray.* He looked at her.

She crossed her arms. "That's Ray."

"I assumed so. Why is he here?" Glen snapped, wishing Mr. Leather Jacket would drive away into the sunset.

"I called him." The roar of the motorbike engine grew louder.

"You called him, and you didn't call me?" What were these emotions boiling through him? He wanted to punch a hole in the wall.

Shannon's glance slid toward him. "Yes, I called him. After I called 911. I. . .I'm not sure why."

Glen's mind was full of ugly thoughts. "How much do you know about him, anyway?"

Shannon's eyes grew wide, and she slammed the cash drawer shut. "You're questioning Ray?" A breath hissed through her lips. "Are you saying you think Ray was behind this break-in? You've got to be kidding. Are you looking at all my friends as suspects? Venus, too? And will you report all of that to Amanda?"

"Report it to Amanda? What are you talking about?" The rumble of the motorcycle engine died.

"You think all my friends are riffraff. Ray happens to be one of my best friends. Like a brother." She paused and slapped her right fist into her left palm. "Yvonne told me horrible things this morning."

Glen heard the sound of footsteps outside. "I didn't *say* your friends are riffraff. And what about what Yvonne said? Yvonne who?"

"Joe's niece. And I know exactly how you feel about my friends. I wish I could trust you, Glen."

Her last sentence hit him like a rock. "I assure you, I'm quite trustworthy."

The back door swung open, and Rebel without a Cause walked in. Shannon stood with her arms crossed. Glen glanced at Ray, who stopped cold, gaze jumping from her to Glen and back again.

"Okay, talk about your awkward entrances. I take it I interrupted something. I can tell by the cold temperature in the room. Should I leave and come back?"

"No," Shannon said.

"Yes," Glen said.

"All righty then. We've got a classic difference of opinions here." Ray leaned against the counter and crossed his ankles. "Shannon, you okay?"

"Of course she's okay," Glen snapped. "She's with me. Do I look like I'm. . .*not trustworthy* to you?"

"Looks can be deceiving," Ray countered and unzipped his leather jacket. He looked Glen up and down. "Still, you're probably all right."

Shannon snorted, and he turned his attention to her. "You sure you're okay?"

She held up her hands. "I'm fine." She pointedly looked at Glen. "I think he was just leaving."

With every muscle in his body tense, Glen kept his anger at bay and simply nodded. "We can talk later."

"Whatever, Glen." Shannon turned her back to him. "Come on upstairs, Ray. I'll make us tea."

Chapter 12

With no memory of driving back to his apartment, Glen exited his vehicle in front of his apartment building, then slapped the car door closed. How had things gone bad so quickly? One moment Shannon was looking to him for protection and responding to his kiss, the next she openly rejected him—in front of Reed. Not trustworthy, indeed. Glen hadn't even had a chance to talk to her about Mike. Maybe he should just let her find out the hard way.

Glen walked into his apartment and flung his keys on the table in the foyer without a care as to marring the expensive marble top. He pulled off his coat and tossed it on the sofa, then kicked off his shoes and left them as is.

"There you have it. A mess." In more ways than one. If he kept this up, his house would look like Shannon's store. But he wouldn't dare tell her that. He went to the kitchen, opened the fridge door, slammed it shut, and opened it again. He drew a breath and snatched a bottle of orange juice from the top shelf. "And I must stop talking to myself."

He reached into the cupboard and knocked two glasses off the shelf. He watched helplessly as they crashed on the tile under his bare feet, sending shards in all directions. *Just great.* He tried to sidestep the mess to get his broom, but a sliver lodged itself into his big toe. The needlelike pain was nothing compared to the pain in his heart. "Forget it. I'll clean it up later."

After an eternal interval of digging out the long splinter of glass, he bandaged his toe and headed back to the living room. There he dropped on the couch and forced himself to take slow, deep breaths.

Shannon. As his anger subsided, reason returned. Today he realized the extent that he'd hurt her in the past with his comments about her store. And to be fair, today he had questioned the honesty of her good friend, Ray. Whether the man deserved her trust or not, Glen should've expected her reaction. Anyone worth their salt would defend someone they considered a friend.

He tried to ignore the spasm of jealousy the thought of Ray brought, but he couldn't. How had Ray managed to become so close to Shannon? Glen couldn't seem to make any progress at all. No matter how hard he tried, he couldn't get things right. If only the spice box would turn up, maybe Amanda would calm down, and he would be able to charm her and Mike into letting things go with Shannon.

At first glance it appeared the missing spice box had caused all the problems that had arisen in the last few days. But in reality, it had only exposed things that were already bubbling under the surface. Festering sores, like Amanda's jealousy of Shannon and Glen's jealousy of Ray. He had to face the fact that Amanda would probably proceed with her petition whether the spice box turned up or not. The only thing he could hope to gain by the return of the box was possibly to keep Amanda's business. And if it weren't for his brother and Glen's outlay of money for Amanda's last order, he would not be interested in keeping that.

Still, the missing box could bite Shannon. She could be sued. So. . .were his and Shannon's suspicions warranted? Did the break-in have something to do with the spice box? And why today? The spice box wasn't there—but who else knew that for sure besides himself and Shannon? Nothing made sense.

There was something more at stake than the spice box. What? Art deco was his forte, and spice boxes were from an earlier period. But he recalled the boxes sometimes had a hidden compartment. Was it possible there was something hidden in Amanda's? Something valuable she wanted to recover? Was she behind the break-ins? How could that be possible? She would have had no way to get the addresses of the homes where the spice box had been. He shook his head. That didn't make sense. He propped his feet on the coffee table. "Think," he whispered, not unaware that he was speaking aloud again.

Glen clamped his hands behind his head and squeezed his eyes shut. His thoughts continued to travel back to Shannon's kiss and how it felt to hold her. His fingers itched to pick up the phone and dial her number. As he reached for his cell to call her, it rang in his hand.

He recognized his father's number and quickly pushed the button.

"Dad! Is everything all right?"

"Yes, I just got in. I went to pick Melissa up from the airport. Thomas will be arriving with the children in a week or so after he gets things settled in Haiti. That's what I called to tell you."

"Thank you, Dad. How's Melissa?"

"She'll see a doctor this week."

"I'll be praying."

"I know you will, son." His father paused. "Melissa told me what you did for them. The money, I mean."

Glen sighed. "I didn't want them to tell you." Last thing he wanted was for them to discover he'd borrowed the money.

"I've asked the Lord to bless you for your generosity. Our church will be taking donations for them as well. And we have some friends who are starting a community fund-raiser."

They chatted a few minutes more, then said their good-byes. Glen pushed the OFF button on the phone. At least one thing he'd done recently had turned out well. Now if he could just fix things for Shannon.

After Shannon and Ray drank their tea and ate salads, she washed the dishes while he sat back in the kitchen chair with his arms behind his head. Truman lay quietly at Shannon's feet. He wasn't nearly so enamored with Ray as with Glen.

"Nice dress," Ray said, pointing at the outfit Shannon had worn to church. She looked down. "Thank you. Vintage sixties."

"So are you ready to talk now?" Ray asked. "You've been oddly quiet, and for once I got more than a few words in edgewise."

"Ha-ha." Shannon couldn't help but smile.

He tapped his fingers on the tabletop. "Why was the air thick with tension between you and Caldwell when I walked in today?"

She placed the washed teacups in the drainer and turned to face him. "Too many things. Glen kissed me, for one. And he was asking questions about you."

"About me? What kind of questions?"

"He insinuated you might be behind the break-in and wondered how well I know you."

Ray nodded. "Is that such a bad thing? Seems like he's just trying to look out for you, don't you think?"

"Don't you go all bossy and superior on me, too, Ray."

"Bossy and superior?"

"Yes. Like Officer D'Amato who didn't believe me. He kept looking around at the mess and wondering how I could know if *anything* was missing." She rubbed her arms. "What a morning. And I can't believe I let him kiss me."

"The police officer?"

Shannon glared at Ray.

A tiny smile crossed his lips. "Okay, let's talk about the kiss and get it out of the way so I can get you to concentrate on the break-in."

She frowned. "What do you mean?"

"I'm not surprised Glen kissed you. Caldwell looked madder than me when Amanda was outside railing at you. Hey, my temper has gotten me into trouble in the past, but even I conceded defeat when I saw the look in Caldwell's eyes."

Shannon sighed. "I don't know what to believe anymore. I found out some things this morning." She related her conversation with Yvonne.

"Ignore gossip. It's healthier." He reached across the table and squeezed her face like she was a kid. "Why don't you simply ask Caldwell if it's true?"

Shannon opened and shut her mouth. "I did, in a roundabout way. But I was getting too angry. Then you walked into the shop."

Ray's expression grew serious. "So, tell me about the break-in."

"I'll start with everything leading up to it." She shared the events of the past few days. Ray moved closer to the edge of his seat, his eyes alight like she'd never before seen them.

"Two break-ins," Ray repeated, "and both occurred where this box was supposedly located."

Shannon nodded, and her stomach churned. "Just talking about it scares me."

Ray scrubbed his hand over his five o'clock shadow. "How do you know someone broke into your place?"

"Well, for one thing Truman was barking when I got home. Also, stuff on my desk had been moved around and the drawers opened." She paused. "Of course no one else would be able to see that."

"And you say the lock wasn't jimmied?"

"No. But someone who knew what they were doing could do that, right?"

He shrugged. "It's possible. Or the key was stolen from your shop. Or someone who had a key came in. Hey, even I have a key to your shop."

She had to concede the truth to his statement. She had copies of her key all over the place. She'd given it to a number of people, as well as having numerous copies for herself. Since things were always getting misplaced, she wanted to make sure she was never locked out. "I think this had something to do with the spice box."

"Hmmm." He tapped his fingers rhythmically against his leg, and a deep line formed between his brows.

"Gee, you're acting like more of a cop than that D'Amato guy." Shannon laughed, waiting for him to join her, but Ray only frowned harder.

"That was the name of the officer who came?"

She nodded.

"Listen, do you know where Venus was this morning?"

Where had the mellow guitar player gone? "You think she did this? No way. She was at church with me this morning. Ray, I'm not kidding. You're acting all weird on me. What's up with that? I was fishing for a little feedback, but—"

"I'm just thinking." Ray smiled at her, but his demeanor wasn't the Ray she knew. Glen's question about how well she knew Ray flashed through her mind, and she forced it away.

"I think there's something about that spice box. Maybe something hidden in it." She paused, unsure of what she was thinking. "Some spice boxes have hidden compartments. They were used to stash valuables."

Ray stared at her intently. "Valuables, huh?"

"Yes. I hate to be suspicious, but I wouldn't put anything past Amanda Franklin." She met Ray's eyes. She refused to cast aspersions on Ray or Venus. She couldn't possibly be that wrong about the people she cared for. "Do you know Amanda?"

"Not personally. I'm familiar with the Franklin family. I'd never met her face-to-face until she verbally abused me."

"I was just wondering if. . .well, she wants that box back badly."

"You're wondering if she's behind the break-ins, including yours today?"

"If there was a break-in here. I'm even beginning to doubt myself." Shannon leaned toward Ray. "What are you thinking? Why are you acting so serious?"

"It's just that. . ." Ray rubbed his head as though trying to force a thought to the fore of his mind. "You might say I'm interested in crimes." He released a long breath and picked up his guitar, holding it against his chest more like a shield than an instrument. "I read about things like unsolved crimes. Keep files of things." He shrugged. "It's probably nothing." He strummed a few chords.

Shannon identified the tune as "Lyin' Eyes." Would Ray lie to her?

"Anyway, I might talk to a few people." He stilled the guitar strings with his open palm.

"If you talk to Venus, don't accuse her of anything. She feels badly enough that she sold the box."

"Don't worry." Ray lifted his hand. "You know me, Shan. I wouldn't do that." He winked. "I'd best get going, but call me if you need anything. Any hour. Got that?"

Shannon nodded, feeling strangely alone.

Ray's deep frown returned as he stood and placed the guitar on the table. "Keep Truman with you, okay?" He leaned down and ran his knuckles over her head. "Hey, knucklehead, if the Brit kisses you again, I say go for it."

Shannon blushed, and Ray laughed. He turned and left, boots clumping down the stairs. "I'll lock the door behind me," he yelled up to her.

She peered out her kitchen window that looked out over the back alley. Ray mounted his Harley and drove away. Truman stood beside her, whining, and she dropped to her knees and hugged him. "I'm glad you're here. You aren't confusing at all like everyone else."

Shannon was filling Truman's water bowl in the kitchen when she heard another vehicle pull into the alley and jumped to her feet. Maybe it was Glen, returning to talk to her. She peered out the window again, and her heart beat faster. Not Glen, but Amanda. As she stepped from her car, Shannon searched her own heart. What was it about Amanda that made her feel like a bag lady? Probably because everything about her was expensive and classy, like the fur coat that billowed around her leather high-heeled boots as she headed toward Shannon's back door.

Shannon twisted the rings on her fingers, then straightened her shoulders, brushed imaginary lint from her dress, and headed down the stairs.

She opened the door wide, and a cold breeze rushed past her, shuffling papers on her desk. "I saw you coming. Does Glen know you're here?"

"Glen? Why would he know I'm here?"

Amanda looked Shannon up and down, but she made no move to shove her way in, and Shannon didn't invite her. Behind Shannon, Truman growled low in his throat.

"Why are you here?" she asked.

"I want my spice box back."

Just like that. No niceties. No hellos. "I don't have it," Shannon said.

"You don't have it, or you're just not giving it to me?" Spittle gathered in the corner of Amanda's mouth. "How could you find anything in that rat's nest you call a store?"

Shannon tilted her chin. She refused to be intimidated. "You can ask Deputy Kroeger of the Benton County Sheriff's Department. He's aware it's missing."

Amanda gasped and backed up a step, nearly losing her balance. "You got the police involved without my permission?"

"Your permission? Why would we need your permission? He was a deputy investigating the break-in at the house from where the box was removed."

"You're telling me the box is gone?"

Oops. Shannon had let the cat out of the bag. Glen hadn't told Amanda yet. Big mouth.

Amanda hefted her expensive leather bag on her shoulder. "If I don't get that box back, losing your business will be the least of your worries." Before Shannon could answer, Amanda whirled on her heel and stalked away.

Losing her business? Was Amanda threatening her? Fear trickled down her back. She shut the door and sank down onto her squishy leather chair. She wasn't the only one who was scared, though. Amanda was terrified. There was definitely something about that box that scared her. And why was Amanda here today, asking about the box, when she'd given Glen until Monday to find it?

Shannon tapped her head with her fist. She needed to go somewhere to think—to be alone with God. And she knew where she could do that. The place she'd gone many times when she was young.

Chapter 13

Shannon's battered truck was parked in its usual place when Glen pulled into the alley. His first reaction was to go rushing into her store, yank her into his arms, and kiss her soundly. But given their last conversation, she'd be more likely to haul off and slug him than to welcome his advances.

He walked into his office, dropped his briefcase on his desk, then went into the showroom where he greeted Charlie with a weary wave.

"Thanks for opening the shop today."

"I'd rather be here than at school."

"Have I gotten any calls?"

"No calls."

"Not even from Amanda?" Glen had expected her to be on the phone nagging him today.

Charlie shook his head. "No, she hasn't called." He grabbed a cloth, turned his back, and got to work dusting.

Frowning, Glen studied him for a moment. Charlie was edgy lately. Could it be that Venus wasn't responding to his overtures? Glen opened his mouth to ask if he wanted to talk, but his cell rang. He yanked it from his pocket and looked at the number on the display screen. It was Amanda. As if mentioning her name had made her call.

"Hello," he said as he walked back to his office.

"I'm calling to give you one more chance." The tone of her voice was chilly.

He sat in his chair asking the Lord for wisdom. "One more chance for what?"

"I want that box, and I want it now."

Glen felt all the frustration of the last week bubbling in his head. "I don't have it. It was stolen. What can I do?"

"Shannon told me you'd talked to the police about the box."

"What? When did you talk to Shannon?"

"Our business relationship is over, Glen. I want my money back. I will arrange for my credit card company to take back my payment."

Glen lost his battle for civility. Amanda's games wearied him. He was sick and tired of being beholden to her. Tired of the way she treated Shannon. "As far as I'm concerned, our relationship is over already. It was over when you broke your word to me. You told me you'd wait until today to talk to Mike about Shannon. But when I met with Mike Friday night, I discovered you'd already spoken with him."

The empty air between them made him wonder if Amanda had hung up.

"I'm not going to apologize," she barked. "This is your fault. Your fault for encouraging that. . .person next door. Don't expect any sympathy from me. And what if I had waited to talk to Mike till today? Would you have been ready to hand over the box?"

"We don't have the box. And Mike has nothing to do with that. You're not making any sense at all." For the first time in his life, Glen wanted to pick up something heavy and break a window. "I have to wonder what's so valuable about that box that you are ready to sever relationships and punish the innocent."

She gasped. "This conversation is over."

As the phone clicked in his ear, Glen knew for certain that he and Shannon were right. Amanda wanted the box for more than just its antique or sentimental value. He sighed. He had burned the bridge between himself and Amanda, and oddly enough, he felt a great sense of relief. Not that there was any logic to that feeling. He'd lost his best client, and he needed the money. *Lord, I need a miracle. I'm trying to do the right thing. Please bless my efforts.*

Now a new worry nagged at him. How far would Amanda go to protect whatever secret the box held?

Glen pushed to his feet, fueled by urgency to find Shannon. He went to the back window and peered out at the parking lot. Shannon's truck was no longer in its usual spot. He grabbed his coat, poked his head into the showroom, and called out to Charlie. "I'm going next door."

Charlie looked up from dusting and stared, as though his mind were a million miles away. "Is this about the spice box?"

"Sort of." Glen headed for the front door, stopped, and called over his shoulder. "If I'm not back before closing time, please lock up."

Charlie nodded, and Glen exited, hurrying next door.

He stepped into Shannon's shop, and Venus spun around and gasped. "Oh, Mr. Caldwell, I nearly had a heart attack. You know someone broke into the shop on Sunday."

"Yes, I heard all about that." Glen tried to smile. "Sorry I frightened you."

"You didn't exactly frighten me, it's just that I'm jumpy, that's all."

Whatever that meant. He looked more closely at the girl. Her eyes weren't as sparkly as normal and seemed sunken in her eye sockets.

"Are you all right, Venus?"

She blinked and clasped her hands together. "I'm fine—why? Why would you ask?"

"Just that you. . .well, no matter. Just being polite."

"I'm fine." She looked everywhere but at him.

"All right then, I need to find Shannon. Do you know where she is?"

Venus sucked in a breath. "She left a few minutes ago with Truman. She won't be back till tomorrow."

"Tomorrow? Where did she go?"

Venus rubbed her hands over her spiky hair. "I—I don't know if I'm supposed to tell anybody where she went."

"Why not?" Glen had a strong desire to take Venus by the shoulders and shake the information out of her. "Shannon didn't go in search of that spice box again, did she?"

"Um, no. Not that. No."

"Listen to me," Glen said. "You must tell me where Shannon went. I'm worried about her safety." After all the unusual activity surrounding the spice box, he'd reached his breaking point. He had to see Shannon and know for himself that she was safe.

"Her safety?" Venus chewed her fingernail.

Another thought occurred to him. "Is Shannon with Ray Reed? Is that it?" Holding his breath, he waited.

Venus wagged her head. "No way."

"Please."

"Well, okay then." Venus twisted her slim fingers. "She went home. To her parents' house. To hike in the mountains." The words tumbled out of her mouth. "But I wasn't supposed to tell. Shannon wants to be alone. She's been through a lot."

Her narrow-eyed perusal indicated that she thought he was partly the cause of Shannon's problem. She was probably right, but he chose to ignore the silent communication.

"Where's home?" he asked gently. "I know her family is from Benton City, but I need the address."

Venus studied him for a moment, sighed, then went to the counter and scribbled down an address.

"If she fires me for doing this, will you promise to give me a job?"

Glen inhaled and realized what he'd asked of the girl. "If I am financially solvent after all of this is resolved, and if Shannon suddenly becomes someone other than herself and fires you for caring about her, then yes. I will give you a job."

"Thank you," Venus said. "Now I know you really love her."

He wasn't sure he followed her logic, but she was right about his feelings for Shannon.

He thanked Venus for the address, hurried to his car, loaded the information into his GPS, and headed toward Benton City. He tried to call Shannon's cell, but instead of ringing through, it jumped right to voice mail. She had her phone turned off. At least she'd taken Truman with her.

"Lord, protect Shannon from all harm. Please."

Amanda wouldn't send somebody to cause bodily injury. . .would she? Glen's heart sped. He couldn't answer his own question.

Chapter 14

After a long trek around town that included a hike along the Yakima River, Shannon arrived back at her parents' double-wide, trailed by Truman whose tongue hung from his mouth. The ache in her muscles from the strenuous hike felt good. She savored the cold air against her skin. The wind was picking up, the prelude to the dust storm.

"Let's sit." She dropped to the ground next to an arthritic oak tree in the backyard and snuggled up against the dog. The exercise had been exhilarating, but it hadn't cleared her head like she'd hoped it would. So many issues crowded her mind, and they were intertwined in each other, like wheels within wheels.

She was losing her shop. After her confrontation with Amanda, she knew it was inevitable. That fact should be upsetting her more, but it wasn't. She'd be relieved to have the drama over with. Now other issues were at the forefront. Amanda was the most threatening of all. What if Amanda sued? Even with insurance, that would be a financial disaster. Shannon shivered. There was something about Amanda that gave her the creeps.

And what about Ray? Why had he suddenly changed so? Was Glen right? Was there something odd with Ray? Shannon shook her head. No, not possible.

She closed her eyes and sighed. She had to look at the bright side. Perhaps by leaving Kennewick, she could regain her self-confidence and return to the person she'd been in Walla Walla. She would leave behind most of the things that bothered her so much, including having a shop next to Glen's.

Glen. Everything always came back to him. Truth be told, she didn't want to leave, but maybe they would have a better chance at love if she weren't next to him making his life miserable. Her heart squeezed in her chest. How had her feelings for him spiraled so out of control? She'd had a thing for him since the day they'd met, but now it was like her mind shut down and her heart had taken flight on its own. And that kiss. She touched her index finger to her lips. She'd never felt that much emotion in her entire life.

She took a deep breath and stared upward. White clouds raced each other across the blue sky. She drew her knees to her chest, wrapped her arms around her legs, and bowed her head. "Lord, please give me guidance. I will do whatever You will for my life."

Truman plopped his head against her shoulder and whined.

"I know, buddy. You love Glen, too. But how can it be? Can you imagine what he'd think if he saw this place?" Shannon got to her feet and brushed dirt off her pants.

Her mother's flock of scraggly chickens scattered at her movement, running pell-mell in all directions, just like her emotions. Truman whined again.

"Yep, I know you're thirsty." She filled his bowl next to the trailer with water from her bottle.

The sound of a car engine drew her attention from her morbid thoughts. Who would be visiting her parents? Hopefully Deputy Kroeger wasn't making good on his promise to come by. Shannon hurried around the corner of the trailer, leaving Truman slurping water. She caught her breath and skidded to a stop. The sleek silver BMW rolled to a stop, and Glen exited his car, smiling.

"Glen! What are you doing here?" This was worse than Deputy Kroeger. She wanted to sink into the ground. She wasn't ready for him to see where she had grown up. She'd wanted time to warn him. But, she reminded herself, this might be a good test. Would he look down his nose at her?

"I can explain," he said just as Truman rounded the corner behind her. Without warning he went ballistic, bounding toward Glen at a full gallop. Shannon opened her mouth to tell Glen to brace himself, but didn't have time. Truman pounced, and Glen went down hard, ending up on his back with the dog on top of him.

"Truman, no!" Shannon ran to Glen's side and tried to shove the excited dog aside. "Back off, Truman. Sit!"

The dog glanced at Shannon, then back at Glen.

"Sit, Truman," Glen said.

Still panting, Truman backed away and obeyed.

"He won't even listen to me anymore when you're around," she griped. "Are you okay?"

Glen groaned dramatically and eyed her from under half-closed eyelids. "I think I dislocated my back."

For some reason, all her fears and worries melted away. "No you haven't, you big baby. You deserve that after all the trouble you've been."

"Trouble? I've been trouble?"

"British invasion." Shannon held out her hand. "Now get up." He grabbed her hand, but as she tried to haul him up, he pulled her down, and she landed on her side next to him. Two chickens cackled as they ran past. Truman licked Glen's ear, and he shoved the dog's head away.

"You deserved that," Shannon said, straightening his glasses.

"Indeed. And now I want to apologize for anything and everything I've done to make you mad at me. And anything and everything I will ever do."

"Anything and everything, you say?"

"Yes. Absolutely."

He still held her hand, and he made no effort to let go or to move. She savored the warmth of his touch.

"All right," she said. "Is that why you're here? To apologize?"

"Partially. I need to tell you that I saw Mike last Friday night and he—"

"Wants to kick me out of my store?"

"You knew about that whole thing?"

"Sort of put it all together after Amanda visited me." Shannon's heart felt light. Glen wasn't hiding anything from her. Ray was right that she shouldn't have listened to Yvonne's gossip.

"She did what?"

"I was planning to come back and tell you. I let it slip that the box really is missing. And I also told her that Kroeger knows, and she totally overreacted to that."

He pushed a strand of hair off her face. "That's what worries me and why I'm here. I don't know why she's so frantic."

Shannon felt the warmth of his care. "Thank you for that, but you could have called me." She patted her cell phone in her pocket.

"It's turned off," he said.

She yanked it out of her pocket. "Oh that's right. I didn't want to be bothered."

He took it from her and turned it on. "Give me your word that you won't turn it off again until all this is over."

"Okay. I promise." His worry was contagious, yet it felt so good to know he cared. "Why were you worried about me?"

"Too many break-ins. Then I talked to Amanda this morning and she's—"

"Threatening us," Shannon finished.

"Yes. You're finishing my sentences today."

She stared down into his blue eyes—she could get lost in those eyes. Then she waved her hand in a wide, sweeping motion. "This is how I grew up. In a rusty trailer, surrounded by chickens and a chaotic mess. I was so scared for you to see it all."

"Come here," he whispered as he put his other hand around her neck and gently pulled her toward him. "I like you for you. I don't care how you grew up or where you came from."

Her lips had just brushed his when the door to the trailer squealed open. Shannon jerked away from Glen and turned in time to see her mother step out onto the rickety wooden deck that ran the length of the trailer. Five cats followed her out the door. Her feet were bare, even in the cold weather.

"Wowzers, look at you kids, playing in the dirt." Mom laughed. "Hey, don't let me interrupt you. Shannon's father and I have been known to—"

"We're not playing, Mom. Truman knocked him over, and I'm helping him up."

"Call it what you want to. That's cool." Mom laughed again.

Shannon hopped to her feet, and Glen followed suit, although at a slower pace, rubbing his back.

"Shannon, baby, where are your manners?"

Shannon huffed out a breath. "Glen, this is my mother, Lois. Mom, this is Glen Caldwell."

Glen brushed off his hands, walked over to the deck and up the stairs, circumventing pots of dead flowers, and held out his hand, but Mom ignored it and gave him a warm hug instead.

Shannon watched, unable to move, fighting total embarrassment. What was Glen really thinking?

"Lois, it's my pleasure. You two look like sisters," Glen added.

"Hear that, Shanny-girl?" Mom smiled her way. "We look like sisters."

"I agree, Mom."

"Why don't you both come inside?"

"Mom—" Shannon felt panic clutch her stomach. What would Glen think when he saw how they lived?

"I think it's a brilliant idea," he said.

Chapter 15

Glen followed Shannon and her mother through the front door, right into the living room. Shannon's demeanor had changed like lightning, and he thought he knew why. He scanned the shabby, cluttered room and the dish-piled kitchen sink and counters, then caught her watching him. She averted her eyes. She hadn't wanted him to see the mess.

Shannon's cell phone began to trill in her pocket, and she pulled it out and answered it. "Excuse me," she whispered and left the room.

"So, Glen, have a sit down," Lois said. She looked around, then laughed. "Oops, it might help if I clear off one of these chairs." She began flinging magazines and papers to the floor.

Shannon returned with a backpack slung over her shoulder. "I have to go."

Lois straightened and stared at her daughter. "Why, sunshine?"

Shannon met Glen's gaze. "Venus called. She's sick."

"She didn't look well when I saw her this morning," Glen said. "Would you like me to drive you?"

"No, that's fine."

"Glen can visit with me for a little while," Lois said.

Glen was loath to let Shannon go off on her own, but good manners dictated he at least be polite and stay for a little while.

"Please keep your phone charged and on," Glen said.

"Okay," she said as Glen followed her to the door and brushed her shoulder with his hand. Her muscles were tense.

"You can kiss her good-bye," Lois chirped. "Kissing is good for the soul."

"Mom!" Shannon shut her eyes and groaned.

Glen laughed, leaned over, and kissed Shannon's head. "Please be careful," he whispered. "And don't worry. I think your mother is charming."

He sensed some of her tension leave, and her lingering look made him feel warm to his toes. "Thank you, Glen."

"Baby doll, you be careful. The wind is picking up, and you know how those dust storms are."

"I will, Mom." She snapped her fingers at Truman. "Come on, boy. Let's go."

He watched until she was in her truck; then he turned to face Lois.

"Sit. Make yourself comfy."

Glen dropped onto the threadbare sofa. "I'm sorry I came unannounced."

She waved her hand. "The best kinds of visits are unexpected." Lois struck a match and brought two candles to life. "My Shannon. She's special, you know."

The candle scent drifted past his nose, and Glen fought the temptation to float off to sleep. "It's been quite a day. Exhausting really."

"I saw stress written all over your face. Shannon's, too. That's why I broke out the candles. Lavender. A scent to soothe the soul," she said with a smile.

Lois's skin, weathered by the sun, didn't hide her fine bone structure and beautiful features. "Yes, soothing, thank you."

"Make yourself at home. You need something to eat?"

"No, thank you," he said hurriedly. Lois might cook like Shannon—bean sprouts and tofu. Not that there was anything wrong with veggie food, except that he disliked it intensely.

Lois pulled up a chair, then sat. "How long have you known Shannon?"

"A little over a year. Since she opened her shop, actually, which is next door to mine." If Shannon had told her mom anything about their relationship, it didn't show on Lois's tranquil face. Her smile remained, and she nodded.

"And how long have you two been in love?"

Her expression didn't change a bit. Was she serious, asking such a personal question? Glen continued to stare at her, mute.

Lois's smile softened. "Okay, that's cool. You'd rather not say." She shrugged. As she watched him with the same disarming hazel eyes as Shannon's, he knew she saw right through his detached facade. He wasn't sure why, but he suddenly felt the need to talk.

"I don't know when it happened or how it happened. One minute we were at each other's throats, figuratively speaking, and then—"

Lois slapped her hand on the crowded coffee table, and Glen jumped. "That's adorable. Isn't that always the way? John and I met in Berkley." She pointed over her shoulder. "John's got a job interview," she said. "Too bad you can't meet him. Anyway, back then his hair was way down past his shoulders, and I was still a snob from the East Coast." She sighed, a faraway look in her eyes. "But he finally got to me. Had me questioning my focus on the material things in life. And politics?" She waved her hand. "I didn't give a hoot about that till John woke me up." Lois shook her head. "I just love that man," she said as though she couldn't help herself.

He found himself wishing he could be as transparent as Lois. Acceptance emanated from the woman, filling the room thicker than the lavender scent coming from the candle. No wonder Shannon was a loving soul. "So then, you think there's hope for opposites, do you?" He looked at her expectantly.

She gazed at him for a long moment. "I know what you want. You want love to be logical, right?" She laughed. "You've got a lot to learn, Glen Caldwell. That's what head over heels means. Kind of like losing your mind.

BOXED INTO LOVE

Losing your heart. Taking risks and jumping off cliffs."

"Even when one should know better."

"Yes! Especially when one should know better." Lois moved to the very edge of her seat. "Or it's not true love." She took a deep breath and squinted at him with intensity. "It's like Truman. He doesn't do the math. He sees you, wags his tail, licks your face. . .maybe even knocks you to the ground. He's thrilled just because you walked into the room. That's how love should feel."

Lois's roundabout conversation sounded so much like Shannon, Glen wanted to smile. He could make the argument that they weren't simple animals, but Lois was on a roll, and he didn't want to contradict her.

"I'm not suggesting we're dogs, if that's what you're thinking."

She was as perceptive as her daughter. He laughed. "That's precisely what I was thinking." He smiled at the gentle woman sitting in front of him.

"Do you believe like my Shannon?" Lois asked, catching him off guard.

"What do you mean?"

"The Bible?"

"Yes," he said.

"That's good. That's very good." She nodded her head gently, and her gaze became distant. "Lately John and I have been reading a Bible and. . ." She stared directly at Glen. "Sometime we must have a talk."

"I would like that very much. I—"His cell phone rang. "Excuse me,"he said.

"Oh, you go on," Lois said. "But using those contraptions is like sticking your head in a microwave."

So that's where Shannon got her theories. He laughed and glanced at the screen. No number was displayed, but he decided to answer just in case. "Hello."

"If you want the box, follow my directions to the letter."

Chapter 16

After seeing Venus off with some aromatherapy oils to inhale, Shannon settled at the store counter with a mug of herbal tea, munching a handful of almonds and raisins. Almost closing time. Things were slow today, no doubt because of the weather. The wind had picked up, and the predicted dust storm was beginning. But nothing could diminish the slightly giddy happiness she felt as she thought of Glen on the ground, Truman's seventy-eight-pound body hovering over him, and then the almost kiss. He had come because he was worried about her. She was tempted to call him on her cell phone to ask if he had finally escaped her mother's hospitality.

Amazing that things could go from bleak to hopeful in such a short time. And all because of an almost kiss. No, it wasn't the kiss; it was because she knew for certain Glen cared.

Six o'clock. Time to shut things down. She locked the front door, counted the cash drawer, then walked back to her office. Headlights winked in the alley, and she went to the window and stared out through the cold pane. Hard to see in the dust driven by the wind, but it looked like Glen was back. She was going to see him. She wanted to finish that kiss.

Pulse racing, she ran upstairs to the bathroom with Truman close on her heels. She brushed her teeth, fixed her braid, then swiped on lipstick.

"You be a good boy," she said to Truman before closing her apartment door. She ran out her back door, hesitating only a second to ask herself if Glen would interpret her visit the wrong way. No, why should he? He started it.

She raised her fist to knock when the door flew open. Glen stood there with a deep frown on his face, holding a briefcase. "Shannon, I'm glad you're here. I was going to call you."

Shannon lost her smile. By the look on his face, she knew she wasn't going to get her kiss now. "What's wrong? Amanda again?"

Glen shook his head. "Not Amanda. I don't want to scare you, but I received an anonymous call. The man told me to meet him this evening at Columbia Park. He's got the spice box."

"What?" Shannon pressed her hand to his arm. "That means it's not Amanda?"

He shrugged. "Not unless she wants money and she's been bluffing. I guess anything is possible."

"You're not going, are you?"

"I am. He'll give me the box in exchange for three thousand dollars. And we'll be done with this, once and for all." Glen's voice was matter-of-fact and void of emotion.

"And you believe him?" Shannon shook her head. "You're not thinking straight. He'll take your money and run. You'll be out three thousand dollars and still have no spice box to show for it. Or worse, he'll hurt you first, then take it all. I don't blame you for not calling the police, but in this case it might be best." She took a deep breath. "This is insane. Our roles have reversed. For once I'm being sensible and you're acting crazy."

"I have to go alone. He—he made a threat against you."

"Against me?" Shannon held her hand to her thudding heart.

"If I called the cops, he warned he would hurt you." Glen cupped his hand around the back of her head and pulled her to him. He kissed her hard, then backed up. "I came here only to get the money from my safe. Please go up to your apartment and lock the door. You've got Truman to protect you."

"How can I let you go alone when I started all this trouble?" Panic swelled her throat, and she had trouble swallowing. What if something happened to him? Looking into his determined blue eyes, she knew beyond a shadow of doubt that she loved him with all her heart. She couldn't bear the thought of losing him. "No, Glen. There's got to be a different way."

"I'm going." He rubbed her upper arm, but Shannon stepped away from him.

She had to think fast to get the information she needed. "At the park? You mean the entrance to the park? Or are you supposed to roam the park all night and wait for him to show?"

"I'm not stupid enough to answer your questions. You'll come to the park after me."

She cut him a defiant look and decided to use a different tack to stop him from going through with this madness. "You can't afford to lose three thousand dollars, Glen. You told me your brother—"

"Look, I must go. Please, I'm doing this for both of us." Glen pulled her into his arms for another quick kiss, then skirted around her and walked to his car. "Go back inside, please."

Glen said something she didn't quite hear as she dashed back inside and began to dig through her desk drawers. "Flashlight. . .flashlight. There it is!" She held it up in triumph. "C'mon, Truman, we've got a job to do."

After Glen had left the alley, she rushed to her truck with Truman, started the engine, and headed to the park. "Lord, protect Glen. I trust You to protect him. And help me."

Truman *woofed* his agreement, just as Shannon caught the dim sight of the taillights of Glen's BMW through the beginnings of the dust storm. "Thank You, Lord," she whispered as she picked up her cell phone and dialed Ray. He didn't answer. All she got was his voice mail, and she left a message.

❧

Glen killed the headlights. He'd been instructed to park at the Kiwanis building, go around back, and leave the briefcase. What was he doing here, in a dust storm, in the pitch-dark in Columbia Park? This was foolish—very foolish. Shannon was right—he should have phoned the police, but the caller had threatened Shannon's life and Glen had made a snap decision to be the hero. Some hero. He cut the engine and tried to visually scan the area, but he couldn't see much through the blowing dust.

He comforted himself with the thought that whoever had the spice box only wanted money in exchange. At least, he prayed that's all they wanted. He grabbed the briefcase off the passenger seat, felt for the flashlight in his coat pocket, and stepped out of the car.

"An even trade," Glen muttered. He flicked on the flashlight and ventured toward the building slowly. An eerie feeling washed over him. He imagined the thief watching him.

Glen drew a breath and stopped in his tracks. This was madness. But he refused to turn back now. Possession of the box meant at the very least that Amanda might reconsider, leave Shannon in peace, and he'd be free to pursue the woman he loved. That is, if Amanda wasn't behind this. Or if he didn't die in the process.

Memories of the caller's words rattled around in his head. "Drop the money on the ground behind the building, then get back in your car. Return in five minutes," he'd said, "and you'll find the spice box behind the building."

The wind howled and blew dust in his face. Glen stopped to wipe grit from his mouth and nose and fumbled with the flashlight. He adjusted his eyeglasses and advanced. The beam from the flashlight did very little to illuminate his way.

When he reached his destination, he did as he'd been instructed and dropped the briefcase. It landed with a dull thud. His fists clenched as he fought the urge to pick it up again and forget the whole deal. *It's for Shannon. Not only will this keep her from danger, but this might make life easier for her.*

He rounded the first corner of the building and heard heavy footfalls behind him. He broke into a jog. *Glen, you were stupid for coming out here. Shannon was right.*

The footfalls came faster. Glen began to run. When he reached the car, he yanked at the door handle.

"You've got your money," he said over his shoulder. "Now keep your word and give me the box."

He heard heavy breathing close behind him as he fumbled to open the car.

It's too late. Shannon was right.

Then a dog barked. Someone yelled...Truman?

The person behind him said something inaudible. Glen glanced over the roof of his car. Through the dust, the beam from a flashlight bobbed. The dog barked again, close enough to hear its panting. A familiarly shaped shadow shot around the front of the car and ran past him.

Glen swung around to watch. "Truman?"

The thief took off running, Truman right behind him.

"Glen?" He whirled at the sound of Shannon's voice. "Glen, are you all right?" She skidded to a stop, but not before she nearly knocked him down.

He grabbed her shoulders to keep them both standing. "What's wrong with you?"

"I was worried about you. I just—"

A deep bellow came from behind the building. Truman barked and growled.

Glen glanced that direction, then back at Shannon. "Go to your truck."

"But I only want to—"

"Now! For once, listen to me, Shannon. You could be hurt."

A shout and yelp followed, and Shannon clutched his arm. "Do you hear? Truman's got the guy."

Truman appeared and rushed toward them. Glen aimed the flashlight at the dog. A bloody piece of sleeve hung from his jaws.

"Truman!" Shannon fell to her knees. "You're such a good boy."

"Stay put," Glen ordered. "I'm sure all is lost. Truman must've scared the guy off."

Glen ran back behind the building, then shined the light at the ground. He saw it—the briefcase and a clear plastic bag beside it. The money...and the spice box?

Glen snatched them both and hurried back to Shannon and Truman.

Chapter 17

Glen placed the spice box on the desk in Shannon's office. Truman sat at his feet, and Shannon hovered behind him. The grit in his mouth, nose, even in his ears didn't improve his mood. "You totally disregarded everything I said." He stared down at her, still furious.

Shannon fisted her hands on her hips. "You'd probably be dead if I hadn't *disregarded* your instructions. Truman saved your hide."

"You don't know that for certain."

"Fine. You wanted to protect me; I wanted to protect you. Let's leave it at that."

"It's just—just not right," Glen stuttered. She was insufferably stubborn. And brave.

She reached up, kissed him full on the lips, then backed away smiling. "That's nice."

He had to agree. His anger was quickly slipping away.

"Okay, let's argue later," she said. "Right now I want to test a theory of mine."

"And that is?" Staying angry with her was impossible.

Shannon slipped around him and began fooling with the box. "Many of these boxes have hidden compartments."

Glen watched her remove the bottom drawer and reach her hand inside.

"If I'm right, there will be a little button kind of thing in here that will release the back cover." She frowned in concentration, then a grin lit her eyes. "Aha, there it is." She turned the box around, dragged it to the edge of the desk, and slid the back off. "Look. Right here at the top. A secret drawer."

Glen leaned over to look. Sure enough, it was a drawer, and the inside was filled with cotton.

Shannon pulled out the cotton and under it lay a gray pouch. She met his gaze, eyes wide. "You look inside the bag," she whispered.

He pulled out the pouch, opened it, and whistled.

"What?" she asked. "What is it?"

He dumped out the contents on the counter. A diamond pendant necklace and two matching earrings caught the light, sending multicolored sparkles in all directions.

"Wow!" Shannon gasped. "No wonder Amanda was so upset. These have got to be worth. . .who knows?"

Her phone trilled in her pocket, and she yanked it out. "Venus again," she mouthed to Glen. "Hey, sweetie. You don't sound so good." She paused and nodded. "Of course you shouldn't come to work tomorrow if you're sick. Promise me you'll get some rest, though." After another pause, Shannon smiled. "That's what I was about to tell you."

Glen listened while Shannon told Venus about the box and its valuable contents. He considered the wisdom of telling anyone about the find until they knew more, but Venus was Shannon's employee.

"I don't know what we're going to do, but you'd better believe the box and this jewelry is going into my safe tonight for protection." Shannon gave a sympathetic hum. "Forget work, you take care, okay?"

She dropped her cell into the pocket of her skirt, and Glen shook his head. "I'm not sure we should keep the box."

"Of course not, but should we call Amanda this late?"

Glen heard the sound of a motorcycle engine, but ignored it. "I need time to think. I don't understand why Amanda didn't just tell us about the jewels." A tickle of dread raised the hairs on the back of his neck.

Shannon looked at the jewels again. "You're right. It doesn't make sense."

"Precisely. Something's impossibly wrong here." He found himself thinking aloud.

"So, what *are* we going to do?" Shannon swiped some strands of hair from her face that had escaped her braid, and he lost his train of thought. He quickly looked away from her and focused on the problem at hand.

"I think we should call the police."

"But what about Amanda?" Shannon asked. "If you don't get it back to her, she said she would never do business with you again."

"Well, I already burned my bridges with her," he said. "I don't think she will bring her business back to me. And I'm quite certain I don't want it, no matter the outcome."

"Well, she said she'd sue us," Shannon said.

"Tell me what you think we should do," he said softly.

The motorcycle engine stopped outside in the alley. Ray had arrived. How did he know Shannon was home?

She shrugged. "I really don't know. We could ask Ray's advice."

That was all Glen wanted to do: ask Ray's advice.

Shannon thumbed through the mail next to the spice box, tossed the flyers aside, and frowned. "I wonder what this is. It's from Mike."

৯

Ray blew through the back door, and Shannon whirled around. Truman, lying on the floor next to the chair, raised his head and wagged his tail.

"I got both your messages," Ray said.

"You're a little late," she murmured as she slipped her finger underneath the flap of a fat white envelope. Maybe Mike had decided she could stay. "We've got the box and the jewels. Now we're trying to figure out what to do. Call Amanda or call the police." She motioned to the spice box on her desk.

"Jewels?" He stalked to the desk, then looked from her to Glen. "Are you kidding me?"

"Messages?" Glen asked at the same time. "You called Ray?"

"Yes, Ray. Jewels. And Glen. I thought we'd need help at the park, but Ray didn't answer his phone. Then I called him again after we recovered the box." Shannon pulled several sheets of paper from the envelope.

"Are you guys crazy? Two amateur detectives." Ray whipped off his leather jacket and tossed it on her chair. "You probably messed up potential evidence."

"What is that?" Glen asked.

Shannon frowned at the letter in her shaky hand and shrugged. "A letter from—"

"I'm referring to Reed here." Glen pointed to Ray, and Shannon lifted her eyes and saw a gun in a holster under Ray's arm.

She inhaled. "Ray? A gun?"

"I have a license to carry," he said.

"Concealed?" Glen continued to stare at Ray. "Who are you?"

"Ray, we need to have a talk. I don't like guns. I want you to take it to your car." Shannon returned her attention to the letter as Ray ignored her instructions and crossed the room to examine the spice box.

She scanned to the bottom of the missive and swallowed hard. "I guess I'm headed back to Walla Walla. Mike isn't renewing my lease. Not that I expected him to." She sighed. "And Ray, you aren't listening to me."

"I suppose you guys had your fingers all over this thing, right?" Ray said.

"Yes, we did," Glen answered.

Shannon flipped to the attachment. The petition was titled "Renew Our Storefronts," and in the paragraph below, her name was mentioned as one of the store owners who should be evicted. She scanned the signatures. At the top of the list in bold, slanted script was Glen Caldwell. Her heart felt like it froze.

She shook the papers at him. "Glen? You signed this? You wanted me out of here?"

"Signed what?" He came to stand beside her, and she held the petition up to his face.

Glen took the papers from her hand and began to read.

Ray pulled a cell phone from his pocket and punched in some numbers.

Shannon tore her gaze from Glen and stared at Ray.

"Yeah," he said. "D'Amato? Ray Reed here." He turned his back to them.

"Yeah, I'm *that* Reed. The one you had coffee with last night. Listen, I'm pretty sure I've run across some stolen jewels at the Quaint Shop." He paused and listened. "Yes, the same place that was broken into. I need a uniform here with evidence bags." He cocked his head to listen. "Good. See you in a few."

He punched the button to end the conversation, then turned back to face Shannon and Glen. "Someone's right around the corner."

"You're a cop," Glen stated.

"Was," Ray said. "I was."

Shannon backed away. "You? My guitar teacher? The musician." She shook her head. "No, Ray, please tell me—"

"I can explain." Ray eyed her, and she saw the cop, not her good friend. Tears filled her eyes.

She slapped the papers on the desk. "I can't believe it." She pushed her way around Ray.

Glen reached for her hand, but she snatched it away. "And you! You sign this petition to get me thrown out?"

"I didn't know—"

"Move, Glen. I'm leaving."

"Hold up, Shan." Ray stood in front of the door, blocking her exit.

"Don't even start with me. You lied to me." She poked his shoulder with her finger. "I should have known. Remember the other day when I said you were acting like a cop?"

"I didn't lie," Ray said. "I told you I didn't want to discuss my past. And there's a reason—"

"I don't want to hear it." Shannon turned and jabbed a finger into Glen's shoulder. "And furthermore, I don't want to hear anything from you, either. You're both. . .not nice."

Shannon snatched her purse from the floor beside her desk. "I want both of you gone when I get back. Come on, Truman. You're coming with me."

❧

Shannon cried as she drove all over the Tri-Cities, from Kennewick to Pasco to Richland and around again. She didn't dare go back to her shop too soon. She wanted to give the police time to arrive and collect the spice box, then time for the two traitors to leave her office. Her curiosity about the spice box and jewels had died in the heartache of discovering how Ray and Glen had misrepresented themselves.

Her stomach growled. On impulse, she pulled into a McDonald's drive-through. "You know what this means, don't you?" she asked Truman.

He wagged his tail.

"It means I'm not as good at reading body language as I thought."

He snuffled her arm, and she stroked his wooly head. Then she sniffled and reached for a napkin from a pile on the floor behind her seat. "I don't even have tissues, Truman. I'm that disorganized. And who knew the two men I trusted most—"

"Welcome to McDonald's."

Shannon swallowed a sob before placing her order. A hamburger for Truman and a fish sandwich with fries for her, along with extra napkins to blow her nose.

She pulled up and paid for the food, ignoring the looks she got from the teen at the window.

Fresh tears threatened as she pulled around, parked, and cut the engine. She unwrapped Truman's burger under his curious gaze, shrugged, and served it to him. "I know. I never eat fast food, and neither do you, but I just don't care tonight."

She took another bite of her sandwich, chewed, and swallowed the food along with a sob. "I still love him—fool that I am. I can't believe he signed that petition and sided with Amanda Franklin, even if he did it weeks ago."

Shannon balled up the trash and stuffed it in the bag. "Let's go home. I've got a lot of work to do. Packing...planning. It'll be a good cure for the blues."

The words brought her no comfort. Glen—and Ray. Why hadn't she seen through their facades?

Shannon pulled into the alley behind her shop and parked. "Come on, Truman." Exhaustion made her muscles ache. Her heart ached more. The dog leaped out of the truck and followed her.

Shannon put the key into the lock, shoved the door open, and froze. "What is this?"

Venus, on her knees in front of the safe, looked up. Louis was standing over Venus with a gun pointed at her head. He swung his gun at her. Truman growled and leaped at Louis. He jerked the gun toward the dog and fired.

Truman fell to the floor. Shannon screamed and flew to his side. Blood puddled beneath him. "Truman!"

Still breathing, he looked up into her eyes and whined.

"That dog took a piece of me tonight. What goes around comes around."

"You were at the park tonight?" Shannon's gaze flew to Louis's arm. It was bandaged.

"You shot my dog," she said, anger lowering her voice to a growl that Truman would appreciate.

Louis laughed. "Shut up, drama queen, and get on the floor next to her." He nodded toward Venus.

"Why do you want the spice box now? You can't possibly think you'll get that much money for it from anyone else but Glen." Shannon blinked, wishing she could erase the surreal scene before her eyes.

"I'm here for what's inside the box."

"Venus?" Had Shannon been betrayed one more time?

"He's been stealing from you, Shannon. I found out a couple of days ago. I've been trying to get him to stop. He knew the box was worth a lot of money. He wanted it. And then he heard you tell me about the jewels and he—"

Louis kicked her. "Shut up. Let's keep things simple and nobody has to get hurt."

"I'm sorry, Shannon," Venus whispered.

"Open the safe," Louis said

Venus's hands were shaking. "I can't. I keep getting the combination wrong."

"Try harder." He pointed at the floor. "I told you to sit."

Shannon crossed her arms. "No. And the box isn't in the safe."

"Really? If it's not, I'll shoot you." He waved the gun in her direction. "I'm probably going to shoot you anyway."

Suddenly she was more angry than frightened. "And go to jail for murder?"

Shannon met Venus's mascara-smeared eyes, and a jolt of fury shot through her—a fire like nothing she'd ever felt before.

"I'm sorry," Venus whispered again.

"I told you to shut up!" Louis slapped her across the head with an open palm.

Venus yelped and sobbed.

Truman came to life, barking and struggling to get to his feet.

Louis turned the gun again at Truman. Shannon exploded, leaping toward Louis. She wondered how fast a bullet would kill her.

Chapter 12

Glen returned to his shop after accompanying Ray to the police station. The police would hold the box and the jewelry until they determined if the jewels were indeed stolen. Now Glen had to make amends to Shannon. He had a plan, but first he had to talk to the landlord.

He pulled into his parking space and heard a muffled explosion like a gunshot or fireworks.

Panicked, he leaped from his BMW. Shannon's truck was parked in its spot. Farther up the alley, he saw Venus's little car parked at an odd angle. Light glowed from the window of Shannon's office, but nowhere else. As he ran toward the back door, he heard Truman bark and Venus yelling.

"Louis, you killed her!" Venus wailed.

"Shut up. Just shut up and get that safe open." The voice was familiar. Similar to the person who had called him.

"Shannon said the box isn't here—"

"I'm sure she lied." Then came the sound of a slap and a scream.

"Louis, why are you doing this?"

Where was Shannon? Glen felt bile in the back of his throat as he pulled out his cell and dialed 911.

Truman barked again. Glen whispered into the phone, "Come, please." Then he left the phone on and stuck it in his pocket.

"I'm going to kill that dog," Louis said.

"Louis, please," Venus begged.

"Open the safe now."

Glen looked up and down the alley for a police car, wishing one was close by. He debated only for a second before he knocked on the door.

Louis murmured something, and Glen pressed himself against the building beside Shannon's door. Holding his breath, he waited till he heard the creak of the rusty door hinges. Slowly Louis stepped outside, gun in hand. Glen shoved the door with all his strength, catching Louis's arm. The gun fell to the ground with a clatter. Glen grabbed it and stepped into the light.

As Louis howled in pain, Glen punched him in the stomach. He went down, and Glen stared into Shannon's office, his gaze searching wildly for her.

"Shannon!" he said. She was slumped on the floor, Venus next to her, and her head was bleeding.

Shannon slowly opened her eyes and wondered where she was. Then she remembered. She was in Allie's guest room. The events of the night before came flooding back into her mind. Louis, Venus, and the safe. Truman bleeding. Glen bursting into the office and holding her. Had he really been crying? And Ray, all cop-ish, running in with other cops, reading Louis his rights. Venus sobbing while she held Shannon's hand.

She heard a soft knock, and Allie's head appeared around the door. "Are you awake?"

"Yes, barely. My head is killing me."

Allie crossed the room and sat on the side of the bed. "No wonder. That monster Louis walloped you something awful with his gun."

"Thank God the doctor at the Kennewick hospital said I was okay. No major concussion."

"Yes, thank God." Allie stroked a piece of hair out of Shannon's face. "I'm glad you called me and Derrick to come and get you."

"I still can't believe what happened," Shannon said.

Allie shook her head. "Based on what we've heard, the jewels were part of a jewelry heist years ago, but I don't know anything else about that."

"A heist? That sounds sort of old-fashioned."

"It is. It happened a long time ago. It involved the Franklin family."

Shannon didn't care much about the Franklins or the box and jewels at the moment. "How is Venus?"

"They treated her at the hospital for cuts and bruises where that monster hit her."

Shannon felt angry all over again at the memory of Louis slapping Venus. "They didn't arrest her, did they?"

"No. They just took her in for questioning."

Shannon reached for Allie's hand. "Thank you. You and Derrick came to my rescue."

"Not really," Allie said. "You'd already been rescued. By two men who care very much for you."

Shannon's stomach clenched. "I don't want to discuss them."

"You have to. Ray called this morning to see how you are. He explained things. He says the police may need another statement from you."

"I already talked to them. And to him. I don't want to again." Shannon sighed. "You know how I feel about the police."

Allie laughed. "Yes, I know."

"And did he explain to you how I spent months getting to know who I thought he was? Pouring out my heart to him?"

"Perhaps it was a good lesson," Allie said.

Shannon frowned. "What do you mean?"

Allie shrugged. "You're the one who's always seeing meaning behind the way everything happens. And here I am having to explain Ray and Glen to you."

"Sometimes it's harder to see things in your own life," Shannon grumbled.

"Okay, I'll explain. It's easy to judge people by their profession or outward appearance. Ahem. Like all farriers are men—and you know I'm a farrier, and I'm definitely not a man. Or. . .like all cops are *fill-in-the-blank*. All antique dealers with ritzy furniture in their shops are arrogant snobs. But when you get to know the person inside, you find they're not anything like what you assumed."

Once again someone was using her own words against her. She picked at the sheet hem.

"I have another surprise for you in that same vein." Allie's green eyes lit with a smile.

"Should I brace myself?"

"Maybe so. Ray told me he got a call from one Deputy Kroeger." Allie's expression was way too self-satisfied.

"Oh boy, how can that be good news?"

"The deputy wanted to know how you were doing."

"No way." Shannon shook her head. "You've got to be kidding."

"I'm not."

"Why did he call Ray?"

Allie smiled. "Several reasons. After Ray and I talked about the box, he called Deputy Kroeger to talk about it. You know how cops are—"

Shannon snorted.

"No, not like that. I mean they tend to be a close-knit group, even if they don't know each other well. Anyway, he was curious about the box. He'd had suspicions after the break-ins. And then he asked about you."

"I find that hard to believe."

"I'll make it easy for you. The deputy is the reason your parents stopped using drugs. That time he arrested your father, he could have arrested your mother as well. Then you would have ended up in foster care. Kroeger agreed to leave her alone if they promised to stop the drugs. He didn't want to see you harmed in any way. They've kept their word, but he still checks on them from time to time."

Shannon was stunned. "Why did he do it? Couldn't he have gotten in trouble for not arresting my mother like that?"

"I don't know," Allie said. "Maybe. But it seems he saw you in your bed, gripping your blanket, terrified. That made a huge impact on him."

Shannon tried to wrap her mind around that. "I've been so wrong," she whispered.

"Yeah. And about a lot of things. Like why didn't you tell me how bad things had gotten with the store and the landlord?" Allie pulled her hand from Shannon's. "Derrick could have intervened."

"I guess I didn't realize how bad it was until it was all too late." She took a breath. "Where is Truman?"

"Don't worry, he's downstairs resting. He'll have a scar on his hip, but the bullet only grazed him, thank God."

"Yes. God definitely protected us all." Shannon sat up. "I can't believe I did what I did."

"You mean leaping at an armed man, trying to rescue someone, and being smacked in the head with a gun?"

Shannon smiled. "Well, yeah, if you want to put it that way."

"You were just trying to protect Truman and Venus. That's how you are. You protect your own."

"It's also like me not to think about the consequences of my actions."

"Too true," Allie said. "You've gotten several other calls. Your parents, Pastor Zach and Laurie, Venus, Charlie. . .and did I mention Glen?"

"Glen." Shannon inched her way to the edge of the bed. "Anyway, what's for breakfast?"

"You're avoiding talking about Glen."

"Yes, I am." Shannon shrugged. "French toast?"

"Don't you care that he called?"

Shannon moved until her legs were hanging over the side of the bed. "All I care about right now is eating. So, what are we having?"

"My famous pancakes." Allie held out her hand. "I know. They aren't what you usually eat, but you need some comfort food right now."

"I agree." Shannon slipped out of bed and stretched. "I'm going to shower. I'll be down in ten minutes."

❧

Allie sat across the table from Shannon with baby Natalie against her shoulder. Shannon smiled, watching her best friend gently rub the little one's back. Allie had taken to motherhood in the same manner she'd taken to mothering her nephew, Danny—with her whole heart and soul.

"I think I'm coming back to Walla Walla. I won't fight the eviction."

Allie frowned. "That's not like you. You seem defeated somehow. Perhaps you should wait and make a decision in a few days, after you've returned to Kennewick. And had time to think."

Shannon chewed a bite of pancake slowly. After she swallowed, she met Allie's gaze. "I guess I *feel* defeated. I've realized a lot of things about myself the past few months. . .well, especially the last month. And the biggest one is I'm stubborn and I don't listen to what other people are telling me, even when they mean to help."

Allie didn't disagree. She dropped her gaze and kissed Natalie's little head.

Shannon's throat grew tight. "Glen was right about a lot of things, even though he did go behind my back." She shivered. "To think Glen would side with Amanda against me."

"Shan, you need to hear Glen out," Allie said softly. "I've spoken with him. You must remember Deputy Kroeger. Things aren't always what they appear."

"Hmm." Shannon stuffed more pancake into her mouth. "These are yummy, by the way. Makes me want to go off my regular weird diet more often."

"Maybe it wouldn't hurt you to be more normal," Allie suggested as she stood and put Natalie in her swing. She collected the dishes and began filling the sink with hot water and soap.

"I'm afraid I don't know what normal is."

"No, you wouldn't. Not the way you were raised." Allie laughed. "But your folks are good people. We're praying that they come to the Lord soon."

"He met my mom." In her mind's eye, she saw Glen, acting as though all families lived like hers. "He was out at their trailer."

Allie whirled around. "You took Glen to meet your parents?"

"No!" Shannon shook her head. "He followed me there."

Allie turned back to the dishes. "Why did he follow you there?"

"Because he was worried about me."

"I see." Allie rinsed a plate and set it in the drainer.

"You see what?" Heat burned a path up her face. Didn't Allie grasp how hurt she was seeing Glen's name on that petition?

"Don't get upset. I just want to know if Glen treated you differently after that. Like you were pond scum or something."

"No, but you don't know Glen like I do. He's—he's charming." Shannon closed her eyes. She didn't want to conjure a picture of the tall, handsome Brit wearing a slight smile. "What I mean is, he's too polite to say what he thought." She sighed. This wasn't coming out right.

"Hmm. Charming. Polite. Not to mention kind and concerned. Bad, bad Glen," Allie's voice dripped with sarcastic humor.

"You know what I mean, Allie. Don't make me explain with this pounding headache."

"Fine, but have you given him a chance to explain about the petition or the restore our street committee or whatever it's called?"

"No, but—"

"Ha!" Allie wiped her hands on a dish towel, turned, and leaned against the counter. "It seems to me that you might be just as guilty of judging him as you think he is of you. He didn't know what he was signing. He just did it in a hurry so she'd leave him alone."

"How do you know that?" Shannon asked.

"He told me."

Shannon began to shred her napkin. "I didn't give him a chance to explain." Her shoulders sagged. "There is another good example why I probably shouldn't be in a relationship at all. It's so much work, and I'm so bad at it. I'm a slob, I can't keep books, I eat weird food, I dress funny, and most of my friends are oddballs."

"Excuse me?"

"I said *most*." Shannon sighed. "I just want to come home to Walla Walla and forget everything. I need time to think. Can I stay for a couple more days?"

"Normally I would tell you to stay as long as you wanted, but this time I won't." Allie bit her lip. "You need to go back. The sooner the better. Tomorrow morning? Get things squared away. Even if you have to shut down your store, you still have a decision to make about Glen. And Ray. They both really want to talk to you."

After a long silence, Shannon nodded. "You're right. I'm being childish and stubborn. I'll go back. But no guarantees after that." That's all she could promise right now. Her head throbbed and her body ached, but her heart. . .

She may as well have handed Glen her heart the first time they'd met. How long would it take to get over him? Months? Years?

Chapter 19

On Wednesday morning, Shannon pulled off the highway to the Tri-Cities, planning her move in her head. She would rent a truck and spend a weekend taking everything from the Tri-Cities store to the shop in Walla Walla. Allie had offered storage in her barn if she needed it.

As she pulled into the alley behind her shop, she saw Glen's car parked there along with Charlie's and Venus's vehicles.

She jammed her truck into PARK, turned it off, and sent up a silent prayer that she wouldn't run into Glen. She couldn't avoid him forever, but she didn't want to face him today.

Glen had challenged who she was. She needed to face her faults. Think about how she impacted other people and not be so determined to do her own thing. Now that she had settled that in her mind, she could begin to change. . .wanted to change. . .with the Lord's help. But she didn't want her motive to be to please Glen. It wasn't fair to him. He needed someone more conventional. Someone more his equal, while she had to define herself on her own terms, not by what Glen or anybody else thought of her.

Shannon exited her truck, went around to the passenger side, and opened the door for Truman. "C'mon, boy." She helped the injured dog down, straining her muscles.

Truman must've sensed her mood. Head hung low, he followed silently.

Shannon stuck the key in her lock, and her heart stilled. After the end of the month, she would never return here again. Turning the knob slowly, she stepped into her office.

A new file cabinet stood against one wall. The floor was clean and had even been waxed. The only thing that remained a mess was the top of her desk. Was Mike already moving someone in? That wasn't legal.

Truman limped past her and curled up next to the leather chair with a sigh.

"Shannon?" Venus shot through the office door and skidded to a stop, her face a question mark.

"Come here," Shannon opened her arms. "I want a hug."

Venus flew across the room and into Shannon's warm hug. "I'm so sorry," she whispered. "You and Truman almost died, and it was all my fault."

"You made a mistake." She pulled away from Venus and put her hands on the girl's shoulders. "You were desperate to be loved, and Louis used that."

"I didn't know what he was going to do." Venus's lower lip trembled. "And he became so mean to me. He threatened me at the end."

"I know that. And that's why you were so stressed out, right?"

Venus nodded.

Shannon rubbed her hands up and down the teenager's arms. "I forgive you."

"Thank you so much." A single tear straggled down Venus's cheek. "And you know what's the stupidest thing?"

"What's that?"

"I wanted love so badly, and here was Charlie, right here. He was worried sick about me." Her face colored. "He loves me."

Shannon grinned. "I hoped you'd say that." She waved her hand around the office. "What's going on here? Is someone else moving in already?"

Venus's smile lit her face, and she grabbed Shannon's hand. "No way. Come with me."

She allowed herself to be led into the shop area. In the doorway, Venus dropped her hand, and Shannon stared, her jaw hanging open. This was her store, but everything was organized and tidy.

"Surprise!" Venus squealed.

"What are you doing? Are you organizing so I can pack more easily?"

"Shannon!" Venus clucked her tongue. "Don't you get it?"

"Get what?"

"You're staying."

"No, you don't understand. Mike—"

"Glen arranged it with Mike. Now that Amanda is out of the picture, she isn't running the show anymore."

"Amanda is out of the picture?"

"Wow, where have you been?" Venus giggled. "Oh, that's right. You were in hiding." She inhaled. "Turns out the necklace and earrings were part of a bunch of stuff taken from a jewelry store robbery. Amanda's father owned the store and faked a break-in. He died like five years ago. The necklace and earrings were what was left. They sold off the rest to live high on the hog."

"No wonder Amanda's mother wanted to get rid of them."

"Yeah. She probably felt guilty or something. People sometimes get that way when they think their life is almost over."

Shannon smiled. Sometimes Venus was very insightful.

"Ray said something about the statue of limitations."

"You mean statute?"

"Whatever. Amanda can't be arrested, but she's not rich anymore. Something about freezing. . .freezing. . ."

"Assets?"

Venus smiled. "Yeah."

The front door opened and both of them turned to look. Glen walked in looking tired and decidedly disheveled in jeans and a T-shirt. He had his hands behind his back. Shannon's heart flip-flopped.

"I'm going next door for a minute." Venus zoomed out of the shop.

Glen's smile was hesitant, and he held up a bouquet of daisies he'd been hiding. "Don't leave until I explain." His words came out in a rush. "Please forgive me. I never meant to keep the petition from you. I never actually read it thoroughly. Amanda told me it pertained to upgrading the area. I only signed it to make her leave me alone."

"I know," Shannon said.

"You do?" He approached her with the flowers held out in front of him. "I'm usually so careful about everything, but she was giving me no peace. I just wanted her to get out of my office. And she led me to believe that you knew about the petition and had refused to sign it."

"Wow." Shannon took the flowers and swallowed. "I'm sorry I walked out before you could explain and that I didn't return your calls from Allie's. I made assumptions that weren't right."

"None of us knew the depths of Amanda's wickedness, especially you. You don't have a vicious bone in your body." Glen looked directly into her eyes.

"How did you do this?" Shannon waved an arm around the room. "How did you talk Mike into letting me stay?"

"With Amanda out of the picture, it was easy."

"What about your business?" Shannon asked. "You needed Amanda as a regular client, and you had all that stuff you'd found for her."

Glen smiled. "Turns out I met someone who wants all of that and more. His name is William Shepherd. Ironically, Mike introduced us."

"Wow," Shannon said again. "That's amazing."

Glen put a hand on Shannon's shoulder. "Can we try again?"

"Try again?" She knew what he meant, and she was stalling to try to figure out what to say.

"You and I. Together. See if it'll work out."

"I don't know." Shannon imitated his hesitant smile. "You and I are so different. I can change, but probably never enough to be like you."

He put his other hand on her other shoulder. "Who said I wanted you to be like me? One of me is quite enough, thank you very much."

Her heart lightened, but she had to be sure. "We'd be like the *Odd Couple*." Venus entered the shop from the back.

"I always liked that old movie." Glen's eyes crinkled in a smile. "Now, can you please forgive me for being bossy?"

"Of course." Shannon stepped closer to Glen. "I'm sorry I never listened or asked for your help, even when I knew you were right. I was embarrassed, I guess. And stubborn."

He came closer, and she couldn't resist. She flung her arms around his neck, and Glen kissed her soundly.

Venus giggled and applauded, then said, "I wondered when you guys would stop yakking long enough to kiss."

Chapter 20

Wednesday night, Ray was slouched in Shannon's leather chair, wooden chopsticks stuck in a white box of Chinese food. "That was good." He put the empty container on the floor.

"Yes." Shannon placed her half-eaten food on her desk. "Dinner was my apology offering."

"And so it should be. You were cruel to me."

Shannon smiled. "You could at least be a little more humble."

He splayed his hand on his chest. "I am your humble servant."

She laughed. "Right. So will you tell me more about your job?"

His smile faded, and he took a deep breath. "Really, you already know the most important things. My spiritual and emotional struggles. Right now, you can just pray for me. I'm deciding whether or not I want to go back into law enforcement." He leaned forward. "So, you've accepted the fact that I'm part of the 'establishment'?"

She nodded. "Yes. And I was so wrong. Me, who prided herself in accepting everyone. I'm really, really sorry."

He smiled and kicked her foot gently with his. "Shan, you're fine. We're all growing in the Lord, and sometimes it's messy."

"Well, I prided myself in accepting everyone, but I wasn't an 'equal opportunity' accepter."

He laughed. "Welcome to the human race. You're not perfect. And we don't need to discuss it again. You and I are fine."

"Good," she said.

"So, what did Caldwell get for his apology offering?"

Shannon blushed. "A kiss."

"I hope he got more than only one after what you put the poor man through."

"Ray!" Shannon's face heated.

"I saw him after you were taken to the hospital. He was a wreck."

Shannon couldn't speak for the emotion that overcame her.

"So," Ray said. "I suppose next you're going to want all the gory details?"

"Yes. The spice box, jewels, the break-ins, and everything."

"I'll tell you what I can." He paused. "You know where the jewels came from and why Amanda wanted them back so badly, right?"

"Yes."

"The DA is figuring things out now. Amanda did not commit insurance fraud. Her father did, years and years ago, but she knew about it and used the money. Statute of limitations is up, but the insurance company will demand restitution. She will also be charged with breaking and entering your office on Sunday morning."

Shannon sucked in a breath. "Amanda did that?"

"Yeah." Ray huffed out a breath. "No matter what, her reputation is shot."

Shannon felt a deep sense of grief. "I didn't like her much, but I would never wish anything like this on anybody."

"I know, but when people break the law, they have to be punished."

"Yes, I know, Mr. Cop." Shannon smiled at him.

He gave her a wink. "And Louis is already in jail. Judge denied him bail. Charged with assault with a deadly weapon, robbery, breaking and entering, to name a few."

"So he is the one who broke into the homes?"

"You got that right."

"Thank you for not involving Venus."

Ray shrugged. "That was partially as a result of Glen's and my intervention at the scene. But she really wasn't guilty of anything but stupidity. She had no clue what Louis was up to until that Monday. And he threatened her if she told."

"So that's why she left work early?"

"Yep. He was afraid she'd cave and tell you. He planned to hit Glen and run away with the box *and* the money. He knew the box was worth money, which was why he originally went after it—apparently Venus exaggerated its worth. But he had no idea the box held anything valuable until you told Venus that night."

Shannon rubbed her arms with her hands. "The Lord was certainly protecting all of us through this."

"Yes, He was." Ray smiled and stood. "And now I must leave, but I've made sure you won't be left alone." He glanced at his watch. "Five, four, three, two. . ."

Someone rapped on the door. Shannon jumped up and opened it. "Glen!"

Ray laughed. "I invited him. It seems a shame for you two to be apart your first evening back."

Glen grinned and reached for her hand. She watched as Ray jogged outside with a backward wave. When he mounted his bike, Glen reached out, pushed the door shut, and pulled her into his arms.

Epilogue

With Truman close on her heels, Shannon scurried from her truck to the back door of the Quaint Shop, hauling her backpack, a bag of spring decorations for the store, and her purse.

She caught a glimpse of Venus's car, unlocked the back door, and strode through her office to the showroom. "Venus?" she yelled. "Why are you still here?"

"Shannon! You're back." Venus popped up from behind the counter, breathless. "I have a date with Charlie, and he's just closing up next door, so I waited."

Venus stepped around the counter and hugged her. "I missed you a whole lot."

"I missed you, too." Shannon let go of Venus, shoved aside a box, and dropped her backpack on the floor. "I brought pictures of Natalie's birthday party. She's a little charmer." Shannon stretched. "I feel so relaxed."

Venus crossed her arms and sighed. "I'll bet you had so much fun with Allie that you wished you could be back in Walla Walla."

"I had fun, but being there for a week confirmed for me that this is my home." She inhaled the scent of her store and realized how true her words felt. She was truly home.

"I'm glad," Venus said. "And I'm sure Glen will be glad you feel that way, too. Did you miss him? Has he called you from London? Is his brother's wife okay?"

"Yes, I miss him. And I hear from him every day. Melissa is making a full recovery from surgery, and the doctors say the cancer is in remission. Glen's having an awesome time with his family. I can't wait until he comes back. Three weeks is a long time not to see him." That was putting it mildly. She wanted nothing more than to be held tightly in his arms.

Venus's cell phone buzzed. "I've got a text message. One sec." While she punched quickly on the phone buttons, Shannon reached under the counter for her notebook containing sales records. She still hadn't succumbed to a computerized record-keeping system, although Glen was slowly convincing her that it would be worthwhile.

Venus shoved her phone into her pocket, then pushed the box on the counter toward her. "This came for you, Shan."

"Okay." Shannon acknowledged the box with a nod. "How is Charlie doing holding down the fort for Glen? It's a good thing this was spring break, huh?"

"Charlie is doing great!" Venus said with pride in her voice. She patted the carton. "Aren't you going to open this?"

After noting that sales had been brisk, Shannon slipped the notebook back under the counter and eyed the package. "It looks like the stationery and business cards and other office supplies I ordered." She yawned. "I'm tired. It can wait until tomorrow."

"But there's no return address on it," Venus said. "Doesn't that make you wonder?"

Shannon pulled the box toward her. "You're right. No return address. That's weird. Maybe it fell off. Could be a bomb."

"That's not funny," Venus said.

Shannon laughed. "Like I'm that important, right?" She pulled at the packing tape, growing more curious. "If it's the office stuff, they used a lot of unnecessary tape. Can you hand me a pair of scissors?"

Venus reached underneath the counter and rummaged around, then stood, triumphant, waving a pair. "Here you go."

The sleigh bells rang on the front door. Shannon looked up as Charlie strolled in.

"Hi, Charlie," Shannon said as she sliced through the tape across the top of the box. "You're just in time to be blown up."

"Hi, Shannon. Um, what?" When he reached them, Venus stepped into his open arms and hugged him tight.

"Kidding. I've got an unidentified package here addressed to me." Shannon looked up. "It's good to see you. Do you miss Glen as much as I do?"

Charlie laughed and draped his arm around Venus's shoulders. "I doubt it. I'm not going out with him. We don't kiss each other."

The reminder of Glen's kisses made Shannon blush. Venus laughed. "You give yourself away."

"Knock, knock, anybody here?"

Shannon twirled around to see Ray enter the shop from her office, smiling broadly. "Howdy, stranger. Missed you, girl."

"Ray. . ." Her heart lifted, and she felt an accompanying pang of sadness. "So, copper, are you still packing to leave town and return to your previous profession with the establishment, or have you changed your mind and decided to continue your music career?"

He crossed the room with long strides and pulled her into a hug. "Yes, I'm still packing to leave. I've decided to return to the *establishment*. Then in my dotage I'll have a good pension and will be able to once again pursue my musical career." He nodded at Venus and Charlie, then looked at the box. "What's in there?"

"It's doubtful we'll ever find out," Venus said. "She keeps getting interrupted. But so far it's either stationery or a bomb."

Charlie pushed at the box. "I'm guessing it's books."

Shannon laughed. "Ray, you want to venture an opinion?"

"Nope. Just open the box. I only believe what I see."

She pulled up the flaps and looked inside. "Lots of packing material." She pulled out a block of blown-in foam and dropped it on the counter. "Hmmm. I think I'll need help with this."

Venus helped her slide out a bubble-wrapped parcel.

"Listen, while you do that, I have something for you," Ray said. "I'll be right back."

"Okay." Shannon paid him little attention as he disappeared into her office.

Venus peeled off the wrapping with her, and Shannon glimpsed the contents and sucked in a breath.

"It's a spice box," Venus said.

Shannon shook her head. "There's been a mistake. I didn't order this."

"Maybe it belongs to Glen," Charlie said.

She heard Ray come back into the store, but didn't look up. Running her fingers across the fine grain wood, she whistled. "It's a beauty."

"Even if it was delivered here accidentally," Charlie said, "I don't think Mr. Caldwell would mind if you looked inside it."

Shannon examined again the label on the box. "It's addressed to me. How can it be an accident?"

"There's been no accident."

Shannon's heart stopped at the sound of the familiar British accent. She looked up. Ray stepped aside revealing Glen standing behind him.

"Here's your surprise." Ray grinned broadly and high-fived Glen.

"You're home early." Shannon slipped out from behind the counter and had to stop, her legs suddenly weak.

Glen's long strides quickly covered the distance between them. He reached her, took her hands in his, and kissed her gently. "You have no idea how much I've missed you."

"I think I do," she whispered.

"What about this?" Venus pointed at the spice box.

"Hmmm." Glen stepped away from Shannon and examined the box. "I see your store has once again been mistaken for mine."

Ray, Venus, and Charlie laughed.

"Very funny, everyone." Shannon eyed each of them. "Coconspirators, I assume?"

"Good guess, Sherlock," Ray said.

Glen draped his arm around her shoulders and kissed her cheek. She faced him for a proper kiss, but Venus cleared her throat.

"Enough smooching right now. I'm curious." Venus hovered close by.

"Do you think this box has a secret compartment?" Shannon couldn't resist pulling open the bottom drawer.

"It's likely," Glen said. "Go on, check it out."

"This box is lovely," Shannon said as she searched for the hidden button.

"Lovely," Glen said, looking into her eyes.

Warmth washed over her, and she gave Glen a smile. "I found the secret button!" She released the back and turned it around.

He moved so close to her she could feel the warmth of his breath on her cheek. If she turned even a fraction, their lips would meet in a kiss. How she longed for his kiss, to be in his arms again. . . .

Shannon slid the wooden back down, pulled out the drawer divide, and found the hidden compartment.

"I wonder if jewels are stashed in this one," Charlie joked.

Shannon's curiosity got the best of her. She pulled open the drawer and gasped. "There—there's a ring in here in a blue velvet holder."

"Not more stolen jewels, I hope." Shaking his head, Ray blew out a breath. "There's been too much crime and mayhem around here. I need to return to police work to escape."

Charlie and Venus laughed.

"Let's have a look." Glen picked up the ring. "It's a yellow and white diamond daisy." He held it out so Shannon could see it.

"A daisy," she whispered, her heart beating fast. Was it possible? "I've never seen a ring this beautiful in all my life."

Glen dropped to one knee in front of her. "You, Shannon O'Brien, have captured my heart and soul and mind."

Looking down at the man she loved with all her heart, tears of joy trickled from her eyes. "Glen, I—I . . ." Aware that her three friends were in the room, the words wouldn't come.

"They already know we're in love." Glen took her hand and looked up into her eyes. "Shannon O'Brien, will you marry me?"

She dropped to her knees in front of him. "Yes, yes, yes."

Glen slipped the ring on her finger, smiling. "I love you." He yanked her into his arms and kissed her soundly.

Ray whistled. "Whoa. And I thought the Brits were cold. I'm feelin' the heat from here."

Charlie and Venus laughed.

Glen helped Shannon to her feet. "Folks, let me present my fiancée and best friend, Shannon O'Brien."

Ray shook Glen's hand.

"Hey," Venus said. "It all started and finished with a box."

MENDING
FENCES

Dedication

To my dad, Walter,
for his love and encouragement all my life.
I love you.

Nancy

To my husband, Kim, my real-life hero.

Candice

Chapter 1

Ray Reed exited Interstate 405, turning his rental truck west toward Bothell. He drove at a sedate pace, eyeing the familiar landscape. Peace settled over him as he breathed in the rain-scented air.

Thank God he was home. He missed Bothell in the months he'd taken leave. Or as his brother, Philip, would say: "You ran away."

Philip was right. Ray had run away, especially from his emotions, but he'd needed a change of scenery. Now he knew without a doubt where he should be. Bothell. What remained to be seen was why and how the Lord would direct him.

The apartment rental he thought was a sure thing had fallen through just yesterday. Tomorrow he'd have to return the truck to the rental agency and put his furniture and most of his belongings in storage. He wouldn't need them. Mabel and Cora offered to give him a room in their home. A smile tugged at his lips. The sisters had been like family to him, at church and at home. It would be like old times.

Ray glanced at the clock on the dash and accelerated. Mabel had told him to pick her up at exactly three thirty in front of the nursing home where she volunteered every Friday. No sense starting off on the wrong foot. When Mabel gave an order, she expected prompt compliance.

Idling at the red light at the corner, he spotted her stocky figure on the sidewalk up ahead, tapped the horn, and waved. Mabel planted her fists on her ample hips. He pulled to the curb, put the truck in Park, and hopped out.

"Ray Reed, look at the time! You gonna stare all day or help me up into this monstrosity?" Mabel glanced skeptically at the truck, then offered him her arm. "I might need a ladder."

"Hello, Miss Mabel." He kissed her cheek. "No need for a ladder. I'll get you in."

"Hello to you, too." Her dark eyes sparkled, belying her gruff words. "Get a move on. You know what I always say, 'Time is a tool—'"

" 'Not to be wasted,'" he finished and laughed.

"Smarty-pants." She grinned.

Mabel had been ordering him around since the day he stood on tiptoes to see her assisting behind the counter at Cora's sweet shop. Nothing like a command from Mabel to remind him he was home. He'd get his life back on track here. He could feel it in his bones.

Ray helped her into the passenger seat, hopped back into the cab, and merged slowly into traffic. "Thank you for taking me in at the last minute."

She glanced at him. "Kind of impulsive of you to make a last-minute decision to come back, but then you always were kind of impulsive. Besides, I'm glad you're home. Means you're coming back to your senses."

Ray shrugged. "I don't know if that's possible."

She sniffed. "Well, did you get rid of that dangerous motorcycle?"

"Not ready to do that, I'm afraid."

"Where is it?"

"In the back of this truck with my furniture."

"Hmm. Then you're right. You haven't come back to your senses."

He hit a bump in the road, and she grunted.

"Sorry, Miss Mabel. The shocks in these trucks aren't the greatest."

"I can feel that." Mabel massaged her neck. "I'm gonna have to see my chiropractor after this ordeal."

"You still see Dr. . . .what's his name? Douglas?"

She nodded. "Sure do. Tom Douglas. And he's still sweet on Cora."

Ray laughed. "They've been sweet on each other as long as I can remember. I'm surprised they haven't tied the knot."

"Neither of them ever been married. Both scared to death. Silly, is what I think." She snorted. "And not the first ones I know who're scared to fall in love."

Mabel had always been straightforward, but Ray had to ask. "Do you mean me?"

"Oh no. You're not afraid of love; you best fine-tune your con meter, though." She laughed. "Anyway, I'm praising the Lord that you've come back where you belong. You miss home?"

"I'll say." Ray eyed her smooth, mahogany skin. "You look good, Miss Mabel. You never change."

She rolled her eyes. "I'm hoping you changed. You shouldn't of left home to begin with. Just my opinion."

Mabel fanned herself with her ever-present handkerchief, filling the cab of the truck with gardenia perfume. He couldn't help pondering the wisdom of her statement.

"Running away doesn't solve anything." As was her habit, Mabel hummed between sentences. "Yep, trust Old Mabel on that. I did some running in my day 'fore I met my Ralphie."

Mabel's husband had passed away fifteen years ago, yet she often spoke of him as if he were still alive. When encouraged to find another man, she protested that Ralph Peter Sanders had been the love of her life. No one could ever replace him. Ray sighed. What would it be like to have a woman who loved him that much? At one time he thought that woman was Bailey. Perhaps she still could be. Only the Lord knew, but Mabel was right—the time he'd spent in the Tri-Cities had brought him to his senses. The distance made him realize how much he missed his home.

"Speaking of running, you heard from your mama?"

He nodded. "Got an e-mail. She's somewhere in the Middle East covering a story."

"Never could handle her grief over your daddy, always being gone for business." Mabel hummed and nodded. "But you never blamed her none."

"Why would I? I had you and Cora." He glanced at her. "Speaking of careers, I was offered my old job back. I drove up last week to qualify." The thought didn't bring him the joy he thought it should.

Mabel tucked her handkerchief into her pocketbook. "Hm-hm. You were a great cop, and you could do that anywhere." Her dark eyes snapped up to his. "So what really brought you back here? Strange decision after you didn't visit all this time. Even before that, we didn't see much of you. Always dating that. . .what was her name? Sally?"

"Bailey." He was struck with remorse. "I'm sorry I didn't visit. I guess I went through a pretty selfish phase."

She patted him on the knee. "No matter about that," she said briskly. "Happens to everyone. Point is, you're home—and don't avoid the question."

He couldn't fool Mabel. She always managed to figure things out. As a kid he suspected she had a phone line to heaven. Now he knew it was a combination of discernment, experience, and common sense. If he were a hundred percent honest, he'd tell Mabel he wanted his old life back. His life before Bailey Cummings cheated on him with Dwight Connor, a local public defender. But he wasn't up for a sermon.

"I feel like God led me back here." Ray shrugged. "We'll see what happens."

"Uh-huh. I believe the first, but you aren't sayin' everything." She clucked her tongue. "No matter. Truth will tell. And you're in good hands now. Cora fixed up the biggest bedroom for you." Mabel chuckled. "It's gonna be nice having you around, son."

"Thanks for letting me stay. I'm not sure I could have found another rental so last-minute."

She slapped his arm. "If you'd gone anywhere else we would have dragged you back to our place. It's a divine appointment. Besides, you helping Cora and me with the repairs on that old Victorian across the street in trade for room and board is a godsend. We can trust you to do things right."

He smiled. "What made you decide to buy the Victorian? It's going to be a lot of work running a bed-and-breakfast."

She breathed a heavy sigh. "After we sold the candy store we found ourselves with too much time on our hands." Mabel wagged her head. "Idleness is the devil's workshop, you know. So we came up with the idea of a bed-and-breakfast. Ralphie left me very comfortable. Might as well put some of that to good use." She grinned. "I always did have my eye on that place."

"One taste of Cora's cooking and the place will be booked every weekend." Ray lingered at the Stop sign and scanned the canopy of tree branches. "I'll only be staying a few months. Once I get your B&B in shape, I'll rent a place of my own in town."

"Hmm, that old Victorian's gonna take a lot longer than a couple months to fix up."

"Philip and a few friends promised to help."

"Still, a lotta work." She smiled. "But that's good. Cora and I, we're gonna love having your company."

"You sure about that?" Ray laughed. "Remember when Miss Cora beat me over the head with a rolled-up newspaper for stealing—"

"Jelly rings." Mabel's shoulders shook with laugher. "Lord, help us all. I thought your daddy was going to do worse than Cora that day. Tan your hide till you couldn't sit." She started laughing again, then rested her hand on his arm. "You were only a kid. A stubborn, willful little boy, but you turned out to be a fine man. Your daddy should see you now."

Ray turned away from her and swallowed past the ache in his throat.

"Here we are," Mabel said as though she needed to point out the cozy Cape Cod where he'd spent more time than he could count as a teen searching for purpose.

"Looks like Cora is home." He pulled up behind their 1960 Thunderbird, went around to the passenger door, and helped her down.

"I'm sorry for bringing up your daddy." Mabel reached up and brushed a finger over his cheek. "The missing never goes away. We just have to trust the Lord to fill the gaps however He sees fit until we see them again."

"You can talk about Dad anytime. It's nice remembering, even though it's sometimes still painful." Arm in arm, Ray walked her to the pristine white picket fence lined with daisies. "He's been gone a long time now."

"Too long. Everybody loved your daddy." She let go of his arm and pointed across the street. "The old Victorian is beautiful, isn't it?"

He nodded. "It will make a great bed-and-breakfast."

"Yes indeedy." Mabel hummed her way up the flagstone path and up the porch steps to the red front door.

Ray began to follow, then stopped and looked around the yard. "Did you hear that?"

"What? I don't hear a thing." Mabel turned and came back down the stairs.

"Some kind of whimpering." Spotting movement in the hedges to his right, he cut across the yard. "What is that?" The low branches stirred, and he hunkered down. Mabel joined him. The whimpering grew louder, and a doe-eyed fur ball limped out. "Look at this," Ray said. "We've got a hurt pup here."

"Oh my," Mabel groaned.

He thought he saw movement out of the side of his eye. He glanced up, but the dog trembled, and he turned his attention back to her. He examined her, but she didn't move to bite him. She stared up into his eyes as though to plead for help. "Poor thing. I'm worried the leg might be broken. We should be careful."

"Looks like one of them little terrier dogs, if you can call something this size a dog. I don't think God made 'em to be this small, like a guinea pig with long legs, but what do I know?" Mabel's eyes and touch were soft, despite her words, and she stroked the dog's tiny head.

Ray picked up the dog and held her in his arms like a baby. "I'd better take her to the animal hospital. Is PetVet still out there on—"

"No, not there! You take that poor baby over to Faith's vet clinic. She'll take care of her."

He started at the name. "Faith? Faith Hart?"

Mabel nodded. "Didn't have time to tell you everything, but while you were exploring your angst, Faith Hart came to town. It's been a long, long time since we seen her. Anyway, she's our neighbor now. She bought her grandmother's old house." She nodded in the direction of a blue-sided two-story next door. "She opened a vet clinic in town while you were gone."

"I figured she was still in the navy."

"No." Mabel stroked the dog's head. "She didn't do that upping thing they talk about."

"You mean 're-upping' into the military?"

"Yes, that's it."

Ray's mind raced with follow-up questions, but he had to tend to the dog. "Will Faith take me without an appointment?"

" 'Course she will." Mabel looked at her wristwatch. "She's open until five tonight, but won't leave until at least six. The door is open anytime she's there, even after hours. Dr. Hart will take good care of the pup." She explained the location of the clinic to him, and Ray headed toward the rental truck.

Doctor Faith Hart. Yes, it made perfect sense. Back in the day during summers with her grandmother, Faith took in every stray in the neighborhood, even box turtles. That's how they'd met—rescuing two sickly kittens from a cardboard box on the side of the road. She had always wanted to be a vet. The warm bundle stirred next to his chest, and he stared into her chocolate eyes, suddenly feeling like a little boy. "Miss Mabel, if Faith can help the dog and we can't find the owner, can we. . ."

A grin lit her eyes. "As long as you take care of the pup, we'll let you keep her." From the open truck window he thought he heard, "Still the same Ray."

She turned and waved. "Just get home in time for dinner. Cora's got your favorites planned." Mabel was chuckling as he drove off.

Chapter 2

Faith inspected an acrylic glass enclosure, then looked at Lindsey, the veterinarian assistant. "When's the last time these cages were cleaned?"

The young woman shrugged. "I cleaned them myself not more than two hours ago, Dr. Hart. Birds will be birds."

Faith felt the bite of impatience and took a deep breath. *Lord, help me change. . . .* Her need for cleanliness at the clinic bordered on obsession. It was a burden for her, not to mention her staff, but she couldn't seem to help herself.

"Here." Faith pointed. "Can't you see this? There's bird breath all over the glass."

"Um, bird breath?" Lindsey shrugged again. "You mean those foggy spots?"

Faith released a noisy breath. "Yes, those foggy spots."

The enclosure held a macaw aptly named Nero who squawked like an angry chicken. A very loud chicken. The parrot had been treated with charcoal for munching on a lily from his owner's anniversary bouquet, and he was not a happy bird.

"There's no such thing as bird-breath spots," Lindsey grumbled as she went to the utility cabinet and grabbed a cleaning cloth. "I'll wipe it down *again* and risk my fingers to that carnivore." She glared first at Faith, then at the parrot, who protested his treatment with more vigor.

Faith closed her eyes. *Lord, help me be patient.* She couldn't risk losing Lindsey. The woman was better with animals than people and excelled in the examining room. A little like herself, come to think of it. She prepared to apologize to Lindsey for nit-picking, hoping it would help the woman's mood, when the sound of the bell signaled that someone had entered the clinic.

"Is Gladys still out there?" Hands clasped, Faith resisted the urge to snatch the cloth from Lindsey's hand and clean the cages herself.

"No. She left early to—"

"That's right. I remember now. I'll go see who it is while you finish cleaning." Faith ignored Lindsey's exaggerated sigh, turned, and hurried down the blue-tiled hallway to the reception cubicle. She stopped at the counter, staring at a tall, dark-haired man. He looked vaguely familiar. Handsome. Very. Her gaze dropped to his arms where he cradled a small wire-haired terrier.

As straight and tall as she stood from military training and being raised in a military family, she had to look up to meet his gaze.

"How may I help you?"

A broad, warm smile creased his cheeks. She almost laughed at the incongruous sight of the big man holding the small dog.

He chuckled. "Tiny, huh?"

Faith blinked and stared into his eyes. Truth dawned. "Ray?"

"Faith?" They spoke at the same time.

He winked, and her breath caught. For a moment she went dizzy as memories flooded her mind. *Ray!* She dashed around the counter but caught herself before she jerked him into a hug. They stood face-to-face for what seemed an eternity.

"We need to catch up, but I have an emergency here." He held the dog out for her inspection.

Her attention dropped to the tiny creature. "What happened? Is she yours?"

"I don't know what happened to her; and no, she's not," he said. "I found her in the bushes between Mabel and Cora's house and your grandmother's—your house. I'm afraid the leg might be broken."

Faith examined the dog. "I've got a lot of questions for you, but right now you need to follow me. I have to x-ray that leg."

"Look at you," he said as they hurried down the hall to the back where she operated on her patients. "You're a real doctor. A vet."

She snorted. "Yes, well, no big deal."

"No big deal? Of course it's a big deal."

Too bad her father didn't think so. "If you say so, I guess it is. What I do know is it's a lot of work." She pointed where she wanted him to place the dog. "Lindsey!"

"What?" Lindsey snapped from the other room.

Ray's eyebrows rose, but Faith ignored his reaction.

"I need your help sedating this dog."

"I'll help, too, if you need me," Ray offered.

As soon as Lindsey saw the dog, her irritation faded, and she jumped right into her job, directing Ray as well.

"No break," Faith said a few minutes later after examining the X-rays. She was amazed at how relaxed she felt in Ray's presence—how easily they were falling back into a comfortable relationship.

Lindsey bustled around, cleaning up. Faith felt doubly guilty for her earlier impatience. "Lindsey, you go on home now. You'll get overtime for staying late. I'll finish up."

"Okay." The young woman left with one last smile for the small dog.

Ray stroked the dog's tiny, still head. "I'm glad she doesn't have any broken bones."

"Me, too, but I wonder how this happened." She glanced up at Ray. "I'm afraid she's been kicked."

"I hope no one did this deliberately." Ray rubbed the dog's ears between his fingers. "Really sad to think that someone might have hurt this gentle animal."

"Makes me furious." Her stomach clenched. "I see so much animal abuse."

Ray patted her shoulder gently. "I've seen a great deal of all sorts of abuse as a cop. It gets very old. The worst is when it's kids."

Anger tugged at her. She couldn't imagine dealing with child abuse cases. With her temper, she'd be tempted to take on an abuser.

They were silent while she finished her work on the dog.

After washing her hands, Faith turned her attention to Ray. "Cora and Mabel told me you took a break from your job. Is that why? All the bad things you saw? Were you burned out?"

Ray inhaled and shifted uncomfortably. "I guess that was part of it." He shrugged. "It's not as bad as life in New York City, I'm sure, but police work can make one cynical, even in Bothell."

He grew silent, and she decided to try a different conversational direction. "Last I saw you I was sixteen, remember? Dad didn't want me hanging around with a 'rebellious musician.'"

Arms spread, Ray chuckled. "And now I'm a keeper of the law." He looked her up and down, making her want to blush. "You were a couple inches taller than me at the time, but still. . .just as beautiful."

She did blush. "Now you tower over me." She took in his visage again. Standing straight and tall, his thick, dark hair mussed, he was more handsome than ever.

"I missed seeing you during the summers after your dad was transferred from Bremerton to Virginia Beach. Your mom died, then your grandmother moved, too, and I never saw you again." Ray's sincere dark eyes searched hers.

"Mom." Faith sighed. "That kind of change in a teen's life changes everything. But that's why Dad accepted the transfer. And why Grandma moved with us. To take care of us in Virginia. She was the saving grace of my life, you know. I missed the freedom of those summers in Bothell." She smiled. "But that's past. Now is now. What were you doing at Mabel and Cora's? Last I heard you'd left town, but my partner just had a baby, and her schedule is erratic. I've been filling in for both of us. I haven't talked to the sisters for over a week."

"I'm going to move in with them."

"Mabel and Cora?" She sounded like a parrot. "Really?"

"It's temporary. The apartment I had lined up didn't work out at the last minute. We're sort of bartering. I'm going to work on the Victorian they bought in trade for rent."

"Nice. They could use the help." She focused on the terrier.

"I'll pay for everything you did for the dog," Ray said. Always the hero.

"Don't worry about that. I'm not worried about the money as much as I am the dog. I'll put out notices and see if I can find the owner." She tightened her lips. "I will need to determine if they are abusive or if something else happened."

Nodding, Ray moved closer to her. The sight of his guitar-string-calloused fingertips brought on a fresh flood of memories.

Faith returned her gaze to the dog and cleared her throat. "This little girl is an orphan for the moment, so I don't have an owner to call. She seems so fragile. . . ." She considered options. "I really don't want to leave her in the kennel. She'll wake and be terrified. Once she comes out of sedation, I'll take her home with me." She toyed with the idea of inviting Ray over to dinner at her place to catch up.

He glanced at his watch. "I didn't realize the time. I've got to go. Mabel ordered me to be home for dinner. Apparently Cora has something special planned."

Faith covered her disappointment with a laugh. "That sounds like Cora. Leave me your number, and I'll keep you posted about the dog."

Ray rested his hand on her shoulder. "Thanks. So good to see you again, Faith. Or do you want me to call you doctor?"

"Doctor? Between friends?" She smiled up into those dark eyes that seemed to read her.

Ray pulled out his wallet and handed her a business card. "The address is wrong, but that's my cell number."

Smiling, she gave him a mock salute. "You'll be hearing from me."

"Good." His full lips turned up in a slow smile. "Look forward to it."

Faith watched him leave the room. He had been her buddy during the warm summers when she'd stayed in Bothell with her grandmother—until her family moved to Virginia Beach. At the same time he started sending her letters declaring his undying love to her. That scared her, but worse was her father's disapproval. What had she really been thinking at the time? It was hard to remember. She guessed her mother's passing had something to do with that—a sort of grief-induced amnesia. And where had avoiding her father's disapproval gotten her? Since she'd left the military, she was a disappointment to him on every level.

The terrier began to move on the table, and she stroked the pup's bony head and found a piece of glitter on her fingertips. "What did you get into, girl? I think I'm going to name you Sparkles till we find your rightful owner." She smiled. "A perfect name for you since you came from Ray."

Faith hummed as she waited for the dog to fully wake up. She was unaccountably happy. Ray looked good. She closed her eyes and pictured him. No, he looked great. Was he seriously dating anybody? Faith frowned and chastised herself. The clinic took all her time. Her father might see her as the prodigal daughter who didn't re-up in the navy—but she would show him. She'd make a success of herself. She'd not get sidetracked with romantic notions. But, oh my. Ray Reed—

Faith checked through the messages Gladys had left on her desk. *Your dad called.* He'd also called her cell phone, but she'd ignored it. Her good mood seeped away. The mere thought of her father made her worry she'd done something wrong. As if she were a teenager and had to hide things from him. Like Ray Reed being back in town. How silly was that? Her father had mostly washed his hands of her anyway.

Snap out of it, Faith! She tried to focus on her tiny patient. Ray would be living with Cora and Mabel—a few steps from her house. Faith couldn't restrain a smile.

Chapter 3

Ray swiped his boots on the outdoor mat, then rang the bell. The red door swung open, and he stepped inside the foyer into Cora's open arms.

"Miss Cora." He kissed her cheek.

"Don't you dare ring the bell," she chided him. "This is your home, you know."

"I've missed you."

"Look at you," she said. "All grown up."

Ray shut the door while he chuckled. "It's not like I've been gone *that* long."

"It's been long enough." She narrowed her dark eyes, so much like Mabel's, and looked him up and down. "You've lost weight."

He stuck his thumbs in his waistband. It was loose. "I had this goofy good friend in the Tri-Cities who fed me health food."

"Bah! Health food." Cora clucked her tongue.

Mabel came bustling up behind her sister and glanced at her watch. "You're right on time. Now, how is that little slip of a dog?"

"Fine. Faith x-rayed that leg. No broken bones." Ray glanced around. Floral paper covered the wall in the hallway, and a gilded mirror hung over a mahogany sideboard. Old-fashioned, just like the sisters. There was only one thing new. A gold-framed photo of Mabel and Cora in their Sunday best hanging in a prominent position in the hall.

"Nice." Ray pointed. "Where'd that come from?"

"Faith snapped the picture of us," Mabel said. "Gave it to us last Christmas."

"We're going to put it in the Victorian." Cora tilted her head, studying the photo. "We're calling it Two Sisters' Bed and Breakfast."

"Great name. And I'm impressed with Faith's work."

"It's her hobby," Cora added. "She says it's a good hobby for her. All about perfection."

"She'll sneak up on you and snap a photo faster than you can blink," Mabel warned. "Don't be surprised."

"Hmm." What other things had changed about Faith in the years they'd been out of contact? "Well, the house looks great. Just like I remember." He planted another kiss on each sister's cheek. "And you guys do, too."

"Flattery will get you everywhere." Cora laughed and swatted him with the dish towel she'd had draped over her shoulder.

"You go wash up and come to the table," Mabel ordered. "Supper's ready."

Ray took an appreciative sniff. "Yes, so it is. I'll be right back."

He hurried to the half bath under the stairs, feeling like the prodigal returned. After scrubbing his face and hands in the washroom, he looked in the mirror and found himself smiling. His first day home and things seemed to be working out well. He hoped it was a harbinger of good things to come. Monday he'd be back to work. What was left was to contact Bailey. He'd heard she was no longer seeing Dwight and went to visit her folks in California to recover. Perhaps. . .

He smiled wider. Then there was Faith. What an extra bonus—having his old friend next door.

Ray exited the washroom and went to the butcher-block table in the center of the eat-in kitchen, which was covered with plates of food.

"Is this what you call supper?" He almost forgot what the sisters considered an evening meal. "This is a feast fit for a king. Yum, fried chicken. And sweet potatoes. And mashed potatoes and gravy."

Cora nodded, eyes shining with pride. "Always been your favorites."

Mabel filled his glass to the brim with sweet tea. "Now sit down, and let's pray before the 'feast' gets cold."

"My pleasure." Ray sat, clasped his hands, and closed his eyes as Mabel uttered solemn words of thanks to God. They said their amens, and the sisters began passing platters. His friend Shannon from the Tri-Cities should see him now. She'd have a cautionary tale about each food group. Shannon with her salads, tofu, and herbal teas.

"So, you saw Faith then?" Mabel's tone was far too casual, which meant she had something to say.

Ray nodded, mouth full, and steeled himself for whatever was coming next.

Cora and Mabel exchanged glances. "She's a good girl," Mabel said. "Tidy, organized, and a good cook."

He didn't need the reminder about her tidiness and organization. Faith's father kept her on a military agenda even as a teen. But the only thing she ever cooked that he remembered was chocolate chip cookies. "I didn't get a chance to ask her how she ended up in Bothell."

"She loved this town. Good memories for her." Mabel waved her fork as she talked.

Cora nodded. "After she opened the clinic, her grandmother's old house came on the market. She snatched it up in a big hurry. Paid more than it was worth, too."

"When her granny passed, Faith was heartbroken," Mabel said.

Poor Faith. Her grandma's house was the one place she could go to escape and be herself. He could only imagine how her life was after they moved and she no longer had a place to visit. "I remember how much she loved her grandma."

"Yes, that's a fact." Mabel passed him the mashed potatoes. "Eat!"

"Don't be shy." Cora added another crispy chicken leg to his plate. "Last July Faith moved in with us for a couple of months while she opened the clinic. Drives us to church, too. Still does. We like to be driven to church on Sunday morning."

"Really?" He stared from one sister to the other. "Don't tell me you let her drive that Thunderbird of yours. You never let me drive it."

Cora studied him with a raised brow. "You're a boy. Reckless."

"I'm a cop. Not reckless."

"High-speed chases," Mabel said.

Ray laughed. "Not if I can help it." He paused. "So Faith goes to Bothell Community Church?"

"Yes, indeed." Cora smiled wide.

"No kidding." Interest piqued, Ray held his tongue while he waited for more.

"Praise God. Faith lost her way for a while, but then she came back to the Lord," Mabel added. "We keep track of kin."

Kin. That's how Mabel and Cora thought of all the kids they'd known and taken in over the years. "I always liked having her around in the summers when we were teenagers." Too late he realized he'd given Cora and Mabel fodder—they were infamous matchmakers.

Cora laughed. "You sure was sweet on her."

Mabel stared at him expectantly.

Yep, this was what he'd signed up for. The sisters would always think of him as a little boy in need of advice. "C'mon, I was a kid. Summer love. Puppy love."

"Puppy love, huh?" Mabel rolled her eyes, then pointed to the front of the house. "You'd be sittin' out there on the porch, strumming your guitar, writing love songs—"

"I was seventeen, Miss Mabel." But they had a point, and Ray couldn't help but laugh. It was the summer of Faith's sixteenth birthday when she said she wouldn't be returning to Bothell for summer vacations. His letters to Faith went unanswered. "I was surprised Faith didn't stay in the navy."

"Mmm, her daddy was, too. Faith was expected to keep up with her two brothers. Rise in the ranks." Cora sighed. "Make the old man proud."

"Poor girl." Mabel dropped a second helping of buttered beans onto his plate. "Four years in the navy. Honorable discharge. Went to vet school. Opened a clinic." She sniffed. "Not good enough for her papa."

"I'd tell him a thing or two," Cora murmured.

"Can't tell you the times I've wanted to call him," Mabel said. "He should be ashamed."

Sympathy stirred in his heart for his friend. "It hurts when you can't be yourself." Ray set down his fork. "Remember when I used to say I wanted to be a musician? I must've sounded like a fool."

"Musician would have suited you, too," Mabel said. "You just didn't have anywhere to do it."

"Some people take to their jobs like a duck to water." Cora chuckled. "Your brother. . .oh, that Philip was gung ho about law enforcement." Both sisters laughed.

"He still is—probably more than me." Ray thought about Faith again and smiled. "I'm glad it all worked out for Faith. She got her wish to become a vet."

"She's beautiful." Cora leveled a gaze at him. "And you two might want to pick up where you left off." She wiggled her eyebrows. "I'm just saying."

"No, no." He had to make his position clear. Nip the matchmaking in the bud. "I'm hoping I can patch things up with—"

"No!" Cora said.

"Oh my, you don't mean. . .her." Mabel's fork hit her plate with a loud clank. "That Sally up and left you for another man. How could you ever trust her again?"

"Her name's *Bailey*." The reminder was like a knife to his heart. Ray released a pent-up breath. "It was partly my fault. I was too focused on my job. I didn't give Bailey the time she needed. I should've—"

Mabel's incredulous glare and Cora's open mouth rendered him silent.

"Such a thing as *faithfulness*," Mabel muttered.

"And being too trusting." Cora nodded.

The doorbell rang, and Ray rocketed out of his chair. "I'll get it," he said, relieved to dodge the subject of Bailey and her infidelity. Had he been too trusting in his personal life? Hadn't being a cop taught him anything?

Ray opened the door. Faith stood there. She had shed her medical jacket, and the deep blue of her blouse emphasized the depth of her brown eyes.

"Hello?" A tiny worried frown wrinkled her brow. "May I—"

"Sure. Come on in." Ray stepped aside. Faith had been a pretty teen, but now. . .

"Who is it?" Mabel called from the kitchen.

"Faith!" He cleared his throat.

"Faith, honey, you come on in here," Cora yelled. "We haven't seen you in too long."

"Guess I'd better." Faith shut the door behind her. "I have a question, and I need to ask them as well as you."

"How's the puppy?" he asked on their way down the hall.

"I've got her tucked in at my house. She'll be fine." At the door to the kitchen, she grinned up at him and her eyes narrowed with humor. "I named her Sparkles for old time's sake."

"Like the stuffed alien bear with sparkly antennas that I won at the fair for you when you were fourteen? You remember that?"

She nodded. "Not only do I remember that, but I still have her. And other things."

"Really?" He kept a plastic bin full of things Faith had given him over the years, too. It warmed his heart to know he still meant something to her.

Chapter 4

Faith straightened her blouse as she walked in the kitchen and made sure it was tucked into her jeans. She greeted the sisters with a smile. "I'm sorry to interrupt your dinner. I didn't even change before I came over."

"Don't you dare get formal with us," Mabel said. "Sis, why don't we set another place at the table?"

"Miss Cora, don't do that. I appreciate the offer, but I can't stay." Faith avoided Ray's gaze. For reasons she couldn't fathom she felt like a jittery schoolgirl around her old friend. "I actually came by to ask if you guys stopped over today or anybody saw suspicious activity around my house."

Ray stepped into her line of vision. "Why? What's wrong?"

Faith searched his concerned eyes. Just like old times. Nobody messed with her during her summertime visits to Bothell. Not with Ray Reed around. She waved her hand in a nonchalant gesture. "No big deal really, but I believe somebody was in my screened-in porch, maybe my house."

"What? And you didn't call the police?" Ray frowned at her.

" 'Course she did." Mabel eyeballed him. "She's here, ain't she?"

"Well, I'm not in uniform," Ray said.

"Don't matter," Mabel shot back.

"Hmm-hmm, you'd better have a look, Ray." Cora glanced at Mabel.

"I'd say so." Mabel nodded her agreement. "You go on over there now, son."

Faith studied the two with narrowed eyes. They weren't. . .matchmaking, were they? They had a reputation for that kind of thing.

"Never know these days," Mabel quickly added. "No sense taking any chances."

Faith's shoulders relaxed. Of course they weren't matchmaking. They knew her situation, and during their last heart-to-heart conversation, they'd concurred there was nothing wrong with staying single to focus on career goals.

"I'll go check it out." Ray took his plate to the sink. "Ladies, thank you so much for the delicious meal. I'll help you clean up as soon as I get back."

"You bet you will or I'll have your hide," Cora said, and she and Mabel laughed.

Ray held open the front door. "They're laughing, but I think Cora's serious."

Faith snickered. Ray was adorable with the feigned worried look on his face. "Cora could still take you. Mabel, too."

"No doubt." He walked behind her through a break in the hedge between her house and the sisters'. The same little opening they had used when they were teens.

"Nice truck." He nodded at her blue Chevy. "Is that your clinic name on the side?"

"Yep. Hart and Downey Veterinarian Clinic." She laughed. "Our last names. Original, huh?"

"The truck is good advertising."

"Exactly."

They reached the gate that led to her backyard, which was surrounded by a split rail fence that was covered on the inside with chicken wire.

"This wasn't here when your grandmother owned the place."

"No. I had it put up after I moved in. Sometimes I'll bring home a dog from the clinic, like I did with Sparkles. Or one of my friends in rescue work will need a temporary place for a dog. It's easier with a fence."

He pointed at an open padlock hanging on the gate. "Do you usually keep this locked?"

"Most of the time." She glanced at the padlock. "I guess I forgot last time I was out here. And someone who is determined could climb the fence. It's not that tall. I just keep it locked so kids can't get back here when I'm keeping dogs."

They stepped through the gate into her backyard. "Where's the puppy?"

Faith's cheeks heated. "In my bedroom in a crate. I know. I'm a sucker."

"Like those kittens you nursed back to health." Ray laughed. "Remember? You let them sleep with you in bed at your grandmother's every night for a week until your father visited and discovered them."

"Yeah. I still can't stand to see an animal hurting, but I don't sleep with them anymore—at least ones I don't know." She bit her lip. "Remember Dad said I'd get fleas or mange? Turns out he was partially right, but I didn't care."

He smiled. "Reminds me of old times. You going on and on about taking care of animals."

"Was I obnoxious?"

"No, it's one of the things I loved about you." Ray gave her a nudge. "I knew we were simpatico ten minutes after we met."

She felt warmed by the reminder. They had been that. Attached from the very beginning. She pointed at the porch door. "Well, this is the scene of the crime."

He glanced around the porch. "Okay, I know this might sound offensive, but did you lock this outside door?"

Faith bit her nail and shrugged. "I guess I wasn't so concerned about this since the gate is usually locked."

His single raised eyebrow said it all.

"I know it's stupid," she said. "And it's weird. I'm so picky about most things, but locks on doors? It's like a brain burp or something."

"Brain burp." He laughed. "Well, everyone has quirks. Yours might as well be burping."

His understanding smile sent warmth through her.

She watched as Ray examined the door to the enclosed porch. His glance slid toward her. "Truthfully, this lock wouldn't be that hard to get through for anyone determined."

"Most houses wouldn't be hard to get into for anyone determined, locked or not," she countered.

"True enough," he agreed.

She swiped an imaginary speck of dust from the glass top of the wicker table and glanced around, fighting a tiny bit of anxiety.

He noticed. "Why do you think someone was here?"

"See that can of birdseed?" Faith pointed at a large tin next to the back door. "I go out every day and put seed in the bird feeder in the backyard. The can was moved."

He pointed at a round indentation where the can originally sat. "You're sure you didn't accidentally kick it or something?"

She shrugged. "I'm not, no. That's why I didn't call the police. I feel stupid."

"Don't," he said. "You know your habits, and I trust your instincts."

She smiled and watched him look around, heart light that he still had faith in her.

"Was anything missing?"

"If there was, it was nothing important. That's the odd part." Faith shook her head and sighed. "I might be missing a banana and an apple, but then I start to question myself. Did I eat them? I might forget locks, but it seems I would know if someone had taken something."

"Right." Ray scanned the porch and nodded. "I can see that. There's a place for everything. Spotless."

Faith's face warmed as she followed his gaze. Did he see her as a neurotic nitpicker, same as the clinic staff?

"Take me inside and show me around the kitchen."

She opened the back door.

"This was unlocked, too?"

"Yes, I think so," she said. "And all the locks are original to the house. No one changed them."

They stepped into her kitchen. The green walls immediately soothed her.

"Nice," he murmured as he looked around the kitchen.

"There's the bowl of fruit." She nodded at the table. "I'm pretty sure something is missing."

Ray studied the room, then sighed.

She pulled back a chair from the table. "Would you like to sit?"

Ray took a seat, and Faith settled in a chair directly facing him.

"If my father didn't teach me 'a place for everything, and everything in its place,' four years in the navy reinforced it."

"Well, it's not a bad thing." Ray's tone was comforting, and she smiled. "Case in point, my friend Shannon back in the Tri-Cities came close to losing her business, a junk shop sort of, and all because..." Ray looked thoughtful, like he was searching for a nice way of making his point. "Shannon had a hard time with 'a place for everything, and everything in its place.'"

Faith couldn't hold back a laugh. "Sounds like a real character."

"You guys would get along great," he said.

"Is she your. . .um." She paused. "Sorry. That's not my business."

"No, she's not my girlfriend." He laughed long and hard. "She'd be so amused to hear that. She's a wonderful friend, and she's engaged to a nice guy."

"Good. I mean, good for her." She looked into his eyes, then quickly glanced away, realizing what a good friend she'd lost when she never returned his letters. "Anyway, this break-in stuff may be the work of teen pranksters."

"Yes, or it might be more serious. I'm officially back to work at the Bothell Police Department Monday. Then I can make a suspicious activity report, but that's all I can do right now. I can't file an official report based on the incidents that have occurred so far but if it happens again, we'll have note of it." He leaned toward her. "You need to remember to lock your doors."

"I will." Her cheeks burned, and she looked down at the floor.

"Sorry. Don't mean to make you feel bad."

She rubbed the toe of her sneaker on the floor. "Thank you."

"It's good to see you again," he said softly, then he inhaled. "I've always wanted to know. Why didn't you write back to me?"

Her gaze snapped up to meet his.

"After you moved to Virginia Beach. You never wrote me like you promised before you left town."

She frowned. How to explain this without telling him the truth? That his intense letters declaring his love scared her to death at a point in her life when nothing made sense. And to make things even harder was the scowl on her father's face when he handed her Ray's letters.

"My father, I guess." Faith looked down at her hands, folded in her lap, remembering the comments her father had made about the "shiftless musician."

"Let me guess." Ray stretched out his long legs and strummed his fingers on the chair arms. "Your dad told you to stay away from me, right?"

She met Ray's dark gaze. "He was trying to control me. He always has."

"Hey, no big deal. It was natural for a career navy man not to want a longish-haired musician for his daughter." Ray laughed good-naturedly.

Tears stung the backs of her eyes. Father dearest. He had always been overbearing.

"Well, that was his prerogative as your father." Ray shrugged. "It happened a long time ago. He was trying to protect you. And you have to admit, I was pretty intense at that point. It would frighten any father."

And me, too.

"It was infatuation on my part, and it's okay." He smiled at her. "And now you're doing what you always dreamed of." Ray leaned forward and placed his finger under her chin, forcing her to look at him. "Faith Hart. A vet. A real doctor."

A breeze from the overhead fan ruffled his thick, dark hair and raised goose bumps on her arms. She forced her father from her mind and concentrated on her friend. "How about you? Did you buck the system along the way?"

"Afraid not. I was an angel." Ray held his thumbs and index fingers above his head to make a pretend halo. "Graduated from guitar to harp—for a while."

Faith giggled. She felt fifteen again.

"Seriously, I went into police work like my granddad, father, and brother. The closest I came to bucking the system was the sabbatical I took last year. I spent time in the Tri-Cities. That's when I met Shannon."

"What did you do to support yourself there?"

A grin flashed across his lips. "Besides using my savings, I gave guitar lessons and played for a Christian coffeehouse. Let's just say I lived cheap and lost weight." He winked at her. "But I didn't grow my hair long to save at the barber."

"Well, there's a good thing. You didn't totally go off the deep end." She paused and studied her old friend. "So, you're still a musician?"

He nodded, and she thought she detected confusion in his eyes, but it disappeared.

"A musician, yes, but I need to make money, so. . .I'm back." He spread his arms wide. "I'm ready to continue the family legacy of police work. For the time being."

She laughed. "Your family must be proud of you, Ray."

"My mother, when I hear from her, is supportive. Philip is ecstatic that I'm back."

"I'm looking forward to seeing Philip again. I remember him being so tall and more than a bit intimidating."

"Well, he's still tall."

Faith giggled again.

"And he can still be intimidating, especially to the bad guys." Ray looked at her long and hard. "So how about you? I'm sure your family is proud of you. It's no small feat becoming a vet."

Faith stood abruptly. "I think my brothers are proud of me. My father. . ." She didn't intend the sarcasm in her voice.

The chair scraped the tile floor, and Ray was beside her, open hand on her shoulder. "Sounds like things are still strained between you guys."

She pulled away from him. "My father hasn't changed, if that's what you mean." Her words sounded harsh.

Ray shifted and bit his lip.

"I'm sorry." Faith waved her hand and attempted a smile. "I have to let bygones be bygones."

"Nah, no explanation necessary. I'm working on that myself. A long story." He glanced at his watch. "Um, listen, I've got to get back, unpack some of my stuff. Just let me know what I can do to help with the dog. Like pay you?"

She considered that. "I'm not sure. Let's see if we can find her owner first. If not, we'll make some sort of deal. You were just a Good Samaritan. I hate to make you pay."

"And I hate to make you work for free."

She grinned at him. "Impasse."

He returned her smile. "Back at you."

How easy it was to fall back into familiarity.

"So, let's make time to talk, okay?"

Faith nodded. She was tempted to ask him to stay, if only for a few more minutes, but she had no reason. "I'm glad we're neighbors."

Ray winked. "Me, too." He glanced around the porch as he backed toward the door. "I'll do what I can about the possible break-in."

Faith gave him a thumbs-up. "Sounds good. See you tomorrow."

She watched as Ray crossed the lawn until he was out of sight. "I *am* glad we're neighbors," she whispered.

Chapter 5

The phone woke Faith at 6:00 a.m. Saturday morning. Only two people called her that early—her father or her partner, Debbie. Faith guessed this time it was the former since she'd forgotten to return his call. Would that be called a Freudian slip?

Reluctantly she picked up the phone. Before she got out a hello, her father reprimanded her. "Why didn't you call me back?"

"I'm sorry, Dad, but I'm busy with—"

"Your clinic."

His harsh tone made her shoulders go ramrod straight.

"No matter. I've got good news. Great news. Your brother, Richard, just made Master Chief. See what happens when you stick to it?"

Faith sighed. Richard had mentioned that he was studying for that, but she'd forgotten. They hadn't communicated in more than a month, and even when they did, it was just surface stuff. So what was the proper response to her father? An apology for disappointing him? Again? "That's great, Dad. I'll e-mail him on board ship to congratulate him."

"You can do it in person, too. The carrier will be back in Bremerton in another month."

Faith continued to look out the bedroom window, watching a red-haired child skirt the trees along the street. She thought it was a girl, but couldn't be sure. The kid disappeared behind a hedge, peeked out, and seemed to look directly at her. Strange. It was pretty early for a youngster to be out and running around, but there were a lot of families with children on the street. And she remembered times during summer vacation when she and Ray would sneak out before breakfast, sit under the trees, and play in the dirt.

Her mind turned, trying to figure out what her father wanted. "Maybe I can drive over there and take everyone out to dinner." The child was still looking at her before she took off down the street, glanced over her shoulder at her house again, then disappeared.

"Your sister-in-law is already planning something," Dad said. "If you're not too busy with that clinic of yours, I'm sure Richard would appreciate you coming. You don't live so far away that you couldn't drive there."

When Faith hung up the phone, her shoulders sagged. She always felt drained after a conversation with her father. Hard as she tried to adhere to

"Honor thy parents," a battle raged within to keep negative thoughts of him at bay. He'd gotten so much worse after her mother passed away—pushy, demanding, controlling. So much so that she was glad he lived in Oregon, hours away. She didn't have to see him regularly. And her clinic offered a great excuse to keep her distance. How awful to feel this way about her flesh and blood. She felt like an utter failure. Even Ray, the soulful musician, had continued the family legacy of police work.

Faith grabbed her laptop from her briefcase, turned it on, and opened her e-mail program. There she noticed an e-mail from her brother telling her about his promotion. She jotted a quick congratulations back to him. Then she went to the bedroom window that faced the side yard between her house and the sisters' place. Gazing across the yard, she forced her mind to good things. Like the fact that Ray was back in town. She sighed. This was the perfect time for a walk. That always improved her mood. She turned back to her bedroom and wondered if Ray was still in the habit of waking early and walking. Back when she came to visit her grandma in the summer, he joined her almost every morning. But Grandma claimed Ray only went for morning strolls when Faith was in town. Grandma had that glint in her eye that spoke much more. A little like the glint in Mabel's and Cora's eyes.

But that was then and this was now, and she and Ray had moved on. Faith changed into her walking shorts and a T-shirt, then made her bed, squaring the corners. Afterward she tidied the room and headed downstairs and outside.

While leaning over the porch rail to do her warm-up exercises, she heard a voice and jumped.

"Sorry I scared you." Ray backed away, hands raised. "I was eating breakfast and wondered if you still walked in the mornings, so I came outside to check."

Her heart warmed, realizing he still remembered. *He's really my friend,* Faith thought. "Yep, and I still fast walk."

"Mind if I join you?"

Faith tilted her head. "Sure. I'm headed to the Burke-Gilman Trail. You ready?"

≈

Keeping pace with the trim and in-shape Faith was heart-pounding exercise, something Ray enjoyed. "I've gotta watch what I eat, or I won't be able to do this anymore. I overdid it again last night. Cora and Mabel—"

"You can't live with them and not gain weight unless you make the effort." Faith laughed. "The couple of months I lived there I gained fifteen pounds and couldn't snap my jeans."

Ray laughed. "You'd never know it looking at you now." She was as near perfect as any woman he'd ever laid eyes on.

"Thanks for that." Faith's shy smile reminded him of all he'd missed about her friendship in the years gone by. He pointed to a grassy area and asked, "Wanna sit for a while?"

"Wimp." She poked him in the stomach and laughed. "Race you to that tree." They reached the large Western hemlock at the same time. Faith laughed and dropped to the grass. He joined her.

"I love this trail and its history. Cool how it used to be part of a railroad." She glanced around, then leaned back against the tree trunk. "Funny how time changes things, but sometimes if we build on the pleasant part of the old, something good comes of it."

"Pretty philosophical for a Saturday morning." Ray tilted back his head and let the July sun warm his face. "This feels good, Faith." Being with her reminded him of summertimes when they were kids. As though he were escaping—a vacation almost.

"Yeah, it's a gorgeous day."

"Right, but I meant being with you feels good. Like old times, huh?" He looked over at her and caught the hint of a blush on her oval face. Maybe it was the hard walking, but he had to know. "Do I make you feel uncomfortable?"

"What? No!" Faith shook her head, and her long, dark ponytail bounced with the action. "Why'd you ask?"

Ray shrugged. "We've been friends forever. You'd tell me if I changed— grew up to be too serious. Right?"

A small frown furrowed her brow. "You? Too serious? You were the most laid-back, mellow guy I knew." Faith tilted her head. "You're asking for a reason, though. What? Somebody accuse you of being a stuffed shirt?"

He should've known she'd get right to it. Ray shrugged. "Not exactly, but I was seeing someone. . .actually engaged to her, and—"

"Oh." An odd look crossed Faith's features. "Don't know why, but that took me by surprise. Go on, please."

He hesitated. "Nah. It can wait." It was too soon to spill the story about Bailey and him. "I'd rather we talk about you." Ray smiled to lighten the mood. "Why didn't you re-up in the navy? What brought you to that decision?"

"Um, okay, change of topic. Mental whiplash." Faith squinted and rubbed the back of her neck.

He chuckled. "Well, it is a serious question."

"And you ask me as if you've got a serious reason for wanting to know." Ray shrugged. "I might, I'm not sure."

"Okay, you know I've always loved animals."

"Always. Can't think of a day you didn't have one creature or another occupying your grandma's house."

"Promise you won't laugh." Faith's gentle brown eyes searched his as though for sincerity.

"You know me better than that," Ray said.

"Short story—I had a defining God moment."

Ray crossed his arms over his chest. "I want to hear the long story. I've got time."

Faith looked pensive for a moment, then nodded. "I was on board ship and had to decide whether to re-up or not. My father was pushing me, of course, but to be honest, I didn't mind being in the navy. He had retired and moved to Oregon, and he seemed to want to continue his career through his kids. The problem was, I didn't feel totally fulfilled. Something was missing, so I began to attend church services and seek the Lord." A tiny grin played on her lips. "I remember those years of Mabel and Cora talking about God's leading." She turned and fully faced him. "Anyhow, we were in port in Spain, and I was walking along, just praying to myself as my friends joked around." She looked off into the distance, as though reliving the moment. "The sun was going down, and I saw this beautiful white stucco church. I stood riveted as the sun hit it at such an angle that a stained-glass tree filled with birds was all I could see." Faith's gaze returned to him. "And I knew, Ray, it was a message from God. He takes care of every sparrow. Maybe it sounds weird, but if God loves the animals enough to take care of them, it's okay if I do, too. Not only that, but then He would take care of me as well."

He sat looking at her for a long moment. "That's beautiful, Faith. I pray He gives me a vision like that for my life."

Faith reached out and almost touched his face but pulled her hand back. "Me, too." She got up and summoned him with a wave of her hand. "Enough rest time. We've got some ground to cover."

Ray nodded, but couldn't take his eyes off his amazing friend. One day she'd make some guy very, very happy.

Chapter 6

Ray paced the kitchen, cell phone to his ear. "All right, I'll talk to you this afternoon. Enjoy your morning with your folks." He ended the call and put the phone on his belt, then he pulled it back and shut it off. He didn't want the phone ringing in the middle of the church service.

"I know that wasn't Faith," Mabel said behind him.

He turned. "Sneaking up on me? Spying on me?" For a woman of her size, Mabel was as quiet as a cat.

"Ray Reed, you know better." She dropped her pocketbook and Bible on the table and faced him in silence.

He sighed. She was waiting for an answer to her unspoken question. "No, it wasn't Faith. It was Bailey."

"Oh well, then you don't know that Faith can't come to church today. Now you can drive us."

"He'll do it?" Cora asked as she walked into the kitchen.

"Of course I'll drive you to church, ladies. I'll have to drive your car, though. No room on my bike."

"I should say so." Mabel checked her earrings.

Ray stood at the kitchen counter, gulped the last of his coffee, then put the empty cup in the sink. "So Faith drives you every Sunday morning, eh?"

Cora nodded and put a lace hankie in her black purse. "When we're so gussied up, we like to have someone else do the driving."

"Like a chauffeur?" Ray asked.

"Like the man of the house, so don't be a smarty-pants." Mabel reached over and straightened his tie even though it wasn't crooked.

Ray summoned a casual tone. "Faith had to go into the clinic today, huh?"

"Yes." Mabel took a lint roller from a drawer in the kitchen and ran it over her skirt. Then she began to run it over Ray's suit jacket. "Lift your arms."

He obeyed as he stifled a laugh, but his thoughts quickly veered toward Faith's safety. "You know, I think I'm going to let Faith keep that doggy. If anybody tries to break in while she's home—God forbid—at least the dog will bark. She can dial 911 right away."

Cora eyed him. "She wouldn't need no dog to protect her if she had a husband."

Ray scowled. "And I suppose it's my fault that she doesn't have a husband."

"There you go being a wise guy again," Mabel said as she finished with his suit. "Well, don't you worry, you'll see Faith later. We told her to join us for lunch today if she could."

Ray turned and looked at the smiling saint. "I wasn't worried, Miss Mabel. I'm only surprised she went into work today because you told me her clinic was open Monday to Saturday."

"Yes, but her partner's baby is sick, there was an emergency, and their fill-in vet couldn't make it either." Mabel examined her image in the small mirror hanging on the wall and adjusted her frilly lavender hat. Cora came up beside her and said, "Don't be a mirror hog, sister."

"That's the pot calling the kettle black," Mabel retorted.

Ray held back a laugh. Did other women at Bothell Community still wear such amazing creations on their heads? "Ready yet, ladies?"

Two sets of dark eyes snapped to his face as though he'd interrupted a solemn ritual. "I'm not rushing you," Ray quickly added.

Cora grabbed her keys off the kitchen table and dangled them in front of Ray. "Go warm up the car. You look like you've got ants in your pants."

Mabel glanced at her watch. "We've still got plenty of time."

That was priceless, coming from Mabel. But he did feel antsy even though it was early. Ray went out to the garage and pulled open the door. Perhaps he could talk the sisters into getting an automatic garage door opener. He stood there admiring the shiny old black Thunderbird. It still looked like new. They had a mechanic who appreciated classics and kept the car in mint condition. He turned the key in the ignition, and the engine roared to life. V-8 and powerful. He had a sudden boyish desire to take it out and see just how fast it could go. Not exactly the best thought for a grown man, let alone a cop.

While the car idled, Ray got out and leaned against the door, arms crossed over his chest. He couldn't help but look in the direction of Faith's house. Too bad she wasn't able to attend church with them. Truth be told, he'd been looking forward to visiting church with her, catching up again on old times. Just as friends. Not that Cora or Mabel would buy that story.

The two sisters walked from the house, arms filled with their pocketbooks and large Bibles.

"What were you looking at?" Cora asked when she reached him.

Ray's gaze shot in her direction. "I'm. . .nothing. I was warming up the car."

"And checkin' out Faith's house." Mabel stood beside the back door of the car next to her sister. "We're ready."

Ray opened the door for them. "What? You're both riding in the back? Like I really *am* your chauffeur?"

No response. Cora slid in beside Mabel. "Go on, now, we know you want to drive this baby."

"Since you were knee-high to a grasshopper," Mabel added.

"Yes, ma'ams." He got in and adjusted the seat and rearview mirror to his height. "You never let me drive this 'baby' before. Why now?"

"We're gonna trust you not to drive it like you did that hot rod Mustang you used to own." Cora grunted, then laughed. "Remember that thing?"

"How many tickets did you get?" Mabel asked. "Five?"

"Um, one." Ray paused. "Well, two if you count the parking violation."

Cora clucked her tongue. "Scalawag."

Ray laughed. The fifteen-minute drive to Bothell Community Church went by in a flash as they continued to reminisce. Ray pulled into a spot at the church, helped the sisters out of the car, and looked intently at the A-frame building where he came to know Jesus at age fifteen. Lord knew he was headed for trouble before that day, but his life had taken an amazing turn for the best.

Cora and Mabel walked in, and Ray followed. Most of the congregation was seated already, but he received a warm welcome in the form of smiles and waves.

He sat in a pew three rows from the front, Cora on one side and Mabel on his other. Soon they were joined by Tom Douglas, who sat on Cora's far side. Ray exchanged a smiling glance with Mabel, who just smiled back knowingly and hummed a soft tune.

While they waited for church to start, he glanced around the building. It had changed little. The stained-glass windows still threw color on the walls as the morning sun flowed through them. His gaze paused at one—Jesus carrying a sheep. Memory hit him like a hammer. That was the window he'd stared at during his dad's funeral. Ray had wished he could be a lamb and get carried away from the funeral service. To a green place where his father was still alive. Where everyone could be happy. The sky was filled with dark angry clouds during the graveside service, like Ray's heart. His mother's face was white and devoid of any emotion, as if she had become an empty shell when her husband died. Ray had watched his brother Philip's face for any sign that it was all right to cry. But Philip, then eighteen, stood strong and stoic, and so Ray, ten years old, clenched his jaw and swallowed a gallon of tears. That's when his Sunday school teacher, Mabel, had appeared from nowhere and hugged him from behind while Cora wrapped her arm around his mother's shoulders.

Mabel patted his arm, bringing him back to the present. "You okay, son?"

"Yeah." What had brought on all this remembering? Seeing Faith again? No matter. All was good. He put his hand over hers and with his other grabbed Cora's. "Thank you," he said softly. "I love you guys." And as if they knew what he meant, they squeezed his hands in return.

Pastor Gary Underwood stood at the altar, and Ray focused his full attention on the minister who knew how to rightly divide the Word of God. He loved most when Pastor Gary would take a word or two from Hebrew or Greek and get to the deepest core of a verse's original meaning.

"I'll get to the sermon in a sec," the pastor said, "but first I've got a request." He looked out over the congregation, smiling. "Why do you all look worried? No, I'm not going to ask for volunteers or take an extra offering." After the laughter subsided, the pastor continued. "Bothell Community is in dire need of a full-time music minister. As most of you know, we haven't been able to fill that slot since our brother, Kenny, retired due to illness." Pastor Gary paused and took a breath. "We need someone who knows music. Someone who can get along with people and flow with the church membership and leadership. Someone with a heart to worship God."

Ray inhaled.

"So please, pray on it, saints. We'll pray in unison now, and if the Lord stirs up the desire in your heart, please get back to me."

From the side of his eye, Ray saw Mabel glance at him, but he stared straight ahead. He was afraid if he looked at her, he'd be unable to contain his desire to run to the front of the church and accept the position on the spot.

Chapter 7

After the service, Tom took Cora's arm and walked her to the back door.

Mabel watched them. "Some folks just don't know when the time is right to step into what God has for them."

Ray glanced at her, but she had already started down the aisle. Had she been referring to Tom and Cora?

At the back door, the pastor and his wife, Nicole, greeted Mabel warmly. Then Pastor Gary turned to Ray and smiled. "Welcome back, son. You still play that guitar?"

"Yes, I do."

"If I called you to fill in, would you mind?"

Ray's heart beat faster. "Not at all."

Pastor Gary smiled, gave Mabel a hug, and moved to the next person.

Ray headed home with the sisters in near silence until Mabel slapped his shoulder from the backseat. "What's wrong, son?"

"Probably my imagination running away with me."

"What're you imagining?" Cora asked.

"I thought I was supposed to go back to law enforcement." Ray nodded to reassure himself. "I mean, look at how things worked out. But something strange happened in the service. . .while we prayed about the ministry position." He blew out a long breath and tried to shake off the feeling. "I'm a cop. I couldn't work full-time as a music minister."

"Hmm." Cora began to hum.

"The Lord give you a nudge?" Mabel asked.

"A nudge? It was more like a shove, which makes me wonder." Ray wagged his head. "No. . .I don't. . .no." He took a deep breath. "I think that punch of desire I felt in the service was my own wishful thinking. I have to be responsible. I have a job to do. I'm not a kid anymore with dreams of being a rock star."

"A rock star?" Mabel repeated, and both sisters broke into laughter.

He glanced into the rearview mirror. "What'd I say that's so funny?"

Cora slapped his shoulder this time. "A music minister is a far cry from a rock star. C'mon now!"

"But he's that good, don't you think?" Mabel asked.

"Yes indeedy," Cora said.

"Thank you," Ray said in his best Elvis voice. "Thank you very much."

Mabel came as near to giggling as he'd ever heard her. They were still laughing when Ray pulled into the driveway, then cut the engine.

"We're going to fix lunch." Cora exited the car and started up the walk.

Mabel took off her hat. "Ray, you go on and sit on the porch. You got some thinking to do. We'll call you when it's ready."

"Ask Him what He wants you to do." Cora pointed skyward before she entered the house.

Ray changed into jeans and a T-shirt, then sat on the porch swing and let the soles of his sandaled feet scuff on the wood porch floor. Had the Lord given him the stirring in his heart when the pastor mentioned a music minister? Or was it Ray's own desire? If the Lord was the One who'd given him the desire, leading him to apply for the position, he couldn't refuse. He'd been out of His will on other occasions and lived to regret it.

"Lord, please make Your desire clear. In the meantime, I'm going to keep heading in the direction I began."

He pushed the swing and noticed a kid wearing a baseball cap standing on the sidewalk in front of Faith's house. He squinted. Looked like a little girl. Probably from the neighborhood, but why was she staring at Faith's place? He immediately thought of someone being in Faith's house, and he stood. The girl noticed him and took off running down the street.

Ray jumped off the swing and started down the stairs, but the girl was out of sight before he could follow. The phone rang inside, and he heard the hum of Mabel's voice as she answered it. He strolled the front yard, then walked to the back, checking things out. Between the sisters' house and Faith's, he noticed some of the chicken wire was coming loose from the fence. He heard the sound of a truck engine. Faith was home. Maybe he'd offer to help her staple it back on. He walked around front and waited as Faith exited her truck, waved, and walked toward him.

"What are you doing in my yard?" she asked, smiling. "Trespassing?"

He saluted her. "I'm from the police. I'm investigating."

Her brows rose. "Investigating?"

"Ma'am, did you know you have loose chicken wire on your fence?"

"Oh dear." She pressed her fingers to her lips in mock horror. "Is that a crime?"

He glanced at the sky, pretending to think. "Well, no, not if you get someone to help you fix it soon."

Faith clasped her hands. "Oh, officer, are you offering to help?"

"Well, it's above and beyond the call of duty, but. . ."

"I'd be ever so grateful." She glanced at him and batted her eyelashes.

He laughed, and she joined him. Soon they were out of breath.

When he'd finally caught his breath, he smiled at her. "I'd be glad to help you mend the fence. Just let me know when."

"Okay."

He frowned. "Now on to something more serious. I saw this kid hanging around your house."

Faith grimaced. "You're thinking of the break-in, aren't you?"

"Sort of. Well, yeah."

"We have lots of kids in the neighborhood."

"This one had on a ball cap. I think it was a girl—"

"Shorter hair?" she asked. After Ray nodded, Faith said, "I've seen her, too. Would a kid do this?"

"Kids are capable of a lot more than you think. They can be as bad as adults."

"Lunch is ready," Mabel called from the back porch.

"I'm going to run in and check on Sparkles. Tell the sisters I'll be right there."

⁊

Faith strolled into Mabel and Cora's kitchen, sniffing the air appreciatively. "Ham?"

"Yes," Cora said, waving a wooden spoon in the air. "Both of you wash your hands."

Ray grinned at Faith. "Race you to the bathroom."

He got there first and wouldn't let her near the sink.

"No fair," she said. "You had a head start."

"Gotta take the advantages given to us." He flicked water at her.

She reached under his arm, put her hand under the running water, and flicked him back. Soon their faces were dripping.

"Children!" Mabel called. "Stop that fooling around and come to the table."

Ray and Faith were still grinning, faces damp, when they got to the kitchen.

"My lands, you'd think these two were teenagers again." Cora placed a heaping bowl of rolls on the table.

"Mmm-hmm." Mabel smiled.

Faith was about to drop into her regular chair when Cora tapped her arm and pointed to an empty seat next to Ray. Still matchmaking. She exchanged a quick grin with Ray. He saw it, too. Oh well. No harm could come from their efforts.

"Let's pray," Mabel said when everyone was seated.

While they ate, they discussed Faith's break-ins.

"You think it might be a child?" Mabel asked, eyes wide.

"Could be." Ray described the kid he'd seen.

"Don't recognize the description, but Cora and I are gone a lot lately." Mabel dabbed her mouth with a napkin. "I just can't believe it's a child."

"Me, either." Cora wagged her head. "Got to be a bad guy."

"Yes indeed," Mabel said. "A bad guy."

"Wasp spray," Cora murmured.

"Wasp spray?" Ray paused, fork in midair.

"Well, Faith doesn't have a man around to protect her. Wasp spray in the face is as good as anything to stop a derelict."

Ray winced. "You know this from experience?"

"Don't ask." Mabel shook her head. "Cora has been chasing men away her whole life. At least she lets that Tom Douglas sit next to her at church."

Cora harrumphed and blushed.

Faith giggled, lifted a fork of herbed potato chunks to her mouth, and her elbow brushed Ray's—again. "Sorry," Faith said. "Remember, I'm a lefty."

"Creative types." Cora dropped another slice of ham on her plate.

Ray glanced at Faith, smiling. "I'm not complaining, am I?"

"Uh-uh, he's not complaining, honey." Mabel emphasized her remark with a wag of her head. "So how's that pup, Faith?" Her attention switched to Ray. "You ought to go over to Faith's to check on your dog."

"He's not mine, Miss Mabel."

"We're going to post an ad in the *Bothell-Kenmore Reporter*. It comes out on Wednesday. We'll see if we can locate her rightful owner. If nobody responds within five days, we—"

"I'll be cleaning up poop," Cora finished and waved her hand.

"Not at the table, sister." Mabel cleared her throat. "Now Ray, tell Faith what happened to you in church."

Faith glanced sideways at her handsome friend. She read his reticence and opened her mouth to change the topic.

"The Lord spoke to him." Cora smiled sweetly. "Go on, tell Faith."

Ray released an audible sigh, and Faith had to hold back a laugh. Poor Ray. They treated him the same as when he was a teen.

"Okay," Ray started, "but I'm not exactly sure that the Lord was speaking to me. Pastor Gary said the church needed a full-time music minister. We prayed, and I felt. . ." He took a bite of bread, which Faith sensed was a diversionary tactic.

"Called," Mabel whispered solemnly. "He felt called. Oh well. Ray was always serenading the neighborhood with his guitar."

"Oh honey, and the music he wrote." Cora closed her eyes. "Heavenly."

Faith felt a push to intercede on his behalf. "Well, but he needs to be very sure." She thought of her own choices, her family's rebuff. "Some decisions are irreversible."

"Amen to that!" Cora fairly shouted. "If it's God, He'll be sure to confirm His wishes."

Ray continued to eat in silence when Mabel slapped the tabletop, giving

Faith a jolt. "I almost forgot," Mabel said. "That Sally person called."

Faith's ears perked up. This time she had no desire to interrupt the sisters to rescue Ray's hide. *Who's Sally?* she wondered, and why did Ray look suddenly animated and interested? Was she the woman he'd referred to briefly during their walk?

"You mean *Bailey*? She called the house phone?" Ray yanked his cell from his belt and groaned. "I turned my phone off for the church service." He turned on the ringer and looked back up at Mabel. "When did she call?"

"About fifteen minutes after you went outside." Mabel started to hum.

"But I was right on the front porch." The frustration in his voice came through loud and clear.

"Prayin'," Cora said. "We wasn't about to interrupt your conversation with God for *her*."

Faith studied the peas on her plate, arranging them, she realized, into a smiley face.

"Okay, so, did Bailey leave a message?"

Gee, he was awfully anxious over a phone call from this Bailey person. Faith swirled the peas, messing up the happy smile, and shoveled them into her mouth.

"Said call her cell. She'll be around this afternoon." Mabel handed Faith a bowl of broccoli. "C'mon now, don't be shy."

"I couldn't." Faith held up her hand.

Ray stood, his chair scraping against the wooden floor. "Great lunch." He brought his plate to the sink, and Mabel and Cora took the opportunity to look at one another and roll their eyes. Faith pretended not to notice.

"Delicious." She stood, empty plate in hand. "I should be getting back. Sparkles needs attention."

"I'll walk you out," Ray offered.

Cora took the plate from her hand, and each sister gave her a hug. "You stop by any time, you hear?" Mabel returned to the sink, and Cora started clearing the table.

At the front door, Ray looked down into her face and tucked an errant piece of hair behind her ear. A fond gesture that she wouldn't allow just anyone to do.

"Listen, if we can't find Sparkles's owner, I want you to keep her. Just extra protection. . .just in case."

"Protection? That little—"

"Noisy dog. Yeah."

"Oh. She's a yapper, true enough."

His gaze had grown distant, and she watched him touch his cell phone. He wanted to call Bailey, whoever she was. Had to be that fiancée of his. Faith patted his arm, said good-bye, and walked down the stairs. She heard the click of the door behind her and suddenly felt vulnerable and sad.

As she entered her house she searched her mind for a reason for her weird emotions. Probably the broken fence. Any woman living alone would have good reason to worry about a potential intruder. But why did she feel sad?

She went to the crate in her bedroom. Sparkles whined as she unlocked it.

"You're adorable, and you're healing quickly." Faith picked her up and snuggled her against her shoulder like a baby. "If we can't find your owner, I'd be happy to keep you, little girl."

They headed for her kitchen, and she set the terrier on the floor where her bowl was filled with dry food. She then went to the fridge for a bottle of water. Four bottles on the shelf. She bent over and looked more closely. "That's odd. . ." She moved the container of milk. Just a couple of days ago she'd put six bottles in here, hadn't she? She shuffled other food items. Worry knotted her stomach. Was she losing her mind? Or had someone really come into her home? To steal water? It made no sense; therefore, she wouldn't make a fool of herself by telling Ray.

Chapter 8

Ray rolled over and took a deep, appreciative sniff of. . .bacon and coffee. His eyes flew open, and he looked at the clock that read 5:00 a.m. on Monday morning. First working day of the week and his first day back at the precinct.

Drifting up from the kitchen were Cora's and Mabel's voices, singing a Psalm in unison. Ray smiled as warm memories flooded his mind. Their heartfelt praises to God soothed his soul.

After a quick shower, he put on his uniform. Was this job what he really wanted to be doing? His thoughts turned to Sunday and the pastor's announcement about hiring a music minister. The desire to take the job had rattled him. He dismissed it from his thoughts as he left his room. No time to think about it right now.

The top step squeaked as he headed down the stairs, and he smiled. That squeak had been like an alarm when he spent weekends here as a young man. He'd had trouble sneaking downstairs without one of the sisters knowing he was up. Hard to take midnight trips to the refrigerator to sneak a snack. And the one time he'd tried to get out to meet a friend in the middle of the night was disastrous.

He paused at the door to the kitchen. Cora was putting bacon on a paper towel to drain. Mabel was at the table reading her Bible. His heart lurched as he realized again how much he loved the sisters.

"Smells wonderful!" Ray announced.

Mabel looked up, smiled, and patted the chair next to her. "Come and sit. You need a big breakfast before you go to work."

Ray slipped a finger into his belt. "Not sure I really need a big breakfast."

"Nonsense," Cora said as she put scrambled eggs on plates. "Sit. Eat."

Ray obeyed.

"You ask the blessing," Mabel told him.

He said a prayer of thanks and dug in. "Hmm, I've been away too long."

"I'll say." Mabel stabbed her Bible with her index finger. "I've got the perfect scripture verse for you today. Look here, Psalm 33:4–5, 'For the word of the Lord is right and true; he is faithful in all he does. The Lord loves righteousness and justice; the earth is full of his unfailing love.'"

"Amen," Cora called from her place at the stove.

Ray nodded. "Amen. I know He's faithful, ladies, and I'm going to need a large dose of His 'unfailing love' this morning. I may end up facing my nemesis."

Mabel set her Bible on the table and tilted her chin. "Now don't go putting all the blame on that other man for what that Sally did."

"*Bailey*, not Sally."

"Takes two to tango," Cora mumbled as she ambled to the table.

Mabel patted the Bible with her open hand. "We heard you on the phone last night, yakking. Was that Bailey?"

Ray had forgotten this part of staying with the sisters. They knew everything. "I can't see it's really anyone's business."

Cora clucked her tongue. "Boy wants privacy."

"Mm-hm," Mabel said. "Privacy? Nothing's private because God knows everything. And we're prayin' about this. It is the rest of your life, you know."

Her logic made sense in a weird way, not that he thought he didn't need privacy.

"You weren't laughing much when you were talking to her." Cora shook her head.

Mabel waved her hand. "No indeedy. Not like with Faith."

He inhaled, ready to argue, but realized he couldn't. Laughter came easily with Faith, but then they had known each other so long, and they didn't have any dark issues to overcome in their friendship.

Cora planted her hands on her hips and wagged her head. "Just look at you. Handsome thing, isn't he, sister?"

Ray was grateful for the change of topic. "Why thank you."

"We'll be praying for you today." Mabel patted his arm. "You're an officer of the law, and that's a godly thing, son. Remember, 'the Lord loves righteousness and justice.'"

"Right." Ray drew a deep breath. "That incident in church yesterday. . . must've been my overactive imagination. I've already got a full-time job."

"We're not saying that either." Cora held his face with her hands and looked in his eyes. "The Lord is faithful. He'll speak to you again on that matter. Got it?"

"Got it." Ray concentrated on his food, and the sisters chitchatted about people he didn't know.

After breakfast he took his plate to the sink and gave each of them a good-bye hug. "I'm off. Philip's going to pick me up so I can drive my patrol car home tonight."

They followed him to the front door with a laundry list of admonitions. "No more bad thoughts. . . . God is good *all* the time. . . . Don't let the devil steal your joy. . . ."

"Morning, bro!" Philip said when Ray climbed into the passenger seat, ears still ringing with the sisters' words.

"Hey." Ray glanced at Faith's house. Her truck wasn't in the driveway.

"You ready for this?" Philip asked, glancing over at him.

"I suppose I am."

"You sound less than thrilled."

Ray shrugged. "Nervous is more like it."

Philip cleared his throat. "I ran into Dwight at the courthouse. He has it in his head to apologize to you."

"Hmm." Ray held his tongue.

"I can imagine how you feel, knowing Dwight and knowing what he did to you, but hitting him again won't solve anything."

"I'll be fine," Ray said. "That will never happen again. With anyone." And he meant it.

For the rest of the drive, Philip updated Ray about the latest, and when he turned onto 101st Avenue, approaching the redbrick building that housed the police department, Ray had relaxed. The tension he'd been feeling had mostly dissipated. That could be from distance, or, Ray hoped, God had done a work inside him. The brawl Ray had started with Dwight took place when he was off duty. To his surprise, Dwight, a lawyer, hadn't come after him. But Ray's chain of command had suggested a short leave to cool his heels.

One month in the Tri-Cities had led to a lengthy leave as the thought of seeing his ex-fiancée with Dwight set him afire with a fury he couldn't fight at first. But little by little, he mellowed. And when Philip phoned to say Dwight and Bailey had split, Ray made his final decision to return home. He had to see if reconciliation with Bailey was possible. And today, armed with the Word of God and Cora's and Mabel's prayers, he was also ready to face his enemy head-on.

When Ray and Philip walked into the building, the first person he saw was Bill Snyder.

"See you in briefing," Philip said and took off down the hall.

"Ray." Snyder came over, shook his hand, and slapped him on the back. "Good to see you, buddy." The older man had been a police officer for years, and he'd known Ray's father. Ray pumped his hand harder.

"You ready for this?" Snyder asked. "You know sooner or later you're going to see Dwight Connor again."

Ray nodded. "Yes, I'm ready."

"Remember, son, once you lose your cool, you can't get it back."

He nodded, knowing Snyder's words were true. He'd never forget that, having learned it the hard way.

Snyder gave Ray a thumbs-up. "Good to have you back."

Ray smiled and strode toward Captain Butler's office and tapped on the door.

"Come in."

He entered, and Captain Butler popped out of his chair, came around, and shook his hand. The tall man, built like a brick, scowled at Ray. That was his normal expression, and it had become etched into his features. "Everything is in order. On paper you're ready to start back, but. . ."

Butler pointed to the chair in front of his desk, and Ray sat. "Yeah, I'm ready."

Butler ran his hand over his buzz-cut, steel gray hair. "Think you can handle working around Connor? He's a public defender. You'll see him again. I don't want any trouble."

The mention of Dwight's name wasn't the hot poker to his heart that it used to be. Ray was surprised. "I'm okay."

Butler looked leery. "You're lucky Dwight didn't sue you. . .and us."

"That's true."

"If it happens again, I can't answer for your future."

"I understand, sir."

"You're one of the best we had, Reed." Butler rested his hands on his desk. "You and your brother. . .it's in your blood."

Ray digested the compliment in silence, wondering if this was confirmation from the Lord that he was to continue in law enforcement.

"Well, welcome back." Butler's mouth turned up, which was supposed to pass for a smile even though it just served to deepen his scowl. Ray had never heard Butler actually laugh.

He shook the captain's proffered hand. "Thanks again, sir."

Back in the hallway, Ray removed his jacket, and he heard two familiar voices behind him. He turned and saw Dwight standing next to Snyder, hands buried in his trouser pockets, rocking heel to toe. That cocky, arrogant air. . .

"Lord, I forgive." Still, Ray couldn't help but wonder. . .how did Dwight face himself in the mirror every day? But Connor had always been that way. Ray hadn't paid much attention until it affected him personally.

Connor turned his head and registered the sight of Ray. His jaw dropped open in mock surprise. His old, sarcastic humor. "Is that. . ." He left Snyder's side and took long strides across the tile floor, hand extended. "Welcome back, Ray."

Ray nodded and grasped Dwight's hand. "Thank you."

Their eyes met, then Dwight's gaze flickered.

"I hear you and Bailey called it quits." Ray blurted out the words before he could stop himself as he released Dwight's hand.

Connor looked up, then dropped his gaze to the floor. "Yeah, um, listen. About that. . ."

"I'm sorry, I shouldn't have said anything." Ray meant it.

"It's okay. It's all behind us now." Dwight met his gaze. "It really is."

Ray knew that was as close to an apology as he was going to get from Dwight, and it was enough. They nodded at each other. Ray walked away, testing his emotions. No anger. No more desire to lash out. The lack of hostility felt odd. Like he was light-headed. Ray shot a thanks to the Lord as he realized that what had happened more than a year ago no longer held him captive.

Chapter 9

Faith's intercom buzzed, and she frowned at the phone as she picked up the headset.

"Dr. Hart," Gladys said, "a man is here to see you. Um. . .his name is Ray."

"Ray is here?" Faith smiled. "I'll be right out."

She walked out into the front waiting area. Ray stood next to the counter. "Hey!" Warmth enveloped her at the sight of her friend.

"Hi. Sorry I didn't call. Just felt like I wanted to do something spur of the moment." Despite his smile of greeting, his eyes lacked their usual mischievous sparkle.

She resisted the temptation to reach out and touch his arm to comfort him. "Are you okay?"

She felt Gladys's stare and realized this was probably the first time she'd seen Faith with anyone besides clients and work staff.

Ray shrugged. "It's just been a strange day. Are you hungry? I haven't eaten yet, and I'm thinking of going to Canyons."

"I like that place." Faith considered her workload for half a beat, then decided everything could wait. As was their agreement, Debbie was handling the evening clients, and if she needed Faith, she could call her cell. Besides, Ray looked as though he could use a listening ear. "I'm game," she said with a smile.

"Good." Ray gave her a thumbs-up. "You don't mind riding on the back of my Harley with me, do you? I'll bring you back here after we're done so you can pick up your truck."

Ah, the mischievous sparkle was back, and she couldn't resist. "It's been a long time since I've been on a motorcycle. Well, really they were dirt bikes and never that big. . . ." Faith chewed her lower lip as she looked at the bike through the front window of the clinic. "Do you have a helmet for me?"

Gladys gasped, but Faith ignored her. Being shocked by Faith's unusual, spontaneous behavior would give her staff something to talk about.

"Sure do." Ray winked. "It's got to be less scary than basic training."

Faith laughed. "All right then. Give me a minute and I'll change."

She hurried to her office in the back where she kept a pair of everyday clothes in a small closet. She spent so many hours at the clinic she should just move in and save herself the monthly mortgage on her house. As she slipped into her jeans, her heart raced, surprising her. *This isn't a date!* Her excitement over having dinner with Ray was simply happiness about being with her friend again.

Faith emerged from her office and asked Gladys to tell Debbie she had gone to dinner. Outside, Ray offered her a dazzling smile. Her friend had certainly grown into a handsome man. She couldn't help but notice.

"I'm ready," she stated simply.

"Don't be scared. I'm a great driver, despite all the undeserved comments I get from Mabel and Cora." Ray took the extra helmet from the back of his bike. "Let me put this on for you."

As he placed the helmet on her head, he tucked in loose strands of her hair. Her skin felt warm where his fingers brushed.

"Beautiful," Ray said.

Beautiful?

He grinned, hopped on his bike, and patted the black seat behind him. "C'mon, m'lady. Your steed awaits."

The picture of Sleeping Beauty riding with her prince on his horse flitted through her mind. *Silly!* Faith mounted the bike in one fast motion.

"Wrap your arms around my waist," Ray instructed.

She did as she was told, then closed her eyes and inhaled deeply. The scent of his leather jacket and the light fragrance of his cologne filled her senses. The rev of the engine made her open her eyes. She tightened her grip at his waist as he pulled away.

The warm wind blew over them, and Faith relaxed, savoring the experience. And for the first time in as long as she could remember, she relaxed. Ray still had that effect on her. Being with him was peaceful.

They reached Canyons in a few short minutes. Too short. She got off the bike slowly, pulled off the helmet, and said, "Thanks for that. I enjoyed it."

"Really?" Ray's smile warmed her heart. Something about him reminded her of a little boy in a man's body. She'd always felt that way about him, that childlike quality that she loved.

They were seated by a window and picked up their menus.

"You want some nachos?" Ray asked.

"Absolutely. And you know what I want for dinner?" She grinned at him. "Ribs."

"Me, too."

After they placed their order, Ray looked antsy.

"What is it, Ray?"

"I could use your advice, Faith."

He spoke her name with such sincerity it took her a second to find her voice. "Yes, right, how can I help?"

"A couple of things really. I need prayer for clear direction on this music ministry position that's opened up at Bothell Community."

"I'm a step ahead of you. After I heard of your experience in church yesterday, I went home and added the request to your name on my prayer list. I know God is faithful. He'll give you clear direction. It's a big step, leaving your present job."

"Yeah, it is," Ray admitted. "And there's something else."

The waiter arrived at their table with the nachos and drinks.

"Thanks," Ray said and took her hand. "Want to bless the food?"

Faith nodded and prayed, grateful that Ray was back in her life. He made her feel important and needed. When they said their amens, she swallowed past the lump in her throat and smiled.

"You were saying?"

Ray looked at her thoughtfully for a long moment. "I guess it's all right to ask a female friend for relationship advice, right?"

His words weren't what she expected and stung. She wasn't sure why. Faith made an exaggerated effort at nonchalance with a wave of her hand and a forced smile. "Of course. That's what friends are for. I can't promise you I'll be much help. The few romances I've had were short and sweet." Faith laughed. "Or not so sweet."

Ray finished chewing a mouthful of nachos and grimaced. "Well then, I'd say it was the guy's loss."

Sure it was, she thought. "No, I always focused on career. It was the navy, then medical school, now it's making a go of the clinic."

"Me, too. Career first, and I'm pretty sure that's how I lost my fiancée."

"Fiancée, eh?" The food in her mouth turned to sawdust.

"Yes. I've got to catch you up on things."

They finished their nachos, and dinner arrived at the table before Ray's story was over. Faith's appetite diminished as Ray talked about Bailey. Overriding the mix of her emotions, anger was bubbling up inside her. She had no right to judge Bailey, but how could the woman have done that to Ray?

"You're such a good guy." Faith dropped her gaze to her plate and finished gnawing a sparerib. As much as she resented what she was about to say, she had to be honest with her friend. "Someone like you doesn't stop loving someone just because they're unfaithful. It's not your nature." His nature was the same as it had always been. Loving and committed.

Dark brows furrowed, Ray gave her an assessing look. "Are you sure you don't mind listening to me?"

Her heart paused as though she'd been caught in deceit. "No, why?"

"It's just that your face looks like you're in pain or something."

That was an accurate description of how she felt, and she wasn't sure why. She pushed her feelings aside. She was here for Ray.

"Not at all. I told you I was willing to listen, and I meant it."

Ray gave her another long look, then nodded. "So, thanks to Mabel and Cora, you already know that Bailey called. And I went ahead and called her back."

Faith swallowed a small bite of coleslaw, forcing her stomach to settle. "So, how'd that go?"

"She's in San Diego, visiting with her parents. We decided to have a talk when she's back in town."

"Hmm." Faith cleared her throat and took a sip of water while Ray looked at her expectantly.

"What?" they said simultaneously.

"Nothing," Faith said. "Just that you seem to have made up your mind already. You want to get back with her, don't you?"

Head tilted, Ray's eyes narrowed. Had animosity come through in her voice? She was not good at disguising her feelings, and her mind raced to come up with a justification.

"I'm just saying. . ." What was she saying? "You—you sort of asked for my input, but you intend to go back with. . ." She couldn't bear to say her name. Worse, she sounded like a woman scorned.

Ray smiled. "You sound a bit like Mabel and Cora."

"I do?"

"Protective. I like that, even though from them it can be overkill."

She sighed with relief.

"So tell me what you think."

"I don't like the idea that Bailey cheated on you, Ray. If she felt you spent too much time at work, she should've given you fair warning." She flicked back her hair and looked him in the eye, feeling the strength of her convictions to her toes. "But in all fairness, I might be the wrong one to ask. I'm personalizing because—"

"It's fine. Most people would feel as you do. Cora and Mabel. . .they have very strong opinions about Bailey—or as Mabel calls her, Sally. My brother"—Ray inhaled deeply—"he's called me a fool more than once."

She wouldn't go so far as to agree with Philip out loud, but the temptation was there.

Ray tapped her plate. "You aren't eating. I'm sorry. I'm spreading a dark cloud. Let's forget romance for the rest of the night and concentrate on friendship and fun."

"Friendship and fun," she echoed. "Sounds good." She began nibbling on a rib to make the effort, but her appetite had fled.

He was as good as his word. He regaled her with stories from work, and soon she relaxed, but in the back of her mind, she couldn't let go of the fear that he would restore his relationship with Bailey. She was worried for him.

No, it was more than that, but what? She watched his animated expression as he told her about the weird man he'd stopped who thought the speeding ticket Ray gave him was a raffle ticket. She'd always loved the way Ray's eyes crinkled when he laughed. A sudden gnawing fear of losing him again came over her. She knew most women weren't keen on their men having female best friends. She didn't like the picture in her head of Bailey whispering in Ray's ear to stop seeing her. She gripped her napkin in her lap as it occurred to her that her feelings seemed an awful lot like jealousy.

Chapter 10

Y o, Ray-mond!"
Ray was leaving the precinct and turned at the sound of his brother's voice. "Hey, Philip."

"What's shakin' today? It's a great day. Fri-day." Philip slapped Ray's shoulder. "You been rounding up bad guys left and right?"

Ray smiled. "Nope. Not really. Just routine stuff. What about you?"

"You know that gas station robbery last week?"

"Yeah." Ray had heard about it in a briefing on his first morning back at work. "Anything new in the case?"

Philip shook his head. "We have suspects, but can't prove anything. I'm just hoping the gas station attendant will come out of his coma."

"What about security cameras?"

"Security cameras weren't working." Philip shook his head. "Why people don't take advantage of technology, I don't know."

They began walking together. "You got plans this weekend?" Philip asked.

Ray hesitated and shrugged. "Not sure."

"How's it going with Bailey?"

Ray shrugged again. "Haven't seen her yet, if that's what you mean. We've talked on the phone."

"I see," Philip said softly. "You're a better man than me."

"What does that mean?"

"If a woman did to me what she did to you? It'd be over. Period. No talking. No nothing."

"But what if it was your fault?"

"Was it really *all* your fault, Ray? Do you know that for sure, or is that what she said to excuse her behavior?"

Ray felt himself growing angry at Philip and reined in his temper. He searched his mind for another topic—one that wouldn't bring such a negative reaction.

"You remember Faith Hart?" Ray blurted.

"Little Faith Hart." Philip grinned. "Of course I remember her. Nice girl. You two were glued at the hip every summer when you were teens." Philip jabbed Ray with his elbow. "She's back in town, you know. In fact, she's living next to Mabel and Cora. I ran into Cora one day, and she told me. You must have seen her."

"I have."

"And?"

"And what?" Ray glanced at his big brother suspiciously. What was he trying to say?

"And, did you talk? Is she nice-looking?"

Ray shook his head. "You're impossible. Don't you see women any other way but 'good-looking' or 'bad-looking'? Yes, we've talked. And, yes. She's nice-looking. She always has been."

"I see," Philip said again as they reached Ray's car. Philip tugged at his uniform collar. "You're wrong, you know."

"About what?"

"How I see women." Philip jingled change in his pocket.

Ray met his gaze. "Really?"

"Yes—at least in this case. It's more how I see people. Actions speak louder than words."

Ray frowned. "Are you being deliberately obtuse?"

"Nope. Just wanting everything to be okay with my little brother." Philip grinned. "I think it is."

"What does that mean?"

Philip laughed. "Exactly what I said. Besides, you got Mabel and Cora on your side. I might not be a religious man, but I sure am glad to know they're praying for us."

They exchanged good-byes, and by the time he reached the house, he'd stopped trying to figure out what Philip had meant. He looked over at Faith's house. No truck. She wasn't home yet. He felt disappointed. It would have been nice to talk to her. He climbed from the car, walked to the porch, and hesitated. What kind of hullabaloo was going on inside? He opened the door, and praise music spilled into the street. In the living room, Mabel and Cora were dancing, a sort of tarantella routine—arms locked and going in circular motions.

They both looked up at him, smiling. "We closed on the Victorian!" Mabel shouted over the din.

"Hey, great news." Ray closed the door and draped an arm around each sister. "Cause to celebrate, for sure."

Cora hit the Off switch on the CD player, fanned herself, and motioned him to the kitchen table. "Yow-wee, Lordy, Lordy! He sure is good to us."

"And look what we have," Mabel said. "The original plans to the house. Why don't you look at them while I go finish fixin' dinner."

"I'm not real hungry," Ray said.

"Nonsense." Mabel spread the plans out on the coffee table. "You need to keep up your strength if you're going to help us with this project."

He and Mabel began studying the original plans to the historic home, and Ray began to share the sisters' excitement. "I can restore this beauty to what she used to be."

"Yes, indeed." Mabel patted his hand. "You always were creative. We would've never trusted anybody else with this work."

Ray's cell phone rang, and he took it from his belt. "Hello?" He sat back on the couch while Mabel pretended not to listen.

"Ray, this is Pastor Gary."

"Hey, Pastor. How can I help you?"

Mabel eyeballed him, and Ray shrugged in response.

"Two things, brother. Do you think you can fill in playing the guitar for us this Sunday? Um, actually, could you lead the worship?"

"Um, I'd be happy to do that, but I'm a little rusty with the songs."

"Huh-uh, the Lord is great and worthy to be praised," Mabel said.

Ray held his finger to his lips, but she just grinned.

"That brings me to my next question," Pastor Gary said. "Would you be willing to attend practice this evening? The worship team practices at seven."

Ray's heart sang with a joy that surprised him. "Absolutely. It would be my honor. I'll be there tonight."

Mabel hummed "Amazing Grace."

Ray hung up, smiling. "I guess you heard. I'm playing my guitar on Sunday."

"Yes indeed." Mabel turned her face toward the kitchen. "Cora? Ray is playing for the service this Sunday."

"Praise the Lord!" Cora hollered from the kitchen.

Good smells wafted into the living room, and Ray felt his appetite return.

"Oh," Mabel said as she stared at the house plan, "did we tell you we invited Faith to dinner tonight?"

Faith pulled into her driveway, put the truck in PARK, and rubbed her tired eyes. As much as she looked forward to dinner with the sisters, and was eager to see Ray again, a part of her wanted to skip dinner, curl up on the sofa with Sparkles, and catch some z's. She sighed. Unfortunately she'd agreed to meet a client for late dessert. Okay, who was she trying to fool? She'd agreed to a date. But now she regretted the impulsive decision. Why had she done it, anyway?

Faith took her keys out of the ignition and caught movement through her rearview mirror. "That little kid again," she whispered. The girl stood beside Faith's front hedges, peering at her. Faith grabbed the handle of the car door, intent on speaking to her. As soon as she stepped foot out of the car, the freckle-faced youngster took off running down the road.

"Hey!" Faith called out. "Don't be scared."

Too late. She watched the girl's retreating form until she rounded the bend. Who was she, and what could she possibly want? She uttered a silent prayer for the youngster's safety before going inside her house.

Sparkles, more hyper than usual, was jumping and whining like crazy. Faith took her out of the crate, gave her plenty of attention, then took her for a walk. "You're in good shape," she said as she watched the dog hop up the front steps to her door. "You're healing well. And I'm going to leave you out of the crate this time." Despite the safety of daylight, an odd feeling washed over her—as if she was being watched.

❧

As soon as she entered the sisters' house, the two women and Ray came out of the kitchen to greet her.

"Good news," Cora said, and Mabel added, "Oh, lots of good news today. Come on in."

Ray stood smiling down at her and winked. "Nice to see you, Faith."

Her gaze latched onto his for a few beats too long, and a giggle bubbled out of her mouth. Awful! She never giggled. Mabel and Cora disappeared back into the kitchen, and the way Ray approached, she almost expected him to give her a welcoming hug.

"Nice to see you, too," she said.

"Come in." He tilted his head toward the kitchen, and Faith followed.

Mabel lined up the ladder-back chairs very close together, then instructed Ray and her to "sit right down," and quickly asked, "How's that precious little dog?"

"Um. . ." Aware that she and Ray were practically glued at the hip, Faith finally managed to find her voice. "Sparkles? Oh, she's doing great."

Ray nudged her with his elbow. "You should be on my other side, lefty."

"Cora says I'm artistic," she whispered, and Ray laughed and nudged her again.

"Have you put an ad in the 'Lost and Found' yet?"

"Yes, this morning. I wanted to first be sure Sparkles was going to totally recover."

"I sure hope nobody abused that baby girl," Cora said, and Mabel came to sit beside her at the table, nodding.

The thought of abusive owners had occurred to her numerous times. She looked down at the stew Cora set before her. "Oh, this smells and looks divine."

Mabel said a prayer of thanks, and as they ate, the sisters relayed their good news about closing on the Victorian.

"The scalloped siding on the Victorian makes it look like a dollhouse," Faith said. But she loved the house she was sitting in even more. "Will you sell this one then?"

"Yes. . ." Tears gathered in Mabel's eyes. "I don't want to think about

strangers living here. Ralphie carried me over the threshold in this house."
Her gaze scanned the kitchen as if she were seeing it for the first time, and
Faith found herself holding back tears. "We scraped together every cent we
had to buy this place." She shrugged. "Oh well. God's got something new for
us." She turned to Cora. "Right, sis?"

"Yes, He does." Cora patted Mabel's shoulder. "We've been praying that
God brings the right people along who'll fill this house with love."

Mabel laughed through her tears. "Oh my. He's gonna bring along the
perfect couple. He told me so."

"Here, here." Ray raised his glass of iced tea in agreement. "If I could afford it I'd buy it myself."

"You never know." Cora looked directly at Faith, and she didn't know what
to make of it.

Ray elbowed Faith. "So what are you doing tonight?"

His question, sudden and out of left field, rendered her mute for a moment. She had nothing to feel awkward about, yet she dreaded having to
respond. "I have a date."

"A date?" Mabel's eyes grew wide as saucers.

"You're going out?" Cora chimed in. "With a man?"

Faith laughed despite her discomfort, but she avoided Ray's eyes. "I think
a date for me would be defined as going out with a man."

Mabel and Cora exchanged curious glances, and Faith turned to Ray for
rescue. He was frowning, and her defenses went up.

"The guy works down the street from me as an accountant. He brought
his dog in one day. . . ." What was she doing justifying her motives? "What
am I supposed to do? Just work all the time? It's Friday night. The start of
a weekend. Most people do fun stuff on Friday night." *Is that why I did this?*

"Well, I would think you'd want to spend more time with Ray." Cora's chin
tilted. "You're just getting reacquainted."

"Hmm, and after all those years apart." Mabel sighed. "A shame."

Speak up, Ray! Faith looked at him again. "He has a life of his own, don't
you, Ray?"

"Not really." His frown had disappeared, and the mischievous smile that
took its place told her he was going to play this for all it was worth. "Other
than music practice tonight"—Ray clasped his fingers—"I usually come
home after work and basically twiddle my thumbs." He demonstrated with
exaggerated motions.

"Hmph." Mabel stood, and Cora followed her to the counter. "Go on and
joke." She nudged Cora. "Before you know it they'll be forty and—"

"Home alone twiddlin' their thumbs."

Faith and Ray exchanged another glance. This time Ray was laughing.

"I'll get you back for this," Faith whispered.

Chapter 11

Faith sat stiff with nerves between Cora and Mabel while Pastor Gary made the Sunday morning announcements. This was Ray's big day. Playing guitar with the worship team. She continued to pray silently for the Lord to anoint his heart, his hands. What would Ray do if he felt the call to full-time music ministry? Scary, but exciting. Her heart thumped hard. She'd been there and back with career choices. Was there ever a right or easy choice—something that would please all the people one loved?

"We have a special treat," Pastor Gary said. "Our brother, Ray Reed, is joining the worship team to help us this morning."

The loudest and longest applause came from Mabel and Cora. Their eyes shone like two proud mamas', fussing over their boy. Sweet, unconditional love. Cora dabbed a tear from the corner of her eye.

Smiling, and with a nod of appreciation, Ray settled on a stool behind the mic and nodded at the other musicians. Then he adjusted his guitar and closed his eyes. After whispering a prayer, he strummed some introductory chords. The other musicians began to play. As his raspy tenor proclaimed the goodness and faithfulness of God and as the instrument in his deft hands sang its own praises, tears sprang to Faith's eyes.

Thank You, Lord, for the gift of music You've given Ray. And now he was giving back the gift, blessing the congregation. Was this Ray's call? Could he walk away from the precinct and not look back? Would he feel regret?

After the worship time ended, silence fell over the congregation. It was as though all were as caught up as she. Faith drew a breath and wiped the tears off her cheeks with a hankie Cora had passed to her.

She stared at Ray. Beautiful inside and out. What if she'd answered his letters so many years ago? Faith watched him walk off the platform, then looked away. Why that thought now? Was she seeing Ray as potentially more than a friend? After all this time. She clasped the hankie in her hands and stroked the soft cloth with her fingertips. Nothing good could come of torturing herself with "what-ifs." She was what she always had been. Unromantic and single-mindedly focused on her goals. Besides, Ray was a man on a mission, intent on getting his fiancée back.

❧

"That was lovely," Cora said from the backseat of the Thunderbird.

Ray turned the key, and the car roared to life.

"A God-given talent." Mabel sat beside her sister, then resumed humming a hymn.

"Anointed," Faith whispered.

Ray felt warmed by the compliments and looked over at Faith, sitting beside him in the passenger seat. "I was surprised how right it felt. It all just flowed. I can't describe it. Now I'm confused."

"I understand." Faith tucked her dark, long hair behind her ear. A nervous habit he found charming. "Maybe you can do both, Ray? Play on weekends for the church and still keep your job."

"Yeah, I could play, but not lead." Ray headed east toward home. "Pastor Gary really needs a full-time music minister. A staff member. Someone to help lead the flock in more than music."

"Pray on it," the sisters said simultaneously from the back. "Pray without ceasing," Cora added.

Their plain talk chased away some of his worry, and he laughed along with Faith.

"Didn't you pray on it, Ray?" Faith grinned.

He looked at her, and understanding dawned. Okay, this was payback because he went along with Cora and Mabel when they told Faith to spend more time with him. "Yes, I did." Ray frowned. "By the way, how'd your date go?"

Faith narrowed her eyes and looked like she wanted to give him a swift kick. "Wonderful! Thank you very much."

"Waste of time," Mabel said, "if you ask me."

"What's that, Miss Mabel?" Ray deadpanned.

"You two, fussin' around with this one and that one. . ." Mabel muttered something inaudible under her breath.

"This one and that one?" Faith glared at Ray. "It was only one date, Miss Mabel. One. It's not like I've dated every single guy in town."

Ray pulled into the driveway. He could see a red stain working up Faith's cheeks. Her temper. Enough teasing for one day. Time for a change of topic. "Do you have the materials to finish your fence? We can do that before lunch."

"Yes. I picked them up this week. Sounds good to me." Faith's face was still red. "I'll go change."

Cora exited the car on a grunt. "Uh-huh, you two need to be mending fences."

"Yes indeed," Mabel agreed. "Mending fences."

※

Faith manned the staple gun as Ray held the wire in place.

"No sign of more break-ins?" Ray asked.

Faith considered the odd feelings she'd had and dismissed them. "Things have been calm, but you know, I'm still seeing that red-haired kid around. Maybe it was her messing around and she's stopped."

Ray sat back. "I saw her again, too."

Faith leaned into the staple gun.

"You're pretty handy with that," he noted.

"Learned to do a lot when my dad was out to sea," Faith murmured.

"Do you talk to him much?"

"I try to avoid him."

His eyes flashed surprise. "Oh."

And his one word spoke volumes. "You don't agree with that?"

He shrugged. "I didn't say that. It's just that. . ."

"What?" Faith felt her temper rising.

"Nothing. It's none of my business. Your face is getting red. I don't want to get yelled at."

She sat back and waited for Ray to stretch more chicken wire over the fence. "You know me too well. And you're right. I don't want to talk about my father. But at least because of him I'm not a sissy."

"Very true. You're definitely not a girlie girl." Ray held the wire.

"So what does that mean?" She jammed the staple gun against the wire fencing and pushed the trigger.

He looked her in the eye. "I didn't mean that in a bad way, just that you can hold your own with the best of them. No offense."

"None taken." Faith shrugged and kept working. "So, is Bailey a 'girlie girl'?"

"Hmm, good question." Ray blew out a long breath and stared off into the distance. "I guess you could say"—he frowned—"she's petite. Feminine." He laughed. "Maybe a diva."

Of course. Faith forced a short laugh. "I guess we're done here." She stood. "Hey, so when's the big day?"

Ray frowned. "Meaning?"

"Your face-to-face meeting with Bailey?" She cleared her throat. Her voice was definitely an octave too high and rang with false cheer. She was feeling a bit hostile toward the feminine girlie diva. The fact that her feelings seemed a bit like jealousy made things worse.

"Oh that." Ray leaned against a fence post. "This coming Wednesday. I don't know what to expect. Haven't seen her in over a year."

A bolt of unpleasant emotion shot through her. Anger? Why should she be angry? "Well I hope you're not nervous or anything." Faith wiped her hands on a rag. "She's lucky you'd consider going back with her. Some men wouldn't. . ." She let her voice trail off as heat rose from her neck to her face.

"Hey." Ray took her hands in his. "If I didn't know better, I'd think you were—"

"Jealous? Well, I'm not."

"No. That's not what I was about to say."

Head tilted, Ray peered at her closely, and her stomach did a backflip. What had gotten into her? She had survived four years in the navy, vet school, and opening a clinic, and suddenly she was an emotional wreck!

"I was just going to say that it was like the old days, when, God forbid, anybody breathed a word against me, you'd come to my defense."

Faith felt her shoulders relax. He'd given her an out. "Yeah, I guess old habits die hard."

"Lunch is ready," Mabel called from the porch.

With a wave, Faith acknowledged that they'd heard. "Be right in."

Faith put the leftover fencing and staple gun on her back porch. They walked together in silence to the back door. She wanted to say so much to him, but no words would come. What could she say when she was unable to sort her own scrambled emotions?

Chapter 12

Ray got in from work, dropped his keys on the table in the foyer, then glanced at the grandfather clock in the living room. He had forty minutes before Bailey would show—if she showed. She said she'd try, if her boss didn't keep the advertising crew late.

Mabel walked down the hall holding the plans for the Victorian.

"I'd like to look at those," he said. "I'm always fascinated by old plans. Be interesting to see if any structural changes were made to the interior."

"And we'd like you to." She hovered a few feet from him. "You gonna take off your gun? Makes me nervous."

"You've got that hunting rifle of Ralph's hanging up in his old office. Why would mine be any different?"

Mabel planted her hands on her hips. "Don't you be mouthy with me, young man. Yours is loaded. Mine has no bullets, lucky for you."

Ray grinned. "Yes, ma'am. I'll go change now."

Mabel swatted his arm. "I'll take these to the kitchen while you get out of that uniform."

"Really amazing that you've got the original blueprints," Ray murmured. He couldn't wait to study them more closely and reluctantly went to his bedroom to shower and change.

He dressed in haste, hurried downstairs, then joined the sisters at the table.

"You going to Wednesday service with us tonight?" Mabel asked.

Aha, he forgot they'd be out of the house this evening. Relief washed through him. "Can't make it tonight."

The sisters exchanged glances, but voiced no objections. Odd. He felt a bit sneaky not telling them he'd made a date to see Bailey. He figured they'd find out once she got here but wanted to avoid a sermon beforehand. Bad enough he'd gotten a strange reaction when he'd told Faith about his ex.

A clap of thunder shook the house, and Mabel let loose an earsplitting hoot. "Lord, have mercy!"

Hand on her heart, Cora shuddered. "Lord, help us all." She got up, went to the kitchen window, and parted the sheer curtains. "I'm not driving in this downpour, I can tell you that."

Ray watched hopefully for Mabel's reaction. Maybe she'd disagree with Cora. A private conversation with Bailey would be nearly impossible with the sisters home.

"Uh-huh, no sense taking any chances," Mabel concurred and looked across the table. "Well, you've got us for company tonight, son."

"You want some blueberry buckle with ice cream?" Cora asked.

Ray groaned, but didn't say no.

After dessert they cleaned up the dishes, and the sisters said they wanted to get back to the blueprints.

Ray looked at his watch. "Maybe it can wait till tomorrow?"

"Huh?" Mabel scowled. "A minute ago you couldn't wait to look at them. Now you want to wait? You feelin' okay? You're acting strange tonight. Sort of nervous."

"Come sit with us." Cora strode into the living room and Ray followed, Mabel on his heels.

He was probably better off occupying his mind with house plans while he waited for Bailey to show. He should tell them now about her visit, but what if she didn't come? He'd endure a good "dressing-down," as the sisters would put it, and for no reason.

They pored over the Victorian house plans, with Cora and Mabel strongly voicing their ideas about decorating style and color.

The doorbell rang, and Cora popped off the sofa. "I'll get it."

Ray got to his feet. "No, I will."

"Sit!" Cora commanded. "You two keep studying that blueprint. Maybe it's Faith."

It would be nice to see Faith again. But he knew better, and the familiar voice at the door confirmed it was Bailey. He felt a surge of nervousness.

"Who is that?" Mabel called out.

Ray got to his feet again. "Excuse me. We'll get back to this later."

"Bailey is here to see Ray," Cora announced from the front hallway. "You can put your umbrella here," he heard her tell Bailey. "My lands, you'll catch a chill in this weather and with no sleeves."

"Bailey? Is calling on you?" Mabel whispered. "In my day women waited for the man to do the—"

"Miss Mabel," Ray warned as Bailey and Cora walked into the room.

Bailey was still beautiful, but her waist-length hair now barely grazed her bare shoulders.

"Ray." Bailey approached with a smile, and he was surprised by how awkward he felt. He reached out to hug her, and she held him tighter and longer than was comfortable, considering their audience. Ray stepped out of her embrace, feeling the stares of the sisters.

"Ohh, honey," Mabel said to Cora. "It's time to take out our Bibles."

"I'll say. We'll have church right here and now." Head held high, Cora sashayed out of the room behind her sister, muttering, "Lord, help us all."

Already they were starting up. Ray pointed to the sofa. "Have a seat, will you?" He was about to apologize for the lack of privacy, but Bailey looked bubbly and happy and didn't seem to care.

"So," they said simultaneously, and Bailey laughed.

"It's great to see you, Ray." She squeezed his forearm. "You're looking better than ever." She searched his eyes, dropped her gaze, and blew out a long breath. "I'm sorry."

Cora's voice traveled from the kitchen. . .something about "binding spirits and loosing the power of God."

Bailey glanced in the direction of the kitchen. "They're really serious about the Bible."

Ray just shrugged. "They missed their Wednesday night Bible study, so they're doing their devotions here instead."

"Whatever. I don't care what anyone else is doing. I'm here to see you." Bailey slipped her slender hand into his. "I don't know how to tell you how sorry I am."

Ray felt oddly ill at ease. He'd waited more than a year to hear her say those words, and now that she was here, next to him, he wasn't sure how he felt.

"I don't know how else to explain it. . . . I guess I fell under Dwight's spell." Her watery gaze softened his heart. Forgive. He had to learn to be more forgiving.

"You were the best thing that ever happened to me, Ray."

Then why? he wanted to ask, but Bailey sniffled and continued, "I want back what we had."

"No," Ray heard himself say. "No, you don't want what we had. You weren't happy with what we had. You want—"

"I was selfish. I wanted more attention from you. Too much attention."

"And that's where Dwight came in, huh? He gave you what I couldn't?" Ray drew a breath. It hurt to think of the two of them together. Would it always hurt this badly? "I know I'm far from perfect, but. . ." The validity of Faith's words came back to him. "You could've given me fair warning."

"I was afraid to," she whispered. "Afraid to pressure you."

"Truth, Lord." Cora's voice rose in prayer. "Reveal all truth."

Bailey inhaled and glanced over her shoulder. "I think they hate me."

"Who?" Ray pulled back and looked down into her face, and Bailey hitched her thumb toward the kitchen.

"Impossible," Ray whispered. "They don't hate anybody." He pondered her answer to his question. Afraid to pressure him? Was it that simple? And if it were, would it happen again? This wasn't the time nor place for a deep discussion on the topic, especially since he wasn't sure what questions to ask or what to say. "So, you still go to church?"

Bailey sighed. "Not every Sunday. I went to your church a couple of times after you left town, but I felt judged. Tried church hopping for a while. Whatever. I guess I became disenchanted."

Disenchanted. Like she'd become with him? Ray inched away on the sofa cushion, putting distance between them. He needed to think clearly. Impossible while he inhaled Bailey's perfume and shampooed hair.

"Are you involved with anybody else?" Bailey held up her hands. "I wouldn't blame you if—"

"No," Ray stated flatly, discounting his friendship with Faith.

Her lips curved in a glossy smile. "Good. That's good."

The doorbell rang, and Ray scowled. "I wonder who—"

"God is good." Mabel bustled past the living room entrance and headed for the door.

"Can we start seeing each other again?" Bailey's words rushed out of her mouth, and she clutched his hand.

Yes, he thought, but the word wouldn't come. Wasn't this what he'd been looking forward to, wishing for? "I think it'll take some time for me—"

"It's Faith," Mabel called out.

"Did you hear that?" Cora dashed into the living room. "It's *Faith* at the front door."

"Yes, I couldn't help but hear that *Faith is here,*" Ray growled, and the sounds of steps coming down the hall told him she and Mabel were headed his way.

"Don't you be a smart mouth," Cora said, swatting his arm on the way to the front door.

"Who's *Faith*?" Bailey mimicked Cora's voice.

"The next-door neighbor, and it so happens, an old friend of mine."

Bailey narrowed her eyes.

"A friend of Mabel's and Cora's, too," he amended.

"I don't want to interrupt him if he has company," Faith protested.

"No bother, honey." Mabel's voice was firm and reassuring. "Go on into the living room."

"None at all," Cora agreed. "You need a police officer; Ray is a police officer."

"Indeed he is," Mabel said. "Handy to have one around when you need one, that's what I say."

Ray came to attention as the three entered the living room, Mabel practically pushing Faith. She was wet and pale and carried Sparkles in her arms.

He slipped his hand from Bailey's and stood. "What's wrong? Did something happen?"

"Someone's been on my back porch again." Faith switched her gaze to the sofa, and her eyes grew wide. "Oh, is this a bad time?"

"No," Ray assured as Bailey approached and echoed, "No."

An awkward moment of silence ensued.

"Since nobody's going to introduce me"—Bailey gave Ray a sideways glance, then stuck out her hand—"I'm Bailey Cummings."

"Oh, right." Faith shook her hand. "Nice to meet you. I've heard a lot about you."

"Good, I hope." Bailey glanced at Ray and then the sisters. "So you're the next-door neighbor Ray was telling me about. Cute dog."

The sisters were silent, arms crossed. Not like them at all. He hadn't exactly referred to Faith as merely a neighbor, but a friend.

Mabel cleared her throat.

Ray faced Bailey. "I need to go check out Faith's place."

Bailey's eyes narrowed again, but she quickly recovered with a smile. "Want me to come, too?"

"Oh no, darlin'," Mabel said. "Too dangerous. We'll keep you company while Ray's gone."

"We will," Cora added. "We need to get to know you, anyway."

Bailey looked like she wanted to run.

"I'll be right back," Ray promised.

"Take your time," Mabel said with a distinct smile in her voice.

So that was Ray's fiancée. *Ex-fiancée,* Faith amended. They didn't look like a match, but Faith had no intention of sticking her nose into his business again. As she walked across the yard with Ray, the wet lawn further soaked her slippered feet. A shiver raced up her spine, and she shuddered.

"You're cold." Ray slipped his arm around her shoulder.

She felt protected in his embrace and quickly reminded herself that Bailey was waiting for him inside. "I'm okay. I shouldn't have run out without my shoes, but I was scared." Sparkles whined. "Hush, little girl," Faith said, kissing the dog's head.

They went straight to the back porch, and Ray examined the door. "Looks like it was forced open. We'll have to fix this."

Faith set Sparkles down to allow the dog to relieve herself, and the little dog ran the perimeter of the yard. Ray smiled. "She's doing well."

"Yes, but it scares me that she was here alone when someone was inside."

When Sparkles was done, Faith dried her off with a towel she had for that purpose on the porch. Then she scooped her up.

They walked into the house, and she put Sparkles down. The dog immediately ran to the door and whined again. "Silly girl."

"Anything missing?" Frowning, Ray glanced around.

"I didn't stay long enough to have a close look." She sighed. "Would you like a soda?"

"No thanks." Ray followed her into the kitchen.

"Well, I need a bottle of water." Faith went to the refrigerator and rummaged around. Her heart sank. "Wait a sec. . . ." She moved aside a gallon of orange juice. "I'm going to sound nutty, but my cold cuts are gone."

"What?" He peered over her shoulder into the fridge. "Not nutty, but that's very odd."

"I wonder. . . ," she murmured. "Nothing of great value is ever missing. I wonder if that little girl is breaking in and taking food." Faith grabbed a bottle of water and slammed the fridge door closed. "This is giving me the creeps, even while I feel sorry for the kid."

"Hey." Ray placed his strong hands on her arms and looked down into her face. "I don't want you to worry. I'm right next door. But if you're home and you hear anything, dial 911 then call me. Okay?"

She nodded.

"I'll make another suspicious activity report. And I'll talk to my supervisor tomorrow and see if I can get permission to look into this further."

Please don't leave. Why was she feeling so desperate? Faith made a valiant effort at a smile. Was she really scared? Or did she just want to be with him? "I'm sorry to have disturbed you tonight. I didn't remember you had a date with your ex, er, Bailey."

A line formed between his dark brows, and he dropped his hands to his sides and shrugged. "Bailey. Not a date really. We needed to talk, but with Cora and Mabel at home—"

"Oh." Faith grimaced. She'd sensed right off that the sisters weren't happy Bailey was there. "I guess you'll be dating again." She felt her smile slipping.

Ray sighed. "I'm working on forgiveness. I believe in second chances."

She heard the "but" in his words. Anger rose up inside her and heated her face as she thought about what Bailey had done to him. "Well, just be careful. . ." *Or she'll walk all over you again.*

"Right. And you lock up after I leave."

With her heart heavy, she walked with Ray through the house to the front door. "Thanks for everything."

He stepped outside. "Anytime, Faith." Halfway across the lawn he stopped and turned. "Remember to call me if you need anything."

Tears pinched the backs of her eyes, but she nodded and tried to smile. She went back into the house, scolding herself for being such a wimp. She'd been happy living alone, feeling she lacked nothing. She prided herself for needing no one. When had the needy little girl surfaced? And why?

"Come on, Sparkles." The little dog followed her to her bedroom. Faith went to the window, lifted the blind slat, and peered across at Cora and Mabel's house. There, on the porch, Bailey stood looking up into Ray's face. Faith felt like a voyeur, watching what looked like an intense exchange between the two, but she was riveted to the spot, praying for the Lord to protect Ray.

Bailey reached up and slipped her arms around Ray's neck. They were about to kiss. She let the blind slat fall into place. She couldn't bear to look.

Chapter 13

R ay pulled his car into the driveway. He'd have to talk to Faith tonight, tell her his supervisor had given him permission to look into the break-ins even though they weren't going to file an official report yet. He cut the engine just as Mabel was walking to the garage with a briefcase that had belonged to Ralphie. It was the color of an old saddle with scars from years of use. He got off his bike and pointed. "Business?"

"Uh-huh." Mabel ran her hand over the bag. "Cora and I are meeting with our accountant to discuss the bed-and-breakfast. We left a plate for you in the refrigerator."

"Thank you," Ray said. "And I checked your oil this morning. That old Thunderbird burns it up."

"Yes, that's what Dilbert at the gas station says." She adjusted the feathered hat on her head and looked at the house. "Now, where is that sister of mine? She's as slow as molasses in winter."

"What time do you have to be at the accountant's, Miss Mabel?"

"Seven." She tapped her foot and clucked her tongue.

Ray bit back a grin. "How long does it take to get there?"

"Twenty minutes. . .with no traffic."

The front door opened and Cora stepped onto the porch and pulled the door shut. Ray glanced at his watch. Quarter after six. He flashed Mabel a grin. "Seems to me she's right on time. You're early."

Mabel pursed her lips. "You watch it, young man, or you'll find yourself scrubbing the kitchen floor on your hands and knees. You know as well as I do that the early bird gets the worm."

Ray laughed and hugged her. "You're so easy to tease."

She slapped his arm. "Shame on you." But she was smiling.

Cora trundled into the garage, black handbag slung over her arm. "You got a message from that. . .Bailey." Cora sniffed. "Said she tried your cell but the mailbox was full. She'll be free on Saturday."

Mabel's head whipped toward him as if she had been slapped. "Ray Reed! You're really going out with her? After what she did to you?"

"Yes, I'm going out with her." Annoyance made him snap.

Cora shook her head and opened the car door. "Mark my words, if she did it once, she'll do it again."

"A leopard doesn't change its spots," Mabel intoned, slipping behind the steering wheel.

They were both voicing his deepest fear—that he'd give Bailey another chance and she'd drop him again. Worry wormed its way into his heart.

Mabel held her hand out the car window, wiggling her index finger. "Come here."

He obeyed as he always did. She snatched his hand and held it. "You're a good boy, Ray. You like to believe the best in people, which is why police work wears you down. And why you get disappointed."

Ray patted her hand. "Don't you worry. My ears and eyes are open this time."

As they backed out of the driveway, Cora wagged her head. "Watch yourself," she said through the open window.

He winked and saluted. "Yes, ma'am."

Inside the house he grabbed his guitar, went to the porch, and sat on the swing. Mabel and Cora couldn't be right about everything. Could they? He had to give the relationship at least one more try.

Ray strummed a few chords and let the music soothe his soul. He closed his eyes and launched into the latest love song he'd written. The lyrics about "forever love" didn't jibe with his present situation—especially the lines on friendship and trust. So many questions swirled in his mind. Was Bailey his friend? Shouldn't a romance be built on a strong friendship? Most important—could he ever really trust her again?

So many questions and no answers.

He heard a foot on the step and opened his eyes. Faith stood there, a soft smile on her face. His heart paused, and he silenced the instrument with his hand.

꙳

"Please, don't stop playing." Faith settled into a lawn chair beside him. "That was beautiful, Ray."

"You think?" He looked thoughtful. "How long have you been listening?"

"Long enough to. . ." *hear about love, trust, and friendship*. Feeling like an eavesdropper, she held that back. "Long enough to know it's a beautiful song. Did you write it?"

Ray settled back and stretched his long legs out in front of him. "Yes, I did." Smiling, he peered at her intently, and a rush of heat warmed her cheeks.

"What?" she asked. A nervous laugh escaped her lips. "What is it?"

"I don't know." He set down the guitar and gave her another lingering look that set her pulse to racing.

Why this reaction?

"The lyrics are odd," he said. "They seemed to have come out of nowhere."

"Out of nowhere?" Faith swallowed past the sudden dryness in her throat. "I—I think I know what happened."

Ray tilted his head. "Do you?"

"Maybe when you met with Bailey the other night, all those old feelings came back and with them, the lyrics."

Eyes narrowed, Ray appeared to be considering her theory. Then he looked at her and shook his head. "No, that's not it. The lyrics came before I saw Bailey. A few nights ago, when I was trying to sleep." He put his guitar in its case. "I've been thinking a lot about friendship and trust."

"And?" she asked, holding her breath.

He didn't answer, just looked out across the yard.

"Ray?"

He looked back at her. "I'm not sure, but I do know that things aren't what I thought they would be."

His words might have been puzzling to anyone else, but not to her. She knew exactly what he meant.

He sat up, and the pensive Ray was gone, replaced by what she could only describe as "cop Ray." She was disappointed and relieved at the same time.

"So, I've got official permission to look into the break-ins in the area. Can't make an official report yet, though." He glanced at her. "Hard to explain, but if it's official, it goes into an FBI database, and we don't like to do that until what's happening is determined to be a real crime." He smiled. "Not that we don't believe something is really happening."

"That's fine." Her mind snapped back to the business at hand. "Who breaks in just to steal food? I own expensive photography equipment, and it's still there. It's got to be that little girl."

Ray got to his feet. "I'll put my guitar inside. Then let's go over to your place, and I'll check it out."

She waited for him and remembered the other news she had.

"I got a call about Sparkles," she said as they strolled across the lawn toward her house. "A man called in answer to my ad."

Ray stopped and looked down at her. "You don't sound happy."

"I'm not on several levels. I guess I have gotten attached, but I always knew she belonged to someone else, so I didn't let my heart go. My bigger issue is that I don't know how she got hurt. I can't let her go until I determine it wasn't her owner. His name is Peter. He's coming by tomorrow night."

"That makes sense." They stepped through her front door. Sparkles greeted them with little yips, then grabbed a toy and began running in circles.

"I call that her 'crazy dog' response," Faith said. "She does it when she's happy."

Ray smiled, then sniffed. "Smells good in here."

"I had a homemaker attack. While you're here you can try my new double-chocolate chocolate chip cookie recipe."

"Cookies, hmm. You know the way to a man's heart," he joked.

Faith blinked and walked to the counter. Why did those words make her think, *I only wish*? "You want coffee?" Faith scooped coffee grounds into the filter.

"Sure. Hey, you mind if I look at these?"

Faith glanced over her shoulder and saw him pointing at a photo album. "Not at all."

After she finished the coffee, she stood beside him at the table, watching him flip through the pictures, one by one. Mabel, Cora, landscapes of the area. Sparkles. The last two were of him sitting on the porch with his guitar. Faith had caught him with a look of what? Melancholy?

"I'm sorry. I'm not spying on you."

"I know you're not. I've seen you with your camera. I knew what you were doing." Ray's muscled forearm brushed hers, and she felt her skin heat.

"Something wrong?" he asked.

"No, of course not." She turned and pulled mugs from the cupboard, then glanced at him. He had that cop expression, like he didn't seem satisfied with her answer. "I—I guess I'm just nervous about the break-in stuff."

"I understand." Ray cleared his throat. "Hey, how'd your date go, by the way?"

"My date?" Faith sat in a chair at the kitchen table, lest the strength in her legs fail her. "That question came out of nowhere."

Ray shrugged. "Yeah, I guess so. But you haven't answered me."

She could give him the truth—that she'd spent half the evening with George comparing him to Ray. Why, she didn't know. Instead she shrugged. "Actually, George is a great guy. He's funny, too." She laughed to prove her point.

Ray pursed his lips and nodded. "Funny? How so?"

Faith's back stiffened. It was just like Ray to put her on the spot, dig for more. "You're a real cop today, you know that?"

He laughed. "We're friends, we can vent to one another. I pretty much tell you everything that goes on in my life. Speaking of which"—Ray glanced at his watch—"I'm going to see Bailey tonight. Wish me luck."

Luck? He'd need more than luck to get himself straightened out about Bailey. "I'll pray for you—that God will show you the truth."

"Whoa, now you sound like the two women I live with." He jutted his thumb in the direction of the sisters' house, and Faith couldn't help but laugh. "That was a slip of the tongue," Ray said. "I'll take the prayer any day before I wait for dumb luck."

The gurgle of the coffeepot sent relief through her. Faith jumped up and went to the counter, fighting the odd feelings bubbling up inside her. She wanted to laugh, to cry, to slip her arms around Ray and rest her head against his chest. What was happening to her?

"You never did tell me about your date," Ray said from his seat at the table.

That was Ray—he wouldn't let it go. He cared about her as a friend and was only looking out for her well-being. She should appreciate his brotherly concern, so why was she irritated?

Faith brought his cup to the table along with three cookies. He thanked her, and she took her seat beside him. Sparkles, worn out from her play, settled on the floor at their feet.

"Nothing for you to eat?" Ray's dark brows scrunched together.

How could she explain she was too confused to eat, and she didn't know why? "Not right now." She smiled. "So, about my date. . .George has a dry sense of humor, and you know how I like that." Not dry enough to make her forget Ray.

Ray swallowed a large bite of cookie and moaned his contentment. "Delicious." He took a sip of coffee. "Actually, I didn't know you liked that kind of humor. Is that like slapstick or something?"

She suddenly felt defensive. "I can't explain it, and it's beside the point. The thing is, I'm going to give it another chance. We're going out tomorrow night."

"Aha, so you are reluctant. 'Another chance' means you weren't gung ho."

Faith crossed her arms over her midsection. "You're giving Bailey 'another chance.' Are you not gung ho?"

Ray nodded slowly. "Point well taken." He set down his cup and looked her in the eye in that unnerving way of his, like she was transparent under his dark gaze. "I'm not gung ho, Faith. What she did to me. . ." He tapped his fingers on the table. "You said something a couple minutes ago that sort of resonated in me."

"What?"

"It was about Sparkles. You said, 'I guess I have gotten attached, but I always knew she belonged to someone else, so I didn't let my heart go.' I wonder if in a weird way that's how I feel about Bailey. I can't let my heart go anymore because she belonged to someone else."

Hurt shone in his eyes, and her heart squeezed in her chest. "I'm sorry, Ray. You guys had a history together. I shouldn't have compared you with my situation with George." What had gotten into her? Every time she heard him speak Bailey's name, a mean streak surfaced.

"Not a problem." Ray finished the cookie and winked. "Thanks. Delicious." He stood, suddenly all business. "Now, let me get to making a list of your missing property."

She'd really done it this time—she and her big mouth.

Chapter 14

Ray leaned back on the soft cushions of the blue couch in Mabel and Cora's living room, once again feeling like he'd taken a trip back in time. The only thing that had changed since he was a kid was a fresh coat of yellow paint in the homey room. He shuffled through pages of music in a notebook, asking the Lord to lead him in picking out songs for the following Sunday. Pastor Gary had asked him to lead the worship again on Sunday morning. Ray had chosen an initial upbeat song in the key of *D*. He needed a couple more, then he would modulate to *G*. Both easy keys for the instrumentalists to play, especially the novice guitar player who was new on the worship team.

He picked up his guitar, and as he softly strummed, Mabel and Cora came and stood in the doorway wearing their "going out" dresses.

"I suppose you're seeing *her* tonight?" Mabel said.

"Yes, I am." Ray wondered how they knew.

"We figured." Cora frowned. "It was inevitable."

"You both look gorgeous. Going somewhere special?"

"To the chiropractor and then to do some research on the Victorian." Mabel had her leather briefcase in hand and set it on the floor next to her feet.

"Chiropractor, eh?" Ray winked at Cora.

She blushed, but Mabel was frowning.

He put his guitar down. "What's wrong? I recognize that look. What did I do? Besides make a date with Bailey."

Mabel snorted, then put her hands on her hips. "Young man, you need to tell us when you eat things from the refrigerator. You're not a teenager anymore. You should know better, eating in the middle of the night. It's not good for your digestion. You'll get an ulcer."

"Or that acid reflux." Cora shook her head. "Destroys your esophagus. Then eats the throat away."

"Can't have that," Mabel said. "If you're that hungry, we'll make a bigger dinner."

Her words reminded him of the many lectures he'd gotten from her over the years. But this time he hadn't earned it. "I didn't eat anything from the refrigerator. And if you make dinner any bigger, I'll be big as a house in a month."

Mabel's frown grew. "You didn't eat any midnight snacks? You used to."

"Yes, I know. I *used* to do a lot of things I don't do now. No. The only things I eat are what Cora makes and sets on the table."

The sisters exchanged glances, then looked at him again. "Someone's been in the refrigerator."

Ray sat up, and a page of music drifted to the floor. "You mean *that* much stuff is missing? You can't be mistaken?"

"Mistaken?" Cora clucked her tongue again.

"Don't be a smarty-pants," Mabel said. "Seems we'd know what's in our own refrigerator, wouldn't we?"

Ray stood. "Believe me, I'm not being a smarty-pants. Please show me."

On the way to the kitchen he explained his suspicions about the kid in the neighborhood, telling them that Faith was missing food, too.

"Oh my," Cora said. "Poor dear. Maybe we should leave the door unlocked so she can come in and eat."

As he scanned the room, Ray shook his head. "Miss Cora, no. I know your intentions are good, but I don't think you understand what kids are capable of."

"Maybe we'll leave food on the back porch then," Mabel said. "We can't have a child going hungry."

"No, please don't. That could encourage more bad behavior. I'm investigating the break-ins. I'll make a report about this. I have to catch her."

The sisters glared at him as if one entity.

"I'm a cop." He shrugged, feeling guilty. "I have rules to follow. And the world isn't nirvana."

"Nirvana? Well, I should say not." Mabel swatted at him. "Don't you go talking about that kind of thing in this house, young man."

"It's only a figure of speech," he mumbled.

"Nirvana, indeed," Cora muttered. "But don't you worry none. We're going to pray about this poor child. God is merciful. He isn't tied down by petty police rules."

"Preach it, sister," Mabel said and pointed at Ray's notebook. "Now you go back to your worship."

"And you promise me you'll keep your doors locked."

His concern seemed to get through to them. They didn't argue.

Ray had to force his mind back to the music as he listened to them drive away. He found a likely song and began to play, singing again, imagining the other instruments playing along. When his cell phone vibrated on his belt, he debated whether or not to pick it up. He hated the interruption, but it might be work. Or Philip. Or the pastor. Or. . .Faith.

He pulled the phone from its holder, looked at the screen, then smiled and hit the TALK button. "Faith, what's up?"

"Ray, I'm sorry to disturb you, but Sparkles is missing." Her voice was higher pitched than normal.

"Missing from your house? Your yard?"

"My house. Totally gone."

"Signs of a break-in?"

She paused and inhaled. "I don't know."

"I'll be right over." He set aside his guitar and music and left the house, locking the door behind him. The conversation with Mabel and Cora made him realize that whether he was pursuing justice with a badge or leading worship at church, he needed to continually pray, and he did as he jogged the distance to Faith's front door where she waited, hand to her heart.

"Ray, I'm not sure what to do. Sparkles isn't mine. Really, I shouldn't have brought her home without her owner's permission, but as you know, I had my suspicions about the injury. I told you the owner was supposed to come by this evening, but I called him and told him not to. I didn't tell him why."

"I'll help you look for her." He impulsively put his arm around her shoulders. She leaned into him for a moment, then stiffened. He let go, surprised that touching her still felt so good, like when they were teens, and he was disappointed she didn't seem to want the contact. "Show me where she was last," he said.

"Okay, okay. . ." Faith led him into the living room and pointed to the sofa. "Sparkles was right there. Right there, curled up on that corner pillow." She looked up at him with worried eyes. "I went to the backyard to put seed in the bird feeder, so I wouldn't have heard anything."

"Did you lock your front door?"

She sighed. "I left the screen door open, and no, I didn't lock it. Anyway, I figured Sparkles would bark."

Ray remained outwardly calm, but the thought that someone had been brazen enough to enter her home while she was there turned his stomach.

"I know it was stupid." She read his expression, although not entirely correctly. "With that child wandering around—"

"Well, I wouldn't go as far as to say stupid, but we all do need to be cautious. Kids, even younger children, are capable of crime. And I don't care where someone lives, the doors need to be locked, even the screen doors. And—"

"And what?"

"For now, I'd recommend you not use the screen door for a breeze. Open windows. Screen doors are too easy to get through."

"Do you think that little girl was in my house again? And maybe took the dog?"

He shrugged. "Could be. You've looked all over the house, right?"

She nodded. "Yes, but you're welcome to do so again if you wish."

He did wish and followed her. He remembered the layout from when her grandmother lived here, but things had changed. A new coat of paint throughout and the wood floors had been refinished. Everything was spotless, like a model home.

"Do you have belongings?" he murmured as he checked the second bathroom. "I think maybe you're only pretending to live here. It's. . .perfect."

She socked him lightly in the shoulder with her fist. "I told you, I'm a neat freak."

"Ow!" He howled. "Brutality. And here I am being nice to you."

"Arrest me," she said and laughed.

After a check of everything, Ray found nothing of interest. They went back to the living room. "Well, let's not waste time. Let's go look around the neighborhood. Remember, I first found her in the hedges."

Faith pulled on her sweater. "True."

He paused. "So, why did you ask the guy to come by here and not your clinic?"

"Besides the fact that I wasn't scheduled to work today, I wanted to gauge the dog's reaction to him in a home-type setting. I just didn't like the fact that she might have been kicked around, and she didn't have tags. I had also planned to have a friend from a rescue organization here with me."

He groaned and motioned for her to follow him outside.

"What?" she demanded. "What are you griping about?"

He shook his head. "I've been a cop too long. I never give anyone information about where I live. I don't care what the reason."

"Hmm. I hadn't thought about that. I suppose I shouldn't have."

"No matter. I'm right next door."

She smiled. "That you are."

They began their search in the bushes where he'd found the dog, then headed down the street. After several minutes, she appeared so dejected he almost slung his arm around her shoulders, like old times, but Faith was all grown up now and obviously didn't want that kind of attention from him. He stuffed his hands in his jean pockets as they walked down the road in the other direction. Soon it was obvious Sparkles wasn't anywhere to be found.

"Only one last place to look," Ray said as they walked back toward home.

"The old Victorian," Faith said. "Remember we used to say it was haunted? And remember the man who used to live there? I wonder if he's still alive."

"His sister is living down the street with her husband." Ray picked up his pace. "But I don't know about him. I do remember they were on the 'outs' because he inherited the house and she didn't. Mabel and Cora would probably know more." He grinned down at her. "Yeah, I remember nights sitting outside with you, and we'd make up stories about what went on in that house."

They crossed the yard, crowded with overgrown bushes and evergreens.

"Do you think Sparkles or the kid are inside?" Faith peered in a window. "Looks cluttered in there."

"They bought it with a lot of the furniture," Ray said. "And I can't imagine the kid being in there with all the activity lately, with the closing and walk-through. Mabel and Cora have been over here every day as well. There'd be no way the kid could hide." Ray poked through the shrubbery, but found no sign of the dog. "But if that kid has Sparkles, it'll make her easier to find. And I think I have enough now to make this an official investigation." He told her about food missing from Mabel and Cora's house. "I'll talk to my supervisor tomorrow."

They headed back across the street to her house.

"I'll call the SPCA and put them on notice to watch for Sparkles. I do pro bono work for them; they'll help me out."

Faith sighed. "Thanks for being here, Ray."

"Hey, you don't have to thank me. I want to be here for you—and find Sparkles, too."

Faith smiled. "You never change, do you?"

"How do you mean that? Mabel and Cora say the same thing." Ray gave her a sidelong glance.

"Just that we haven't seen each other in years and yet here you are, helping me, just like you used to. Not only that, you seem to bring out the best in me." Faith's face colored.

Ray stopped midstep, turned to her, and took her hands in his. "I think that's the nicest thing anybody's ever said to me. . .that I bring out the best in them." For sure Bailey never spoke anything close to that, and he felt the sting to his core. "You know, you bring out the best in me, too, Faith."

"Do I? How so?"

"You, accepting me at face value. You're probably the only person on the planet who knows me inside out."

She squeezed his hands and smiled. "Ditto. It's nice to be with someone who knows me so well. Someone who doesn't mind my humanness." Faith glanced at her watch. "I've got to get ready for my date with George tonight."

"Hmm." Ray nodded. "You think anything will come of it?" She frowned, and he went on to clarify. "I didn't mean that you had to have marriage in mind to go on a date. But wondered if you thought it might be a possibility."

"I don't know. He's a great guy. This'll be the second time we've gone out. Really, I'm not good at the getting-to-know-you phase of dating. I like the familiar." Faith clamped her teeth on her lower lip as though to stop her flow of words.

"Hey, I'm familiar." Ray laughed, but had to wonder why he felt unsettled about her going on a date and even more so about George being a permanent part of her life. Perhaps he was falling back into the protective role, maybe a big-brother thing. "I'm going out with Bailey tonight."

She eyed him with an unreadable expression. "Aha, so you like the familiar, too."

"Possibly," he said. *Or maybe I'm just a sore loser who has to win back what he lost?* The thought was disturbing. It meant seeing Bailey was more about ego than love. "Okay, I'd better get a move on."

Faith went inside her house, and Ray jogged across the lawn, hoping to outrun the fire burning in his chest. He reached the house, then heard the slam of a car door and turned.

A blond man was climbing from a blue Ford pickup truck. Was that Faith's date?

Chapter 15

I'm sorry," Faith repeated to Peter, the man who had called about Sparkles, who stood at her door. His bulk blocked the light coming into the house. "I called and left you a message. Told you not to come tonight. The dog isn't here." She glanced at her watch and tried to quell her irritation. The search for Sparkles had taken longer than she planned. George would arrive in less than an hour, and she wasn't quite ready to go.

"Where is it?" he asked.

It? Didn't he know the sex of the dog? "Not here at the moment. Did you bring proof that the dog is yours?"

His face grew red. "I want my dog. I could sue you."

Being sued was always in the back of her mind as a vet and owner of a clinic. The fact that he prodded that fear pushed her irritation to anger. "Yes, you could. And then I would point out that the dog had no collar and no tags. That's irresponsible. As far as we could tell, *it* was a stray. I cared for the dog myself rather than take her to the pound. If you want to pursue this legally—"

"Are you threatening me?" He took a step toward her.

Faith's irritation grew, but she also felt a bit vulnerable. The man was big. "I'm reminding you that I treated a dog for which I had no guarantee of ever being paid." She had a guarded feeling about the man standing in front of her. "What did you say the dog's name was?"

"I don't have to pay for anything I didn't authorize," he said, his stance challenging her.

Faith threw her shoulders back and slipped around his large frame, letting her door fall shut behind her, and stood at the top of the porch stairs. "I'm expecting company. I'll call you and keep you updated. Next time bring proof the dog is yours. What did you say your last name is?" She tried to make eye contact, but his heavy lids hooded his eyes.

"Yeah, yeah, my last name's Davis. What about it?"

Faith looked across the yard, and her heart jolted. "Ray, hi there!" He stood on the sisters' porch, muscled arms crossed. "Oh, there's my neighbor." She pointed. "He's a cop. He's as interested as I am in getting the dog back to its rightful owner."

Peter narrowed his eyes.

"I'll call you soon, and we can arrange another time for you to pick up the dog."

"Right. Good." He gave her one last scathing look and hurried down the sidewalk to his truck, jumped inside, and took off.

Ray walked across the lawn, and his gaze followed the truck. He reached her and frowned. "Was that George? Did he leave you stranded?"

Did she look desperate? "No, that *wasn't* George. No date of mine would leave me like that." Faith tamped down her irritation now that Peter was gone, narrowed her eyes, and pulled in a breath. "That man was a bully, and I don't date bullies."

"Takes one to know one, I guess." Ray winked, glanced at her again, then grew serious.

Warmed by his affectionate humor, she smiled. Still the tease, Ray was adorable. "That was Peter, the dog owner. Well, he says he's Sparkles's owner, but didn't refer to her by sex or name. I guess the dog could have belonged to one of his kids or something, and he's not that engaged with them. But I got a bad feeling from him."

Ray's brows were furrowed. "I should have gotten his license plate number."

She shrugged. "How would you know he was weird? I'm supposed to call him and tell him when it's convenient to come see the dog again."

"If you do that, tell me. I'd like to be here."

"Will do." She glanced at her watch. "I've got to get ready. George will be here in just a few minutes. Fortunately it's not formal."

"Have a good time," Ray mumbled. "My date isn't for another few hours." He started across the lawn.

"You have a good time with Bailey as well," Faith called out, but her heart wasn't in her fond farewell.

❧

I'm not spying, Ray decided as he settled on the front porch with his guitar. If he happened to catch a glimpse of Faith's date, so be it. What was Faith's type? When they were teenagers, she never kept posters of movie stars on her walls. She never had a steady boyfriend back then that he knew of. Always focused on her goals, she carried a day planner even as a teen. He wondered if she'd had a serious relationship as an adult. Or if she'd ever been engaged.

Ray picked at the guitar strings with no particular song in mind. Tonight he'd find out if there was anything left to salvage of his relationship with Bailey. He ought to be looking forward to their time together—but he felt neither joy nor sadness. Odd after the anticipation he'd felt when he knew he was returning to Bothell, knowing she was available again. He searched his heart, frustrated that he couldn't put a name to his emotions.

The rev of a car engine grabbed his attention. Ray leaned forward in his chair, unsure if the foliage around the porch hid him from view. A man got out of a red Chevy Malibu, and Faith stepped out onto her porch to greet him. She was smiling.

"George," Ray muttered. He was tall and had to lean down to kiss Faith on the cheek. A flare of some strong emotion went off in Ray's chest. For sure, he wasn't angry. Odd that he was so emotionally confused tonight. He shook his head. "What's up with me?" He wasn't Faith's bodyguard. He was her friend. Still, wasn't the guy acting too familiar with her? It was only a second date.

Ray settled back in his chair. Who was he to judge? He'd kissed Bailey on the lips on their second date. He let that thought rattle around in his head for a while, stood, and took another look across the yard. Yeah, but that was Bailey. Faith was different. She was always conservative. Chaste.

Faith looked up, and Ray knew he was busted. He made a show of waving a big hello.

She smiled, that little smile he loved so much, then nodded a hello. Her date held open the car door for her, and Faith got in without giving Ray another look.

Ray drew a deep breath and went inside the house. He was going to see Bailey tonight—that was probably a good thing. He had to get his mind off Faith. It was none of his business whom she dated.

Chapter 16

Bailey patted her soft blond hair and looked him in the eye. "Great place," she said again, then glanced around the dining room in Canyons.

They were seated one table away from where he and Faith had been sitting. He'd enjoyed that meal, which was probably why he wanted to return. The only spoiler had been their conversation about Bailey. Maybe it was a mistake to take Bailey here. He wanted to remember Faith sitting across from him.

"I've been thinking about us," Ray said, then speared a piece of steak. He suddenly became aware that his plate was almost clean, but Bailey had hardly touched her food.

"Me, too," Bailey said hopefully. "I know it's a big deal to ask you to forgive me. I'm not stupid. I can't really say I'd forgive you if you'd done the same to me." She swiped a tear from the corner of her eye.

Ray set down his fork. "I appreciate your honesty, but it's not about forgiveness." He paused. "Well, that's not exactly true. I am struggling with forgiveness, but it goes deeper. I don't know if what we had is still there, Bailey." She looked on the verge of tears, and he hesitated to continue, but this meeting was about getting it all out on the table. "My feelings for you. . .over the past year, my feelings have run the gamut. It's not a matter of recovering what's lost. It's starting over. I can try—"

"We have to try." Her voice was high-pitched and panicked. "You don't think we deserve one more chance? Think about how wonderful it was!"

He tried to call back to memory the good times. There had definitely been a strong physical attraction, and they'd had laughs together. But. . .his gaze snapped to hers. "Do you think I've got a good sense of humor?"

Bailey blinked. "Talk about out of left field." Her brows arched. "Is that the criteria? If I think you're funny"—her tone got lighter—"we can date again?" She laughed.

Ray shrugged. In all fairness to Bailey, the question was out of line. He knew why he'd asked—Faith said George was funny, and he wanted to know how his sense of humor compared.

"Of course you're funny," Bailey said. "I think you're wonderful." She reached across the table for his hand.

He gripped hers for a moment, and when the waiter arrived, he let go. He ordered regular coffee and Bailey ordered decaf, then Ray settled back in his chair and leveled a gaze at Bailey. "Trust is key in a relationship. Before anything can be repaired, you and I need to discuss what happened. I want to know why your relationship with Dwight ended."

She colored and glanced at the table. "I guess you could say he ended it."

"He ended it?" Ray's muscles tensed.

"Well, yes. He—he just didn't think we were working out."

Ray unclenched his tight fists. "So is that the only reason you're here? It didn't work out with Dwight?"

Bailey's eyes flashed. "I think it should count for something that *I* didn't end the relationship with him."

"Like you did with me?"

Tears pooled in her eyes. "I can't win here, can I?"

"It's not a matter of winning or losing. I don't know if this hurdle's too big to jump."

She swallowed. "Can you try?"

Their coffee arrived before he could answer, which gave him time to think. For so many months all he'd wanted was to win Bailey back. Now, faced with the reality, he couldn't commit.

He met Bailey's teary gaze. "I can tell you I'll try. I can't give you any guarantees. But you need to give me time. Don't rush me."

Her lips firmed. "I'll prove myself to you. You won't be sorry."

He wasn't so sure.

❧

"You seem a million miles away, Faith." George walked her from the burger joint out to his car with his hand at the small of her back. "Things okay at the clinic?"

"Things are good. Debbie is back full-time now." She was determined to make the best of their date. Get Ray and Bailey off her mind. But the truth was, she didn't want to date George. She didn't see him that way.

"I thought we'd go bowling." George opened the car door for her. "You mentioned you liked bowling."

"Bowling, right." Faith tried to smile. George was trying hard to please. He remembered what she said she liked.

As they rode toward the bowling alley, she looked over at him. George's bushy hair was graying at the temples, which gave him an air of distinction. He wasn't playing at dating. From the first time they'd met when he brought in his dog for shots, she saw the admiration in his eyes. What made her think they could just hang out and be friends? It was now or never.

"George, in all fairness, I've got something I must tell you."

"Uh-oh, I don't like that tone." There was humor in his voice, but he was frowning. He pulled his car into a parking spot in front of the bowling alley and cut the engine. "All right, shoot."

"These, um, dates. . .I'm not ready for a real relationship. I've had a great time with you, but I don't want to give the wrong impression. I see us as friends. If you want more than that—"

"I do," he stated flatly. "I appreciate your honesty, but I don't see you as a female buddy."

"I'm sorry." Faith scanned his face and shrugged. Tonight would only be their second date, but she should've made herself clear from the start. "It's nothing personal. Just that I've got to focus on my career."

"And you can't do that and have a boyfriend?" George looked at her thoughtfully. "Are you sure you're not commitment phobic?"

"No!" Her shoulders tensed. "At least I don't think so."

"But you're not sure, are you?" He studied her face. "I felt your walls up ever since I met you. I wasn't sure what was wrong, but they were still up during our first date. I thought it was me, but you accepted my second invitation."

"It's not you," she said. "Really."

He patted her arm. "When was the last time you had a boyfriend?"

"A real boyfriend?" She hesitated to say it aloud, glanced at George, and decided she could trust him. "That's easy. It was back in the navy." But she had never really loved the guy.

"I see." He stared at her for a moment more, then pointed to the building. "You ready?"

"If you'd rather turn around and take me home, that's fine."

"Nope. I can handle this." George smiled and exited the vehicle, came around, and opened the door for her. "This may be God's timing. There's a good chance I'll be transferred to San Diego soon."

A rush of relief came over her and eased a bit of her guilt. "San Diego— that's a beautiful city."

They got their shoes and balls and began to bowl. When they were done, they got colas at the snack bar. George was an exceptionally nice guy; funny, too. Faith found herself wishing she could love him. "I'm pretty sure you won't be on the market for long, George."

He laughed. "That's what my sister says. She's been trying to hook me up with 'the perfect woman for me' for months now. Maybe I should take her up on that. Sometimes our friends and family know us better than we know ourselves."

Faith's thoughts traveled to Cora and Mabel and their matchmaking efforts. "I wonder. . ." She clamped her mouth shut. She'd just told George she was career-minded and had no interest in a romantic relationship.

"What is it?" George tilted his head. "Is there someone else? Was that the guy next door?"

Faith felt the color drain from her face. She stared at him, mute.

"I didn't mean to upset you." George took a sip from his can of cola. "But you should've seen your face."

"How did you know about the guy next door?"

"He was watching us as we pulled away."

Faith smiled. Ray had been watching. "That's the guy my friends are trying to set me up with. Yes. But we're only friends. He doesn't think of me that way."

"But you think of him that way, right? You should see your face now, too." George was being a good sport, but she found herself getting more agitated by the second.

"No!" Faith shook her head. "As a matter of fact, he's trying to reconcile with his ex-fiancée."

"I'm sorry." George looked genuinely empathic. "But if it's meant to be—"

"No, no, it isn't meant to be." She paused. "What did you mean about my face?"

"What?" George looked baffled then smiled. "Oh, your face lit up when we started talking about him. What's his name?"

"Ray," she whispered. Her heart flipped. She was in love with Ray.

Chapter 17

After double-locking her front door, Faith strolled toward the sisters' house, the morning sun warming her head. Would she be able to look Ray eye to eye? Mabel and Cora stood beside the Thunderbird with him like two bodyguards. Before she got within ten feet of them, Mabel pointed at the passenger side door. "Faith, honey, you get in front. Cora and me, we'll sit back here. Ray will do the driving."

"O-kay."

Mabel and Cora sat primly in the backseat, holding almost identical purses in their laps. They were clearly in charge, and today she had no objection to their matchmaking efforts, even though she believed they were wasted. She didn't have the courage to act on what she felt to her core—the revelation had hit hard. Smack dab in the middle of her date with George she realized she was in love with Ray Reed. Perhaps she'd always been in love with him.

Ray glanced at her, and they exchanged a smile, but she couldn't hold his glance. He looked great in a suit. What would Ray think if he could see into her dark heart? He innocently thought of them as friends. He'd trusted her with his deepest secrets—and she'd stayed up half the night praying he wouldn't reconcile with Bailey. Some friend. She'd betrayed his trust. Not that God would honor her selfish prayer.

"So, no sign of Sparkles, eh?" Cora wagged her head.

"None." Faith's heart sank a notch. "I've done all I can."

"I'm sure you have," Cora said.

"Don't you worry none." Mabel nudged her shoulder. "We're prayin'. We have a feeling about this. We think that little puppy is fine. Maybe even with that hungry child."

"We thought the same thing," Faith said. "But if she is, I wish the girl hadn't come into my house to get her."

"Judith down the street had her bananas taken right out of her car while she was unloading her groceries." Mabel groaned.

Ray's head snapped up. "Why didn't she report it to the police?"

"Because we told her we had a good idea who was doing it. Poor little tyke."

"You find out anything more about her, Ray?" Cora asked. "I worry she's an orphan and she's hungry."

Mabel nodded. "We need to catch her and feed her."

"Like she's a rabbit?" Ray laughed.

Mabel huffed. "Like we did you, smarty-pants."

"You didn't have to catch me. And no, I didn't find out anything else."

"Well, get busy with that," Cora demanded. "Now, you best get us to church. You've got worship to play for."

"Yes, ma'am." Ray smiled, and Faith couldn't help admiring his handsome profile.

"Faith, honey?" Mabel nudged her out of her daydream.

"Yes?" Faith turned to see Mabel's knowing look and prayed Mabel wouldn't give away her secret.

"Would you do me and Cora a big favor?"

"Yes, sure, anything."

"When we start work on the house, we want you to take pictures."

"Yes," Cora said. "Like a diary of how it changes."

Faith smiled. "Absolutely. I'd love to."

Ray shot Faith a covert glance. "Did you talk to Peter again about the dog?"

That was something else that had kept her tossing all night. "No."

"Just remember, don't you ever open the door to him again unless I'm with you, understand?" Ray's face was rigid, his tone adamant.

"I won't." She liked the big, protective side of Ray. Surprising. She normally hated to be fussed over, especially by a man. She smiled. She loved everything about him. If he ever knew what she was really thinking—

"Ray told us about Peter." Cora sniffed.

"And if Ray's not home, we'll help," Mabel said, slapping her purse. "Nerve of him. You just call us. Cora's got that set of cast-iron skillets. Take a man down fast."

Faith giggled, picturing the sisters walloping someone to protect her. Ray reached across the seat and squeezed her hand.

"Huh-uh." Cora laughed. "There you go."

"You two look cute," Mabel said.

Ray released her hand and set his on the steering wheel. "We're not teenagers anymore, Miss Mabel."

"And too bad for that, ain't it?" Mabel moaned.

"What's that supposed to mean?" Ray's brows pulled together.

"Just that some people take detours when what they need is sittin' right there in front of them." Mabel swatted the back of Ray's head, and Faith offered him a sympathetic look.

Of course Ray was frustrated. He must've had a wonderful time with Bailey. She imagined them chatting and laughing. Reminiscing. "How'd it go last night?" Faith blurted and wanted to bite her tongue.

Ray gave her a long look, then indicated with his eyes that they were in mixed company.

"Oh, he had a bad time, yes he did," Mabel uttered, her voice dripping with sympathy.

"Miss Mabel. . ." Ray's jaw clenched.

"Um." Faith sat stiffly. What had she started? "I'm sure he had fun." After opening Pandora's box, she felt obligated to intercede on Ray's behalf.

"Ray's always a gentleman, but he couldn't hide it from us. No sirree." Cora jutted her chin. "It was all those short answers at breakfast. 'Yes, it was fine. Sure, it was fun.' Not the words of a man who had a good time with the woman he wants to spend the rest of his days with."

"Sure ain't," Mabel punctuated.

Ray glanced at Faith. She looked everywhere but at him. She opened the clasp on her handbag and gazed into it. "Anybody have a mint?"

"We know our Ray too well," Cora said, ignoring her question. "God is good."

"Yes, He is." Mabel hummed for a bit. "Faith, darlin', you coming to lunch at our house after church?"

She should decline. The unexpected addition of emotions into her already hectic life would ruin her appetite. And then Ray might see right through to her heart. But on the other hand, her refusal could open a whole new line of questioning she wasn't ready for. "Sure, sounds good."

❧

After church Ray sat at the kitchen table in silence. He mindlessly ate whatever Cora and Mabel set on his plate. His world had been turned upside down during worship. Did anybody notice?

"You played well, son. Even better than last week." Cora's voice was gentle, like she could see the questions churning in his head. "The Lord will show you the way."

His smile was meant to end the conversation. He'd have to make his decisions in the prayer closet—just God and him.

Faith nudged him with her elbow. "Your voice. . ." She set down her fork and sighed. "You're truly anointed, Ray. God gave you an amazing gift."

And therein was the problem. "I don't know. I love playing and singing for the church." Ray settled back in his chair and paused. "But I like being a cop, too. I like protecting Bothell's fine citizens." He half-jested to lighten the mood.

"Don't you worry none. It'll all be good. Just like with that little dog. She'll come back. We been prayin'. We got a feeling." Mabel dropped a heaping spoonful of sweet potatoes on Faith's dish. "Well? Faith, honey, how'd your date go last night?"

"Miss Mabel!" Ray stared at her. He appreciated the change of topic, but had to play interception on Faith's behalf. "Delicious lunch, ladies, I appreciate—"

"It was fine. . . . I mean, yes, we had fun." Faith fumbled with the napkin on her lap.

"Mm-hm." Cora carried the platter of leftover ham to the stove, then returned to the table wearing a bright smile.

"What I thought," Mabel said.

Ray looked at Faith and perceived a storm behind her brown eyes. "Want to go for a walk? We could go to Bothell Landing Park."

"I'd like that. I'll grab my camera." Faith smiled and nodded as the doorbell sounded.

"I'll get that," Cora said.

"Let's go." Ray pulled out Faith's chair for her, ready to make a hasty retreat, then heard Bailey's cheery voice and held back a groan. *Great!* He needed time to think, and Bailey wasn't about to give him the time nor space. Had she always been this pushy? Come to think of it, yes. He had to wonder if Dwight really had done the initial pursuing of Bailey—or had she pursued him?

"It's Bailey!" Cora yelled.

"Bailey," Mabel echoed and looked sadly at Faith and Ray. "No walk in the park. Guess it's time for some Sunday afternoon prayer."

Faith sighed. "I better get home, anyway. I have bills to pay. Don't want to fall behind."

She looked like she could use a friend. "I'm sorry," Ray said just as Bailey flounced into the kitchen behind Cora.

"Ray!" Bailey went to him, wrapped her arms around his neck, and kissed him on the cheek. He pulled back, just slightly. His gaze shot to Faith. She was balling up her napkin, and her lips were narrowed. He wanted to apologize. For what, he didn't exactly know.

"Thanks so much for lunch." Faith stood.

"You don't need to go yet, do you?" Mabel scowled.

Cora stood. "We have pie."

"No, thanks." Faith gave Mabel a hug, then Cora. "Nice seeing you again, Bailey." She disappeared from the kitchen in a flash.

After a long moment of silence, and several sympathetic moans from the sisters, Cora set a plate at the table next to hers.

"Go on and sit." Mabel pointed at it.

Bailey glanced at the chair next to Ray, but he didn't say anything. He was still pondering why Faith had run off. Bailey finally obeyed and perched on the edge of the chair.

"Would you like some lunch?" Mabel gave Bailey an assessing look, and Ray prayed silently that the sisters wouldn't say anything crazy.

Bailey glanced at the food on the table. "Um, no thanks. I had some sushi and miso soup in town a little while ago."

"Ohh, that's raw fish, ain't it?" Cora stood and murmured, "Pin worms. . ."

Mabel frowned. "Me-soul-soup?"

"Miso. It's a fermented soy product and. . ." Bailey looked at Ray for help.

"Fermented?" Mabel asked. "Isn't that what—"

"It's good soup," Ray said. "I've had it." He patted Bailey's arm. "They don't do Asian food."

"What's wrong with good old country cooking is what I want to know?" Cora said. "Raw fish, indeed. Hmpf."

Ray winked at Bailey, hoping she wouldn't take offense. "I happen to like sushi—"

"I call it bait," Cora interrupted. "We used it to catch catfish when I was growin' up."

Ray accepted that this was a battle he couldn't win. He just smiled.

"Have some iced tea then." Mabel slapped a glass in front of Bailey.

"Does it have sugar?" Bailey bit her lip. It was clear she was trying to be polite. "I'm sorry. I'm just…well, I avoid sugar to keep my weight at a good place."

"What kinda tea doesn't have sugar?" Mabel planted her hands on her hips and looked Bailey up and down. "Besides, you could use a little meat on your bones."

Ray squeezed Bailey's arm and bit back a grin. "It's southern sweet tea. Delicious."

"Well, I can't. . ." Bailey's voice trailed off as the sisters stared at her incredulously. "Um, I'll make an exception. I'm sure it's wonderful." She took a big gulp.

"Why don't we go sit in the living room?" Ray nodded at Bailey.

Mabel and Cora were next to each other, looking like one solid unit.

"We'll be cleaning up," Cora said.

"And praying," Mabel said over her shoulder as she turned to the sink.

"They pray a lot," Bailey whispered when they reached the living room.

"You don't know the half of it." Ray took her arm to lead her to the sofa when Bailey turned to him.

"Can we sit out on the porch instead?" She looked over her shoulder at the kitchen door.

"Sure." He held the door open for her, and they settled into chairs on the porch.

"You can pour that into the bushes, if you'd rather not drink it." Ray pointed at the glass of tea she held in her clenched fist.

"Are you sure?" Her gaze settled nervously on the windows as if she was afraid Mabel and Cora were watching.

"Here, I'll take it." He pried it from her hand and downed it with three gulps.

"Thank you," she said.

"You're welcome. You don't need to worry. Mabel and Cora are sweet, but opinionated and sometimes overbearing. You just gotta go with the flow."

"I guess." Bailey's voice was small.

Ray put the glass on the floor. "Okay, I don't want to be rude, but why are you here? I told you I needed some time to think—"

"I know." She slipped her hand in his. Her smile was shaky, unsure. "It's just that I stayed up all night thinking about you. About us. I couldn't wait another minute to talk to you."

"You could've called. It's not like I wouldn't take your call."

Her eyes teared, and Ray took her other hand in his. "I'm not going to lie to you. I don't know if this relationship can be fixed."

Bailey sniffled. "That's why I knew I had to come over today. We need to talk. I don't want to lose you." She squeezed his fingers. "I made the biggest mistake of my life dating Dwight. I love you, Ray. I've loved you all along. I guess I never learned coping skills. I felt ignored, and I did the next best thing."

Ray leaned forward and hugged her. It hurt to know he was the cause of her tears. "I forgive you, Bailey, but I just don't know."

"Please?" Bailey leaned back and looked into his eyes. "A few more dates. How can that hurt? I believe in my heart we're worth another chance."

What could it hurt? He pondered the question, recalled their good times together. They'd been so in love once. Ray drew a breath and nodded, then heard the slam of a door.

Bailey glanced over his shoulder, and her eyes narrowed. He turned to follow her gaze. Faith was rushing toward the house, crossing the yard in a steady jog.

She stopped at the bottom of the porch steps. "I'm so sorry to interrupt but—"

"That's okay. What's wrong?" Ray offered Bailey an apologetic nod and stood.

Faith's face was set, almost angry. "It's my back porch and the back door."

Ray walked down the stairs. "What?"

"I went in the front door and walked down the hall to the back door. It was open. There's dog food spilled all over the porch. It might be that kid, and it makes me nervous. I don't know if anybody's still in the house. Food is missing again, too."

"I'll go check things out now." Ray turned to see Bailey, arms crossed tight against her midsection, anger emanating from her eyes.

"I'll be back," he said.

Mad as Bailey looked, Faith's safety took precedence.

"I'll go with you," Faith said.

"No. You and Bailey go inside."

"It's fine," Bailey said. "I have somewhere to go. I'll call you later, Ray." She glanced at Faith. "You're in good hands."

Chapter 18

I'll be there, Miss Mabel," Ray said into his cell. He clicked the OFF button and put the phone on his belt.

Philip walked into his cubicle and dropped onto a chair.

Ray eyed his brother. "You look exhausted."

Philip stifled another yawn. "I think single life is catching up with me."

Ray shook his head. "Still the playboy—out all hours. Even on a Sunday night?"

Philip grinned. "At least I'm not tied down."

"Well, I'm not either anymore, but I do get decent sleep." Ray laughed when Philip slumped in his chair and pretended to snore. "Maybe I shouldn't ask, but what are you doing after work?"

Philip sat up. "What? Why? Will there be pretty girls there?"

"Oh brother!" Ray shook his head. "Pretty girls? Yes. Cora and Mabel."

Philip grinned. "Beautiful inside and out. If I could find a woman that good—and that good in the kitchen." He sighed. "That could be the ticket. These women I'm dating. . .doesn't anybody cook anymore?"

"Gotta look in the right places for them." Ray thought he should take a dose of his own advice.

"So what's up?"

"That was Mabel on the phone. She and Cora want me to start measuring at the Victorian, make a supply list. Faith's coming to take pictures. You up for that? I need your input since you'll be helping me anyway."

Philip rubbed his eyes and his stomach, then groaned dramatically. "Can we eat first?"

"I've got one better for you. Cora's bringing over her fried chicken. They want to celebrate in the new place. Good?"

"I'm there." Philip grabbed his car keys off the desk. "And it'll be good to see Faith again. Give me an hour."

❧

Ray walked across the street to the Victorian while dialing Faith's cell number.

"Hello, Ray."

The sound of her cheery voice brought a smile to his face. "Did Mabel and Cora call you and tell you the good news?

"Yep. That's why I'm home. Debbie is working her normal evening shift.

I'm coming over in a minute after I finish changing."

"I'm at the Victorian. They gave me a key and one for you, too. If you come over now, we can explore before all that energy arrives in the form of two sisters we both know and love."

She laughed. "You've got that right."

Minutes later Faith arrived, camera hanging around her neck. Ray held the front door open for her, and she brushed past him smelling of perfume and shampoo with just a faint touch of antiseptic, a scent he was beginning to associate with her.

For a moment he thought she was going to hug him, but she didn't hold his gaze. Instead she began to look around the foyer.

"Wow. This is amazing." She wandered from the foyer to the wood-floored hallway. "And the mess is amazing, too."

Old furniture crowded the rooms. It was difficult to distinguish clutter from trash. "Yeah. The owner is in a nursing home apparently, and his family didn't take the time to clean things out. Well, except for some of the nicer antiques. They made sure to take those, and they made a mess while they pawed through stuff. But the sisters bought it as is."

"They'll find some treasures in here, I'm sure." Faith looked cute in her jeans and T-shirt. Nothing fancy, but it suited her. "Look at this molding." She snapped a picture. "And that staircase." She took another.

"And especially note all the work that needs to be done," Ray muttered, tugging on a hanging strip of wallpaper.

She aimed her camera at him. "That's what you experts are here for."

He posed, pretending to wipe sweat from his brow.

"Do a muscleman," she said.

He struck a weight-lifter stance.

She laughed, a contagious sound that he couldn't help but join. "We've got our work cut out for us, that's for sure."

Faith snapped another picture, then looked pensive. "Did you check for signs of that kid being in here? Or Sparkles?"

"I did a quick walk-through before you got here, but it's hard to tell if things were left by the owner or by someone in the house."

"What did you find?"

"A banana peel in a trash can and a couple of apple cores."

"Well that wouldn't be from the previous owner, but maybe Cora and Mabel ate here."

He shrugged. "Could be. We'll ask them. The front door was locked. I didn't hear or see anything unusual."

She began clicking more pictures, and he walked into a large room to the left, off which were two sets of french doors.

"If I understand things right, this is going to be a dining area." Ray scanned the room, imagined what it could be, and smiled. "They want to have tables outside on the terrace in warm weather."

More camera clicks behind him. "Got it," Faith whispered.

He gave her a lingering look as she walked past him into the room. She seemed to be blooming before his very eyes. Hair wild, a smile on her face, she was in her element doing what she loved. She looked. . .good. He intentionally glanced away and focused on the fireplace mantel made from bird's-eye maple. "Lots of work here, too."

"This is amazing," Faith said. "I would love to live in a house like this, but you know what my dream house is?" As though the hearth had been ignited, Faith's warmth filled the high-ceilinged room.

"No, tell me. What's your dream house?"

"Hands down, Mabel and Cora's place. It's so. . ." She walked to the right set of french doors and grabbed the handle. "Homey. I feel at home there."

"I thought you loved your grandmother's house."

"I do, but it's not big enough to raise a family in."

Faith's face took on a dreamy glow. "If I had the money, I'd buy Cora and Mabel's house. It would be great for a family—if I ever have a family." She sounded suddenly sad.

Ray patted her back but wanted to yank her into his arms, camera and all. The conversation reminded him of a long-ago day she'd been upset about something her father had done and she'd started to cry. Ray had felt so helpless. He hugged her. Now he remembered the feel of her—soft, leaning into him. The slow dawning in her eyes when the hug continued longer than normal. But she'd withdrawn when it was over, and not too long after that, she moved away. No, he couldn't think about her that way.

Ray swiped his hand through his hair and turned away. Why was his mind going that direction? Perhaps insecurity about the decisions he had ahead made him look to the past for good feelings. He took a deep breath and cleared his throat.

"Everyone will be here any minute. And Philip is coming as well."

"Good," she said, disappearing into the room on the opposite side of the hall.

Please, please come soon. Ray felt himself losing the battle. "We'll look through the house when they get here."

"Okay," she called.

Relieved she was out of sight, he tried to focus on the work to be done. What was wrong with him that he couldn't keep his eyes off Faith? He heard the sound of a car engine and voices and breathed a prayer of thanks to the Lord as he walked back to the hallway.

"Yoo-hoo, it's me." Mabel traipsed through the front door, carrying a picnic basket. Cora followed with two more. "Me and Cora."

Faith appeared. "Smells delicious." She took a basket from Cora. "Which way to the kitchen?"

"Follow me," Mabel said. "It's at the back of the house."

"Let me help." Ray tried to take the other basket from Cora.

"You go out to the car and get the cooler of drinks," Cora ordered.

"You drove *all the way* across the street?" Ray snorted a laugh.

"Yes, Mr. Smarty-Pants. You think we were going to carry all this food?" Mabel said over her shoulder.

"I would have helped you."

Cora and Mabel exchanged glances and tiny grins. "We were giving you time to show Faith around our new place."

Ray shook his head. Matchmakers!

Chapter 19

Faith glanced around the makeshift table in the kitchen at Ray, Philip, Mabel, and Cora. It was easy. Comfortable. Like those summer meals so long ago when she was young. She hadn't realized until now how much she'd missed this. And just how much she'd missed Ray. Her heart ached thinking she could lose it all again. If he and Bailey got together, that would change everything. Bailey wouldn't want to share Ray. Faith would lose him as a friend. She'd caught enough of her sharp glares the few times they'd been together.

Mabel patted her knee. "Don't you fret now. Take that frown off your face."

"How could anyone frown with all this good food?" Philip said. "Pass more of those mashed potatoes, please." He pointed at the large plastic container.

"Watch it," Ray said. "You won't be able to button your shirt tomorrow."

"Like you?" Philip shot a grin at Ray while he dropped a generous helping on his plate.

"Ray, don't you bother your brother none while he's eating." Mabel blew out a sigh.

Cora nodded. "You always used to do that, you scamp."

Faith smiled. "Really?"

"Yes indeedy. Ray would poke and prod Philip until he poked back. Then Ray would play the innocent."

Ray wiggled his eyebrows at Faith, and she giggled.

"Gravy, please," Philip said.

"But he didn't get away with it. No sirree." Mable handed Philip the gravy boat.

"We knew. We always know." Cora hummed under her breath and glanced from Faith to Ray.

"How's work, Philip?" Mabel asked. "You still enjoying your job?"

"Except for the cases I can't solve." He shoveled another spoonful of food into his mouth.

"The gas station robbery," Ray clarified.

Philip nodded. "Attendant is still in a coma. But he's showing signs of coming around."

"I remember reading about that," Faith said. "No witnesses?"

"Not that we can find yet."

"We'll pray for a miracle," Mabel said.

Cora nodded. "God is in control."

Faith sat quietly while everyone finished their meal. She couldn't eat another bite, and surprisingly the sisters let her alone, not nagging her to clean her plate. *This is family,* Faith mused. They talked and shared laughs in that easy way that she'd never known with her real family, even before her mother passed away. She'd always felt like a misfit in her own home.

"Earth to Faith," Ray said, tapping her foot with his under the table.

She blinked. "What?"

Mabel chuckled. "We been talking to you, honey, but you were somewhere else."

"Yes, I guess I was." Not really. She was here, heart and soul.

Cora stood. "Time to tidy things up."

"I'll help you wrap the leftovers." Faith joined Cora.

"You boys start making your list of things that need to be done," Mabel ordered, pointing first at Ray then at Philip.

"From that we'll decide which projects we want done first," Cora said.

"Everything done decently and in order," Faith and Mabel said at the same time.

Everyone laughed, then Ray slapped his brother on the shoulder. "Let's start upstairs."

As she and the sisters repacked the baskets, Faith tried to put her feelings into words. "This is going to sound crazy." She put lids on the containers. "But I feel like I'm home."

"You are." Mabel tucked foam plates and plasticware into a trash bag. "No hot water here yet. The electricity will be turned on tomorrow. And we ordered us a humongous refrigerator."

"Side-by-side," Cora said with pride in her voice.

"Big enough for three turkeys." Mabel patted Faith's arm. "When will you understand?"

Cora leaned against the counter, smiling.

"What?" Faith looked at the two and shrugged. "What do you mean?"

"Our home is your home. . .and Ray's," Mabel said, and Cora nodded. "But we two best make haste." Mabel eyed her sister.

"Oh yeah." Cora removed her apron. "We've got a prayer meeting at our place with Sister Judith. Huh-uh. We gotta go right now."

Faith helped them load the leftovers in their car and returned with them to the kitchen for more. "Leave the cooler and drinks for Ray and Philip," Mabel ordered.

"Okay, and I guess I'll get going, too. Leave the guys to their work." Faith reached for her camera, but Cora clamped a hand on her arm.

"Can you stay a bit longer? Take more pictures?" Cora asked as Mabel exited the kitchen.

Now what were they up to? Faith shrugged. "I—I guess so."

Cora gave her a warm hug. "Don't bother showing us to the door. We know our way out."

Ray walked into the kitchen with Mabel at his side. Faith's heart sped. She had to get over this—over him—and quick.

"You kids have fun," Mabel said, and the slam of the front door followed shortly.

She stood staring at Ray. If she was supposed to speak, she was at a total loss.

"Did you need me?" Ray clipped the tape measure to his belt and walked toward her.

Faith spread her hands in question. "Need you?"

A frown started at his brows, followed by a slow smile that made her go weak at the knees. "That's what Mabel said."

"Me?" Faith pointed an accusing finger at her shoulder. "I didn't say that."

"Interesting." Ray walked around the table and looked down into her eyes.

"I was helping them clean up. Now I have orders to take pictures. That's all. Just take pictures." Why did she feel guilty? Because she loved Ray's eyes? His muscular arms? "I have no idea why Mabel told you that." Faith tilted her chin defiantly, which brought her eye-to-eye, nose-to-nose, and nearly mouth-to-mouth with Ray.

He wrapped his hands around her upper arms, sending warmth through the cotton of her T-shirt. Her breath came faster. With no conscious thought, her hands reached around his neck in a reckless embrace.

Their lips touched, as though she'd been waiting all her life for this moment. His fingers tightened on her arms. She leaned against him, feeling how strong and solid he was.

"Oops, bad timing."

Faith and Ray jumped apart. Philip stood in the doorway of the kitchen shielding his eyes. "Sorry, folks."

"No, we were just. . ." Faith looked to Ray for rescue, but he seemed glued in place, glancing from her to Philip.

"I'll be upstairs." Philip ducked out of the room in a flash, and she heard his retreating footfalls. Her face heated.

Ray suddenly came to life. "Are you all right?" He rubbed her arm.

She ignored the warmth of his touch. "I'm fine," she snapped, pulling away from him.

"You're mad. Why are you mad?" He frowned.

"If you don't know, I'm not going to explain." She knew her words and tone made her sound irrational, but she felt irrational.

"I have to leave now," she said, afraid if she talked, she'd burst into tears, and she hated weakness.

"Leave? Now?"

"Yes, now."

His eyes glinted. "I'm sorry, Faith. That shouldn't have happened."

His words only made things worse. "I agree." She glared up into his face. "Excuse me, please."

Ray stepped aside. "Fine, but I think we need to talk. I still don't understand why you're angry."

"Later." She slipped out the front door, hurried down the steps, and ran across the street toward her house. "Need to talk, my foot," she whispered.

Faith stepped onto her front porch and skidded to a stop. A tiny, dark form huddled next to her front door. "Sparkles!" She scanned the area before reaching the pup, knelt down, and scooped her up. "You're shivering."

How did she get back here? Faith glanced over her shoulder before unlocking her door. She went inside, set down her camera, and cuddled Sparkles closer to her chest. The little dog frantically licked her chin, then yapped a hello.

Faith grabbed the phone and dialed the sisters' house. She'd have to let them know she'd found Sparkles. . .and tell them to pass the information on to Ray. There was no way she wanted to face Ray Reed again tonight.

Chapter 20

Ray woke early, the bright sun in total opposition to his mood. What had happened? He'd kissed Faith...his friend. And liked it. Of course he did. He was a man. Didn't most men like kissing women? And she'd looked and smelled irresistible.

He crawled out of bed and went to the shower. No, kissing Faith hadn't been a mere physical response. He enjoyed it because he liked her. *And* because she looked good. How could he call himself her friend? Sending her mixed signals. Telling her he wanted to reconcile with Bailey one minute, taking her in his arms the next.

After treating himself to a cold shower as punishment, he dressed and peered out the window. The sisters were shopping for wallpaper for the Victorian so he wouldn't have to deal with them. He'd managed to avoid them last night, too, and found the note they'd left explaining that Faith phoned to say she'd found Sparkles on her front lawn. Why hadn't Faith phoned him instead?

Simple, you idiot. She was offended and angry...and embarrassed. He'd seen it in her eyes. But would she avoid him forever?

Ray went downstairs, grabbed two sweet rolls from a plastic container on the counter, and hurried out the door. He looked over at Faith's house. She wasn't there. Good. It was best not to see her again until she cooled down. Then he'd try to reason with her. Tell her she had nothing to be embarrassed about.

He went to his car, unable to take his mind off the kiss. Yes, he'd made her uncomfortable and self-conscious. But...

She *had* kissed him back. Fastened her hands around his neck and pulled him closer. He wasn't mistaken about that. He dug his keys from his uniform pocket, but before he could give the matter deeper thought, he saw the kid, this time hanging around in front of the Victorian.

He hustled down the drive. The kid looked over and saw him. Her little mouth opened in a silent *O*, and she broke into a run. Ray gave chase for more than a block, but the kid disappeared between two houses, and Ray couldn't find her.

Even though he wasn't due to work yet, he called dispatch to report in. Before he returned to the Victorian to look around, he stopped at the houses on either side to ask the residents if they were missing things. He got one negative from a woman who worked nights. The other house was owned by a retired couple who said they rarely left home.

Ray suddenly recalled that this was where the sister of the man who had owned the Victorian lived. "One more question," Ray said.

The elderly couple opened the door wider. "Coffee?"

Ray declined but thanked them all the same. "Have you seen a young girl... looks to be around ten, eleven? She's got red hair, freckles. Hangs around the neighborhood all day it seems."

"That kid do something?"

"Not that I know of, but I need to find her."

The man studied Ray's face. "My wife was feeding the kid. Dirty little urchin. Had her sleeping in the shed. But I took care of that."

"What do you mean you *took care of that*?"

"I told her to go home," Ernest said. "Edna, she was upset. She treated the kid like a pet. . .when she remembered she was there." His wife went back inside and sat on the sofa, mumbling. "Doctor says it's Alzheimer's," Ernest whispered.

"When did you tell the kid to leave?"

"Last night. She had a dog, too."

"Would you mind showing me the shed?"

Ernest walked Ray around the house and pointed to a ramshackle wood building. "I never use it. That's why I didn't know the kid was there. But I cleaned it up after the kid left. There was trash here and some dog stuff."

"Why didn't you report this to the police?"

"Police cause me trouble," Ernest grumbled. "Don't like 'em. Sorry."

"I am, too. We're not all bad."

"Could of fooled me." Ernest sounded bitter.

Ray wished he could pursue the conversation but didn't have time. He disliked having his uniform stand between him and people in need—especially those in need of God. Many were often intimidated and even nervous around him.

He pulled out a business card. "I live right down the road at the moment. With Mabel Sanders. If you need anything, call me."

Ernest's face softened for a moment. "Mabel and Cora. Good people." He blinked. "No, I don't think so. I told you, don't have much time for the police." But he took the card anyway.

Ray thanked the man and walked back to the Victorian. What did the kid want? Ray checked all the doors to the Victorian. Everything was locked tight. He walked around the building, noting the overgrown shrubbery. This would all have to be torn down. He noticed some of the plant life was smashed down, probably from the real estate people and the building inspection. He pushed aside the bushes, and behind them was a basement window.

He knelt in the dirt and pressed his hand against the window. It was open.

❧

Faith nearly fell over the trash receptacle in her office and kicked it out of her way. It rolled into the hallway, where she left it. "Stupid cleaning people can't put things back," she said to no one in particular as she dropped heavily into her chair. Good thing the clinic wasn't open yet. She was in such a bad mood she wasn't fit for human contact. She yanked some files from her inbox. "What am I looking for?" she mumbled.

"Doc, I'm cleaning cages in the kennel," Lindsey shouted as she walked quickly past her office door.

"Wonderful!" Faith hollered in return as she leaned over her desk to study reports from the lab.

There was a tap on her door, and Gladys peeked into her office. "Dr. Hart?"

"What?" she snapped.

Gladys glanced from her to the trash can in the hall. "Um, I . . ."

Faith stared at her. "What do you need?"

Gladys took a step back. "I just wanted to know if you'd like me to start billing today."

"Yes. It is billing time. It happens the same time every month. And shut my door, please."

Gladys obeyed without saying another word, shutting the door with more force than necessary.

Faith knew she was being obnoxious, but couldn't seem to help herself. Well, that wasn't true. She *could* help herself, but she wasn't trying very hard. She stared at the lab reports, but the words and numbers were like gibberish. Instead, her errant mind insisted on imagining Ray's eyes and lips. She had kissed him—and she'd liked it. She slapped her hand on her desk. If she relived the kiss one more time she might throw more than a trash can across her office.

"Is that the sound of violence I hear? And look, a dented trash can. I wonder who did that." Debbie's voice floated through the door.

It opened, and Faith blew out a long breath. "You of all people should understand. The door is shut for a reason." She glared at her friend.

"I had to make sure you weren't doing any more damage. We do share the expenses around here." Debbie strolled across the oatmeal-colored Berber, trash receptacle hanging from her fingertips. "Lose this? Looks like someone abused it and put it in the hallway."

"Very funny. Just set it next to my desk."

"Yes, ma'am." Debbie's tone was sarcastic as she placed the receptacle down with exaggerated gentleness. "And I thought I was crabby from lack of sleep with my colicky baby. Your hair is sticking up all over the place. That only happens when you're stressed, and the last time I can remember it being this bad was during final exams in vet school." She crossed her arms. "Everyone is whispering in the office so as not to disturb you, even Lindsey."

Faith felt the bite of guilt. Come to think of it, she was acting a lot like she had in the navy when she'd been on board ship and sleep deprived. And, like Debbie said, during final exams. *Lord, I am one impatient person.*

"So, what's happened to bring this not-so-charming side of you out?"

"I'm sorry," Faith said. "I called that guy Peter to tell him I found Sparkles again. He's coming by the house this evening."

"So, you found the dog—that's good news. The guy who might be the owner is coming by—and maybe he'll pay the bill. Doubly good news." Debbie frowned. "I don't get it. *That's* why you kicked your trash can into the hall?"

"No." Faith picked up a folder and flipped through it, unseeing. "It's because I have to call Ray. He wants to be there the next time Peter comes by. Says there's something weird about the whole thing. And about Peter." She sighed. "I have to agree. The guy gave me the creeps."

"I don't understand." Debbie's frown deepened, and she leaned against the desk, arms folded. "Ray's a cop. He'll be there to protect you. Why is that bad?"

"That's exactly the problem. *Ray* will be there."

"I admit I haven't had my second cup of coffee, so all my cylinders aren't running yet, but what am I missing? The guy's a creep. Ray is going to keep you safe. Did something happen between you guys?"

"A kiss!" Shame heated her face. "That's what happened." Faith slapped the folder down. Papers slid all over the desk. "And I liked it. Wrong, wrong, wrong."

"What? A kiss? And what's wrong with that?" Debbie laughed, but Faith glared at her, and she sobered. "I'm sorry, but do you know how weird you sound?"

Faith shook her head. "Didn't you hear me? I—kissed—Ray."

"Okay." Debbie's eyes widened. "So why is this so bad?"

Faith glanced at her partner, then counted out on her fingers. "First, he's my best friend. *Was* my best friend. Second, he's still pining for someone else. Third—third. . .I'm so stupid. I think my feelings are more than. . .well, more than friends. . .I'm. . ." She let her voice trail off.

"In love?" Deb asked in a solemn whisper.

Faith ran her finger over the papers that had slipped from the file and let her breath out slowly. "I. . .well. . .maybe." *Yes.*

"I don't think there's any *maybe* about it." Debbie stared at her long and hard. "You're in love. I've been watching you since Ray came into town. You glow. Your eyes sparkle. And you're smiling a whole lot more."

"That can't be right," Faith murmured. She wouldn't admit it aloud. Doing so would make it all too real.

"Ah, love." Debbie sighed. "I remember when Lance and I first met." Her smile lit her face. "We were ice-skating at—"

"No, this is different, Deb." Faith closed her eyes to collect her thoughts. "Ray's still got his ex-fiancée on his mind. Worse, I'm afraid I ruined one of the best friendships I've ever had." Tears made her blink. "I intentionally refused a date with Ray when we were teens. I didn't want to ruin our friendship then, and I don't intend to destroy it now."

"Interesting. That's not how you told it back in college. It was your father who put the kibosh on it."

Faith felt the blood drain from her face. Had she been blaming her dad for her fear of failure? "My father was a big, big part of my decision." Not exactly true. If she'd wanted to pursue Ray, she could have. At that point her father might have backed off. Faith had Ray's phone number. She swallowed around the lump in her throat and started again. "Okay, I didn't want to disappoint my father—"

"And you didn't want to disappoint yourself if things didn't work out," Debbie stated boldly.

"That's beside the point." Faith stood and jammed her hands in the pockets of her jacket. "I want to stay friends with Ray. Friends don't kiss in *that* way."

Debbie rolled her eyes toward the ceiling. "Lord, please help this woman see common sense." She screwed up her face and blew out a breath. "Did you force him to kiss you?"

"No, but I liked it and encouraged it."

"And he didn't push you away? He didn't run screaming in torment because you locked lips?"

Faith shook her head. "Of course not. Don't be facetious. His brother walked into the room."

"Oh, that's rich." Debbie grinned. "I would have loved to be a fly on the wall when those two talked."

Faith blushed again. "Right. How embarrassing is that?"

Debbie straightened and tucked her hair behind her ears. "I think the biggest problem here is that both of you are dumb as rocks."

Faith blinked. "Dumb. . .what?"

"You heard me."

"That's insulting."

"It was meant to be. Now get your act together and quit scaring the staff." Whirling around, Debbie laughed. "I'm leaving before I get hurt by a trash can hurtling through the air." She disappeared out the door, then poked her head around the corner. "By the way, I have a good feeling about things." She withdrew like a turtle.

"A feeling? You sound just like Cora and Mabel!" Faith yelled at the empty doorway. "And right now *all* of you are irritating me."

Debbie's only response was more laughter.

Chapter 21

R ay, here's some joe." Philip pushed a cup of coffee across Ray's desk. "You look like you need it."

"Yeah, thanks." Ray didn't look up from the report he was typing, just snatched the coffee cup and pulled it toward him. He'd hoped his job would take his mind off his personal life, but it wasn't working. Between exhaustion from tossing and turning at night and frustration with so many decisions and so few answers, he could barely think. Not to mention a kid running around the neighborhood breaking into houses and stealing stuff.

"Earth to Ray." Philip waved his hand in front of his face.

Ray glanced up. "Sorry. And thanks for the coffee." He lifted the cup to his mouth.

"Watch out—"

Ray took a big gulp before Philip finished his sentence. The coffee hit his tongue and the roof of his mouth like fire, then burned its way down his throat.

"—it's hot," Philip finished.

Ray set the cup back on the desk and swallowed several times, blinking back tears of pain. "Really hot," he said hoarsely.

"That would be why steam was coming off the top." Philip squinted and waved his hand in front of Ray again. "You all right? Something wrong with your eyes?"

"Don't get smart with me." Ray swallowed again and cleared his throat. "Just because you're older doesn't mean I can't take you down."

"You and what army?" Philip snorted a laugh and flexed his arm. "I've started lifting three days a week. Hired a personal trainer at the gym."

"And you're making me feel like a slob." Ray glanced down at his stomach. He was fast developing a paunch.

"Helps relieve the stress of the job," Philip said. "So, what are you working on?"

Ray turned his monitor so Philip could read it. "The break-ins in my neighborhood. This morning I found a basement window open on the sisters' new place. I went inside, but found nothing. I went door-to-door earlier and found out that more locals than I thought have had things stolen. I think I know who the culprit is. This kid who's been hanging around the neighborhood." He explained about the old man's shed and how his wife fed the kid.

"You talking about Ernest and Edna?"

Ray nodded.

"She's the sister to the guy who was living in that monstrosity that Mabel and Cora own now. Bad blood there between them, the brother and sister."

"So I hear," Ray said.

Philip dragged a chair to the side of Ray's desk and stared at the monitor. After a moment, he looked up. "A kid, huh?"

"Yep. She's fast, though. I chased the little bugger through the neighborhood this morning. Couldn't catch her."

Philip laughed. "Maybe you need to cut out Cora's fried chicken and take up jogging."

"You might be joking, but I'm thinking the same thing." Ray sat back in his chair and pointed at the monitor. "Knowing who's doing the breaking in only leads to more questions."

"Doesn't it always?"

Ray nodded. "This kid is tied up with the dog somehow and then tied up with this dude who scared Faith when he came to claim the dog. She left a message for me and said—"

"Left a message?" Philip's brow lifted.

"Yes," Ray said. "She left a message and said the guy is coming by her house in an hour and a half. I told her not to see him again unless I'm there." He shook his head. "I can't believe she gave a stranger her home address to begin with."

"I see." Philip smiled.

"It's not funny," Ray said. "The guy is a creep."

Philip shrugged, still smiling. "Not arguing that point."

He stared at his smirking brother. "Then what?"

"You, being so concerned about your neighbor—Faith."

Ray's frustration boiled to the surface. "I'm a cop," he snapped. "I'm investigating crimes."

"And you're very concerned about your neighbor."

"I'd be concerned about anyone in a case like this."

"Uh-huh. Right. Any chance you're thinking about that little escapade I walked in on the other night? The one you tried so hard to explain away?"

Ray felt his face heat. "I told you, it was nothing. We're friends."

Philip laughed. "Wish I had more friends like her."

"We *are* friends," Ray protested.

"Okay, and so?" Philip took a swig of coffee. "You can be friends and fall in love. Kissing friends. All the better, I would think."

"No. You don't understand. It can't be that way."

Philip shook his head. "You are stupid. Really, really stupid." His cell phone rang on his belt. He looked at the number and grabbed it. "Yo, Reed here."

His eyes lit up. He stood and punched the Off button. "That guy came out of his coma."

Ray's mind went on full alert. "You mean the gas station attendant?"

"Yep. C'mon, let's go."

❧

Faith opened her front door and tossed her purse on the sofa, expecting the little terrier to come running from the bedroom like she always did. "Sparkles, where are you, girl?" Apprehension tickled her spine. Her cell phone rang in her purse, but she ignored it and walked down the hall to her bedroom. Sparkles's bed was empty.

"Sparkles?" Faith hurried back up the hall to the spare room. No dog. Almost running now, she hurried to the kitchen. "Sparkles!" The back door to the porch was open. She peered into the screened-in porch. The door to the outside was open, too. Sparkles was gone. Again.

Back in the kitchen, she bit her nails and glanced at the clock on the wall. Peter would be here in a little over an hour. Once again, she wouldn't have the dog. "Calm down," Faith whispered. Ray would be here. He was scheduled to arrive thirty minutes before Peter. She didn't want the time alone with Ray, but she wanted to be alone with Peter even less. Meantime, she'd look for Sparkles outside.

Her cell phone beeped, indicating the person who'd called had left a message. She hurried to the living room and dug her phone from her purse. *Missed call.* She pushed a button, and the screen indicated the call had come from Ray.

She dialed her voice mail to retrieve the message while she opened the front door to go outside, and she slammed into Sparkles's supposed owner.

"Whoa, lady," Peter said, taking a few steps backward from the force of her hit.

"Sorry." Faith looked up into his hard face. "You're early." Had her heart stopped beating? She couldn't breathe.

"Yeah, I got off work early. I've waited long enough to get my dog back."

Like last time, he didn't refer to the dog by name or sex. Faith took a step backward and fumbled for the knob to shut the door. She'd be safer on the front porch.

"What's wrong with you?" Peter frowned down at her. "You lost your voice?" He glanced over her head and scanned the room. "Where's my dog?"

Faith cleared her throat. Time for damage control. "Well. . .she's not here right now."

"What?" He took a step toward her. "I came here for nothing?"

"Well. . .a friend of mine has her. He's bringing her in a minute." Breathing a prayer to God to ask forgiveness for lying, she continued. "You *are* early."

"I can't believe it. You let someone else take my dog?" Peter's face reddened.

"For a vet, you're awfully irresponsible."

Faith glimpsed movement from the side of her eye and turned. The young girl was peering through the bushes.

Peter followed her glance. He narrowed his eyes and swore. "That kid!" he hollered as he ran down her porch stairs. "Probably took the dog."

The little girl took off running.

"No!" Faith hurried down the porch stairs to follow Peter. "Leave her alone!"

Her view of Peter disappeared behind trees and hedges on neighboring properties. As much as she hoped Peter wouldn't catch the kid, she knew she was no match for the man. She needed help. She hurried back into her house, locked the door, and dialed Ray. While the phone rang, she heard footsteps on her front porch. Then bangs on the door. "Hey, lady! Let me in."

Peter was back—and he was fuming.

"I'm calling the cops," Faith yelled. She got Ray's voice mail and left a hurried message.

The pounding stopped suddenly, and the footsteps retreated. She heard the roar of an engine and ran to the window. He was leaving. She had just enough time to note his license number. Then her cell phone rang.

Chapter 22

"Faith?" Ray said into his phone. He was speeding toward her house as they talked. "Did you get my message?"

"No, I didn't get a chance. But Peter was here. He came early."

"Was there?" he shouted, grasping the steering wheel tighter and feeling sick.

"Yes, was," Faith shouted back. "You're going to break my eardrum if you yell any louder. He was here, but he's gone. It was pretty scary. I was about to call 911."

"Sorry." Ray loosened his hold on the steering wheel. "Is your door locked?"

"Yes. It's locked."

"Good. Stay inside," he ordered. "Now tell me everything that happened."

"Why? What's going on? You're scaring me."

"Just tell me what happened, and then I'll explain."

After he'd listened to what she had to say, he swallowed. She could have been hurt or even killed, and he wouldn't have been there to help. "You sure your door is locked?"

"Yes. Now please tell me why you're so frantic."

He arrived at her house and swerved into her driveway, wheels spitting gravel. "I'm here. As soon as I'm inside, I'll tell you everything."

She was waiting at the front door.

"I thought I told you to lock the door," he growled as he stalked past her.

"I did," she snapped. "But I unlocked it when you arrived." She glared at him. "I'm not a child."

He faced her and sighed. "I know. I'm sorry. I was scared. You could have been hurt."

She relaxed a bit. "I was scared, too."

He wanted to yank her into his arms, hold her tight, and promise to protect her always, but the memory of the kiss was too fresh. Besides, they needed to talk.

"Can we sit?" he asked. He tried not to look into her beautiful brown eyes. He didn't want to be tempted again.

"Spill it," she said.

"Remember that gas station robbery Philip was talking about last night?"

Faith licked her lips and nodded.

"The gas station attendant came out of his coma today. Peter was the man who had robbed the gas station, only that's not his real name."

"I didn't think so," Faith said. "Liar. I hate being lied to." She felt her anger growing.

"The gas station attendant identified a mug shot of Peter. That is his first name, but Davis isn't his last name." Ray smiled grimly. "It gets more serious. A kid with a dog witnessed the robbery."

Faith put her hand to her heart. "Oh no. Maybe Sparkles and the little girl? Remember, Peter chased the kid." Faith pulled a slip of paper from her jeans pocket. "I got his license number."

"Good. Give that to me. I'll call it in, then I'll tell you more."

He called dispatch with the information, and when he was done, he pulled out his notebook. "I need information from you."

Faith nodded. "To think a guy like that was in my home. No wonder he made my skin crawl." She brushed her hands over her bare arms, and he felt another strong pull to hold her.

"So you think it's our kid?" she asked. "The one wandering the neighborhood?"

"Not sure."

Faith gave him a rundown of the events. As he took notes, he could feel the unanswered questions hanging between them. The kiss. Why did it happen? He forced the thought from his mind.

"So what can you tell me?" she asked. "Why was he looking for the dog? That makes no sense."

Ray stood, putting physical distance between them, and dropped his gaze to the notebook in his hand. "There was a kid in the gas station when everything went down. A girl with a dog and a cell phone." He tapped the paper.

Faith breathed. Their eyes locked, and he saw her thoughts click into focus. "You're still thinking it's the kid we've been chasing around the neighborhood, aren't you?"

He nodded. "That's what Philip and I suspect. We also think Peter wanted to use the dog as bait to lure the girl out of hiding." He studied her for a moment, then went to the door. "I have to go back to work. I want you to stay safe. Lock all your doors and keep your cell phone with you." He backed toward the front door. "I'll call Cora and Mabel on my way out to tell them what's happened. They need to keep their doors locked, too."

"Okay." Faith took a step back, and he felt the wall go up. "I'll probably join them. We'll lock ourselves up together."

He was reluctant to leave. "Listen, Faith, we need to talk."

The look in her eyes, her stance, told him her walls got higher.

"Haven't we been talking?"

"Yes, but I mean about the other night. It's sort of—"

"Awkward?"

"Yes, it is that."

She was blinking hard. Was she about to cry? "I'm sorry I upset you."

She shrugged. "Maybe some things are better left unsaid."

"Is that the way you feel?"

"Maybe. I don't know."

"Okay, I'll see you later then. And we'll see." He turned before he walked out. "Remember to lock your door."

He went to his car with a heavy heart. He never meant to hurt Faith. She was his best friend, when they were teens and now. Ray stood beside his car and called dispatch to ask where he was needed. While he waited, he glanced at Faith's house, reluctant to drive away and leave her alone.

At the sound of a vehicle coming down the street, he turned. Had Peter returned? He waited until the car came into sight. It was Bailey. She pulled alongside his car and opened her window. "I've got to talk to you."

"Now? I'm on duty. We've got a crisis."

His words didn't dissuade her. She got out of her car and smiled.

"This is going to have to wait, Bailey. I've got to—"

"This will take less than a minute. I promise." Bailey pulled in a breath like she was summoning courage. "Ray, I love you." She grasped his arm. "But I feel like you're avoiding me. I've got a surprise planned for you tonight."

"Tonight?" Why was she making plans without consulting him?

"Yes." The smile on her face died as if he'd slapped her. "You don't look happy. I guess—I guess the real question is, can we make this right?"

Truth hit like a wake-up slap to his face. If they were truly a couple, her making plans wouldn't annoy him. He was confused about a lot of things—his calling to the ministry, his occupation, kissing Faith, but this was for sure. "You're forcing me to talk on the run. But if you need an answer right now, I have to say I'm sorry, but it's over." The second he spoke the words, he felt at peace.

Bailey released her grip on his forearm. Her face changed from repentant to callous. "I sort of knew it was too late. I just wish you would've been man enough to tell me right away."

Her anger stemmed from hurt, but he couldn't help that. "I was sincere about trying again. But what happened is too much to overcome." He opened his car door.

Her eyes darted toward Faith's house. "It's *her*, isn't it? Something else you should've told me."

"Her? Faith?" Ray examined the feelings stirring in his heart and shrugged. "Faith and I have been friends since we were kids. We've got a history together, but it's not like that. And I know she doesn't feel that way about me." He remembered the kiss and suddenly wished she did.

"Then you're blind." Bailey took a step back. "Well, I'm not about to crawl, so I guess this is good-bye."

Ray nodded. "I wish you the best, Bailey. I truly do."

Her eyes filled. "Do I get a good-bye hug?" She didn't wait for his response, but stepped up to him and slipped her arms around his chest.

Ray patted her back, but tried to politely step out of her lingering embrace. His radio crackled. Philip was requesting his help. "Listen, I've got to go."

Bailey pulled away, a shaky smile masking her tears. "Take care, Ray. I wish the best for you, too." She ran to her car without a backward glance.

Ray sat behind the wheel with one thought in his head. Bailey said he was blind. Did she see something in Faith's feelings for him that he'd missed? He glanced at Faith's house before pulling away from the curb. With surprise and a sudden lightness of heart, he found himself praying that was true.

Chapter 23

Faith paced her living room, a mix of feelings swirling inside her heart. Confusion, worry, fear, hope, anger—it ran the gamut. She stumbled over a dog toy. Did the little girl have Sparkles? Ray had been very concerned.

Faith stood in front of her window and couldn't resist pulling aside the curtain to look out and see if Ray had driven away yet.

He hadn't. Faith blinked and leaned so far forward that her nose pressed against the glass. Was that Bailey? Hugging Ray? In broad daylight, in front of the whole world? Where had she come from? Faith clenched her fists and ordered her feet to stay put, otherwise she'd run from the house screaming and rip Bailey from Ray's arms.

After a torturous moment, she let the curtain drop. *Voyeur!* she chided herself as she stomped to the kitchen, wishing it were morning and she could go to work. How she loved the distraction of the busy clinic. But she should have the right to look out her own window and not have to watch scenes like that! She took a deep breath and unclenched her fists, forcing her body to relax. "I'm sorry, Lord. It's my temper again."

She opened the refrigerator door, then shut it again. She couldn't rid her mind of the picture of Bailey and Ray.

I love him. The thought kept returning, each time with more certainty— and trepidation. When had she fallen in love with Ray? As a teenager? Probably. Back then it was young love, but love nonetheless. And like Debbie said, she was scared of failure, so she let him go rather than take a chance. But through the years he had always been the standard by which she had judged other men, even in the navy. That was probably why she'd never fallen in love with anyone else.

Faith shook her head. Ray wasn't available. She'd seen it with her very own eyes two minutes ago. He had a thing for Bailey Cummings, despite the fact that she'd cheated on him. And Bailey definitely had a thing for him. Maybe Ray's kiss in the kitchen of the Victorian had been a sort of payback for Bailey's indiscretion.

"I kissed him back," she said with a mocking laugh.

She'd always been Faith the control freak. Faith the woman who kept everything in order, even as a child. As an adult, she realized the habit was more than a personality quirk. She did it so she could keep her emotions orderly. If they weren't orderly, she fell apart, like she had in the office that morning. And all in an effort not to let anything break through the walls she'd built around herself. Now Ray was back, and he had managed to hammer through those walls. She'd let him in, despite her best efforts—a man who was in love with another woman.

She needed to get ahold of herself. She grabbed her sweater and marched to the front door. She'd go see Mabel and Cora. The sisters were supposed to be working on the new place. Just being around them calmed her. Besides, there was safety in numbers.

Faith locked her door, then hurried across the street. There were cars parked along the curb, but none looked like Peter's. She entered the Victorian using a key the sisters had given her and heard noise in the back of the house.

"Cora? Mabel?" She rushed down the hall to the kitchen, all the while calling their names. "There you are!" Faith said.

Mabel held a sponge against the old wallpaper. "Land sakes, child, what a commotion." She dropped the sponge into a bucket and descended the ladder. "You worried about that criminal?"

"Not now. I guess Ray called you?"

"Yessiree. Told me all about it. Said you were safe, praise the Lord for His protection." Mabel pointed at a chair in the middle of the kitchen. "Sit down. You look pale."

Faith complied, but couldn't keep her hands still. She kept tapping her fingers on her thighs.

"I hate to say this, but you're a mess looking for a place to happen. You look like you're going to pop." Mabel moved the bucket aside, wiped her hands on her work apron, then put them on her hips. "Do you need to eat? Cora will be here shortly. She says she has something important to tell me."

"Not hungry, but I could go for some coffee."

"That's the last thing you need. Your hair is already standing on end." Mabel studied her with narrowed eyes.

Faith shook her head. "I'm sorry to bother you. I'm probably not fit for human company today."

"Hush now," Mabel warned. "You know better. You never bother me."

Faith bit at her nails. The image of Ray's eyes when he bent down to kiss her was superimposed in her mind with the image of him and Bailey hugging.

Mabel pulled up a chair next to her. "Now talk to me."

Faith bit her lip, reluctant to blurt the whole truth; but wasn't that why she'd come here? And where did she start? With something safe, she decided. "I'm worried about Sparkles and the little girl."

"So are we. We prayed, and we're believing God is in control. He's doing a good work."

"Maybe for some people." As soon as the words were out of her mouth, she knew she sounded like a child. Her problems were nothing compared to the young girl running around the neighborhood alone.

They heard the front door open.

"That would be Cora," Mabel said. "I recognize her footsteps."

"I brought weapons," Cora said as she walked into the kitchen and put a sack on the counter.

"What?" Faith asked.

The plastic rattled as Cora removed a can from the sack. "We're gonna be ready for him if he comes. Why do you think the good Lord made wasp spray?"

Faith laughed. "What would I do without you two?"

"I have some news for you," Cora said as she removed duct tape, trash bags, sponges, and several containers of cleaning products from the sack.

"What are you planning to do?" Faith pointed at the supplies.

"Clean," Cora said, then she waved the duct tape. "And fix a couple of loose things around here until Ray can do it right. Duct tape is good for lots of things." She grinned and put it back in the bag. Then she wiped her hands and turned to Faith and Mabel. "My news can wait for a minute. Looks like this is a serious discussion."

Mabel nodded. "Faith is troubled, but she hasn't told me why yet."

Cora crossed the room and laid her hand on Faith's head. "Lord bless you, child. Talk."

Faith swallowed hard, trying to find a way to open a discussion about her feelings for Ray and what she'd just witnessed from her window. "I, um, just saw Ray."

"Huh-uh." Mabel laughed. "Is that all that's stuck in your head after you were almost accosted by a robber? Ray told us all about it."

" 'Course it is," Cora said, smiling. "Our boy is good-lookin' and charming. A real catch, I say."

"I'd be smiling with you if I hadn't seen Ray and Bailey from my window . . .hugging." Faith searched their faces for a reaction. Nothing. "They were hugging for a really long time," she added, feeling a new wave of anger.

Mabel and Cora exchanged glances, then Cora held up her hand. "Now let's not jump to any conclusions, right, sis?"

Mabel tilted her chin. "I don't blame Faith. I don't like that huggin' stuff either." She tapped Faith's hand. "You ought to have come out of the house with a broom and shooshed that girl away."

As heavy as her heart felt, Faith laughed with the two. "Believe me, I wanted to do worse, but I—"

"If you did that, Ray would know you loved him." Cora looked thoroughly satisfied with her conclusion.

"I. . .well. . ." Faith still couldn't say the words out loud.

"Bless your heart," Cora said. "It's like faith. Like accepting Jesus. You just got to screw up your courage and say it out loud."

As usual, the sisters saw right through her. Faith blew out a breath, ready to confess all. "Yes, all right. I'll admit I'm in love with Ray. But what's the point? He's after Bailey, and she's after him. Nobody hugs that long if—"

"He don't look at Bailey like he does you." Mabel's smile got wider. "And Bailey don't look at Ray the way you do."

"Then why the dating? Why the hug?" The sisters were usually right, but maybe they wished so hard for her and Ray to get together that they were blindsided this time.

"What's that poet say?" Cora appeared thoughtful for a moment. " 'Better to have loved and lost than not to have loved at all.'"

"Now that's a fine howdy do." Mabel slapped Cora's arm. "We're trying to encourage Faith. Besides, you should talk, Cora Mae." Mabel rolled her eyes. "You with your beau of a hundred years, Dr. Douglas."

"You don't know nothin'." Cora turned to Faith and winked. "Now honey, you lovin' Ray despite what you see with your eyes, that makes you human instead of a machine who won't let herself feel nothing."

"That's right," Mabel agreed. "It's time you become normal. We been prayin' about that, too. You need to forgive your daddy for being a dumb man. And don't you think we won't investigate that huggin' stuff that went on today. We'll nail that boy to the wall. Bad enough he thought to give that Bailey a second chance. We prayin' for her, don't you think we're not. And we don't wish evil for her, but she's not the one for Ray. No sirree. It would never work."

Cora clapped, sending a shot of adrenaline through Faith. "Lord, show Ray the truth." She grabbed her sister's hand and Faith's in a spontaneous act of prayer. "Arrest that boy's heart right now, Father, and tell him what You've told us, that they belong together. We pray this in Jesus' name, amen."

Faith nodded her agreement and found herself smiling. She loved these sisters with all her heart and deep inside believed everything would be all right, though she couldn't fathom how that would happen.

"One more thing," Faith said. "I—I kissed Ray."

Both sisters' faces lit with hundred-watt smiles.

She frowned. "I don't think you heard me right. I said we kissed. Right here. In this kitchen."

Cora sniffled and dabbed her eyes with her fingertips. "Now isn't it just like God to make it happen in our new house. A sign of more good to come."

"Amen." Nodding, Mabel stood and pointed at Cora. "Now sis, tell us your good news."

Cora beamed. "You know how I found the grandson of the man who built this house?" She clasped her hands. "He told me a secret. C'mon." She motioned to the basement door. "I'll show you. It's a surprise."

Faith followed the sisters down the sturdy wooden stairs. A rock-walled basement room spread out before them. It smelled dusty, but not damp. Cobwebs hung from the large beams on the ceiling. "Are there other rooms?"

"Don't you know it." Cora's beam grew.

"We gotta clean this up," Mabel said, poking at a low-hanging cobweb.

"Come on!" Cora led them through a wooden door to a room on the right. A couple of windows stood at the top of the walls.

Faith heard a dog whine. Sparkles?

Cora stopped.

"I'm hearing things," Faith said.

"If you are, I am, too," Mabel whispered. "I heard that doggy."

Cora walked to a set of shelves that ran from floor to ceiling and pulled on them. Like a door, they opened, and behind them was a cavity lined with rock that extended beyond the house.

And crouched on the floor against the back was a little girl. A cell phone lay at her feet. She was curled up, crying, holding Sparkles to her chest.

Chapter 24

Ray and Philip stood in the small house not far from Mabel and Cora's. Mrs. Wilson, the little girl's grandmother, cried silent tears, clasping and unclasping her hands. "I should have known Sasha was missing, but I thought she was with her mother."

Ray couldn't help but agree with her. She *should* have known the girl was missing, although perhaps he was being too judgmental. He just couldn't stand the thought of kids in danger.

"You haven't called your daughter?"

"Daughter-in-law. Actually, ex-daughter-in-law." Mrs. Wilson looked so pale, he thought she might faint.

"Perhaps you should sit down," he said.

"No! How can you expect me to sit when my Sasha is in danger?" She inhaled. "Has anyone seen Lucky?"

"Who's Lucky?" Philip asked.

"Her dog. They are inseparable."

"A little terrier?" Philip asked.

She nodded, looking at them with a spark of hope.

"The dog has been seen," Ray said.

"But you don't know where Sasha is." The older woman paced across her sparsely furnished living room, tears still falling down her cheeks. An old television flashed commercials in the background. She turned to Philip and Ray. "This is my fault, you know. I got Sasha that cell phone for her birthday. She was twelve. It was all she wanted. I worked extra hours to get her what she wanted. It took pictures—imagine a phone taking a picture. If I hadn't gotten her that phone maybe this wouldn't have happened." She stopped pacing, lowered her head, and sobbed.

Ray and Philip exchanged glances. They had to get her back on track.

"Ma'am, we're sorry, but we have to get more information from you." Philip pointed to the threadbare sofa. "Why don't you have a seat? Can one of us get you something? A glass of water?"

She shook her head and dropped onto the sofa. "No, nothing. I just want my granddaughter back."

"Can you tell us what happened the day she disappeared?" Ray still wondered why the woman hadn't reported Sasha missing.

Mrs. Wilson nodded. "She said she was going for a walk with Lucky, to take some pictures, and then go to her mama's. Her mama lives two blocks away. She's got custody, you know. Next thing I know, Sasha calls and says she's at her mom's and is going to stay there for a while."

"You didn't call her mother?" Ray tried to keep the cynical tone from his voice when what he really wanted to do was ream her out.

" 'Course I did." Mrs. Wilson shook her head. "Her mama wouldn't answer. She refuses to talk to me. That's one reason I got Sasha the phone. So she could call me. But she hasn't answered her phone. I've been so worried. Her mama. . .she's bad news. Her and them people she brings in." She began to cry again. Ray cleared his throat, and Mrs. Wilson continued. "When Sasha's daddy, my son, died, I went to court and tried to get custody. I lost. She could make things bad for me. . . . She's got this boyfriend. . . ."

She kept rubbing her worn hands, her eyes filled with fear. Ray and Philip exchanged glances.

"We need a picture of Sasha," Philip said.

Mrs. Wilson stood and went to an old spinet piano where a series of pictures showed the growth of a girl who was obviously Sasha. "Here's the latest." Her hand trembled as she held the framed photo out to Philip.

"We'll bring it back," he said, indicating the photo, then he nodded at Ray.

Ray pulled a sketch of Peter from his pocket. "This is the man involved in the robbery. Do you recognize him?"

She took the paper from Ray and frowned at it. "Yes." She inhaled and her face hardened. "That's him! My daughter-in-law's boyfriend. He sometimes lives with Sasha's mother. Stays for days at a time." She gave them the address, and Philip called it in.

"Is he involved?" she asked.

Ray hesitated, and Philip nodded. "We believe so."

"Do you think Sasha is okay?" Mrs. Wilson looked up at Ray, fear etching her face with deep lines. "Will my baby be okay?"

"We hope so," Ray said. He hated this part of his job. Watching people suffer and not being able to help them the way he wanted to because of rules. He had to be politically correct. But as the woman wrung her hands, he crossed the room and put his hand on her shoulder. "Do you go to church, ma'am?"

She blinked. "Yes, I do."

The mic on Philip's shoulder crackled to life, and he excused himself.

"Do you believe in prayer?"

"Yes, I do." The hope in her eyes grew.

"Just know that people are praying for Sasha. I know that for a fact. Let me pray for you and Sasha now."

When they were done, she cried again, but this time with hope. She grasped his hand. "Thank you, officer. You don't know how much that means to me."

Ray felt as if he'd been hit with lightning. *I'm in the wrong career. Now I know. It's like Faith said—that when it happens. . .it's a defining God moment.*

But before he could follow the thought, Philip burst back into the room. "They found the guy's car at Sasha's mother's house. They're interviewing the mother now, but she. . ." Philip paused, and Ray knew he wasn't telling him everything in front of Sasha's grandmother. "Peter took her car, and he's gone."

"He hurt her, didn't he?" Mrs. Wilson said. "He did that a lot."

"I'm sorry, ma'am, we need to go," Philip said.

Ray took Mrs. Wilson's hand. "You just keep praying."

❧

Along with Mabel and Cora, Faith coaxed the frightened girl upstairs to the kitchen.

"What's your name, baby doll?" Cora asked the girl.

"Sasha," she whispered, clutching at Sparkles so hard the dog yelped.

Faith pulled out her cell phone to call Ray. Mabel shook her head violently and pulled Faith into the hallway.

"That child is scared to death. Let us settle her down before we call in the police. They'll just come roaring in here, lights going, and they'll bring Social Services or something. Poor little tot needs to be prepared for all that commotion." Mabel turned as though the matter were settled.

Faith thought the word "tot" didn't apply. The girl looked to be almost twelve, but she wasn't going to argue the point. "I'm worried. I think Ray needs to know."

Mabel turned back to her. "We won't wait long to call him. Just enough to get some food into her and settle her down."

"Mabel?" Cora called from the kitchen. "The electricity is on now. I'm going across the street to get that pot of chicken soup from the refrigerator. And biscuits. I'll need your help. And we're safe together."

"Right!" Mabel said from the hallway. She pushed Faith back into the kitchen. "You keep that child company. You can talk to her about the dog. She'll like that. You two got a lot in common. We'll get food and be right back. And don't worry, we'll call Ray, too."

The sisters bustled from the house, and Faith was left alone with Sasha, whose wide eyes left no doubt she was just as stunned as Faith by the whirlwinds called Cora and Mabel.

Faith reached down and stroked Sparkles's head.

"You took good care of Lucky, didn't you?" Sasha looked up with a watery gaze.

"Lucky? Is that her name?"

Sasha nodded, and a smile broke through.

Faith pulled a chair up and sat next to the girl, but Sasha drew back as though afraid of being touched. She recognized something in the child that she saw in herself. Walls. *Don't let anyone too close. You might get hurt.*

Faith scooted her chair back to give Sasha space. "Lucky is a good dog."

"I know." She hugged the dog. "I was so scared that day. I was running away from Peter." She inhaled. "My mama doesn't live far from here, but I couldn't stay with her. Peter would find me. Anyway, Lucky got away from me, and I had to chase her." Sasha watched Faith warily, her blue eyes wide.

Faith reached out to brush the girl's bangs out of her eyes, but pulled back her hand. She needed to make Sasha feel safe first. "You've been taking food from people's houses, now haven't you?"

Sasha nodded, and fresh tears filled her eyes.

"How did you get into this house? And how did you know about the secret room?"

"A lady down the street. She let me stay in her shed until her husband found out. She told me where to hide so no one could find me, and I crawled in the basement window. But you did find me."

"Yes, we did."

"I'm going to jail, I know I am," she whispered. "If I don't die."

"If you don't die? Why would you die?"

"Peter said he'd kill me and Granny and Lucky if I told anybody about what he did."

Faith's heart lurched. "When did he say that to you?"

"After he robbed the gas station. I tried to run away, but he grabbed my shirt and said that. Then I kicked him hard and ran." Sasha twisted her small hands in her lap, and her chest rose and fell as though she could see Peter.

"Oh, sweetheart." Faith swallowed around the lump in her throat.

"I saw him in his car watching my granny's house, so I couldn't go back there. I wanted to. And I wanted to call Granny, but my phone battery died. I didn't know what to do. . . ." Her voice broke.

Anger like fire hit Faith that the poor child had been threatened by Peter. "Don't worry. My friend Ray will take care of Peter." *I'd like to take him on myself for what he's done.* She took a breath, willing her anger to simmer. "Can you tell me what happened? How did Lucky get hurt?"

Sasha nodded. "I got this glittery card and a new cell phone for my birthday, and I went to take pictures."

"I love taking pictures," Faith said, trying to bring levity to the situation. "It's my hobby. And your grandma allowed you to go to the gas station alone?"

Sasha raised her chin. "I'm twelve."

"I know," Faith said. She didn't want to judge, but in this day and age—

Sasha sucked in her lower lip. "The gas station is at our corner. Lucky started pulling me in that direction. I got money for my birthday, too, so I wanted to buy candy."

"I see." Faith brushed her hand over Sasha's hair, and this time the girl didn't shy away.

"Peter. . .he's a drug dealer. I knew that because sometimes he did it at my mom's house."

Faith's heart broke for this young girl who had seen too much. A sudden flash of insight hit her like a slap. Her life hadn't been as bad as she'd allowed herself to believe. In fact, she was blessed. Mabel was right. She needed to forgive her father. He might have been strict, too strict, and distant—not nearly as loving as he could have been—but Faith had never had to deal with the horror Sasha had been through.

"I was already in the store when Peter walked in. When he started robbing the gas station man, I hid behind where the potato chips are and took pictures of him. But Lucky started barking, and Peter saw me." Sasha's lip trembled again. "He kicked Lucky, and he grabbed my shirt. He said, 'Give me that phone.' But I kicked him and got away. I kept on running. . . ."

"That was smart, Sasha." Faith brushed a tear off her cheek, and a new thought struck. "You took Lucky both times before Peter came to my house to get her. How did you know he was coming for Lucky?"

"I was hiding in my mom's house and heard Peter say it." Sasha lowered her gaze. "And. . .the other time I heard you talkin' on the phone. . ." Fresh tears filled the girl's eyes.

Faith held her close. "It's going to be all right, Sasha. Do you believe me?"

The sound of the front door opening behind her sent relief through Faith. Footsteps came down the hall. "Ray?"

Sasha let loose a bloodcurdling screech.

Faith turned. "Oh no. . ." She leaped to her feet and grabbed Sasha to run.

"Don't move," Peter said, brandishing a pistol. "It's my lucky day. I can take care of my problems all at once."

Chapter 25

Lucky barked frantically, wiggling in Sasha's arms.

"How did you know I. . .we. . .were here?" Faith drew Sasha closer.

"Been parked down the street. Knew those two old women left. You were here alone, I thought. But now. . .I've got what I was looking for." He pointed the gun at Sasha. "It's time to come home."

Lucky growled and leaped from Sasha's arms.

"No!" the girl screamed.

Faith tried to grab the little dog, but she ran past them, right for Peter's legs. Without taking his eyes off Faith, Peter gave the animal a swift kick. Lucky yelped, then limped under the table and collapsed.

Sasha was sobbing now, hanging on to Faith.

"The police are on their way," Faith threatened, taking another step back.

"No way. Not yet. They're busy with Sasha's mom. After I got done with her, she's not gonna talk."

Faith saw motion over his shoulder. Cora and Mabel appeared in the doorway. Mabel had her finger to her lips. Faith's heart sped faster. Sasha's wails and the dog's yapping must have covered the noise of them coming into the house. Faith kept her face rigid. The sisters would know what to do—as long as Peter didn't hear them.

Faith had to keep talking. "You won't get away with this. The police will find you and you'll pay."

"Shut up," he spat.

Faith fought for deeper breaths. She had to do something to keep Peter from hearing the sisters and so pretended to break down in sobs.

Mabel held a basket in one hand. Cora walked into the kitchen, balancing a pot in her hands.

"What are you going to do with us?" Faith wailed louder.

Cora lifted the pot above her head.

"I ask the questions," Peter said. "Now shut your mouth and stop that infernal noise."

Cora lifted her arms higher and then dropped the pot on Peter's head. Chicken soup sloshed everywhere, and the pot and lid hit his shoulders and clanged to the floor.

Peter staggered and lunged for Faith, but he slipped on the soup and fell

373

flat on his face.

"Shame on you!" Mabel yelled. "You're lucky that soup wasn't boiling, you hoodlum!" She dumped the contents of the basket on Peter, and biscuits bounced over his head and onto the floor.

"For once, I wish your biscuits weren't so fluffy," she said to Cora.

Peter struggled to stand again, but Mabel knocked him over with a single shove.

"Glory to God!" Cora yelled and sat down hard on the small of his back. "This'll teach you, young man. You hear me? Ain't nobody gonna hurt our kin."

"Vengeance is mine, sayeth the Lord!" Mabel pointed at him. "Trying to hurt a child. Hurting her mother. And kicking a dog. Not to mention *thinking* about hurting Faith. You are a bad man!"

Peter struggled under her. "I—can't—breathe."

"That's the least of your worries," Cora said. "Officer Ray Reed is on his way. You'll be answering to the law soon." She planted herself harder on his back. He gave up with a moan. "Sister," Cora pointed at the bag on the counter. "Get the duct tape."

Mabel did so and fastened his feet first, then, without too much of a struggle, she taped his hands together. "Like Cora said, this stuff is good for nearly everything."

Silence reigned for nearly a minute. Faith gazed at the scene. Noodles, bits of celery, onion, carrot, and pieces of chicken littered the kitchen floor. The pot was lying on its side. Biscuits were strewn from one end of the room to the other. Mabel and Cora were like rescuing angels. Even Sasha had stopped crying, although she wouldn't have been able to continue with her mouth gaping open like it was.

Mabel looked down and pointed at Peter. " 'The Lord's curse is on the house of the wicked, but he blesses the home of the righteous!' Proverbs chapter three, verse thirty-three."

"Preach it, sister!" Cora bounced on Peter's back with more exuberance.

Sasha started to giggle. "I've heard of people being *socked*, but not *souped*."

Faith high-fived the girl. Mabel grinned. Cora snorted. Then they all began to laugh.

As Faith wondered what they were going to do with the "souped" bad guy, she heard the front door bang open over the laughter and Ray call her name.

"That boy never did learn how to come into a house quietly." Mabel clucked her tongue.

Cora shook her head. "Gets hisself all worked up and then dents the wall with the doorknob."

Faith wiped tears from her eyes. "In the kitchen, Ray," she said between gasps of laughter.

"Faith! Are you okay?" His question was followed by the sound of several people storming down the hallway. Ray skidded into the kitchen and stopped. Philip slammed into his back. Their wide gazes took in the scene.

"What—what. . .happened here?" Ray asked.

Philip walked around Ray and into the kitchen. "For crying out loud! This is the most amazing thing I've ever seen."

"Calm down and arrest him!" Mabel ordered, pointing at Peter.

"Let me up," Peter groaned.

"How did you. . .never mind." Ray took cuffs from his belt and started for Peter, walking gingerly on the messy floor.

"You won't need them things." Cora pointed at the handcuffs.

Peter wiggled. "Get me away from these crazy women. You're the police, help me!"

"You hush, young man." Mabel pointed at Peter's hands. "Nope, you won't need those, Ray. He's trussed better than a Thanksgiving turkey."

"I can see that," Ray said, exchanging a grin with Philip. He glanced over at Faith. "Are you all right?"

She nodded, feeling suddenly shy.

Ray took a deep breath. "I was so scared—"

He was interrupted by yelling from the front of the house.

"It's all clear," Philip hollered. Thundering footfalls raced down the hall.

"Lord, have mercy," Cora said. "Sounds like an army."

"See what I mean by all that cop commotion?" Mabel glared at Faith, but she was having trouble keeping her eyes off Ray.

Several other officers charged into the room and halted, and like Ray and Philip, stared wide-eyed at the suspect on the floor.

"I've never seen anything like this in my life," one of them whispered in awe.

"Perhaps we need to hire you ladies," Philip said.

"Not in this lifetime," Mabel said. "I got other work to do than catch bad guys for the police."

Everyone started laughing, but Faith continued to gaze at Ray. He looked so handsome. *Always the hero,* she mused and felt her emotional walls crumbling and her love for him growing. But was it too late?

"That man made me waste a perfectly good pot of chicken soup," Cora grumbled. "I made it from scratch."

"Well, it's like I always say." Mabel planted her hands on her hips. "Chicken soup is good for whatever ails you."

Chapter 26

The next afternoon Ray walked into the Cape Cod, and the sisters were waiting for him in the living room, their arms crossed over their midsections.

"I just got off work and went over to see Faith. She's not there." He rubbed his tired eyes and recounted in his mind for what seemed like the hundredth time how near he came to losing her.

"Sit down," Cora demanded, and he caught one of Mabel's dirty looks on the way to the sofa.

"What's wrong? What did I do this time? Is everybody okay?" Ray searched the two frowning faces.

"Oh, everybody's okay," Mabel said, "if we're not counting Faith's feelings."

"Faith's feelings?"

"Hush, young man and sit yourself on the couch." Mabel pointed. "And make sure your gun is turned off in this house."

Ray obeyed, flipping the safety, feeling like he was twelve.

Cora began to pace. "Huggin' up like that." She shook her head side to side. "In broad daylight, with a woman you aren't in love with."

"What?" Ray scrubbed his hand over his five o'clock shadow. "Did I miss something?"

They both chuckled in that way that told him nothing was funny, then Mabel harrumphed. "In my day you didn't go huggin' up in public for all the neighbors to see. Especially with someone you have no business huggin' up to."

"Like it's something to be proud of," Cora added.

"Huggin' up?" Exhausted, he fought to get their meaning. "I've had a long day helping to wind up this case. Trying to make sure Sasha doesn't get charged for breaking and entering and stealing stuff...and...I'm so confused. Can we start from the beginning?"

Cora stopped in front of him. "We'll discuss Sasha in a moment, so don't you get all cop-ish with Miss Cora and Miss Mabel. You might have a badge, but you're in our house now, and we're in charge. We have more important fish to fry at the moment. Besides, that child will be just fine."

"Yes indeed," Mabel said. "We have connections."

"Connections...," he mumbled.

"That means we're taking care of Sasha," Mabel said.

"Now don't change the subject," Cora said. "We were discussing your misbehavior."

Ray shifted on the sofa cushion, wishing he'd stayed at work. "I'm sorry, but I have no idea what you're talking about."

"You'd better not be playing dumb on purpose." Mabel lowered her lids like he wasn't worth a second look. "It's that Bailey, and right outside Faith's house, putting her paws all over you."

"You think we don't know." Cora snorted and looked him in the eye.

"Bailey?" Ray whispered. "Bailey had her paws all over me? When did you see Bailey with her paws, er, hands all over me?"

"Not us. *Faith* saw Bailey," Mabel said. "And you."

"Faith saw Bailey and me—"

"That's what we're sayin'," Cora huffed. "For such a smart boy, you aren't acting it."

"Okay, I give up. I'm clueless today. When did Faith see this?"

"Yesterday," Mabel hissed. "In her driveway."

Light dawned. Ray couldn't help but smile.

"What're you grinning about?" Cora looked over at Mabel, then back at Ray. "You come home to mend a relationship—"

"Aha, I get it now." Faith was mad because she'd seen Bailey hug him. That was very good news. "I was saying good-bye to Bailey—"

"And you have mended fences," Mabel said, "but not the one you thought needed mending."

"It's over with Bailey."

Cora and Mabel both stopped and stared down at him.

"I agree with everything you've both said. Bailey was only hugging me good-bye, and it wasn't my idea." Ray looked from one lovely sister to the other. "I love her. With all my heart."

"You best be talkin' about Faith." Cora gave him a challenging glare.

"I am. I'm talking about Faith. I love her."

"It's about time!" Cora shouted.

"Then what are you doing sittin' here?" Mabel pointed to the front door. "Faith's at the clinic. Get yourself in gear and get over there now."

Ray stood. "Shouldn't I change my clothes first?"

Mabel wagged her head. "Land sake Ray, you oughta know better."

"Women love men in uniform," Cora said, and both sisters laughed.

❧

Lucky was bruised, but thankfully she had survived another attack by Peter. Lucky, indeed. Her name should be Blessing. This one little dog had done more to bring people together and help mend relationships than any pet she'd ever met. Faith set her on a cushion in her office and patted her head.

Lucky sighed and stared at the door.

"I know—you want Sasha. Just you wait. Her grandma is bringing her to get you."

Faith shook her head as she sat down at her desk and began to doodle. Mabel and Cora had pulled some strings to help Sasha. Who knew they had those kinds of connections? Not only was no one charging Sasha for stealing and breaking into their homes, but Social Services had given temporary custody to her grandmother until things could be permanent in court.

She looked down at her doodles. All hearts. That told her exactly whom she was trying not to think about. *Ray.* She hadn't seen him since he took Peter away the night before. She'd gone straight home, dropped into bed, and fell into a dreamless sleep. For the first time in months, she slept straight through the night. As though the Lord had healed something inside her— and He had. For the first time in her life, she wasn't afraid to love. She looked down at the heart doodles again. *Ray, I love you.*

She'd have to tell him, even if he couldn't return her feelings. That way she'd be free to move on.

"Dr. Hart?" Gladys peeked her head in the office.

Faith dropped her pen and looked up. "Yes?"

"Your father is on the phone. Says it's important."

Her father. "Okay. I'll take the call."

Gladys hesitated. "Mr. Rees is in examining room one with his three Dobermans."

"Are Thor and Zeus huddled against his legs, shaking? And is Samson retching in the corner?"

Gladys nodded. "And Mrs. MacInnis is in examining room three with her cat. She's got hair balls."

"Mrs. MacInnis has hair balls?" Faith smiled.

After a hesitant chuckle, Gladys shook her head. Faith had a ways to go before her staff wouldn't be nervous around her. "Ask Lindsey if she'll go in and do the initial work. I'll be there in a couple of minutes. And thank you."

"Um, you're welcome," Gladys said and shut the door.

Faith stared at the phone and thought about Sasha and once again realized she had much to be grateful for. Though her dad had never been affectionate... Faith sighed. Okay, even by normal standards he'd be considered too strict. But he'd always given her everything she needed. Maybe she needed to give him a break. Crack the ice and see what kind of potential lay underneath.

She picked up the phone. "Dad?"

"Faith! I got a call from some person named Mabel. She said you were involved in a kidnap attempt. What's happening there?"

Faith paused. How did Mabel get her father's phone number? There was a lot she didn't know about the sisters. "Mabel said all that?"

"Yes. And you helped capture a known felon."

"I'm not sure it's quite like that," Faith admitted.

"Well, what happened?" he demanded.

Faith explained, and after a long pause, he groaned. "You could have been killed." It was a statement, not a question. "All for a dog and a little girl." Another statement.

"Sort of, I guess," Faith said, waiting for the criticism.

"I see." His voice was lower than normal.

After thirty seconds she realized he wasn't going to criticize her, and her heart felt lighter. "Dad, I have something to tell you."

"What's that?"

"I've been thinking lately and—and I want you to know that I appreciate everything you've ever done for me."

"Well. I should think so." He harrumphed. "Your brother will be coming into port soon."

For the first time she wondered if this was her father's awkward way of carrying on a conversation. Fact or not, she would take it as such. "Yes, I know. And I will attend the picnic celebrating his return."

"Good," he said. "Richard will like that."

There was a knock on her office door. "Faith? We need you," Debbie called.

"Dad, I have to go. I have clients. Oh—I love you." She didn't give him a chance to respond, just hung up. Let him think about that for a while.

"What is it?" she asked. "Come in."

Debbie cracked the door and poked her head through the opening. "You're wanted out front."

Faith drew a breath and shook her head. "I've got two examining rooms full. Can you deal with it?"

"No, I cannot." Debbie's voice was firm. "You must come out front. Please."

"Who needs me?"

"Faith, do I ever intrude on your day for trivial tasks?"

"No. I'm sorry." Faith stood and straightened her white jacket and followed Debbie to the front.

"What is it?" she whispered.

"Some guy said he has to see you. . .right now. It's urgent."

Faith gave up asking questions. She opened the door to the waiting room area and halted.

"Ray?"

He stood in his uniform, tall and posture ramrod straight. Three other clients sat in chairs watching her with wide eyes. They probably thought he was there to question her.

Ray walked the few steps toward her slowly. "Thank you for coming out here, Dr. Hart."

Faith took a step toward him. Why was he calling her doctor? She glanced at her clients as though they had the answer, but they looked how she felt—worried.

"The other night your actions caused some serious issues."

She took two steps toward him, motioning him with a finger to her lips to keep his voice down. "What are you talking about? Issues with what?"

"You and me. You're going to have to be taken into custody."

"What? What do you mean?" She moved closer until she could smell his aftershave. "Ray, if this is a joke. . . ," she whispered. "You're in uniform. My clients think I've committed a crime."

"You have." Ray placed his hands on her upper arms and pulled her to him. "You've stolen my heart."

The elderly Mrs. Bancroft smiled, then covered her mouth with her hand. The man sitting two seats away from her turned down his mouth and nodded as though he were proud of Ray's boldness. Tracy Como chewed her nail like she was watching a scary movie.

Had Faith heard him right? "What are you saying?"

"You've stolen my heart. So you have to pay a fine. I need yours in return."

"You need my. . .heart?"

Ray looked over his shoulder. "I just told her what I want, didn't I?"

All three of her clients nodded as Ray dropped to one knee in front of her. "I love you, Faith. If you love me, too, we'll get married and fill our house with lots of babies."

"Married? Babies?"

"Just say yes," Debbie squealed.

"Yes?" Faith heard herself say.

"Say you love him, too," Lindsey said behind her.

"I love you, too." Faith blinked, and the full impact of what was happening finally hit. She reached for his outstretched hands. "I think I've always loved you, Ray Reed."

"Will you marry me?"

Nodding and smiling, she said, "Yes!"

Ray stood, and a single tear ran down his cheek. "You need to know I'm going to be a music minister, not a cop."

"Oh Ray," she whispered. She wiped his tear with her index finger. "My sensitive musician. That's the perfect job for you."

He cupped her face with his hands and kissed her soundly. When he was done, he backed up and smiled. "I'll bet Mabel and Cora would approve of *that* public display of affection."

"Oh, I have no doubt," she said and threw her arms around his neck.

Epilogue

The October sky was never brighter or bluer. After quickly crossing the road from her house, making sure that Ray was nowhere in sight, Faith stood on the steps of the Victorian mansion in jeans and a sweatshirt, her long hair still in rollers. She tapped at the front door before going in, then stood in the large entry hall and visually scanned the room and the staircase. Colorful bunches of flowers were tied to the banisters as far as she could see. Chrysanthemums filled vases everywhere, and a white runner stood beside the french doors off the dining room, waiting to be unfurled.

Faith stood in silence, alone, hand over her heart. Today she would become Faith Anne Reed. She looked down at her sparkly engagement ring. In just a while she would don a matching wedding band.

"I thought I heard the front door open." Mabel came waltzing up to Faith and wrapped her in a tight hug. "Now get upstairs and get dressed. The girls are waiting."

Faith nodded. "Thank you for all this, Miss Mabel. How will I ever repay you and Cora?"

Cora came down the staircase. "You and Ray live a long and happy life together and raise your children in the admonition of the Lord."

"Teach them His ways," Mabel added. "That's repayment enough. Now git!" She pointed up the staircase, and Faith laughed.

Debbie, her matron of honor, greeted her with a squeal. "Look at my make-up." She batted her eyelids. "We've got a real makeup artist."

"You look fabulous," Faith said. "Do I go next?"

She was summoned over by Lori, the cosmetologist, so she scooted past Debbie and settled in the chair.

"Your bone structure is perfect," Lori said. "You won't need much to make you shine."

"Thanks. I don't wear heavy makeup, so that's good." Faith folded her shaky hands on her lap. In two hours she'd be Mrs. Reed. She closed her eyes and thanked God she would marry her best friend and the man of her dreams.

A knock came at the door, and Debbie went off to open it.

Faith heard the deep rumble of her dad's voice and felt her heart sink. Today she needed his affirmation and approval. "Please, Lord," she whispered.

Debbie stepped back, and her father entered the room with military bearing and an expression she could not decipher.

"Excuse me, Lori." Faith stood, straighter than usual, and approached him. "Hi, Dad, what's wrong?"

He clamped his hands behind his back. "Why does something have to be wrong?" His lips turned up in a smile. "You are beautiful." He reached out awkwardly, gave her a hug, stepped back, and took her hands in his. "Did I ever tell you how proud I am of my daughter?"

Faith laughed through a sudden spate of tears. Her dad almost always spoke of his children in third person.

"Don't cry," Lori and Debbie said almost simultaneously. "Your makeup," Lori added.

Faith sniffled. "I'm not sure you ever told me you're proud of me, Dad." She shrugged. "Or maybe I've forgotten."

He nodded slowly. "Maybe I didn't say it enough. Things were hard after your mother died. But you did turn out fine." Despite his tough words, he was blinking back tears. For the first time in her life, Faith thought he might shed tears. He tilted his chin and cleared his throat. "I'm proud of you, Faith. Now"—he glanced at his watch—"it's twelve hundred hours. I'll leave you to get ready."

When Faith returned to the chair, Debbie was trying to hide tears. "Your makeup," Faith warned with a little laugh. "This is the happiest day of my life," she said with all the conviction in her heart. She again closed her eyes and thanked her heavenly Father.

❧

Ray paced the large kitchen in the Victorian, distracting himself by watching Mabel and Shannon interact. He was thrilled that his good friend from the Tri-Cities was able to attend the wedding with her husband, Glen. And she and Faith had become fast friends.

"Now what's this stuff you're mashin' up?" Mabel asked. Cora stood beside her sister, shaking her head.

Shannon continued to assemble the dish. "It's couscous with broccoli and—" She gasped and put her hand to her stomach. "He's kicking again."

Both sisters smiled broadly. "You know it's a he?" Cora asked.

Shannon's eyes grew wide, and she wagged her head. "Oh no, I'm just guessing. I wouldn't get a sonogram."

"Quite right." Glen looked up from where he sat at the kitchen table, sipping tea. "Shannon says the high-frequency waves disturb the baby's inner peace."

Ray held back a laugh. "Some things never change."

"Indeed," Glen said with a sneaky smile.

"Have you seen the sunroom, Ray?" Shannon asked. "It's amazing beyond words."

Ray shook his head. "No, Miss Mabel and Miss Cora said I'm not allowed in there yet."

"That's right," the sisters said. "You try to sneak a peek again"—Cora grabbed a magazine off the counter and rolled it up—"I'll hit you in the head with this."

"I believe it." Ray laughed long and hard with the other guests, then sobered. "Miss Cora beat me a few times," he announced. "And she'll do it again."

His brother and best man, Philip, poked his head into the kitchen. "She beat me, too."

Ray couldn't resist hanging an arm around each of the sisters' strong shoulders. "That's what all moms do."

Mabel swatted him with a dish towel but couldn't hide the tears in her eyes. "You sure look handsome, son."

"Uh-huh." Cora was nodding and dabbing at her face. "Now where'd your mama go? We're glad she managed to fly back for the wedding."

Ray tilted his head toward the sunroom. "She said she wouldn't have missed it. She's somewhere around here talking to people. You know how she is."

The sisters nodded.

"Okay, everybody." Pastor Gary entered the kitchen, smiling. "It's time. Take your places."

Ray followed his brother into the sunroom. "You should have done this first. You're old, you know."

"Ha!" Philip shook his head. "It'll be a couple of years before I get single life out of my system."

"We'll see." Ray scanned the beautiful room, his heart overflowing with appreciation for all the work Mabel and Cora put into preparing the place. He nodded a greeting to his mom, and she blew him a kiss.

They stood at the altar. How had this all come together so quickly? Ray smiled and answered his own question. *The hand of God is on our lives,* he mused. *Thank You, Lord, for bringing Faith back into my life.*

The music commenced, and the sunroom doors were opened by white-gloved attendants. Ray's breath caught at the sight of his beautiful bride. He suddenly got choked up and came close to tears.

Promising to love and cherish Faith all the days of his life would not be an effort. He had loved and cherished her since he'd been a teen. They'd both taken detours in life, but God brought them right back to Bothell, to their old neighborhood. The Lord worked all things out for the good.

Faith slipped her hand in his, and they faced one another as Pastor Gary had them repeat their vows—the words spoken in the Bible by the Lord Himself.

"The Lord God said, 'It is not good for the man to be alone.'" Pastor Gary looked into their faces. "And He brought Faith Anne Hart into Ray Reed's life a long, long time ago." He smiled and winked at Ray. "I wondered for a long time when I'd be officiating at their wedding."

"Oh, amen to that!" one of the sisters called out.

After the giggles from the congregation, Ray slipped the wedding band on Faith's slim finger. "I love you so much, Faith."

"I love you more," she whispered.

They kissed to the sound of applause from the wedding guests.